For Winifred with love

Contents

It was ten of April morn by the chime;
As they drifted on their path,
There was silence deep as death
And the boldest held his breath
For a time.

From *The Battle of the Baltic*
by THOMAS CAMPBELL

I

We Happy Few

Admiral Sir George Beauchamp held his thin hands towards the blazing log fire and rubbed his palms slowly together to restore his circulation.

He was a small, stooped figure, made fragile by his heavy dress coat and gold epaulettes, but there was nothing frail about his mind or the sharpness of his eyes.

It had been a long, tiresome ride from London to Portsmouth, the journey worsened by autumn rain and deeply rutted roads. And Beauchamp's one night's rest in the George Inn on Portsmouth Point had been ruined by a fierce gale which had changed the Solent'into a raging mass of white horses and made all but the largest vessels scurry for shelter.

Beauchamp turned from the fire and surveyed his private room, the one he always used when he came to Portsmouth, like many important admirals before him. Now the gale had receded and the thick glass windows shone like metal in sunlight, a deception, because beyond the stout walls the air was chilled, with a hint of winter to come.

The little admiral sighed aloud, something he would never have done if company had been present. Late September 1800, seven years of war with France and her allies.

Once, Beauchamp had envied his contemporaries, at sea in every quarter of the globe, in their fleets, squadrons or flotillas. But in weather like this he was more than satisfied with his office of Admiralty where his shrewd mind as a planner and strategist had won him much respect. Beauchamp had sent more than one flag officer to ignominy, and had placed his confidence in other, more junior men whose experience and ability had been previously overlooked.

Seven years of war. He turned the thought over in his mind. Victories and defeats, good ships left to rot until the enemy were almost at the gates, brave men and fools, mutinies and triumphs. Beauchamp had seen it all, had watched new leaders emerging to replace the failures and the tyrants. Collingwood and Troubridge, Hardy and Saumarez, and, of course, the public's darling, Horatio Nelson.

Beauchamp gave a thin smile. Nelson was what the country needed, the very stuff of victory. But he could not see the hero of the Nile enduring the work of Admiralty like himself. Sitting at endless policy meetings, smoothing the fears of King and Parliament, guiding those less eager towards positive action. No, he decided, Nelson would not last a month in Whitehall, any more than *he* would in a flagship. Beauchamp was over sixty and looked it. He sometimes felt older than time itself.

There was a discreet tap on the door and his secretary peered warily in at him.

'Are you ready, Sir George?'

'Yes.' It sounded like *of course.* 'Ask him to come up.'

Beauchamp never stopped working. But he enjoyed seeing his plans come to fruition, his choices for leadership and command rising to his severe standards.

Like his visitor, for instance. Beauchamp looked at the polished doors, the sunlight reflecting on a decanter of claret and two finely cut glasses.

Richard Bolitho, stubborn about some things, unorthodox in others, was one of Beauchamp's rewards. Just three years ago he had appointed him commodore over a handful of ships and sent him into the Mediterranean to seek out and discover the French intentions. He had been a good choice. The rest was history; Bolitho's swift actions and the later arrival of Nelson with a full fleet at his disposal to smash the French squadrons into defeat at the Battle of the Nile. Bonaparte's hopes for a total conquest of Egypt and India had been destroyed.

Now Bolitho was here, but as a newly appointed rear-admiral, a flag officer in his own right with all the doubts behind him.

His secretary opened the door.

'Rear-Admiral Richard Bolitho, sir.'

Beauchamp held out his hand, feeling the usual mixture of pleasure and envy. Bolitho looked very well in his new gold laced coat, he thought, and yet the transition had left the man unchanged. The same black hair with the rebellious lock above his right eye, the level gaze and grave expression which hid the adventurer and at the same time concealed the man's humility which Beauchamp had discovered for himself.

Bolitho saw the scrutiny and smiled.

'It is good to see you, sir.'

Beauchamp gestured to the table. 'Pour, will you. I'm a mite stiff.'

Bolitho watched his hand as he held the decanter above the glasses, steady and firm, when it should be shaking with the excitement he really felt. When he had seen his own reflection in a mirror he had scarcely been able to accept that he had made the final, definite step from captaincy to flag rank. Now he was a rear-admiral, one of the youngest ever appointed, but apart from the uniform, the gleaming epaulettes, each with the solitary silver star, he felt much as before. Surely something should have happened? He had always assumed that the move from wardroom to captain's cabin would alter a man. But the stride from it to the right of hoisting his own flag was like ten leagues by comparison.

Only in others had he seen any real difference. His coxswain, John Allday, could barely stop himself from beaming with pleasure. And when he had visited the Admiralty he had seen the amusement on his superiors' faces when he had shown caution with his ideas. Now, they listened to his suggestions, when before someone might have crushed him into silence. They did not always agree, but they heard him out. That was a change indeed.

Beauchamp eyed him severely above his glass. 'Well, Bolitho, you've got your way, and I've got mine.' He glanced at the nearest window, steamy with the room's heat. 'A squadron of your own. Four ships of the line, two frigates and a sloop of war. You'll be receiving orders from your admiral, but it will be up to you to translate them, eh?'

They clinked their glasses, each suddenly wrapped in his own thoughts.

To Beauchamp it meant a fresh, young squadron, a weapon to fit into the complex of war. To Bolitho it meant a lot more. Beauchamp had done everything to help him. Even to his choice of captains. All but one of them he knew well, and with good reason, and some he knew like old friends.

Most of them had something in common in that each had served with or under him in the past. Bolitho glanced around the room. In this same room, nineteen years ago, he had been given his first major command, and in many ways his best remembered. In her he had found Thomas Herrick, who had become his first lieutenant and his loyal friend. In the same unhappy ship he had also met John Neale, a twelve-year-old midshipman. Neale was in his squadron now, a captain commanding a frigate of his own.

'Memories, Bolitho?'

'Aye, sir. Ships and faces.'

That said it all. Bolitho had gone to sea, like Neale, at the age of twelve. Now he was a rear-admiral, the impossible dream. Too many times he had stood eye to eye with death, too often he had seen others fall about him to hold much confidence beyond the month or the year.

'Your ships are all gathered here, Bolitho.' It was a statement. 'So there's no sense in wasting time. Get 'em to sea, exercise them as you know how, make them hate your guts, but forge them into steel!'

Bolitho smiled gravely. He was eager to leave. The land held nothing for him any more. He had visited Falmouth, his house and estate there. It had affected him in the same way as before. As if the house had been waiting for something. He had stood before her portrait in his bedroom several times. Listening to her voice. Hearing her laugh. Yearning for the girl he had married and lost almost immediately in a tragic accident. *Cheney*. He had even spoken her name. As if to bring the picture to life. When he had left to make for London he had turned in the doorway to look at her face once more.

The sea-green eyes, like the water below Pendennis Castle, the flowing hair with the colour of new chestnuts. She, too, had appeared to be waiting.

He shook himself from his thoughts and remembered the one enjoyable thing he had shared when Herrick had returned to England in his old *Lysander*.

With surprisingly little hesitation Herrick had married the widow Dulcie Boswell whom he had met in the Mediterranean.

Bolitho had made the journey willingly to the small Kentish church on the road to Canterbury. The pews had been filled with Herrick's friends and neighbours, with a good sprinkling of blue and white from fellow sea officers.

Bolitho had felt strangely excluded, the feeling made harder to bear when he had recalled his own wedding at Falmouth, with Herrick beside him to offer the ring.

Then, as the bells chimed and Herrick had turned from the altar with his bride's hand on his gold-laced cuff, he had paused by Bolitho and had said simply, 'You being here, sir, has made this just perfect for me.'

Beauchamp's voice intruded again. 'I would like to take lunch with you, but I have business with the port admiral. And no doubt you've much to do. I'm obliged to you for many things, Bolitho.' He gave a wry smile. 'Not least for accepting my suggestion for a flag lieutenant. I've had my fill of *him* in London!'

Bolitho guessed there was a lot more to the request than that but said nothing.

Instead he said, 'I shall take my leave, sir. And thank you for seeing me.'

Beauchamp shrugged. It looked like a physical effort. 'Least I could do for you. You have your orders. You're not being offered an easy passage, but then you'd not have thanked me for one, eh?' He chuckled. 'Just keep a weather eye open for trouble.' He fixed Bolitho with a flat stare. 'I'll say no more than that. But your deeds, your rewards, well earned though they were, will have made you some enemies. Be warned.' He held out his hand. 'Now be off with you, and mark what I said.'

Bolitho left the room and strode past several people who were waiting to see the fierce little admiral. For advice, for favours, for hope, who could say?

At the foot of the stairs, standing near a crowded coffee room, he saw Allday waiting for him. As always. He would never alter. The same homely face and broad grin whenever he was pleased. He had thickened out a bit, Bolitho thought, but he was like a rock. He smiled to himself. At any other time an inn servant would have hurried a mere coxswain round the back to the kitchens, or, more likely, outside into the cold.

But in his blue coat with its gilt buttons, new breeches and polished leather boots he looked every inch an admiral's cox-swain.

And how Allday had struggled over the past three years to call him sir. Before, he had always addressed Bolitho as captain. Now he was having to get used to a rear-admiral. Just that morning as they had left for Portsmouth from a friend's house where Bolitho had been staying for a few days, Allday had said cheerfully, 'Never mind, *sir*. It'll be Sir Richard soon, and I can manage that well enough!'

Allday handed him his long boat-cloak and watched as Bolitho tugged his cocked hat firmly over his black hair.

'This is a moment, eh, sir?' He shook his head. 'We've come a long road.'

Bolitho looked at him warmly. Allday usually managed to put his finger on it. Times and places, blue seas and grey ones. Danger with death swiftly on its heels. Allday was always there. Ready to help, to use his cheek as liberally as his courage in every situation. He was a real friend, although he could do much to try Bolitho's temper when he wanted to.

'Aye. In some ways it feels like beginning all over again.'

He glanced at himself in the wall mirror near the entrance, much as he had done when he had gone out to take command of the frigate *Phalarope*, younger then than any captain in his new squadron.

He thought suddenly of the country house where he had been staying, recalling one of the housemaids, a pretty girl with flaxen hair and a trim figure. He had seen Allday with her on several occasions and the thought troubled him. Allday had risked his life and had saved Bolitho's many times. Now they were off again, and Allday, because of his dogged loyalty, was being taken from the land once more.

Bolitho toyed with the idea of offering him a chance of free-dom. To send him to Falmouth where he could live in peace, to stroll the foreshore and drink ale with other seafaring men. He had done more than his share for England, and there were plenty who never risked life and limb aloft in a gale or standing to the guns while the air was rent by the enemy's iron.

He saw Allday's face and decided against it. It would hurt and anger him. He would have felt the same way.

Bolitho said, 'There'll be a few fathers looking for the sailor who wronged their daughters, eh, Allday?'

Their eyes met. It was a game they had learned to play very well.

Allday grinned. 'My thoughts, too, sir. It's time for a change.'

Captain Thomas Herrick walked from beneath the poop and stood with his hands behind his back while he allowed his mind and body to adjust to the ship and the cold, damp wind which dappled her decks with spray.

The forenoon was almost over, and with practised eye Herrick noted that the many seamen working about the decks and gangways, or high overhead on the yards, were moving more slowly, probably dwelling on the midday meal, the thoughts of rum, a moment's respite in the crowded life between decks.

Herrick let his gaze stray around the broad quarterdeck, the stiff-backed midshipman of the watch, obviously conscious of his captain's presence, the neat lines of guns, everything. He still could not get used to the ship. He had brought his old command, the *Lysander* of seventy-four guns, home after many months of continuous service. Age, storm-damage and the heavier strains of battle had left deep wounds in the old ship, and it had been no surprise to Herrick to be told to pay off his command and be prepared to turn *Lysander* over to the dockyard. He had gone through a lot in that ship, had learned even more about himself, his limitations and his skills. As flag captain to Commodore Richard Bolitho he had discovered more paths of duty than he had known existed.

Lysander would never stand in the line of battle again. Too much damage had taken its toll, and her many years of service would probably be ignored and she would end her days as a store-ship, or worse, a prison hulk.

Her complement had been scattered throughout the fleet in an effort to feed the unending appetite of a navy at war. Herrick had seen it all before, and had wondered more than once what his own fate would be. To his astonishment he had been given this ship. His Britannic Majesty's seventy-four-gun ship of the line *Benbow*, absolutely new from her builders in the main dockyard at Devonport, the first new vessel Herrick had ever served in, let alone commanded.

He had been with her for months, worrying and working while the dockyard completed their part and *Benbow* grew and grew to her present appearance.

Everything was strange and untried, not least the men who were gathered into her eighteen-hundred-ton hull, and Herrick had blessed every ounce of experience which he had gained on his long climb up the ladder of advancement and service.

Luckily, he had been able to hold on to a few of his old professionals from the *Lysander*, some of her 'backbone' of skilled warrant and petty officers who, even now, after the previous night's howling gale, were to be heard bawling around the upper deck as they, like their captain, grew conscious of their responsibility and what the next hour would bring.

Herrick looked up at the mizzen masthead and felt the spray stinging his cheeks. Even at anchor it could be lively at Spithead. Soon now the flag of a rear-admiral would break at the mizzen truck. They would be together again. Different tasks, harder responsibility, but they would surely be unchanged.

Herrick walked to the hammock nettings and looked at the misty shoreline. Even without a glass he could see Portsmouth Point with its buildings crowded together as if fearful of toppling into the sea below. The church of Thomas à Becket, and somewhere to the left was the old George Inn.

He climbed on to a bollard and looked down at the swirling water alongside the stout black and buff hull. Boats were bobbing about, tackles rising and falling as last minute stores were swayed aboard. Brandy for the surgeon, wine for the marine officers, small comforts which would have to last them how long?

The past months had been not only demanding on Herrick but intensely rewarding, too. From a poor sea officer without influence or property he had become a man with roots. In Dulcie he had discovered a warmth and happiness he had not dreamed of, and to his utter surprise, which was typical of him, he had found himself to be married to a woman who, if not rich, was extremely well off.

She had stayed near the ship while the finishing touches had been completed. Yards crossed, fresh rigging blacked-down and made taut. Canvas spread, guns hoisted aboard, all seventy-four of them, and the miles of cordage, hundreds of blocks, tackles, crates, casks and equipment which turned a hull into the most modern, the most demanding and probably the most beautiful creation of man. *Benbow* was now a man-of-war, and not only that, she was flagship of this small squadron anchored in Spithead's fleet anchorage.

He said sharply, 'Mr Aggett! Your glass, if you please!'

Herrick had always been good at remembering names. It took him longer to know their owners.

The midshipman of the watch scurried across the quarterdeck and handed him the big signals telescope.

Herrick trained it across the starboard nettings, seeing the hazy humps of the Isle of Wight beyond the other anchored ships. He studied each vessel with slow, professional interest. The other three two-deckers, looking almost bright in the dull glare, their closed gunports presenting a chequered pattern above the choppy wavecrests alongside. *Indomitable*, Captain Charles Keverne. With each ship Herrick pictured her captain in his mind's eye. Keverne had been Bolitho's first lieutenant in the big prize *Euryalus*. The *Nicator*, Captain Valentine Keen. They had served together in another ship on the far side of the earth.

Odin, a smaller two-decker of sixty-four guns. Herrick smiled despite his list of anxieties. Her captain was Francis Inch. He had never imagined that the eager, horse-faced Inch would ever have made post-rank. Any more than he had expected it for himself.

The two frigates, *Relentless* and *Styx*, were anchored further astern of the squadron, and the smaller sloop, *Lookout*, was showing her copper in the watery sunlight as she rolled sickeningly to her cable.

All in all it was a good squadron. Its officers and men lacked experience for the most part, but had the youth to make up for it. Herrick sighed. He was forty-three and senior for his rank, but he was content, although he would not have complained about dropping a few years from his age.

Feet thudded on the quarterdeck and he saw the first lieutenant, Henry Wolfe, striding to meet him. Herrick could not imagine what he would have done without Wolfe in the past months of commissioning *Benbow*. In appearance he was quite extraordinary. Very tall, well over six feet, he seemed to have difficulty in controlling his arms and legs. They, too, were gangling and lively, like the man. He had fists like hams and feet as bulky as swivel guns. Dominating all these things, his hair was bright ginger, jutting from beneath his cocked hat like two vivid wings.

He was old for his appointment, and had served in merchantmen when laid off from naval service in peacetime. Collier brigs, speedy schooners with lace from Holland, men-of-war, he had been in them all. It was rumoured he had even been in the slave trade, and Herrick could well believe it.

Wolfe slid to a halt and touched his hat. He took several deep breaths, as if it was the only way he knew of controlling his energy, which was considerable.

'Ready she is, sir!' He had a harsh, toneless voice which made the nearby midshipman wince. 'I've just about got everything in place an' a place for everything! Give us a few more hands an' we'll make her show her paces!'

Herrick asked, 'How many more?'

'Twenty prime seamen, or fifty idiots!'

Herrick added, 'Those I saw brought aboard yesterday by the press, are they useful?'

Wolfe rubbed his chin and watched a seaman sliding down a backstay to the deck.

'The usual, sir. Rough-knots and a few gallows-birds, but some good men also. They'll be fine when the boatswain has had his say.'

A tackle squeaked and some canvas covered cases were hauled up and over the gangway. Herrick saw Ozzard, Bolitho's personal servant, fussing around them and directing a party of seamen to carry them aft.

Wolfe followed his gaze and remarked, 'Have no fear, sir. *Benbow*'ll not let you down today.' In his blunt fashion he added, 'It's a new experience for me to serve under an admiral's flag, sir. I'll take whatever guidance you see fit to offer.'

Herrick studied him and said simply, 'Rear-Admiral Bolitho will tolerate no slackness, Mr Wolfe, no more than I will. But a fairer man I never met, nor a braver.' He walked aft again adding, 'Call me the moment you sight the barge, if you please.'

Wolfe watched him leave and said to himself, 'Nor a better friend to *you*, I'll wager.'

Herrick went to his own quarters, aware of bustling figures, the smells of cooking and the stronger, unused scents of new timbers and tar, paintwork and cordage. She felt new all right. From keel to mainmast truck. And she was *his*.

He paused by the screen door and watched his wife sitting at the cabin table. She had pleasant, even features, and brown hair like his own. She was in her mid-thirties, and Herrick had given her his heart like a young lover to an angel.

The lieutenant with whom she had been speaking stood up instantly and faced the door.

Herrick nodded. 'Be easy, Adam. You are not required on deck as yet.'

Adam Pascoe, the *Benbow*'s third lieutenant, was glad of the interruption. Not that he did not enjoy talking with Captain Herrick's lady, it was not that at all. But, like Herrick, he was very aware of today, what it could mean to him personally when his uncle's flag broke to the wind, what it might mean for them all later on.

He had been under Herrick's command in *Lysander*, beginning as the junior lieutenant, and because of the advancement or death of his superiors had risen to fourth lieutenant. Even now, as *Benbow*'s third lieutenant, he was still only twenty years old. His emotions were torn between wanting to stay with Richard Bolitho or going elsewhere to a smaller, more independent vessel like a frigate or sloop.

Herrick watched his face and guessed most of what Pascoe was thinking.

He was a good-looking boy, he thought, slim and very dark like Bolitho, with the restlessness of an untrained colt. Had his father been alive he would have been proud of him.

Pascoe said, 'I had better attend my division, sir. I'd not want anything to go badly today.' He bowed slightly to the woman. 'If you'll excuse me, ma'am.'

Alone with his wife, Herrick said quietly, 'I worry about that one sometimes. He is still a boy and yet has seen more action and fearful sights than most of the squadron.'

She replied, 'We were speaking of his uncle. He means a lot to him.'

Herrick passed her chair and laid his hand on her shoulder. *Oh dear God, I have to leave you soon.* Aloud, he said, 'It is mutual, my love. But it is war, and a King's officer has his duty.'

She seized his hand and held it to her cheek without looking at him.

'Oh, stuff, Thomas! You are talking with me now, not one of your sailors!'

He bent over her, feeling awkward and protective at the same time. 'You will take good care when we are away, Dulcie.'

She nodded firmly. 'I will attend to everything. I shall see that your sister is provided for until her marriage. We shall have a lot to talk about until you return.' She faltered. 'When may that be?'

Herrick's head had been so much in a turmoil with his new command and his unexpected marriage that he had not thought much beyond sailing his ship from Plymouth to Spithead and assembling the little squadron together.

'It will be north, I believe. May take a few months.' He squeezed her hand gently. 'Never fear, Dulcie, with our Dick's flag at the masthead we'll be in good hands.'

A voice yelled overhead, 'Secure the upper deck! Side party to muster!'

Calls shrilled like lost spirits between the decks and feet thudded on the planking as marines bustled from their quarters to fall in at the entry port.

There was a sharp rap at the door and Midshipman Aggett, his wind-reddened eyes fixed on a half-eaten cake on the table, reported breathlessly, 'First lieutenant's respects, sir, and the barge has just shoved off from the sallyport.'

'Very well. I will come up.'

Herrick waited for the youth to leave and said, 'Now we will know, my dear.'

He took his sword from its rack and clipped it to his belt.

She stood up and walked across the cabin to adjust his neck-cloth and pat his white-lapelled coat into place.

'Dear Thomas. I'm so *very* proud of you.'

Herrick was not a tall man, but as he left the cabin to meet his admiral he felt like a giant.

Unaware of what was happening in his flagship, or indeed the whole squadron, Richard Bolitho sat very upright in the barge's sternsheets and watched the anchored vessels growing larger with each stroke of the oars.

He had recognized several of his old bargemen from the *Lysander* as he had stepped aboard, back at sea again probably without even a sight of their homes and families.

Allday sat near him, his eyes everywhere as he watched the white-painted oars rising and falling like polished bones. A lieutenant no less was in charge of the boat, *Benbow's* most junior officer, and he seemed as much ill at ease under Allday's scrutiny as he did in his admiral's company.

Bolitho was wrapped completely in his boat-cloak, with even his hat held firmly beneath it to prevent it from being whipped into the sea.

He watched the leading two-decker, recalling what he knew of her as she took on form and substance through the blown spray.

A third-rate, the strength in any sea fight, she was slightly larger than *Lysander*. She looked very splendid, he thought, and guessed that Herrick must be equally impressed. He saw the figurehead standing out as if to signal the barge with its raised sword. Vice-Admiral Sir John Benbow, who had died in 1702 after losing a leg by chain-shot. But not before he had lived to see the execution of his captains who had deserted him in battle. It was a fine figurehead, much as the dead admiral must have been. Grave-eyed, with flowing hair, and wearing a shining breastplate of the period. It had been carved by old Izod Lambe of Plymouth, who although said to be nearly blind was still one of the finest in his trade.

How many times he had wanted to go across from Falmouth to see Herrick in the final stages of getting his ship ready for sea. But Herrick might have taken it as lack of trust in his ability. Bolitho more than once had been made to accept that a ship was no longer his direct concern. Like his flag, he was above it. He felt a shiver lance up his spine as he studied the other members of his squadron. Four ships of the line, two frigates and a sloop of war. In all nearly three thousand officers, seamen and marines, and everything which that implied.

The squadron might be new, but many of the faces would be friends. He thought of Keverne and Inch, Neale and Keen, and of the sloop's new commander, Matthew Veitch. He had been Herrick's first lieutenant. Admiral Sir George Beauchamp had kept his word, now it was up to him to do his part.

With men he knew and trusted, who had shared and done so much together.

He smiled in spite of his excitement as he thought of his new flag lieutenant when he had tried to tell him his feelings.

The lieutenant had said, 'You make it sound exclusive, sir. As the bard would have it. *We happy few.*'

Perhaps he had been truer than he had understood.

The barge turned, swaying over a trough, as the lieutenant headed towards the flagship's glistening side.

There they all were. Red coats and cross-belts, the blue and white of the officers, the mass of seamen beyond. Above them all, towering as if to control and embrace them, the three great masts and yards, the mass of shrouds, stays and rigging which were incomprehensible to any landsman but represented the speed and agility of any ship. *Benbow*, by any standard, was something to be reckoned with.

The oars rose as one while the bowman hooked on to the main chains.

Bolitho handed his cloak to Allday and jammed his hat firmly athwartships across his head.

Everything had gone very quiet, and apart from the surge of the tide between the ship and the swaying barge it seemed almost peaceful.

Allday was standing, too, and had removed his hat while he watched and waited to lend a hand should Bolitho miss his footing.

Then Bolitho stepped out and upwards and hauled himself swiftly towards the entry port.

He was aware of the sudden bark of orders, the slap and stamp of marines presenting arms simultaneously with the fifers breaking into *Heart of Oak*.

Faces, blurred and vague, loomed to meet him as he stepped on to the deck, and as the calls shrilled and died in salute, Bolitho removed his hat to the quarterdeck and to the ship's captain as he strode to greet him.

Herrick removed his hat and swallowed hard. 'Welcome aboard, sir.'

They both stared up as some halliards were jerked taut by the signal party.

There it was, a symbol and a statement, Bolitho's own flag streaming from the mizzen like a banner.

The nearest onlookers would have watched for some extra sign as the youthful-looking rear-admiral replaced his hat and shook hands with their captain.

But that was all they saw, for what Bolitho and Herrick shared at that moment was invisible but to each other.

2

Flagship

By dawn the following day the wind had backed considerably, and once again the Solent was alive with angry wavecrests. Aboard the flagship, and all the rest of Bolitho's small squadron, the motion was uncomfortable as each vessel tugged at her anchor as if determined to drive aground.

When the first dull light gave colour to the glistening ships, Bolitho sat in his stern cabin re-reading his carefully worded instructions and trying at the same time to detach his mind from the sounds of a ship preparing for a new day. He knew Herrick had been on deck since dawn, and that if he went up to join him it would only hamper the business of getting *Benbow* and the rest of his command ready to weigh.

It could be bad enough at any time. War had left severe shortages of ships, material and experience. But most of all trained seamen. In a new ship, as part of a freshly formed squadron, it must seem even worse to Bolitho's captains and their officers.

And Bolitho *needed* to go on deck. To clear his mind, to get the *feel* of his ships, to be part of the whole.

Ozzard peered in at him and then padded across the deck with its covering of black and white chequered canvas to pour some more strong coffee.

Bolitho had not got to know his servant much more than when they had first met aboard Herrick's *Lysander* in the Mediterranean. Even in his neat blue jacket and striped trousers he still looked more like a lawyer's clerk than any seafarer. It was said he had only escaped the gallows by running to hide in the fleet, but he had proved his worth in loyalty and a kind of withdrawn understanding.

He had shown the other side of his knowledge when Bolitho

had taken him to the house in Falmouth. Laws and taxes were becoming more complicated with each new year of war, and Ferguson, Bolitho's one-armed steward, had admitted that the accounts had never looked better than after Ozzard's attention.

The marine sentry beyond the screen door rapped his musket on the deck and called, 'Your clerk, sir!'

Ozzard flitted to the door to admit Bolitho's new addition, Daniel Yovell. He was a jolly, red-faced man with a broad Devon dialect, more like a farmer than a ship's clerk. But his handwriting, round like the man, was good, and he had been quite tireless while Bolitho had been preparing to take over the squadron.

He laid some papers on the table and stared unseeingly at the thick glass windows. Dappled with salt and flying spray, they made the other ships look like phantoms, shivering and without reality.

Bolitho leafed through the papers. Ships and men, guns and powder, food and stores to sustain them for weeks and months if need be.

Yovell said carefully, 'Your flag lieutenant be on board, zur. He come off shore in the jolly boat.' He concealed a grin. 'He had to change into something dry afore he came aft.' It seemed to amuse him.

Bolitho leaned back in his chair and stared up at the deck-head. It took so much paper to get a squadron on the move. Tackles rasped over the poop and blocks clattered in time with running feet. Despairing petty officers whispered hoarse curses and threats, no doubt very aware of the skylight above their admiral's cabin.

The other door opened noiselessly and Bolitho's flag lieutenant stepped lightly over the coaming. Only a certain dampness to his brown hair betrayed his rough crossing from Portsmouth Point, for as usual he was impeccably dressed.

He was twenty-six years old, with deceptively mild eyes and an expression which varied somewhere between blank and slightly bemused.

Lieutenant the Honourable Oliver Browne, whom Admiral Beauchamp had asked Bolitho to take off his hands as a favour, had all the aristocratic good looks of comfortable living and breeding. He was not the sort of officer you would expect to find sharing the hardships of a man-of-war.

Yovell bobbed his head. ' 'Morning, zur. I have written in your name for the wardroom's accounts.'

The flag lieutenant peered at the ledger and said quietly, 'Browne. With an "e".'

Bolitho smiled. 'Have some coffee.' He watched Browne lay his despatch bag on the table and added, 'Nothing new?'

'No, sir. You may proceed to sea when ready. There are no signals from the Admiralty.' He sat down carefully. 'I wish it were to be a warmer climate.'

Bolitho nodded. His instructions were to take his squadron some five hundred miles to the north-western coast of Denmark and there rendezvous with that part of the Channel Fleet which patrolled the approaches to the Baltic in all weathers under every condition. Once in contact with the admiral in command he would receive further orders. It was to be hoped he would have time to whip his squadron into shape before he met with his superior, he thought.

He wondered what most of his officers were thinking about it. Much like Browne probably, except that they had cause to grumble. Most of them had been in the Mediterranean or adjacent waters for years. They would find Denmark and the Baltic a bitter exchange.

Yovell passed his papers to Bolitho for signature with the patience of a village schoolmaster. Then he said, 'I'll have the other copies ready afore we weigh, zur.' Then he was gone, his round shape swaying to the ship's motion like a large ball.

'I think that takes care of everything.' Bolitho watched his blank-faced aide. 'Or does it?' He was still unused to sharing confidences or revealing doubts.

Browne smiled gently. 'Captains' conference this forenoon, sir. With the wind remaining as it is, the sailing master assures me we may weigh at any time after that.'

Bolitho stood up and leaned on the sill of the tall windows. It was good to have old Ben Grubb aboard. As *Lysander's* sailing master he had been something of a legend. Playing his tin whistle as the ship had sailed to break the enemy's formation and the decks had run with blood around him. A great lump of a man, the breadth of three, his face was brick-red, ruined by

wind and drink in equal proportion. But what he did not understand about the sea and its ways, the winds to carry you through
ice or a tropical storm, was not worth the knowing.

Herrick had been delighted to have Grubb as his sailing
master again. He had said, 'I doubt if he'd have taken much
notice if I'd have wanted otherwise!'

'Very well. Make a signal to the squadron to that effect. To
repair on board at four bells.' He smiled gravely. 'They'll be
expecting it anyway.'

Browne gathered up his own collection of signals and papers
and then hesitated as Bolitho asked abruptly, 'The admiral with
whom we are to rendezvous. Do you know him?'

He was amazed just how easily it came out. Before he would
no more have asked a subordinate's views on a senior officer
than dance naked on the poop. But *they* said he must have a flag
lieutenant, someone who was versed in naval diplomacy, so he
would use him.

'Admiral Sir Samuel Damerum has spent much of his time
as a flag officer in India and the East Indies of late, sir. He was
expected to move to some high appointment in Whitehall, even
Sir George Beauchamp's position was mentioned.'

Bolitho stared at him. It was a different world from his own.

'Sir George Beauchamp *told* you all this?'

The hint of sarcasm was lost on Browne. 'Naturally, sir. As
flag lieutenant it is my place to know such matters.' He gave a
casual shrug. 'But instead Admiral Damerum was given his
present command. I understand he is experienced, and well
versed in matters relating to trade and its protection. I fail to
see what Denmark has to do with such knowledge.'

'Carry on, if you please.'

Bolitho sat down again and waited for Browne to depart.
He walked with easy grace, like a dancer. More likely a duellist,
Bolitho thought grimly. Beauchamp's way of giving him an
experienced aide and saving the man at the same time from
some unpleasant enquiry.

He thought about Damerum. He had seen his name rise
slowly up the Navy List, a man of influence, but always seeming to be on the fringe of things, never in the places of action
and victory.

Perhaps his knowledge of trade was the reason for his

present post. There had been an unexpected flare-up between Britain and Denmark earlier this same year.

Six Danish merchantmen, escorted by the *Freja*, a forty-gun frigate, had refused to allow a British squadron to stop and search them for contraband of war.

Denmark was in a difficult position. On the face of it she was neutral, but she depended on trade, nevertheless. With her powerful neighbours, Russia and Sweden, as well as with Britain's enemies.

The result of this encounter had been sharp and angry. The Danish frigate had fired warning shots at the British vessels, but had been forced to strike her colours after half an hour's fierce battle. The *Freja* and her six charges had been escorted to the Downs, but after hurried diplomatic exchanges the British had been faced with the humiliating task of repairing the *Freja* at their own cost and then returning her and the convoy to Denmark.

Peace between Britain and Denmark, friends of long standing, was preserved.

Perhaps Damerum had had a hand in the original confrontation, and was kept at sea with his squadron as an example. Or maybe the Admiralty believed that a constant presence of their ships at the approaches to the Baltic, *Bonaparte's back door*, as the *Gazette* had called it, would prevent any more trouble.

There was a tap at the door and Herrick walked into the cabin, his hat jammed beneath his arm.

'Be seated, Thomas.'

He watched his friend, feeling the warmth he held for him. Round-faced and sturdy, with the same clear blue eyes he had seen on their first ship together, here at Spithead. There were small touches of grey on his hair, like hoar-frost on a strong bush, but he was still Herrick.

Herrick gave a great sigh. 'It seems to take them longer not shorter to get things done, sir.' He shook his head. 'Some of them have thumbs instead of fingers. There are far too many folk with pieces of paper to shake in the faces of the press-gangs, prime seamen we could well do with. Hands from the Indiamen, bargemen and coasters. Dammit, sir, it's their war, too!'

Bolitho smiled. 'We've said that a few times, Thomas.' He

gestured around the cabin with its green leather chairs and well-made furniture. 'This is very comfortable. You have a fine vessel in the *Benbow*.'

Herrick was as stubborn as ever. 'It's men who win battles, sir. Not ships.' He relented and said, 'But it's a proud moment, I admit, *Benbow*'s a good sailer, fast for her size, and once we put to sea again I might raise another knot by shifting some more iron shot further aft.' His eyes were far-away, lost in a captain's constant struggle to keep his ship trimmed to best advantage.

'Your wife? Will she go straight to Kent?'

Herrick looked at him. 'Aye, sir. When we're out of sight of land, she says.' He gave a slow smile. 'God, I'm a lucky man.'

Bolitho nodded. 'So am I, Thomas, to have you as my flag captain again.' He watched the uncertainty on Herrick's homely features and guessed what was coming next.

'It may be impertinence, sir, but have you ever thought? I – I mean, would you consider . . .'

Bolitho met his gaze and answered quietly, 'If I could bring her back, old friend, I'd cut off an arm to do it. But marry another?' He looked away, recalling with sharp anguish Herrick's face when he had brought word of Cheney's death from England. 'I thought I'd get over it. Lose myself. Heaven knows, Thomas, you've done your best to aid me. Sometimes I am so near to despair . . .' He stopped. What was happening to him? But when he looked at Herrick he saw only understanding. Pride at sharing what he had perhaps known longer than anyone.

Herrick stood up and placed his coffee cup on the table. 'I'd best go on deck. Mr Wolfe is a good seaman, but he lacks a certain gentleness with the new men.' He grimaced. 'God knows, he frightens me sometimes!'

'I shall see you later at four bells, Thomas.' Bolitho turned to watch a gull's darting shape as it flapped past the quarter windows. 'Adam. Is he well? I spoke to him briefly when I came aboard. There is so much I'd like to know.'

Herrick nodded. 'Aye, sir. High rank makes higher demand. If you'd entertained young Adam yesterday, the others in the wardroom might have sniffed at favouritism, something which I know is foul to you. But he *has* missed you. As I have. I think

he yearns for a frigate, but fears it might hurt the pair of us,
you especially.'

'I shall see him soon. When the ship is too busy for gossip.'

Herrick grinned. 'That'll be *very* soon, if I'm any judge. The
first really good squall and they'll be too worn out to stand!'

For a long time after Herrick had left him Bolitho sat quietly
on the green leather bench below the stern windows. It was his
way of getting to know the ship, by listening, identifying, even
though he was unable to share what was happening above him,
or beyond his marine sentry.

The stamp of feet and squeal of blocks. He shivered, recog-
nizing the sounds of a boat being hoisted up and over the gangway to be stowed on the tier with the others.

The bustle of many men, guided and harried by their warrant
and petty officers. The seasoned hands being spread thinly
through the watch and quarter bill to make the raw and untrained ones less of a hazard.

Volunteers had come to the ship in Devonport, and even here
at Portsmouth. Seamen tired of the land, men running from
the law, from debt or the gibbet.

And the rest, hauled aboard by the press-gangs, dazed, terrified, caught up in a world they barely understood, except at a
distance. This was a far cry from a King's ship under a full
head of sail standing proudly out to sea. Here was the harsh
reality of the crowded messdecks and the boatswain's rattan.

It was Herrick's task to weld them by his own methods into
a company. One which would stand to the guns, even cheer if
need be as they thrust against an enemy.

Bolitho caught sight of his reflection in the streaming windows. *And mine to command the squadron.*

Allday entered the cabin and studied him thoughtfully. 'I've
told Ozzard to lay out your best coat, sir.' He leaned over as the
deck tilted steeply. 'It'll make a change not to fight the
Frenchies. I suppose it'll be the Russians or the Swedes before
long.'

Bolitho looked at him with exasperation. 'A *change*? Is that
all you care about it?'

Allday beamed. 'It *matters*, o' course, sir, to admirals, to
Parliament and the like. But the poor sailorman.' He shook his
head. 'All he sees is the enemy's guns belching fire at him, feels

the iron parting his pigtail. He's not caring much for the colour of the flag!'

Bolitho breathed out slowly. 'No wonder the girls fall for your persuasion, Allday. You had *me* believing you just then!'

Allday chuckled. 'I shall give your hair a trim, sir. We've a lot to live up to, with Mr Browne amongst us.'

Bolitho sat back in a chair and waited. He would have to put up with it. Allday would guess how much he might worry until they were at sea in one company. Equally, he would make certain he was not alone for a minute until the captains came to pay their respects. With Allday you could rarely win.

Two bells chimed out from the forecastle, and seconds later Herrick came aft once more to Bolitho's cabin.

Bolitho held out his arms for his coat and allowed Ozzard to tug it into place, to make sure that his queue was lifted neatly above the gold-laced collar.

Allday stood by the bulkhead, and after some hesitation took down one of the swords from its rack.

It was glittering brightly in spite of the grey light from the windows, beautifully fashioned and gilded, and when drawn from its scabbard would reveal an equally perfect blade. It was a presentation sword, given and paid for by the townspeople of Falmouth. A gift, a recognition for what Bolitho had done in the Mediterranean.

Herrick watched the little tableau. For a few moments he forgot the pain of leaving Dulcie so soon, the hundred and one things which needed his attention on deck.

He knew what Allday was thinking, and wondered how he would put it.

The coxswain asked awkwardly, 'This one, sir?' He let his eyes stray to the second sword. Old-fashioned, straight-bladed, and yet a part of the man, of his family before him.

Bolitho smiled. 'I think not. It will be raining soon. I'd not wish to spoil that fine weapon by *wearing* it.' He waited while Allday hurried across with the other sword and clipped it to his belt. 'And besides,' he glanced from Allday to Herrick, 'I'd like *all* my friends about me today.'

Then he clapped Herrick on the shoulder and added, 'We will go on deck together, eh, Thomas? Like before.'

Ozzard watched the two officers leave the cabin and said in a mournful whisper, 'I don't know why he doesn't get rid of that old sword, or leave it at home.'

Allday did not bother to reply but strolled after Bolitho to take his own place on the quarterdeck.

But he thought about Ozzard's remark all the same. When Richard Bolitho parted with that old sword it would be because there was no life in his hand to grasp it.

Bolitho walked out past the helmsmen and ran his eye over the assembled officers and seamen. He felt his eyes smarting to the wind, the chill in the air as it whipped around his legs.

Wolfe looked across at Herrick and touched his hat, his ginger hair flapping from beneath it as if to escape.

'All cables are hove short, sir,' he said in his harsh, toneless voice.

Equally formal, Herrick reported to Bolitho. 'The squadron is ready, sir.'

Bolitho nodded, aware of the moment, of the faces, mostly unknown, around him, and the ship which contained all of them.

'Then make a general signal, if you please.' He hesitated, turning slightly to look across the nettings towards the nearest two-decker, the *Odin*. Poor Inch had been almost speechless with the pleasure of seeing him again. He finished it abruptly. '*Up anchor.*'

Browne was already there with the signal party, pushing urgently at a harassed midshipman who was supposed to be assisting him.

A few more anxious moments, the hoarse cries from forward as the capstan heaved in still more of the dripping cable.

'*Anchor's aweigh, sir!*'

Bolitho had to grip his hands like twin vices behind his back to contain his excitement as one by one his ships weighed and staggered violently downwind beneath a mass of thrashing, booming canvas.

The *Benbow* was no exception. It seemed an age before the first confusion was overcome, and with her yards braced round, her courses and then the topsails hardening like metal breast-plates to the wind, she steadied on her first tack away from the land.

Spray thundered over the weather gangway and up past the hard-eyed figurehead. Men dashed out along the yards or scurried in frantic groups to add their weight to the braces and halliards.

Wolfe had his speaking trumpet to his mouth without a break.

'Mr Pascoe, sir! Get those damned younkers of yours aloft again! It's a shambles up there!'

For an instant Bolitho saw his nephew turn and stare along the length of the deck. As third lieutenant he was in charge of the foremast, about as far from the quarterdeck as he could be.

Bolitho gave a quick nod and saw Pascoe respond just as swiftly, his black hair ruffling across his face. It was like seeing himself at the same age, Bolitho thought.

'Mr Browne. Signal the squadron to form line astern of the flagship.' He saw Herrick watching him and added, 'The frigates and our sloop will know their part without unnecessary instructions.'

Herrick grinned, his face streaming with salt spray. *'They'll* know, sir.'

Beating hard to windward, the frigates were already thrusting through bursting curtains of spray to reach their stations where they would watch over their ponderous consorts.

Bolitho walked to the larboard side to look at the land. Grey and shapeless, already losing its identity in the worsening weather.

How many had watched the squadron getting under way? Herrick's wife, Admiral Beauchamp, all the old crippled sailors thrown on the beach, flotsam of war. Once they had cursed the Navy and its ways, but there would be a few tight throats amongst those same men as they watched the ships make sail.

He heard Wolfe say scathingly, 'God, look at him, will you! All ribs and trucks, even his coat looks like a purser's shirt on a handspike!'

Bolitho turned to see who Wolfe had described and saw a thin, flapping figure scurrying towards a companion and vanishing below. His face was pure white, like chalk. Like a death's-head.

Herrick lowered his voice. 'Mr Loveys, the surgeon, sir. I'd not want to see his face looking down at me on the table!'

Bolitho said, 'I agree.'

T.I.S.—B

He took a telescope from a midshipman and levelled it towards the other ships. They were working into line, their sails in confusion as the wind swept across their quarter and thrust them over.

Before they made their rendezvous they would have improved considerably. Sail and gun drill, testing and changing. But if they met with an enemy squadron before that time, and for all Bolitho knew a whole French fleet might be at sea, he would be required and expected to lead his squadron into battle.

He glanced at the companion hatch as if expecting to see the surgeon's skull-like face watching him. It was to be hoped that Loveys would be kept unemployed for a long while yet.

Order was returning to the upper deck. Tangles of cordage had changed into neatly flaked lines or belayed coils. Seamen were gathering at the foot of each mast to be checked and counted. And above all of them, their silhouettes as lively as squirrels in a galeswept forest, the topmen worked to make certain the sails were set and drawing to perfection.

It was time to leave. To give Herrick back his command.

'I will go aft, Captain Herrick.'

Herrick matched his mood. 'Aye, sir. I shall exercise the upper batteries until dusk.'

For nearly a week the squadron battered its way across the North Sea in weather which even Ben Grubb admitted was some of the worst he had endured.

Each night the reeling ships lay to under storm canvas, and with the coming of first light had to repeat the misery of finding their scattered companions. Then, in some sort of formation once more, they proceeded on their north-easterly course, drills and repairs being carried out whenever the weather allowed.

Throughout the squadron there had been several men killed and others injured. The deaths were mostly caused by falls from aloft as repeatedly the dazed and salt-blinded men fought to shorten sail or repair damage to rigging.

In the *Benbow* several hands had been hurt by their own ignorance. On darkened decks it was possible to be cut down by a line as it was hauled madly through a block. The touch of it on a man's skin was like a red-hot iron.

One man vanished without anyone seeing him go. Washed overboard, left floundering for a few agonizing moments as the two-decker faded into the darkness.

Everything was wet and dismally cold. The only heat was from the galley stove, and it was impossible to dry out clothing in a ship which seemed intent on rolling herself on to her beam-ends.

Whenever he went on deck, Bolitho could sense the gloom around him like something physical. Knowing Herrick as he did, he guessed that nothing more could be done to ease the men's suffering. Some captains would not have cared, but would have ordered their boatswain's mates to flog the last man aloft or the last man down from a duty. But not Herrick. From lieutenant to captain he had remained unswerving in his determination to lead rather than drive, to understand his men rather than use fear as his right of command.

Yet, in spite of all this, three men were seized up and flogged after Herrick had read the relevant Articles of War and the ship had continued to smash her way up and through every succession of crested rollers.

Bolitho had stayed away from the punishments. Even that was no longer his concern. He had paced up and down his cabin, hearing the regular swish and crack across a naked back in time with a marine drummer's staccato beat.

He was beginning to wonder what he, or any other admiral, had to do to remain sane during such periods of misery.

And then, quite suddenly, the wind dropped slightly, and small isolated patches of blue appeared between the banks of cloud.

Seamen and marines paused to look up and draw breath, hot food was hurried through the messdecks as if in a battle's lull or that the cook could not believe his galley would remain in use for long.

Bolitho went on deck just before midday and felt the difference. The midshipmen, their faces suitably expressionless as the master and his mates watched over their efforts with sextants to check and estimate the ship's position. The men working high above the deck no longer held to each vibrating spar or shroud but moved more easily about their varied tasks. The first lieutenant, leading a little procession of experts, passed down the larboard gangway, pausing to look for anything which needed repairing, painting or splicing. He was followed by Drodge, the gunner, Big Tom Swale, the gap-toothed boatswain, Tregoye, the carpenter, and several of their mates.

By the forward companion, Purvis Spreat, the *Benbow*'s purser, was speaking confidentially with Manley, the fifth lieutenant. More food for the wardroom perhaps? Too much madeira being consumed? It might have been anything. Spreat looked a typical purser, Bolitho thought. Sharp-eyed, suspicious, just honest enough to stay out of trouble. He had to feed, clothe and supply every man aboard, with no excuses for bad weather or faulty navigation to sustain him.

The marines were standing easy in two long scarlet lines, swaying from side to side in the ship's regular motion. Bolitho watched them, putting names to faces, trying to gauge the skills or the lack of them. Major Clinton, with Lieutenant Marston, his junior, walked slowly along the ranks, listening to whatever Sergeant Rombilow was telling them about each man and his duties in the ship.

The marines were a strange breed, Bolitho thought. Jammed as tightly as the seamen in the *Benbow*'s fat hull and yet completely apart, so different in their ways and customs. Bolitho had seen them in America during the Revolution, when as a youthful lieutenant he had taken the first step towards his own command. In the Mediterranean or the Caribbean, the Atlantic and the East Indies, they all had one thing in common. Reliability.

Bolitho saw the afternoon watch gathering below the quarterdeck in readiness to take over the ship for the next four hours.

Here and there a jaw was still champing on the first good, hot meal for days. A few eyes were studying the changing weather with professional interest or, in the case of the new men, obvious relief.

But most of the men were darting glances at their rear-admiral as he paced restlessly along the weather side of the quarterdeck. They were quick to look away whenever Bolitho turned towards them. The usual mixture. Interest, curiosity, resentment. Bolitho knew from past experience that if he wanted more it was up to him to earn it.

He heard Pascoe's voice as he strode aft and touched his hat to Speke, the second lieutenant, who was about to be relieved.

'The watch is aft, sir.'

Across on the other ships it would be the same. Routine and tradition. Like a well-tried play where everyone had changed roles on many occasions until he was word-perfect.

The two lieutenants examined the compass, the log, the set of the sails, while the other players moved round them to their stations. The helmsmen and quartermaster, the midshipman of the watch. Bolitho frowned. What was *his* name? Penels, that was it. The youngest aboard. Just twelve, and a fellow Cornishman. He smiled. Hardly a *man*.

'Relieve the wheel, if you please.'

Eight bells chimed out from the forecastle and the forenoon watchkeepers hurried to their messes for their food and a good, strong tot.

Bolitho crossed the quarterdeck and said, 'You are looking well, Adam.'

They moved away from the double-wheel and its three helmsmen and walked side by side to the weather nettings.

'Thank you, sir.' Pascoe shot him a sideways glance. 'Uncle. You, too.'

When Bolitho eventually pulled out his watch he realized he had been speaking with his nephew for an hour. It had seemed like minutes, and yet they had conjured up a far different picture from the one around them. Not sea and sky, spray and taut canvas, but country lanes, low cottages and the grey bulk of Pendennis Castle.

Pascoe was very tanned, as dark as a gipsy.

Bolitho said, 'We shall all be shivering soon, my lad. But perhaps we may be able to set foot ashore. That was why I could never stand blockade duty in the Bay. The British people become moist-eyed when they speak of their "wooden walls", the weatherbeaten ships which keep the French fleet bottled up in port. They would speak less warmly if they knew what hell it can be.'

Midshipman Penels called nervously, 'Signal from *Styx*, sir.' He purposefully looked at Pascoe. '*Man overboard*, sir.'

Pascoe nodded and seized a telescope to train it on the distant frigate.

'Acknowledge. I will tell the captain presently.'

He watched the frigate's shape shortening as she came up into the wind, her sails aback and in confusion. It was to be hoped she could get her quarter boat away in time to recover the luckless man.

Bolitho watched Pascoe's expression as he studied the frigate's swift manoeuvre. He thought, too, of her captain, John Neale. He had been Penels' age when the mutiny had broken out aboard his *Phalarope* during the American Revolution. A small, plump youth, he could see him clearly. He could even smile about it now. How he and Herrick had rubbed the naked mid-shipman all over with rancid butter to force him through a vent hole to free him from the mutineers and rouse assistance. Neale had been small, but it had been a hard struggle all the same.

Now Neale was a post-captain, and he knew exactly what Pascoe was thinking as he watched his ship-handling through the glass.

Bolitho said quietly, 'As soon as possible, Adam. I'll do what I can. You've earned it.'

Pascoe stared at him, his eyes wide with astonishment. 'You knew, Uncle?'

Bolitho smiled. 'I was a frigate captain once, Adam. It is something you never quite lose.' He looked up at his rear-admiral's flag streaming from the mizzen truck. 'Even when it is taken from you.'

Pascoe exclaimed, 'Thank you very much. I – I mean, I want to be with you. But you know that. I just feel I am marking time in a ship of the line.'

Bolitho saw Ozzard hovering below the poop, his thin body screwed up against the damp wind. Time to eat.

He chuckled. 'I think *I* said much the same, too!'

As Bolitho ducked below the poop, Pascoe began to pace slowly up and down the weather side, his hands clasped behind him as he had seen Bolitho do so often.

Pascoe would not have said anything about his hopes to either Bolitho or Herrick. He should have known he could not hide a secret from either of them.

He quickened his pace, his thoughts exploring the future, which no longer seemed an idle dream.

3

The Letter

It was another full day before Bolitho's lookouts sighted Admiral Damerum's squadron, and then because of the lateness of the hour an extra night passed before they could make contact.

Throughout the following morning, while Bolitho's ships changed tack to run down on the larger formation, Bolitho studied the admiral's squadron through a powerful telescope and wondered at the sense of keeping such a force employed in this fashion. The British fleets, in summer and winter alike, were expected to blockade the Dutch men-of-war along the coastline of Holland, the Spanish at Cadiz and, of course, the powerful French bases of Brest and Toulon. Apart from that, they were entrusted to patrol the vital trade routes from the East and West Indies, to protect them from the enemy, from privateers and even common pirates. It was an almost impossible task.

And now, because Tsar Paul of Russia, who had little liking for Britain and a mounting admiration of Bonaparte, might be expected to break his neutrality, even more desperately needed squadrons were wasted here at the approaches to the Baltic.

Herrick joined him and said, 'The third ship, sir, that'll be Sir Samuel Damerum's.'

Bolitho moved his glass slightly and trained it on the one which wore the Union Flag at her mainmast truck. He was very conscious of the difference between the slow-moving vessels and his own small squadron. Patched canvas, weather-beaten hulls, in some cases whole areas of paint stripped away by wind and sea, they made a marked contrast with his newly refitted two-deckers.

Far beyond the heavier ships Bolitho could just make out the topgallants of a patrolling frigate, the admiral's 'eyes', and he guessed that their lookouts could also see the Danish coast.

'Call away my barge, Thomas. We will be up to them within the hour. See that the stores for the admiral are sent across in another boat directly.'

It was always a strange feeling when ships met each other. Those which had been at sea for a long period were always craving for news from home. The new arrivals had the additional anxiety of ignorance about what might be waiting for them.

His flag lieutenant strode across the quarterdeck, his face pinched with the keen air.

Bolitho said, 'There is the admiral's flagship. The second-rate.'

Browne nodded. 'The *Tantalus*, sir. Captain Walton.' He sounded as if he did not much care.

'You will come across with me.' He smiled grimly. 'To ensure that I do not do something indiscreet.'

Herrick said, 'It might all blow over, sir. And we'll be back at Spithead for orders before you know it.'

Bolitho was in his cabin collecting his despatches from the strongbox when a clatter of blocks and the stiff crack of canvas told him that *Benbow* was coming about under shortened sail so that the barge could be lowered safely alongside.

When he went on deck again the scene had changed once more. The admiral's ships, moving very slowly under fully braced topsails, were like an enemy fleet, with *Benbow* about to break through their line of battle. It was only too easy to picture, and although many of *Benbow*'s people had never heard a shot fired in anger, Bolitho, like Herrick and some of the others, had seen it many times.

'Barge alongside, sir.' Herrick hurried towards him, his face lined with the responsibility of controlling his ship and the rest of the squadron in Bolitho's absence.

'I will be as quick as I can, Thomas.' He tugged his hat firmly across his head, seeing the marines at the entry port, the boatswain's mates moistening their silver calls on their lips in readiness to speed him on his way. 'The admiral will not wish me to be an enforced guest if the sea gets up again, eh?'

A midshipman, unusually neat and tidy, was standing in the pitching barge, and beside him Allday was at the tiller, his rightful place. He must have impressed upon somebody that the rear-admiral would prefer his coxswain to a ship's lieutenant. If Allday got his way, the next time there would be no midshipman either, he thought. Browne, too, was in the boat, somehow managing to appear elegant.

'Attention in the boat!'

The calls shrilled, and Bolitho jumped the last few feet into the sternsheets as the barge rose sluggishly against *Benbow*'s rounded flank.

'Bear off forrard! Give way all!'

Once clear of the two-decker's lee, the barge dipped and staggered through the waves like a dolphin. When Bolitho glanced at the midshipman he saw that his face was already ashen. His name was Graham, and he was seventeen, one of the senior 'young gentlemen'. His chances of promotion to lieutenant might be marred if he was sick in the barge carrying his admiral to meet another.

'Sit *down*, Mr Graham.' He saw the youth staring at him, startled at being addressed by one so senior. 'It will be a lively pull yet.'

'Th-thank you, sir.' He sank down gratefully. 'I shall be all right, sir.'

Across his shoulders Allday grinned broadly at the stroke oarsman. Only Bolitho would bother about a mere midshipman. The funny part was, that Allday knew the luckless Graham had been eating some pie he had brought from England. It had doubtless been going mouldy when he had stepped aboard. After days at sea in a damp, cheerless midshipman's berth, it must be as near poison as made no difference.

Bolitho's arrival aboard Damerum's flagship was no less noisy than his departure from his own.

He got a hasty impression of glittering bayonets and red coats, of stiff-faced lieutenants, and then the admiral himself, thrusting forward to meet him.

'Come aft, Bolitho. God's teeth, this chill is enough to pierce your marrow!'

The *Tantalus* was a good deal larger than the *Benbow*, and Damerum's quarters more lavish than Bolitho had ever seen in

a King's ship. Apart from the movement, and the muffled shipboard noises, it could have been part of a rich chamber. If the
ship ever had to clear for action in a hurry, the fine drapes and
expensive French furniture would suffer badly.

Damerum gestured towards a chair while a servant took
Bolitho's hat and boat-cloak.

'Sit you down, sir, and let's have a good look at you, eh?'

Bolitho sat. Sir Samuel Damerum, Knight of the Bath,
Admiral of the Red, was, at a guess, in his early fifties. He had
a brisk, lively way of moving and speaking, but his greying hair,
and an obvious thickening about his middle which even an
immaculately tailored waistcoat could not conceal, made him
seem older.

He said, 'So you're Richard Bolitho.' His gaze fell briefly on
the gold medal which Bolitho wore around his neck for this
formal visit. 'The Nile medal, no less.' He shook his head.
'Some people have all the luck.' In the same quick manner he
changed tack again. 'How's the squadron?' He did not wait
but added, 'You took longer to reach me than I'd hoped, but
can't be helped, what?'

Bolitho said, 'I'm sorry about that, sir. Bad weather, raw
landsmen. The usual.'

Damerum rubbed his hands, and as if by sorcery a servant
appeared.

'Brandy, man. And not that muck we keep for captains!' He
chuckled. 'God, what a war, Bolitho. On and on. No damn end
to it.'

Bolitho waited, not yet at ease with this erratic man. He
spoke a lot, but so far had said nothing.

Bolitho said, 'My flag captain is sending some stores across
for you, sir.'

'Stores?' The admiral's eyes were on the brandy and the two
glasses which his servant had carried to a table. 'Oh, yes. Mr
Fortnum, my grocer in London, does his best to keep me sup-
plied, y'know. Not easy these days.'

Bolitho did not know who Mr Fortnum was, but felt he
should have done.

The brandy was mellow and warming. Much of it and Bolitho
knew he would be asleep if he was not careful.

'Well, Bolitho, you will know that you are to assume the

duties of the inshore squadron. The Danish affair seems to have
cooled down for the present, but my information is that the
Tsar of Russia is eager to join with the French against us. You
know about the pact he has been trying to make with Sweden?'
Again he did not wait for an answer but hurried on. 'Well, he
is still set on that idea. In addition, he has the backing of
Prussia. Together they may force the Danes against us also. It
is never easy to live in peace next to a raging lion!'

Bolitho pictured his small squadron trying to stem the
advance of the combined Baltic fleets. Beauchamp had said that
his task would not be an easy one.

'Will we enter the Baltic, sir?'

Damerum signalled to his servant for the glasses to be refilled.

'Yes and no. A great show of strength would be wrongly
interpreted. Tsar Paul would use it to fan the flames. We'd be
at war in a week. But a smaller force, yours, can go with peaceful intent. My ships are known to all the spies who flit past my
frigates. It will soon be common knowledge that a new squadron
is here. Smaller, and so a lessening of tension and suspicion all
round.' He smiled, showing very even teeth. 'Besides which,
Bolitho, if there was real trouble we are helpless until next year.
March at the earliest. We could not get to grips with the Tsar's
ships while they are in harbour, so we must wait for the winter
ice to melt. Until then,' he fixed Bolitho with a calm stare, 'you
will keep an eye on things at close quarters.' He chuckled. 'At
very close quarters to begin with. You are instructed to enter
Copenhagen and meet with a British official there.'

Bolitho stared at him. 'Surely you, as senior officer, would be
a better choice, sir?'

'Your concern does you credit. But we have to tread warily.
Too junior an officer and the Danes will feel slighted. Too
senior and they will see this for something sinister, a threat
perhaps.' He wagged a finger. 'No, a young rear-admiral would
be about right. The Admiralty believes so, and I have confirmed
my support.'

'Well, thank you, sir.' He did not know what to say. It was
all happening so quickly. A squadron, a new station, and almost
at once he was off again on something quite different. He had
a feeling he was going to find Browne very useful after
all.

Damerum added suddenly, 'In any doubts at all, send a fast vessel to find me. Half of my ships are returning to England for overhaul, the remainder are to reinforce the Dutch blockade. It is all in the written instructions which even now my flag lieutenant is handing to yours. They are lucky men. They handle the destiny of a fleet, but take no part in the skill of responsibility for it, damn them!'

Water dashed against the stern windows like pellets. It had begun to rain or worse.

Bolitho stood up. 'I shall find my fresh instructions interesting reading, Sir Samuel.' He held out his hand. 'And thank you for the trust you have placed in me.'

As he said it he realized the true meaning for the first time. It was like having a line severed. The instructions were for him to interpret as he saw fit. There was nobody nearby to run to for guidance or advice. Right or wrong, it was his decision.

'I'll not see you over the side, if you don't mind, Bolitho. I've letters to write to catch the courier brig for England.' As they walked to the screen door, beyond which Browne was conversing with a very weary looking lieutenant, he said, 'So good luck in Copenhagen. It's a fair city, I'm told.'

After a perilous descent down the flagship's side, Bolitho and Browne wedged themselves in the sternsheets and wrapped their boat-cloaks around their bodies.

Through chattering teeth Browne asked, 'All well, sir? I should have been *with* you, but the admiral's aide was waiting to head me off. I did not even get offered a glass, sir!' He sounded quietly outraged.

Bolitho said, 'We are going to Copenhagen, Mr Browne.' He saw the lieutenant's eye light up. 'Does that suit?'

'Indeed it does, sir!'

It was good to be back aboard *Benbow*. New she might be, and as yet untried, but already she had a personality, a warmth which had been lacking aboard the ship he had just visited. Perhaps it was Herrick's influence at work. You never knew for certain with ships, Bolitho thought.

Herrick joined him in the cabin and waited patiently while Bolitho rid himself of his dripping cloak and hat.

'Copenhagen, Thomas. We will lay a course for The Skaw at once, and I shall inform the squadron what is to happen.' He grinned at Herrick's grave expression. 'When I know myself, that is!'

It was a hundred miles at least to The Skaw, the northernmost point of Denmark. It would give him ample time to study his instructions, and perhaps even to read that which had been left out.

Bolitho lay back in a chair while Allday finished shaving him. It was early morning and barely light beyond the salt-streaked windows, but Bolitho had been awake for an hour, preparing himself for a testing day and going over his instructions to see if he had missed anything.

Bolitho was surprised he was so relaxed. He was able to drowse while the razor slid smoothly up his throat, to listen to the sluice of water overhead and the attendant march of bare feet as the decks were washed down.

He thought he heard the boatswain's thick voice, too. Swale, Big Tom as he was called, had a strange sounding tone, almost a lisp, caused by the loss of most of his front teeth. In battle or brawl, Bolitho did not know. Herrick had said he was a good boatswain, and at this moment he was probably examining the poop and quarterdeck again. It was always a strain for the first weeks at sea for a newly built ship. Timber, not always as well seasoned as it should be after years of war and shortages, could do strange things with the hull rolling about in all directions.

Benbow certainly sailed well, he thought. Several times the other two-deckers had been forced to spread more canvas to keep up with her. A fine ship. She alone must have taken the best part of a forest to build.

Bolitho jerked upright in the chair, making Allday exclaim, '*Easy*, sir! I all but parted your windpipe just then!'

Then he said, 'I heard it, too. Gunfire!'

Bolitho started to rise and then lay back again. 'Finish the shave, please.' He controlled his sudden excitement. 'It won't do for me to go rushing on deck.'

It was hard, all the same. He had always been used to going at once to the quarterdeck to assess the circumstances for himself. He recalled one of his first captains, when as a midshipman he had been ordered to pass an urgent message aft to that same lordly presence.

The captain had been drinking in his stern cabin. Bolitho could picture him without effort. As he had stammered out the message, the captain had turned merely to nod and say, 'My compliments to the first lieutenant, Mr Bolitho. Tell him I will come up *shortly*. That is, if you have still the breath for it!'

Perhaps he, too, had been dying to see for himself, as Bolitho was now.

There was a tap at the screen door and Herrick entered the cabin.

'Good morning, Thomas.' He smiled. It was wrong to play games with Herrick and he added, 'I heard firing.'

Herrick nodded. 'From the bearing I would say it is *Lookout*, sir, to the nor'-east.'

Bolitho wiped his skin with a towel and stood up, feeling the deck quiver as the rudder fell heavily in a trough. *Lookout* was the little sloop-of-war, and her captain was Commander Veitch, Herrick's previous first lieutenant. A stern-looking man from Tynemouth, utterly dependable, who had earned his promotion the hard way. If he was tackling something on his own, then it was small and agile. Veitch obviously considered there was no time to inform his flagship or call for assistance. He was not that sort of man anyway.

Herrick suggested, 'Probably a blockade runner, sir.'

Ozzard hurried in with Bolitho's coat and held it out like a Spaniard tormenting a bull.

Bolitho said, 'Are either of the frigates in sight yet?'

More explosions echoed against the *Benbow*'s side. Short and sharp. *Lookout*'s bow-chasers from their sound.

Herrick replied, 'Not when I was on deck, sir. *Relentless* should be away to the sou'-west and *Styx* down to lee'rd as instructed.'

'Good.' He slipped into his coat. It felt damp. 'Let us see for ourselves.'

The sky was much brighter when they walked from beneath the poop, and Wolfe hurried to meet them.

'Masthead reports *Lookout* in sight, sir. She's in company

with another smaller craft. Either a brig or a ship with one mast shot out of her!' He bared his teeth.

Bolitho could read his mind. An early capture. Prize-money. A command for somebody. Even a temporary one as prize-master was all it needed in wartime. And some luck. Bolitho had had both, and had so won his own first command.

People bustled about the quarterdeck, securing the pumps and scrubbers, faces still obscured in shadow. But all well aware that their admiral was up and about. What did it mean to them? A sea fight? Death or mutilation? It would certainly be a break in the monotony of daily routine.

Bolitho saw some of the officers on the lee side of the deck. Byrd and Manley, the fourth and fifth lieutenants, and, younger still, Courtenay, the sixth, whom Allday had ousted from his barge.

He must find time to meet and get to know them. He was lucky to know the minds of the officers who captained the squadron, but if the *Benbow* was driven into a hard battle, a young lieutenant could find himself in command after one devastating broadside.

Wolfe had a telescope to his eye and said, 'Here comes *Relentless*! I can just see her sky-scrapers. She scents the smell of battle, sir.'

Bolitho could imagine the activity aboard the thirty-six-gun frigate. He had met her young captain, Rowley Peel, only twice. He was the odd one out in the squadron, but was quick to move when need be. Dashing down from his station to protect his heavier consorts, to harry the enemy, to attempt whatever was so ordered by the flagship.

Old Grubb rumbled, 'Better day today. Fine an' clear.' He lapsed into silence again, his hands thrust deeply into his shabby watch-coat.

Wolfe saw Pascoe on the larboard gangway and called harshly, 'Would you go aloft, Mr Pascoe. Take a glass and see what you can determine.'

Pascoe threw his hat to a seaman and ran to the weather shrouds. He was amongst the black tangle of rigging and beyond the mainyard before Bolitho could watch his progress. Bolitho thought of his own hatred for heights, what it had cost him at Pascoe's age. He felt his mouth lift in a smile. It would sound

ridiculous to tell somebody that one of the fruits of his promotion had been that he no longer had to climb up those head-
spinning shrouds.

Pascoe called down, his voice clear above the drumming beat
of canvas and rigging.

'*Lookout* has grappled, sir! The other one is a brig. She wears
no flag but they are hoisting our colours now!'

Several of the idlers on the gangways and gundeck cheered,
and Herrick exclaimed :

'So soon. Well done. Well done.'

Bolitho nodded. 'You trained your old first lieutenant well,
Thomas.'

Lieutenant Browne appeared through the after companion,
buttoning his coat and saying, 'I heard something. What is
happening?'

Wolfe said to the sailing master, 'A lot of use *he'll* be!'

Herrick answered, 'We have taken a prize, Mr Browne. I fear
you have missed it.'

Several of the nearby seamen were grinning and nudging
each other. Bolitho sensed the change. There was a better feeling already.

'Deck there! Land on the lee bow!'

Herrick and the master bustled to the chart room beneath the
poop to consult their findings.

That would be The Skaw. As far as the strange brig was concerned, it had been a near thing. An hour earlier and she would
have slipped away unseen.

Bolitho said, 'I will take breakfast now. Let me know when
Lookout is near enough to exchange signals.'

Herrick stood by the chart room entrance, shading his eyes
as if he expected to see the other vessels.

'Mr Grubb thinks we should be off The Skaw before noon if
the wind stays with us.'

'I agree. Once there you may signal the squadron to anchor
in succession.' Bolitho nodded to the other officers and made his
way aft.

Herrick gave a great sigh. He tended to worry when Bolitho
was nearby, but he worried all the more when he was gone.

Pascoe slithered down to the deck and retrieved his hat. He
was about to approach the quarterdeck when a small figure

stepped from between two eighteen-pounders and said, 'Excuse me, sir!' It was Midshipman Penels.

'Yes?' Pascoe paused and studied the boy. *Was I ever like that?*

'I – I don't know how to explain, sir.'

He sounded and looked so despairing that Pascoe said, 'Speak out.'

It was virtually impossible to find any privacy in a ship-of-war. Apart from the captain, and possibly a man deep in the ship's cells, there was always a crowd.

Pascoe knew very little about the newest midshipman. He was from Cornwall, and that was all he had to go on.

He said, 'You are from Bodmin, I believe?'

'Yes, sir.' Penels looked around like a trapped animal. 'There's someone in your division, sir. Someone I grew up with back in England.'

Pascoe stood aside as a file of marines stamped past on their way to one of their complicated drills.

Penels explained, 'His name is John Babbage, sir. He was taken by the press-gang at Plymouth. I didn't know until we were at sea. He worked for my mother after my father died, sir. He was good to me. My best friend.'

Pascoe looked away. It was not his place to interfere. In any case, Penels should have gone to the first lieutenant or the master.

But he remembered his own beginning. The long, hungry walk from Penzance to Falmouth. Just a boy, and quite alone.

'Why did you approach me, Mr Penels? The truth now.'

'My friend said you are a good officer, sir. Not so sharp as some.'

Pascoe formed a mental picture of this unfortunate Babbage. A wild-eyed youth, nearer his own age than Penels', he would have thought.

'Well, we are with the squadron now, Mr Penels. Had you come to me in port I might have been able to do something.' He thought of Wolfe and knew it would have made little difference even then.

A ship needed men. Every hand she could get. Wolfe was a good officer in many ways, but he was short of sympathy for any catch brought aboard by the press.

But it must be hard for both Penels and his friend of boyhood
days.

In the same hull, yet neither knowing the other was aboard
until the ship was standing out to sea. Separated not only by
rank and station, but also by the ship's own geography. Penels
served with the afterguard for sail drill and duty with the
quarterdeck nine-pounders. Babbage was classed as a landman
in his own division at the foremast. Babbage was young and
agile. With luck he should soon learn to run aloft with the
topmen, the aristocrats of seamanship.

He heard himself say, 'I will look into it. I'll not promise
anything though.'

He strode away, unable to bear the gratitude in Penels' eyes.

Commander Matthew Veitch arrived in Bolitho's cabin and
looked around him curiously. On his left shoulder the single
epaulette denoting his rank glittered in bright contrast to his
shabby sea-going coat. Veitch had served with Bolitho before
and knew he would get no thanks for wasting time to change
his clothing before he reported to the flagship.

Bolitho said, 'Sit down and tell me about it.'

It felt strange to be at anchor again. The four ships of the
line were all lying to their cables in close formation, with the
Danish coast clearly visible through the quarter windows. The
frigates were still on patrol, like watchdogs, they rarely rested.

The sloop, with her prize, were also at anchor off Skaw Point,
which in recent months had become the fleet's general rendezvous and resting place.

Veitch stretched his long legs. 'The prize is a merchant brig,
sir, the *Echo* out of Cherbourg. Slipped through our patrols in
a storm last week, her master says. She made a run for it, so I
raked her promptly.'

Bolitho glanced at the bulkhead door. Beyond it Browne,
who had a good knowledge of French, was busy going through
the *Echo*'s papers which Veitch had brought aboard.

A French brig. Without obvious cargo or passengers. She had
taken considerable risk in running the blockade, more again
when she had attempted to outsail the *Lookout*.

'Where bound?'

Veitch shrugged. 'Her master had false papers, I suspect. But the charts were found stuffed in the lazarette by one of my midshipmen with the boarding party.' He grinned. 'The lad was searching for food, no doubt, but I'll not spoil his glory because of that!' He became serious again. 'Two points were marked, sir. Copenhagen and Stockholm.'

Herrick moved restlessly away from the quarter windows and said, 'It smells, sir.'

Bolitho looked at him. 'You think as I do, Thomas? The French are in some way mixed up with Tsar Paul's discontent?'

Herrick replied, 'I feel certain of it, sir. The more they can put under arms, the better it is for them. We'll have the whole world against us if they have their way!'

The door opened and Browne entered the cabin. He held one letter in his hand, the broken seal shining dully like blood. He raised his eyebrows questioningly.

'What does it say?' Bolitho had noticed that Browne never shared a single word of information with anyone else present without his permission.

'It is addressed to a French government official in Copenhagen, sir.'

They all looked at each other. It was like some prearranged gathering of friends and enemies alike.

Browne continued in his unemotional tone, 'It is from the military commander in Toulon, and has reached this far via Paris and Cherbourg.'

Herrick could not contain his impatience. 'Don't keep us in suspense, man!'

Browne merely glanced at him. 'The French forces in Malta have surrendered to the British blockading squadron, sir. It happened last month.'

Herrick sounded perplexed. 'Well, surely that's *good* news? With Malta in our hands the Frenchies will have to tread warily in the Mediterranean in future!'

Browne did not smile. 'It should be known, sir, Tsar Paul of Russia had become the so-called head of the Grand Knights of Malta. When the French captured the island he was furious. This letter explains that the French government had offered to transfer the rule of Malta to the Tsar, knowing full well, of course, that the island would fall to the British anyway.'

Herrick spread his hands. 'I still don't see where we come in?'

Bolitho said quietly, 'The British will not leave Malta, Thomas. It will be too valuable to us, as you just remarked. The French have made a clever move. What better way of turning the Tsar and his friends finally against us? We and not the French are now between him and his precious Knights of Malta.'

Browne said, 'That sums it up, sir.'

'Obviously, Sir Samuel Damerum knew nothing of this. Because of bad weather the news has moved slowly.'

Veitch cleared his throat. 'But *you* have the letter, sir.'

Bolitho smiled gravely. 'I have indeed, thanks to you.'

'Will you act on it, sir?' Browne watched him impassively.

Bolitho walked to the windows and stared at the anchored ships.

'There is no one else here. I think the sooner we act the better.'

Herrick said, 'It's all getting beyond me, sir.'

Bolitho came to a series of decisions. It would all probably be too late, couriers could have reached Copenhagen overland if necessary. But if not, he would get no thanks from the Admiralty for dragging his feet.

'Send for my clerk. I'll make out orders for the brig. Commander Veitch, you may select a prize-crew for her. I want her to go with all speed to Great Yarmouth. Choose an intelligent prize-master, for I'll need him to take my despatches by the fastest means to London.' He looked at Herrick. 'I will shift my flag to *Styx*. Signal her accordingly.' He saw all the arguments, the protests building up on Herrick's round face and added quietly, 'I'd not ask you to take *Benbow* under the batteries of Elsinore, Thomas, if we are already at war! And if we are still at peace, a frigate will present a less threatening image.'

His clerk, Yovell, was already in the cabin, opening up his little writing desk which he kept available for such occasions.

Bolitho looked at Veitch. 'You will take over *Styx*'s duties for the present.'

From a corner of his eye he saw Yovell preparing his pens and ink ready to write new orders for the brig, a report for the Admiralty, a sentence of death, too, if that was asked of him.

To Herrick he said, 'You will command the squadron until

I return. If I am longer than a week without sending word, you will act accordingly.'

Herrick saw he was beaten. 'And when will you leave?'

'I hope to be aboard *Styx* and under way before we lose the light.'

After Herrick and Veitch had left to carry out his instructions, Bolitho asked the lieutenant, 'Do you think I am acting unwisely?' He saw Browne's rare uncertainty and added, 'Come on, man, you should know me better after more than a week at sea together. I'll not bite off your head if I disagree with what you say. But I may not heed it either.'

Browne shrugged. 'In a way I share the flag captain's apprehension, sir. I know your background, and I have read of many of your past exploits with admiration.' He looked Bolitho straight in the eyes. 'Like Captain Herrick, I see you as a fighting sailor, not as a diplomat.'

Bolitho recalled his visit to Damerum's flagship. He had thought it strange then that Damerum had not taken the initiative himself. He was a senior flag officer and well respected. Most such men would have expected it, demanded it in many cases.

Browne added quietly, 'But you are left with little room for manoeuvre now, sir. I would merely suggest, from my own experience with Admiral Sir George Beauchamp, that you tread warily. A victor is one thing, but a scapegoat is often more easily discovered.'

Herrick came back rubbing his hands. He looked cold.

'*Styx* has acknowledged our signal, sir. May I suggest you take some extra hands with you?' He grinned ruefully. 'I know there's no point in me protesting any more, so I took the liberty of telling Mr Wolfe to detail thirty seamen and a couple of junior officers. One lieutenant, and I thought a midshipman for messages and so forth.'

Bolitho nodded. 'That was thoughtful, Thomas. I think Captain Neale will appreciate it, too.'

Herrick sighed. '*Captain* Neale.' He shook his head. 'I still think of him as that greasy cherub we pushed through the vent-hole!'

Bolitho steadied his thoughts again. They were too often racing ahead like halliards gone mad and fouling their blocks.

What Browne had said made sense.

'Well, Yovell, write what I shall tell you.'

Herrick was about to leave again and asked, 'Which lieutenant, sir?'

'Mr Pascoe.' He smiled. 'But I expect you already thought of *that*, too!'

4

The Ajax

Allday and Ozzard carried a small chest of Bolitho's clothing and personal effects and laid it in the *Styx*'s stern cabin.

Captain John Neale watched Bolitho's reactions as he looked around and said, 'I hope you will be comfortable, sir.'

Neale had not changed all that much. He was just a larger edition of the chubby midshipman whom Herrick had described. But he wore his rank and command well, and had used his early experience to good effect.

Bolitho replied, 'It brings back memories, Captain Neale. Some bad, but many good ones.'

He saw Neale shifting his feet, eager to be off.

'You carry on, Captain. Get your ship under way again and make as much progress as you can. *Benbow*'s sailing master assures me there will be fog about.'

Neale grimaced. 'That could be dangerous in the narrows, sir. But if old Grubb says fog, then fog there will be!'

He left the cabin with a nod to Allday, who murmured admiringly, 'He's not spoiled, sir. Always liked him.'

Bolitho hid a smile. '*Spoiled?* He's a King's officer, Allday, not a piece of salt pork!'

From the quarterdeck they heard Neale shouting lustily, 'Get under way, Mr Pickthorn! Hands to the braces, roundly, if you please! And I'll want the t'gan's'ls on her once we clear the anchorage!'

Feet pounded along the decks, and Bolitho felt the cabin dip as *Styx* responded willingly to the sudden press of canvas. He sat down on the bench seat and surveyed the cabin slowly. He had commanded three frigates during his service. The last one, the thirty-six-gun *Tempest*, had been down in the Great South Sea. That was when they had first heard about the bloody revolution in France. The war had started soon afterwards, and had gone on ever since.

He wondered if Pascoe was exploring the ship, mulling over his uncle's promise to help him get an early transfer. It would be painful to lose him so quickly again. Anything else would be selfishness, Bolitho knew.

Allday murmured, 'We're passing abeam of *Benbow*, sir.' He smiled. 'She looks big from down here!'

Bolitho watched her as she slid away across the frigate's quarter. Black and buff, shining with spray and damp air. Her upper yards and loosely furled canvas did look hazy, so Grubb's prediction was coming true already. That would give Herrick something else to worry about.

Eventually, Browne came aft to report that *Styx* was standing well clear of the anchorage, and that Pascoe had arranged for the additional seamen to be quartered throughout the ship.

He said, almost as an afterthought, 'The captain seems to think we can make good time around the point, but after that he believes the fog will come down.'

Bolitho nodded. 'Then we shall anchor. If the fog is bad for us, so too will it prevent others from moving.'

At this time of year fogs could be as common as icy gales. Each had its own special kind of danger, and both were respected by sailors.

But once the frigate had completed her passage around The Skaw and changed tack to steer south along Denmark's opposite coastline, Neale was able to report that the fog was little more than a thick sea-mist. The densest part was clinging to the land, and in all probability was trapped in the anchorage they had left astern.

Herrick could cope with that all right. Pay Herrick a sincere compliment and he would be speechless. Put him before a lady and he would be tongue-tied. Gales, fog or the roaring horror of battle and he was like a rock.

They sighted very few craft, and only small vessels at that. Coasters and fishermen, staying near the land, and certainly wary of the lean-looking frigate as she thrust further south towards the narrow sound between Denmark and Sweden. The gateway to the Baltic. A shelter or a trap, according to what your intentions might be.

As soon as it was dark Neale asked permission to anchor. As *Styx* swung slowly to her cable, and the mist filtered through her spars and rigging to make her like a phantom ship, Bolitho walked the quarterdeck, watching the pale stars, the occasional gleam of a light from the land.

Styx showed only an anchor lantern, and the watch which moved about the forecastle and gangways were fully armed. Mr Pickthorn, her first lieutenant, had even spread boarding nets.

Just to be on the safe side, as Neale had put it.

Pascoe emerged from the darkness and waited to see if it was convenient to speak.

Bolitho beckoned to him. 'Here. Let's walk a while. Stand still for long and the blood feels like glacier water.'

They paced back and forth, meeting and passing the men on watch or some of the ship's officers who were also trying to take some exercise in the keen air.

'Our people are settled in, sir.' Pascoe shot him a quick glance. 'I have Mr Midshipman Penels with me as messenger. I thought him a bit too young, but Mr Wolfe said he's got to start sometime.' He chuckled. 'He's right, I expect.'

'Tomorrow we will enter Copenhagen, Adam. There, I am to meet a British official of some standing.'

He looked towards the tiny lights on the shore. The news would be there already. An English man-of-war. One from the new squadron. What did it mean? Why had she come?

'There are a few questions I will want answering for my own content, too.'

Pascoe did not break into Bolitho's thoughts, even though he was speaking them aloud. He was thinking of Midshipman Penels and his friend Babbage. By some accident, or a petty officer's indifference, Babbage was aboard *Styx* also.

Bolitho asked suddenly, 'How are you getting along with my flag lieutenant? The Honourable Oliver Browne?'

Pascoe smiled, his teeth white in the darkness. 'With an "e", sir. Very well. He is a strange man. Far removed from most sea officers. *All*, in my own experience. He is always so calm and untroubled. I think that if the Frenchies were to storm aboard at this moment he would pause to finish his meal before joining the fight!'

Captain Neale came on deck and Pascoe excused himself and left.

Bolitho said, 'It seems very quiet, Captain.'

'I agree.' Neale peered through the sagging boarding nets. 'But I'm careful. Captain Herrick would spit me if I allowed his admiral to run aground, or worse!'

Bolitho bade him good night and went to his borrowed quarters. He had not realized before just how well known Herrick's devotion had become.

'Take in the maincourse, Mr Pickthorn.' Captain Neale stood very still, his arms folded, as the frigate glided ahead under topsails, forecourse and jib.

The cold air, the icy droplets of moisture falling from the heavy weather canvas like rain were forgotten as the *Styx* moved slowly towards the last channel.

Two great fortresses, Helsingborg on the Swedish side of the Sound Channel and Kronborg on the Danish, were enough to awe even the most hardened man aboard.

Bolitho took a telescope and trained it on the Danish fortress. It would take an army, and months of siege, to breach it, he thought grimly.

It was almost noon, and the nearer the frigate had drawn to the narrows and the protective batteries on either side, they had sensed the excitement *Styx*'s appearance was causing. But if there was no sign of welcome, there was no hostility either.

He glanced along the upper decks. Neale had done well, and his ship looked as perfect as she could be. The marines, conspicuous in their bright uniforms, drawn up in squads on the poop deck. None in the tops, and no swivels had been mounted there either. Seamen moved about their duties, while others stood ready to spread more sail and flee or take in the remaining canvas and anchor.

Neale looked at Bolitho questioningly. 'May I begin the salute, sir?'

'If you please.'

Neale said sharply, 'Remove the tampions and open the ports.'

He was probably thinking that once he had fired a full salute

to the fortress his guns would be empty. But to man his broadsides with anything more than the men required for this ritual
might appear like a threat of war.

'Run out, if you please.'

Squeaking and rumbling the *Styx*'s guns poked their black
muzzles into the harsh light.

'Stand by to dip the colours!'

Bolitho bit his lip. Still no hint from the land. He looked
across at the great artillery emplacements. The wind had
dropped considerably. If the Danes opened fire, *Styx* would be
hard put to come about and beat clear.

She would be hammered into submission in minutes under
such conditions.

'Commence the salute, Mr Pickthorn.'

'Fire *One*!'

The bang echoed across the choppy water, to be followed gun
for gun by a battery below the fortress. Then, the Danish flag,
standing out like a flake of bright metal from a tall staff, dipped
slowly in salute.

Allday wiped his mouth with his wrist. 'Phew! That was a
near thing!'

Bolitho saw *Styx*'s gunner marching from cannon to cannon,
beating out the time with his fist, oblivious to everything but
precision.

There were people visible on the shore now, some running
and waving, their mouths soundless in the telescope's lens.

The final gun crashed out, the smoke fanning ahead of the
frigate's figurehead.

Captain Neale touched his hat to Bolitho and said, 'I think
we are accepted, sir.'

Browne, who had been clasping his ears during the salute,
said sourly, 'But by no means welcome, sir.'

'Guard-boat approaching, sir!'

'Take in the forecourse, Mr Pickthorn. Stand by to receive
our visitors!'

Men swarmed out along the yard, fisting and cursing the big
foresail as they struggled to furl it with extra smartness, watched
by the distant crowds of onlookers.

The guard-boat was an interesting craft. Far longer than a
ship's boat, it was propelled by the biggest oars Bolitho had

seen outside of a chebeck. Two men to each oar, while just abaft of the deadly-looking prow was a solitary but heavy cannon. Under oars, this miniature gunboat could outmanoeuvre anything larger than a frigate and throw heavy balls through her poop with total safety. Even a frigate would be in trouble if she lost the wind.

Bolitho studied the figures in the ornate cockpit. Two Danish sea officers and two civilians, one, if not two, of the latter obviously English. They looked more suitably dressed for a stroll around Hyde Park than crossing open water in October.

'Man the side! Marines, *fall in*!'

Mr Charles Inskip, the important government official whom Bolitho had been instructed to assist in every possible way, sat stiff-backed in one of Captain Neale's chairs and examined the captured French despatches. He held them at arm's length, and Bolitho guessed his sight was not what it should be. His companion, Mr Alfred Green, apparently less important, stood beside the chair, peering and pouting at each newly turned sheet.

Bolitho heard the Danish sea officers talking and laughing beyond the bulkhead, and guessed they were being traditionally entertained by Neale and some of his lieutenants. Governments could create war from almost anything. Sailors, meeting on their home ground, rarely fell out.

Browne glanced meaningly at Bolitho as Inskip re-read the letter with the broken seal.

Bolitho noticed that when seamen rushed across the deck above, or some heavy block and tackle fell on the planking, Inskip did not even blink. He was obviously a much travelled man, well used to ships of every sort.

Inskip was about fifty, he decided. Neatly but not flamboyantly dressed in a green coat and breeches of similar colour. His head was almost bald, the remaining hair and unfashionable queue hanging down his collar like a rope's end.

He looked up sharply. 'This is bad news, Admiral.' His voice was incisive, a bit like Beauchamp's. 'I thank God you managed to intercept it.'

'Luck, sir.'

A small smile, pushing the years from the man's features. 'Where would we be without it?'

His companion said, 'You would have had a warmer reception, Admiral, had the brig *Echo* got here ahead of you.'

Inskip frowned at the interruption. 'I have made some progress with the Danish government. They do not wish to join with the Tsar of Russia's proposed alliance, but pressure is mounting. Your arrival may be timely. I thank God you had the good sense to come in a small ship-of-war and not a three-decker or something. It is a powder-keg here, although the Danes, being Danes, are trying to ignore it. I would love to return in happier times.'

Bolitho asked, 'Will you wish me to come ashore, sir?'

'Yes. I shall send word to you. The guard-boat will lead you to the advised anchorage.' He glanced quickly at the door. 'There is a French frigate in Copenhagen, so you must warn your people to avoid any contact with her.'

Bolitho looked at Browne. An added complication, and they had not yet begun.

Inskip tapped the letter. 'Now I have read this I think I understand the purpose of her presence. I was sent by His Majesty's Government with the intention of preventing Danish involvement. The French may be here to provoke the opposite. Your small inshore squadron would not stem the flood if the worst happened before we could muster a fleet. Even then, the Russians and the Swedes are said to have sixty line-of-battle ships between them, and the Danes another thirty in commission.'

Bolitho warmed to this nondescript man. He knew everything, even the size of his own small squadron. The fact he had brought Inskip some information he did not already have made him feel humble rather than superior.

Inskip stood up, waving Ozzard and a loaded tray aside as he said, 'Not just now, thank you. Clear heads are needed.' He smiled. 'So I suggest you order your captain to approach the anchorage. You have roused plenty of curiosity and speculation. To see you actually step ashore should add to the gossip, eh?' He picked up his hat and added, 'I am sorry you missed meeting with a fellow English traveller.'

Bolitho allowed Allday to buckle on his glittering presentation sword for this formal occasion, but saw the distaste in his eyes.

'Oh, who was that?'

'Rupert Seton. I understand he is the brother of your late wife?'

Bolitho stared at Allday, his mind suddenly frozen. He could see Seton as a young midshipman during the ill-fated attempt to retake Toulon for the French Royalists. A slightly built youth with a stutter. With a sister so beautiful that she was rarely absent from Bolitho's memory.

'He told me about the tragedy, of course.' Inskip was unaware of the havoc he had caused. 'A fine, intelligent young man he is, too. He has a good post with the Honourable East India Company. Where *I* should be if I had any sense. There are more kicks than guineas working for Mr Pitt's administration.'

Bolitho asked quietly, 'You met him *here*, you say?'

'Yes. Taking passage for England. I told him to make haste, otherwise he'd still have been here. But the war could spread any day, and I'd not wish one of John Company's people to become interned!'

Bolitho said, 'Escort these gentlemen to Captain Neale, Mr Browne. My compliments to the captain, and tell him we are finished our business and ready to proceed.' He looked impassively at the two officials. 'I'm certain you'll wish to get ashore ahead of me?'

Inskip shook his hand warmly. 'We will meet again.' He dropped his voice. 'I am sorry if I have roused some painful memories. I meant it for the best.'

As the door closed behind Browne and the others Allday exclaimed brokenly, 'Oh, *God damn it*, sir! After all this time, it's not right, not *fair*!' He controlled his outburst and added, 'Shall I fetch Mr Pascoe, sir?'

Bolitho sat down and unbuckled the sword. 'No. But I would take it kindly if *you* would stay.' He looked up, his eyes pleading. 'Will it never end? I've acted foolishly, done things to shame my friends, hoping perhaps to find peace again!'

Allday crossed to the table and almost tore a goblet from Ozzard's hand.

'Here, drink this, sir, and damnation to the war, and all who fan its fires!'

Bolitho swallowed the brandy, almost choking on its fire.

He could see her framed in the church door, her hand on her brother's arm, just as Herrick's own bride had been led up to the altar.

Almost to himself he said, 'Maybe it is as well we did not meet. Perhaps he blames me for Cheney's death. She was alone when she needed me. I was at sea. Sailors should never marry, Allday. It is a cruelty to those they leave behind.'

Allday jerked his head at Ozzard, who backed from the cabin as if mesmerized.

'To some, mebbe, sir. But not the special ones.'

Bolitho stood up and replaced the sword at his hip. 'And she *was* special.' He looked at Allday and gave a brief nod. 'Thank you. I am ready now.'

Allday watched him square his shoulders, then duck automatically beneath the deckhead beams as he strode towards the quarterdeck.

That was a bad one, Allday thought. Worse than for a long while. It was always there, hiding like a wild animal, ready to break cover and destroy.

He followed Bolitho into the keen air, watched with the same fascination as he shook hands with the two Danish officers before seeing them over the side into their boat. A smile to Neale, another handshake with the Danish water pilot who was to assist the master with the last part of the journey.

Pascoe passed him with a handful of seamen to prepare the frigate's boats for swaying out when required.

Again, Allday saw their quick exchange, like brothers, no words spoken or needed.

But for once Allday would have gladly done without the privilege of knowing and sharing this close relationship. He knew Bolitho too well to be deceived by his outward calm. It was not an easy secret to hold.

Being ashore in a beautiful city like Copenhagen was a strange experience for Bolitho. He would have liked to explore its squares, dominated by high green spires and impressive buildings which looked as if they had been there forever. And there were inviting little lanes which he saw from the window of a carriage sent by Inskip to collect him from the harbour.

Inskip, like the Danish authorities, wanted to know where a visiting British admiral was at all times of the day, and Bolitho wondered what the coachman would do if he suggested a different route.

As he had prepared to leave the ship for his first visit to Inskip's headquarters he had seen Neale and his officers studying the harbour, not least the French frigate which was anchored as far away as was prudently possible. The anchorage was crowded with Danish men-of-war, but in spite of their impressive size and numbers, the attention on the waterfront or the many small craft which plied back and forth was fixed on the two frigates. Separated by a stretch of water and a wary guardboat, they represented the war and all that went with it. The war, which if Russia had any say would engulf the Danes also.

The French frigate was called *Ajax*, a powerful vessel of thirty-eight guns. As aboard Neale's command, the seamen went about their daily tasks, apparently blind to their enemies and their intentions.

The carriage wheels rumbled noisily over the cobbles, and Bolitho saw many people pausing in the cold air to watch him pass. They were a nice looking race, he thought. Perhaps that was how a country became without constant wars and strife.

Browne, who had been watching the passing panorama with rapt attention, said, 'We have arrived, sir.'

The carriage clattered beneath a low archway and into a neat private square. The buildings around it looked in some way official, and Bolitho saw two footmen hurrying down some steps to greet him.

It felt colder, and Neale's sailing master had warned of snow. Fog, then snow, it was like listening to Grubb.

Inskip was waiting by a blazing fire. He was wearing a wig, but it made him look older than the opposite effect, which was suprising.

He said, 'Good of you to be so prompt. I have been making further inquiries about the Frenchman. They say she is here to carry out storm repairs. Denmark has no wish to provoke France by refusing the *Ajax* permission. My guess is that she was waiting for the letter, or some other relevant instructions concerning Malta. Your sudden arrival will have put the cat amongst the pigeons!' His eyes twinkled.

Bolitho said, 'When *Ajax* leaves, Captain Neale will be eager
to bring her to battle.'

Inskip shook his head firmly. '*Ajax* arrived first, and in peace.
She will be allowed a day's grace before you may follow.'

Browne coughed discreetly. 'It is an unwritten law, sir.'

'I see.' Bolitho looked at the fire. 'Then there is nothing for
me to do but wait, kick my heels, while the Frenchman calls
the tune? Another courier may come here any day, any time.
Could you not send a fast messenger overland to make contact
with my squadron? With another frigate to seaward I could
soon put a stop to the French captain's plan of action.'

Inskip smiled. 'You are indeed a man of action. But I am
afraid the Danes would probably take even less kindly to that
misuse of their, er, hospitality, and seize your ship for good
measure!'

Bolitho remembered Browne's remark on board the *Benbow*.
I see you as a fighting sailor, not as a diplomat. In his inability
to sit still and wait for some unknown factor to play its part, he
had more than proved Browne to be right.

'They could *try*!'

'Make no mistake, they could and would. I have heard
through my own sources that there are plans to blockade the
harbour and remove all buoys and leading marks if need be.
The Danes have assembled a considerable fleet, as you have seen.
Believe me, they can give good account of themselves.' He
pounded one fist into his palm. 'If only the French had not given
up Malta or, more to the point, our own Navy had for once
been less successful.'

Browne said quietly, 'I suggest they would have found other
fuel for their fires, sir. Appeasement buys a little time, but not
very much.'

Inskip raised his eyebrows. 'Your aide is shrewd, Bolitho. A
pity he wears the King's coat. I could find a place for him in
Whitehall!'

Bolitho sighed. 'What do you suggest, sir?'

Inskip replied instantly, 'Wait. I will see the Danish minister
tomorrow and try to discover his feelings. I may need you with
me, so I suggest you remain ashore in this house tonight. It will
save time and be less conspicuous. If the French captain decides
to sail, he will probably meet up with your squadron after he

T.I.S.—C

has rounded Skaw Point. If he steers west into the Baltic he may intend to make contact with the Swedes, or even the Russian fleet if the ice is not too dangerous.'

A bewigged footman glided through a pair of ornate doors.

'I beg your pardon, sir, but there are two, er, *persons* below demanding to be brought to the rear-admiral's presence.'

Inskip asked mildly, 'Who are they?'

In the same lordly tone the footman replied, 'Seafaring fellows, I believe, sir. One says he is a coxswain, the other is some sort of servant.'

Bolitho grinned. Allday and Ozzard.

'I am glad you did not attempt to send my coxswain away. The outcome might have been worse than facing the Frenchman!'

Inskip instructed the footman to show Allday and his companion to a room with a fire.

Then he said, 'Well, at least it brought a smile to your face, Bolitho. That's more like it, eh?'

Bolitho turned to Browne. 'Return to the ship and explain matters to Captain Neale. Tell him to keep note of any craft which go alongside the *Ajax* or unusual preparations.'

It was unlikely that Neale would need telling.

When Bolitho was alone with Inskip he asked, 'Just suppose the Tsar discovers the fate of Malta before you can gain a firm declaration of neutrality from the Danes, what then?'

Inskip eyed him gravely. 'The Tsar may be able to revive his idea for an Armed Neutrality of the North. He has made threats before that he would seize all British ships in his ports. It would be an act of war, and Denmark would find herself in the forefront of the battle.'

Bolitho nodded. 'Thank you for explaining it to me without frills. These are facts I can recognize. I have no doubt Bonaparte will have ensured that several messages were despatched to the Tsar. That we have been lucky enough to capture one will *not* be known yet.'

Inskip regarded him thoughtfully. 'I suppose you may be right. But that is your concern, not mine, thank heaven.'

Three hours later Browne returned from the ship. The *Ajax* was still at anchor and doing nothing to excite suspicion. Her captain had been seen to go ashore, probably to pay his respects to the port admiral before leaving. Equally, he might have gone to seek information about Bolitho.

That night, as Bolitho tried to accustom himself to the vastness and stillness of a large bed, he considered what Inskip had said. So much could depend on the weather as far as the Russian ships were concerned. He listened to the wind moaning around the roof-tops, and played with the idea of leaving the house without telling anyone. He would find one of the noisy taverns he had seen, lose himself in the crowd, just for a precious hour or so.

He must have fallen asleep, for the next thing he knew was that Inskip, looking like a goblin in a long sleeping cap, was shaking his arm, while lanterns and candles bobbed into the room from what appeared to be a crowded passageway.

'What is it?'

He saw Allday, grim-faced and watchful, as if expecting a surprise attack, and Ozzard dragging the chest across the floor like a wrecker with a prize.

Inskip snapped, 'I have just had word. The Frenchman has weighed, though God knows how well he will do. It is snowing like the devil!'

Bolitho was on his feet, groping for a shirt, as Inskip added soberly, 'A schooner brought worse news. Several British ships have been taken by the Russians. Now, whatever the Danes want, they will be forced into a war.'

Browne pushed through the footmen and servants. Surprisingly, he was fully dressed.

Bolitho shouted, 'Fetch a carriage!'

Browne replied calmly, 'I heard the news, sir. I've already got one. It's waiting below.'

Inskip stood between Bolitho and the frantic Ozzard.

'You know the rules. You must not sail until a day has passed.'

Bolitho looked at him gravely. 'Where will the British merchantmen be held, sir?'

Inskip was taken off guard. 'The island of Gotland, I'm told.'

Bolitho sat on the bed and jammed his feet into his shoes.

'I'm going after them, sir, not back to my squadron. And as for the rules, well, I've often found them to be like orders.' He touched Inskip's arm impetuously. 'They have to be moulded to the requirements of the moment!'

As they bundled into the carriage and the wheels moved soundlessly over a thickening carpet of snow, Browne said, 'I'll lay odds that the Frenchman knows about the British ships, too, sir. He'll cut them out without anyone raising a finger to stop him.'

Bolitho settled back against the seat and composed his thoughts. 'Except us, Mr Browne. Except the *Styx*.'

5

Trust

Bolitho gripped the quarterdeck rail and peered along the frigate's upper deck, his eyes slitted against the snow and bitter air.

It was a weird, unnatural scene, with the rigging and guns glistening in snow, while seamen slithered and blundered from one task to another like cripples.

He tried to plan clearly, to compress his thoughts on what might lie ahead. But from the moment they had weighed anchor and the first excitement of slipping out of harbour in a snow squall, the weather had defied even the power of thought.

They had been at sea for twelve hours, and by rights it should be daylight. But as they had fought their way south-east, battered and harried by a strong wind from the coast of Sweden, their movements had become jerky, their actions taking longer and longer with each change of watch.

And all the while the blizzard had swept down through shrouds and running rigging, until time and distance had shrunk to the width and length of their ship.

It was all Bolitho could do to prevent his teeth from chattering uncontrollably, and despite his thick boat-cloak he was chilled to the marrow. He had watched the wretched lookouts being relieved from the masthead after less than an hour's duty, and even then they had barely been able to clamber down to safety.

And suppose it was all wasted? The thought grew stronger with each reeling mile, and Bolitho supposed every man aboard was cursing his name as the day dragged on. Or suppose the Frenchman had gone elsewhere? He might even now be running under Herrick's guns, or heading somewhere else entirely.

Captain Neale staggered across the quarterdeck, his chubby features glowing with cold.

He said, 'May I suggest you go below, sir? The people know you are aboard. They'll also know you're with them whatever happens.'

Bolitho shuddered and watched the spray surging over the beakhead to freeze like jewels on the nettings. Neale had ordered the lee gunports to be opened. Water trapped long enough to freeze in the scuppers had been known to build up so rapidly it could capsize a vessel far larger than a frigate.

He asked, 'Where are we now?'

'The master *assures* me that the island of Bornholm is on the lee bow, some five miles distant.' Neale wiped his streaming face with his fingers. 'I have to take his word, sir, for we could be *anywhere*, as far as I am concerned!'

Neale turned as his first lieutenant hurried towards him, and Bolitho called, 'Don't worry about me, Captain Neale. If nothing else, this wind is keeping my head clear!'

He thought of the swift departure from Copenhagen, and wondered if anyone had seen them weigh. He doubted it. But when daylight arrived there would be a few awkward questions for Mr Inskip to answer.

Browne had been as blunt as he had dared. 'I think you are wrong to chase the Frenchman, sir. You are sending *Styx*, that is enough. Captain Neale knows the risks, and you might be able to save his name if things go wrong. But if you are with him, who will save *you*?'

Sometime later, as *Styx* had tacked violently clear of the Swedish mainland, Bolitho had heard Pascoe speaking to the flag lieutenant in an angry whisper.

'You don't understand! The admiral has been in far worse situations! He's always managed to fight out of a trap!'

Browne had replied sadly, 'He was a captain then. Responsibility is an axe. It can cut either way.' There had been the sound of his hand on Pascoe's shoulder. 'But I admire you for your loyalty, believe me.'

Pascoe was up forward at this moment, working with some hands to clear the foretopmast blocks. If they froze, or the cordage, already swollen with snow, followed suit, the *Styx* would be helpless. Like a phantom she would sail on, deeper and deeper into the Baltic.

Allday crossed the deck, his shoes slipping on the slush.

'Ozzard's got some soup, sir.' He glared at the white-crusted sails and added, 'I'd rather be becalmed than in this!'

Bolitho watched the next party of seamen clambering down from aloft. It was to be hoped they would find something hot below, too. Knowing Neale, he decided he would manage something for his men.

He looked up at the bulging canvas, following Allday's gaze. Iron hard, and brutal for the seamen who had to fight and control it. And yet it had a strange beauty. The small realization helped to drive his anxieties back into the shadows.

'Then I'll come down. I'd relish some soup, though I doubt if I could keep much else in my stomach!'

Allday grinned and stood aside to allow Bolitho to reach the companionway.

In the years he had served Bolitho he had never once seen him seasick. But there was said to be a first time for everyone.

Right aft, with the stern lifting and falling into a quarter sea, the scene was more like a grotto than a cabin. The windows were laced with fine ice, so that the filtered light made it seem colder than it was.

Bolitho sat and consumed Ozzard's soup, amazed that he could feel his appetite responding readily. More suited to a skinny midshipman than a flag officer, he thought.

Neale joined him later and placed his chart on the table for Bolitho's inspection.

'If the British merchantmen are in fact at Gotland, sir,' Neale jabbed his brass dividers on the chart, 'they will be lying here, on the north-western coast.' He looked at Bolitho's intent features. 'Below the guns of the fortress, no doubt.'

Bolitho rubbed his chin and tried to transfer the lines and figures into the sea and land, wind and current.

'If the ships are *not* there, Captain Neale, we have come in vain. But Mr Inskip strikes me as a man who is very shrewd and careful with his information. In theory, the ships will be in Swedish waters, but as the Russians seized them, and the French are showing interest, it seems I have little alternative but to cut them out. With the ships freed the motive for war is removed and any hope of the Tsar's success in invading England will melt with the snow.'

Neale pouted, his face full of mixed emotions.

Bolitho watched him and said, 'Speak your mind, Captain. I am too well used to Captain Herrick's ways to exclude you from free speech.'

'I doubt that the French will be expecting us to arrive, that is, assuming the *Ajax* is on the same course as ourselves. I will be eager to get to grips with her, sir, my ship owes a few scores. But to speak plainly, I think you have more chance of starting a war than preventing one.' He spread his hands helplessly and looked like a midshipman again. 'I cannot imagine why our admiral failed to act on these threats long ago.'

Bolitho glanced away, recalling Browne's words and Admiral Beauchamp's warning. Was Admiral Damerum the root cause of the warning? If so, why? It did not make any sense at all.

'How is the weather?'

Neale smiled, knowing Bolitho was giving himself time to think.

'Still snowing, sir, but no worse. My sailing master believes it may clear towards dawn.'

They both looked meaningly at the chart. By that time, events might have been decided for them.

Close-hauled on the larboard tack the frigate *Styx* drove steadily to the north, the sea sluicing over the weather bulwark and smashing down on the opposite side in regular assaults. Men too numbed by the wet and cold to speak kept a constant watch on running tackles and the trim of each yard, minds blank to all else but the pain and the danger.

Unseen on one beam was the Swedish coastline, and then as the frigate passed the southernmost point of Gotland the sea became choppier but less violent as she began the final part of her journey.

Bolitho was up and dressed before first light, so restless that Allday had a harder time than usual shaving him. The ice was still clinging to the stern windows, but when the dawn eventually broke through it was brighter, and even promised a hint of sunlight.

Bolitho snatched up his hat and looked at Allday. 'God, you take your time, man!'

Allday wiped his razor methodically. 'Time was when admirals had patience, sir.'

Bolitho smiled at him and hurried on deck, the breath knocked instantly from his body by the keen wind.

Figures bustled about on every hand, and when Bolitho took a glass from the rack he saw the sprawling island of Gotland to starboard, blurred and humped in the dim light, like a sleeping sea-monster. It was said to be a strange place, with its fortified city and tales of raids and counter-raids going back over hundreds of years. It was not difficult to picture the Viking long-ships sweeping towards that inhospitable coast, he thought.

Neale crossed the deck and touched his hat.

'Permission to clear for action, sir? The people have been fed, but the benefit of a hot meal will soon fade if they are not kept busy.'

'Carry on, if you please. You command here. I am a passenger.'

Neale walked away, hiding a smile.

'Mr Pickthorn! Beat to quarters and clear for action!' He turned and held Bolitho's gaze, cutting back the years. 'And I want two minutes lopped off the time, d'you hear?'

The sun probed through the drifting flurries of snow and touched the taut sails with the colour of pewter. Everything shone, even the sailors' hair as they ran to obey the urgent tattoo of drums had droplets of melting ice as if they had been dragged up from the sea-bed.

Pascoe strode past buckling on his curved hanger and calling the names of the *Benbow*'s men. Bolitho noticed that when he called one in particular, a new hand named Babbage, he paused and studied him gravely, separating him from the crowd with a quick scrutiny.

A candidate for promotion, or someone to be warned for carelessness? Bolitho caught his nephew's eye and nodded to him.

'Well, you have a frigate, Adam. How does it feel?'

Pascoe smiled broadly. 'Like the *wind*, sir!'

The first lieutenant, puffing with exertion and red from the keen air, called, 'Ship cleared for action, sir!'

Neale closed his watch with a snap. 'Smartly done, Mr Pick-thorn.'

Then he turned and touched his hat to Bolitho.

'We are yours to lead, sir.'

Browne watched the preparations and then the sudden still-ness along the gundeck and said half to himself, 'But to where, I wonder?'

Bolitho moved the telescope carefully along the grey shoreline. If only the snow would go altogether. Yet in his heart he knew it was their only ally, their one guard against detection.

Figures moved restlessly around and past him. The occasional clink of metal or the scrape of a handspike intruded into the telescope's small, circular world to distract him.

He tried to recall everything he had studied on the chart and in Neale's notes. A headland should be standing out somewhere on the lee bow, and around it would lie the ships.

Bolitho bit his lip to contain his racing thoughts and anxieties. *Maybe, could, might, perhaps*, they were useless to him now.

He heard Neale say, 'Shall I run up the colours, sir?'

'Please do. I suggest you hoist an ensign to the fore and main also. If our captured merchantmen are over yonder, they'll need all the convincing we can offer.'

He glanced up at the mizzen truck where his own flag had been broken when he had transferred from the *Benbow*. It might make the French, and anyone else who would otherwise try to attack them, imagine that other ships were on their way in support. Even very junior admirals were not expected to stray about in frigates.

Bolitho asked, 'How is the wind?'

The master replied instantly, 'Shifted a point, sir. Nor'-westerly.'

Bolitho nodded, too absorbed in his thoughts to notice how an edge had come to his voice.

'Let her fall off three points, if you will. We'll weather the headland as close as we can.'

The sailing master said, 'Well, I dunno, sir . . .' Then he saw the look in Neale's eye and cut his protest short.

The big wheel creaked over, three helmsmen, legs wide apart to keep their balance on the icy deck planking, watching sails and compass like hawks.

Eventually the master said, 'East by north, sir.'

Bolitho ignored the seamen as they ran to retrim the yards and braces, the heavy tramp of the afterguard as they followed suit. Neale had learned a lot. Stripped to topsails, forecourse and jib, *Styx* was responding well, leaning forward under her ice-hard canvas as if eager on her own account to do battle.

He looked at the gun crews, huddled together for comfort but ready. The sand on the deck around the long twelve-pounders to prevent the men from slipping already changing to liquid gold.

How bright the marines' coats looked in the strange light. With snow gathering on their hats they could have been a child's toys at Christmas time.

He saw Pascoe by the forward guns, one hand resting on his hanger, his slim outline swaying easily with the regular plunge of the stem. He was talking to another junior lieutenant, probably discussing their chances. It was often like that. Trying to appear calm, to remain sane when your heart was gripped in a vice and you imagined every seaman near you could hear its frantic pounding.

'Land on the lee bow, sir!' A slight pause. 'Almost dead ahead!'

Neale called sharply, 'Leadsman in the chains, Mr Pickthorn. Begin sounding in fifteen minutes.'

If he was afraid of his command running aground he concealed it very well, Bolitho thought.

Bolitho steadied his glass once more. The land looked very close. An illusion, he knew, but if the wind veered suddenly, or they lost it entirely, they would be hard put to claw away.

Neale said, 'Take in the forecourse.' He moved closer to Bolitho. 'May I bring her up a point, sir?'

Bolitho lowered the glass and looked at him. 'Very well.'

He stared up at the bright flags at each masthead and gaff. He could feel the snowflakes melting on his eyes, moistening his lips. It helped to steady him.

The big forecourse was already booming and flapping reluctantly up to its yard, the seamen spread out above it fisting and kicking the frozen canvas like apes gone mad. Slivers of ice fell through the nets above the gun crews like fragments of broken glass, and Bolitho saw a petty officer stoop to retrieve a piece before jamming it into his mouth.

Another familiar sign. The mouth like dust, when you craved for beer, water, anything.

If only the people in England could see them, he thought grimly. These same sort of men throughout the fleet lived in squalor but fought with dignity and incredible courage. Sweepings from jails some of them perhaps, ill-used ashore and afloat, but they were all that stood between Napoleon or anyone else who became an enemy. He almost smiled as he recalled something his father had once said. 'England must love enemies, Richard. We make so many of them!'

The first lieutenant called, 'Permission to load, sir?'

Neale glanced at Bolitho then replied, 'Yes. But not double-shotted, Mr Pickthorn. With the breeches almost frozen solid, I fear it would do more damage to us than the Frenchies!'

Bolitho gripped his hands together behind him. So confident in him, they even had a mental picture of their enemy firmly fixed. If the bay was empty, that trust would fade just as swiftly.

The leadsman's thick arm was revolving in a slow circle, then he released the lead and line and craned over to watch it splash down beyond the bows.

'By the mark ten!'

Bolitho sensed the master shifting restlessly by the wheel, imagining the craggy bottom gliding beneath the coppered hull.

The lead splashed down again.

'An' a quarter *less* ten!'

Bolitho clamped his jaws together. They had to get as near as possible. He saw the great slab of land rising above the bowsprit and jib-boom, filled with menace.

'By the mark seven!'

The ship's marine lieutenant cleared his throat nervously and one of the quarterdeck seamen jumped with alarm.

'By the mark five!'

Bolitho heard the master whispering to Neale. Thirty feet of water. It was not much with the shelving bottom so close.

'Deep four!' The leadsman sounded quite unperturbed again.

As if he was convinced he was about to die and there was noth-ing he could do about it.

Bolitho levelled the glass again. Two isolated dwelling houses, like pale bricks on the hillside. Drifting smoke, too, or was it? The snow made it hard to see anything clearly. Smoke from an early morning hearth? Or some forewarned battery heating shot to give the impudent *Styx* a hot reception?

He saw the surf boiling below the headland, the sharp glitter of ice caught in the reflected glare.

'Bring her up two points, Captain Neale.'

He shut the glass with a snap and handed it to a midshipman.

The seamen had been poised for the order like athletes, and as the braces squealed and the yards added their confidence to the rudder, the frigate headed up further to windward, the headland moving back like a great stone door.

The leadsman called, 'By the mark ten!'

Somewhere a man gave an ironic cheer.

'Nor'-east, sir! Full an' bye!'

Bolitho gripped the quarterdeck rail as he had done so many times in so many ships.

Any moment now. The wind was right, with the ship sailing as close to it as she could and still keep the canvas drawing. Once round the headland it must be quick and definite, the shock of surprise like ice water across a sleeping sailor.

'Run out, if you please.'

Bolitho looked away from the little group of officers. If the bay was empty they would laugh at his pitiful preparations. But if they lost precious minutes to save his pride they would curse him with justification.

As the second lieutenant dropped his hand the guns trundled to the ports, trucks squealing as the crews controlled their down-hill advance with tackles and handspikes. It was no easy task with the planking so treacherous.

Almost together the black muzzles of the twelve-pounders thrust through the ports, while here and there a gun captain reached out to brush snow from his charge.

'Starboard battery run out, sir!'

'Deck there!' The tension was broken momentarily as the masthead lookout yelled excitedly, 'Ships at anchor round the point, sir!'

Bolitho looked at Neale, and beyond him where Allday was moving his big cutlass back and forth through the air like a wand.

Then forward again, to where his nephew had climbed on to a gun truck to see beyond the nettings.

If every other man-jack aboard had doubted him, these three had not.

'Stand by to wear ship!'

'Hands to the braces there!'

As topmen and others employed at each mast dashed to obey, only the gun crews remained motionless, each captain watching his small world which was held in a square port like a picture.

Neale held up his hand. 'Be easy, lads! *Easy* now!'

Bolitho heard him. It was like someone calming a nervous horse.

He stared hard across the nettings, barely able to control his feelings. It was all there. Half a dozen merchantmen anchored close together. Somehow dejected in their coatings of white snow, their crossed yards devoid of movement or life.

Allday had moved up to his shoulder, as he always did. To be near. To be ready.

Bolitho could hear his heavy breathing as he said, 'English ships, sir. No doubt about it.' His thick arm shot forward. 'And look yonder! The damn Frenchie!'

Bolitho snatched the glass again and trained it through the masts and rigging. There she was, the *Ajax*, as he remembered her. Further inshore was a second man-of-war, larger and more cumbersome. Probably a cut down two-decker. The escort for the seized merchantmen, waiting to ride out the weather or await orders.

The paler outline of the fortress walls were almost lost in drifting snowflakes, but somewhere a trumpet gave a strident blare, and Bolitho pictured the startled, cursing soldiers as they ran to man their defences. No man thought too well when roused from a warm bunk to face this kind of weather.

'Now, Captain Neale! Alter course and cut astern of the merchantmen!'

A long way off a gun boomed out, the sound without menace in the snow. A testing shot? A call to arms? Bolitho could feel the excitement welling up like madness. It was too late, whatever it was.

He put his hand down to steady himself as the wheel went over and the *Styx* changed tack towards the anchorage. His palm touched the brilliantly gilded hilt of his presentation sword, and with something like shock he remembered he had left his old blade in the *Benbow.*

Allday saw his uncertainty and felt the same anxiety.

Bolitho turned and looked at him. He knew that Allday understood and would be blaming himself.

'Never fear, Allday, we did not know our visit to the Danes would end here.'

They both smiled, but neither was deceived. It was like an omen.

'The *Ajax* has cut her cable, sir!' A midshipman was dancing with excitement. 'They are in a real confusion!'

Bolitho watched the first scrap of canvas appear on the other frigate's yards, the steep angle of her masts as wind and current carried her towards the shore.

Neale had drawn his sword and was holding it above the nearest gun crew as if to restrain them. The French ship was standing higher through the snow now, taking on shape and personality. More sails had appeared, and above the din of spray and canvas they heard the rumble of gun trucks, the urgent shrill of a whistle.

Across his shoulder Neale called, 'Don't let her fall off too much! We'll hold the Frenchman 'twixt us and any shore battery!'

Bolitho studied the enemy frigate as she appeared to move astern. Neale had forgotten nothing. From the corner of his eye, even as the *Styx* completed her slight change of tack, he saw the captain's sword slice down.

'As you bear! *Fire!*'

6

Quickly Done

Bolitho felt his eyes smarting painfully as a freak breeze brought some of the gunsmoke down across the quarterdeck. He watched the guns hurling themselves inboard on their tackles, the fiery orange tongues ripping through the swirling snow, his ears half-deafened by the noise. Then the quarterdeck six-pounders added their sharper notes, the balls falling short or beyond the other ship, some even hitting her.

Like madmen the crews were already sponging out their weapons, ramming home fresh charges and balls before throwing their weight on the tackles once again.

And still the French captain had failed to fire a single shot in reply.

The hands of the gun captains were raised in a ragged line, and the first lieutenant yelled, 'Stand by! *Fire!*'

Bolitho shaded his eyes to watch the dense smoke being driven downwind towards the other ship. They were on a converging tack, the slightly heavier *Ajax* spreading even her topgallants to fight her way into more open water.

There was a cheer as the *Ajax*'s topsails danced and shook to the onslaught, the wind exploring the shot holes and ripping the maincourse apart like an old sack.

Then the enemy replied. At a range of perhaps a cable, the broadside was ill-timed and badly aimed, but Bolitho felt the iron smashing into the *Styx*'s hull, and a stray ball striking further aft beneath his feet. The deck rebounded as if being struck by a great hammer, but Neale's gun crews did not even seem to notice.

'Stop your vents! Sponge out! Load!'

All the drills, the training and the threats had paid off.

'*Run out!*'

The smoke writhed between the two ships, its heart bright with red and orange as if it contained life of its own. Then the balls crashed into the *Styx*'s side once more even as she returned the broadside.

Bolitho saw one gun overturned, some of its crew writhing across the deck, leaving patterns of scarlet to mark their agony. Holes appeared in the sails, and Bolitho heard a ball tear above the quarterdeck within feet of where he stood.

Neale was pacing back and forth, watching the helm, the sails, his gun crews, everything.

'*Fire!*'

Whooping and yelling the men threw themselves on their guns again, barely pausing to see where their shots had gone before they reloaded.

Bolitho walked aft, his feet slipping on slush as he raised his telescope to seek out the other man-of-war. She was still at anchor but her decks were crammed with sailors. But she was not making sail or even running out her artillery, and as he moved the glass further he saw the blue and white flag of Russia. The Tsar wished more than anything else to be a respected friend and ally of Napoleon. His captain obviously thought differently, probably still stunned by the ferocity of *Styx*'s attack.

A ball slammed through the nettings behind him and he heard a chorus of cries and shrieks. The line of marines, who had been training their muskets over the tightly packed hammocks in readiness to engage, had been parted by bloody confusion. Men crawled and staggered through the smoke, and two were smashed to bloody gruel on the opposite side.

Their sergeant was yelling, 'Stand fast, marines! Face yer front!'

The marine lieutenant was sitting with back to the bulwark, his face in his hands, his fingers the same colour as his coat.

Neale shouted, 'The Frenchman has recovered his wits, sir! He'll try using chain-shot presently!'

Bolitho stared quickly around. It had been only minutes, yet felt an eternity. The cluster of English merchantmen were as before, but small figures dashed along their yards and gangways, cheering or calling for aid, it was impossible to tell.

Neale saw his glance and suggested, 'I'll send the quarter

boat, sir! Those poor devils may have no officers to help them escape.'

Bolitho nodded, and as men rushed aft to the quarter boat he said to Browne, 'You go.' He clapped him on the shoulder, expecting him to be as relaxed as he looked. But his shoulder was like a carriage spring, and he added quietly, 'Captain Neale has enough to contend with.'

Browne licked his lips and winced as more enemy shots crashed into the side, throwing up cruel splinters, one opening a man's arm and hurling him to the deck.

Then he said, 'Very well, sir.' He forced a smile. 'I shall have a fine view!'

Moments later the boat was pulling lustily towards the merchant ships. Somebody had even had the presence of mind to hoist a British ensign above the transom.

The *Ajax* was moving closer, her gunports flashing fire at regular intervals. But the wind was holding her over, and many of her balls shrieked above the *Styx*'s gangway, bringing down oddments of cordage and severed blocks like dead fruit.

Bolitho looked along the gundeck, seeing Pascoe's white breeches faintly through the smoke and snow as he directed the forward guns towards the enemy.

The broadsides were getting more ragged, the men too dazed by the din and thunder of battle to keep up their original timing.

Some lay dead or badly injured, others tried to drag them clear of the recoiling cannon, their faces masks of determination and shock.

There came a wild chorus of yells from the forecastle, and Bolitho saw the Frenchman's foremast part like a carrot, the upper spars and yards, complete with thrashing canvas and rigging and not a few men, plunged across her forecastle. Even through the roar of battle they heard it, like a cliff falling, and the effect was instantaneous. As most of the topmast staggered over the side, trailing broken shrouds like black weed behind it, the frigate swung drunkenly into the wind, the wreckage acting as a giant sea-anchor.

Neale cupped his hands, his sword dangling from his wrist, as he yelled, 'Full broadside, Mr Pickthorn! Double-shotted with grape for good measure!'

Wallowing helplessly while her seamen tried to hack the

trailing wreckage away, the *Ajax* drifted end-on towards Neale's battery. There was no fear of the double-shotting splitting the breeches now, Bolitho thought. The guns were so overheated that he could feel the nearest one like an open furnace.

He saw one old gun captain cradling each shot in his hard hands before allowing it to be rammed home. It had to be perfect this time.

Neale clambered up into the lee shrouds and snatched his first lieutenant's speaking trumpet to shout, 'Strike your colours! *Surrender!*' He sounded almost as if he were pleading. But the only answer was a volley of musket shots, one of which clanged against his sword like a bell.

He climbed down to the deck, his eyes bleak as he stared at the raised fists of his gun captains.

'So be it then.' He looked at his first lieutenant and gave a curt nod.

The broadside, which thundered with mounting fury from bow to stern, gun by gun, as the *Styx* sailed slowly past the enemy's figurehead, was terrible to see. Wreckage flew high in the air and the mainmast fell in a great swooping crash to join the other broken spars alongside. Bolitho thought he saw the frigate drop her bows under the murderous weight of iron, and he saw a young midshipman biting the sleeve of his coat with horror as long tendrils of blood ran from the *Ajax*'s scuppers, as if she and not her people were dying.

A master's mate shouted, 'The merchantmen are weighing, sir.' He sounded beyond understanding, past belief.

Bolitho nodded, still watching the beaten frigate. Vanquished in battle, but her tricolour was still flying, and he knew from hard experience that she at least would live to fight again.

He guessed that Neale and many of his men still had fire enough to try and seize the *Ajax* as a prize. But they had done plenty, and far more than he had dared hope. To go further, and flaunt the authority of the Swedish commandant and the one-sided neutrality of a Russian warship, would be pushing the odds too far.

He looked instead at the merchantmen. There were six in all, their sailors busily spreading more sails and trying to avoid collision with one another as they steered towards the small frigate which flew four flags for all to see.

Neale wiped his smoke-grimed features and said, 'Your flag lieutenant will not be the same again, I fear, sir.' He sighed as a wounded man was carried past. 'Nor any of us, for that matter.'

He turned to watch the nearest merchantman passing abeam, her larboard gangway alive with cheering men.

He added dryly, 'We did what we came to do, sir. I think it only fair we borrow a few of their prime seamen? The least they can do to show their gratitude!'

Pascoe came aft and touched his hat. He waited for Neale to walk away to deal with the countless problems left behind by the fight, then said, 'That was quickly done, sir!'

Bolitho rested one hand on his shoulder. 'Barely twenty minutes. I can scarce believe it. Captain Neale is a fine seaman.'

Pascoe did not look at him, but his mouth twitched in a smile.

'I believe he learned a lot in his first ship, Uncle?'

Mr Charles Inskip strode back and forth through the high-ceilinged room as if it were no longer big enough to contain him. Even his wig, which he had donned to lend dignity to his authority, was knocked awry with his agitation.

'God damn it, Bolitho, what am I to *do* about you?' He did not wait for a reply. 'You abuse the Danish neutrality and slink off in the night with some cock-and-bull scheme for a cutting-out expedition, and now you are back here in Cophenagen! You do not even have the sense to stay away!'

Bolitho waited for the squall to pass. He could sympathize with Inskip's unwelcome role here, but he had no regrets about the released ships. By now they would be passing through the narrows and out into the North Sea. To have left them in the Tsar's hands, to be handed possibly to the French as some kind of gift or bribe, was unthinkable. It would have been even more cruel to leave their luckless crews to rot in some prison camp or freeze to death in alien surroundings.

He said impassively, 'It was the least I could do, sir. The merchantmen have no cause to fear attack from the Danes. They were wrongly seized, much as the Danish ships were impounded by us this year. But if I had not anchored here again,

had trailed my coat instead beneath the shore batteries of the
Sound Channel, I would have provoked a disaster.'

He thought suddenly of the passage back. No one had had
time to precede them and yet rumour had outpaced everything.
The waterfront had been packed with silent townspeople, in
spite of the bitter cold, and later, when permission had been
granted by the port admiral to carry out repairs and to carry the
dead ashore for burial, something like a great sigh had gone
up from the watchers.

Inskip did not seem to hear him. 'I might have expected
such action from one of your captains. But the flag officer of a
squadron, *indeed not*! Just by being there you represented your
King and Parliament.'

'You mean that a mere captain could be dismissed, court
martialled, if things went against him, sir?'

Inskip paused in his agitated pacing and said, 'Well? You
know the risks as well as the rewards for command!'

Bolitho knew he was getting nowhere and said, 'Anyway, I
should like to send word to my flag captain, if that is possible.
I told him I might be away from the squadron for a week at
the most. It is that now.'

Inskip glared at him. 'Oh dammit, Bolitho. I did not say you
could not achieve what you set out to do. It was your method I
doubted.' He gave a wry grin. 'I have already sent a message to
your squadron.' He shook his head. 'I cannot imagine what they
will say in Parliament, or here in the Palace, but I'd have given
a lot to see you free our merchantmen! My aide has already
spoken with your Captain Neale. That young man told him that
the *Styx* dished up the enemy in no more than twenty minutes!'

Bolitho recalled Herrick's comment. *Men, not ships, win
battles.*

'True, sir. It was the fastest frigate action I have yet wit-
nessed.'

Inskip regarded him calmly. 'I suggest you were more than
a mere witness.' He crossed to the window and peered at the
square below. 'The snow has stopped.' Almost off-handedly he
added, 'You must prepare yourself to meet the Adjutant General
while you are here. Possibly this evening. In the meantime you
will remain as my guest.'

'And the ship, sir?'

'I am assured she will be allowed to leave when temporary repairs are completed. But . . .' the word hung in the air as he turned to face Bolitho, 'your stay will be rather more permanent if the Danes request me to hand you over to them.'

He rubbed his hands as an elegant footman entered with a tray and said, 'But for now we will toast your, er, victory, eh?'

Later, when he had been joined by Lieutenant Browne, Bolitho dictated a full report of his discovery and the action against the French frigate. He would leave higher authority to draw its own conclusions about the rights and wrongs of it.

By permitting the French ship to interfere with seized merchantmen within Swedish waters, and in the presence of one of the Tsar's own vessels, it would be a hard knot to untangle, he thought.

He sat back and watched Browne's face. 'Have I forgotten anything?'

Browne eyed him for several seconds. 'I believe, sir, that the less you put on paper the better. I had time to think while I was boarding the merchantmen, time to place myself in a position where I would have to *act* instead of suggest. You won a battle, nothing to change the face of the world, but the very sort to give heart to the people at home. They hate to see ordinary folk like themselves put upon and humiliated by some foreign power. But others may not be so kindly towards you, sir.'

Bolitho smiled gravely. 'Go on, Browne, you have my full attention.'

Browne said, 'Admiral Sir Samuel Damerum, sir. He will not be pleased. It might make him look a fool to some, a man who lacks the courage to fight for small causes as well as great ones.' He gave a smile, as if he had gone too far. 'As I said, sir, I have had time to change places with the mighty while I have been away. Frankly, I am glad to be a lieutenant, especially a privileged one.'

Bolitho rubbed his chin and glanced at the presentation sword which was lying on a chair. Even the omen had been false. He had been right to act, and though Neale had lost ten men killed it had been worth it. As Browne had pointed out, it was no great panorama of battle, but it would put a small edge to their pride and show that, even standing alone, England would not hesitate to act for her own people.

An hour later he was in a carriage with Inskip being driven to the Palace.

It was late and the streets almost empty. More like the setting for an assassination than an enquiry, he thought. Allday had pleaded to come with him, but Inskip had been adamant.

'Just you, Bolitho. That is an order.' He had been unable to resist adding, 'Even you should find this one difficult to mould to suit your requirements!'

Through some gates and then the carriage halted by a narrow side entrance.

Stamping snow from their shoes they were ushered through several doors and into another world. A fairyland of glittering chandeliers and great paintings along the walls. Sounds of music and feminine voices, a place of power and absolute comfort.

But that was as near as they got. They were shown into a small but beautifully decorated room with a blazing fire and walls completely lined with books.

One man was waiting for them. He was elegant like the room, and beautifully clothed in blue velvet. He had heavy gold cuffs which all but reached his elbows, and had the air of a man who never acted hastily or without dignity.

He studied Bolitho thoughtfully, his face almost in shadow. Then he said, 'The Adjutant General is not able to be here. He has gone to the mainland.' He spoke with barely an accent, his tone almost caressing in the warm room.

Then he continued, 'I will deal with this matter, Rear-Admiral Bolitho. As his aide I am well versed in the whole affair.'

Inskip started to speak. 'The fact is, sir, that . . .'

One hand moved up, like a priest about to offer a blessing, and Inskip fell silent.

'Now, let me say this. You saved those six English ships by your action. In their turn they saved you by being there. Had you attacked a French vessel in Scandinavian waters, no matter upon what ideal, neither you nor your ship would have reached England again, be certain of that. Your war is with France, not with us. But we must exist in a world turned upside down by London and Paris, and we shall have no hesitation about drawing our swords to protect what we hold dear.' His voice softened. 'That is not to say I do not understand, Admiral. I do, better than you realize perhaps.'

Bolitho said, 'Thank you for your understanding, sir. We are an island race. For a thousand years we have had to defend ourselves against attackers. People at war too often forget the rest, and for that I apologize, sir.'

The man turned to the fire, saying gently, 'I think my own people invaded your country a few times in the past?'

Bolitho smiled. 'Aye, sir. They still say that the girls on the north-east coast got their flaxen hair from the Viking invaders!'

Inskip cleared hs throat nervously. 'In that case, sir, may I take Rear-Admiral Bolitho with me?'

'Please do.' He did not offer his hand. 'I wanted to meet you. To see what sort of man you are.' He gave a brief nod. 'I hope that if we meet again it will be under happier circumstances.'

Bolitho followed Inskip and two footmen down the same passageway, his mind still in a whirl.

He said, 'I believe I might have fared worse with his superior. I think this one just wanted me out of his country.'

Inskip took his cloak from a footman and waited for the cold air to greet him through the open door.

'Quite possibly, Bolitho.' He glanced at him wryly. 'That was the Crown Prince himself!' He shook his head and walked towards the carriage. 'Really, Bolitho, you've such a lot to learn!'

Captain Neale entered the cabin, his hat tucked beneath one arm.

'I thought you would wish to know, sir. We have cleared the Sound and are standing into the Kattegat.' He looked both tired and elated as he added, 'Our escorts have gone about and left us.'

Bolitho stood up and walked aft to the windows. The snow had completely dispersed and the water looked hard grey and uninviting. The Danes had taken no chances. The *Styx* had been followed by two frigates from the moment she had weighed, and when Bolitho had been driven down to the jetty he had seen soldiers manning the artillery near the fortress. Not a threat. A warning perhaps.

'Thank you.'

Bolitho listened to the doleful clank of pumps, the muffled sounds of hammers and saws as the ship's company continued with the repairs of the short, savage engagement.

It would mean that *Styx* would have to be sent to England where she could carry out a proper and more lasting overhaul. She had earned it, as had her whole company.

He said, 'I shall feel at a loss aboard my flagship again. Like a horse in a larger field!' He became serious. 'I have completed a full report for you to carry to England. Your part in it will reach the proper authority.'

Neale smiled. 'Thank you, sir.'

'And now, I'll leave you in peace to run your command as you will and carry me to the squadron as quickly as possible.'

Neale began to withdraw, then said, 'My first lieutenant is very pleased with the new hands that he took from the merchantmen, sir. All prime seamen, although at this moment they seem uncertain what is happening, or whether they have exchanged one hell for another.'

The following morning, as Bolitho was finishing his breakfast, one which Ozzard described as more fitting for a prisoner of war, Neale came down to report that his lookouts had sighted a sail, confirmed almost immediately as the frigate *Relentless*.

Almost before she had topped the horizon the *Relentless* was hoisting signals to be seen and repeated by the sloop-of-war *Lookout* to the remainder of the squadron.

Bolitho could imagine their feelings. Herrick's patrols would have sighted the released merchantmen, and what he had not discovered from them he would have guessed.

A first blood for the new squadron. Something to brag about when the weather got a man down and the food was too vile even to discuss.

Later when Bolitho went on deck he noticed that Allday had preceded him with his sea-chest, as if he too was more than eager to be getting back to the *Benbow*.

He saw Pascoe and the small midshipman, Penels, standing

on the larboard gangway pointing towards the ships, and then as the anchored squadron hove slowly into view he saw him turn and look aft, his expression puzzled.

Neale said, 'Hand me a glass.' He trained it beyond the other frigate as she went gracefully about and steered back towards the squadron. 'Captain Herrick is prepared to weigh, it seems.' He handed the glass to Bolitho and watched his reactions.

Bolitho levelled the telescope on the *Benbow*'s shining hull as she swung tightly to her cable. Neale was right. The sails were loosely brailed up and not furled neatly as he might have expected. The cable was all but hove short, as were those of the other two-deckers. He felt suddenly uneasy but said as calmly as he could, 'We must be patient.'

Neale nodded doubtfully and then called, 'Get the royals on her, Mr Pickthorn! We are in a hurry this morning!'

The *Benbow*'s signal midshipman lowered his telescope and reported, 'The squadron has weighed, sir!'

Bolitho gripped the hammock nettings and watched first one and then the next ship heeling over to the wind, sails filling and emptying until they had completed their manoeuvre. Wolfe, the first lieutenant, was doing most of the work on the quarterdeck, which was not Herrick's way at all, and gave some hint of his anxiety.

It had been barely fifteen minutes since Bolitho had clambered through the entry port, fifteen minutes of bustle and outward confusion while the seamen had dashed out on the yards or hauled at halliards and braces as if they had been timed to act at the very moment of his appearance.

In between his many duties, Herrick had said, 'A courier brig came from the Nore, sir. Her commander had despatches for Admiral Damerum, but of course his squadron had already gone its different ways.' Some of his anxiety had left his face as he had added thankfully, 'By God, it is *good* to have you back, sir. I was at my wits' end as to what course to take.'

Piece by piece, in between exasperating delays while Herrick ordered a change of tack or the reduction of sail while the squadron formed into line astern, Bolitho discovered what had happened. He did not once interrupt or hurry Herrick. He wanted it in his own words and not in some carefully prepared oration for his benefit.

One fact stood out above all else. A French squadron had broken out of Brest and had vanished into the blue. It was known to be under the flag of *Vice-Amiral* Alfred Ropars, an experienced and daring officer. He had taken advantage of the terrible weather, but more than that, he had sent out two of his frigates under cover of darkness to attack and seize the only British patrol which was close enough inshore to see what was happening. Bolitho thought of Inskip's views on a captain's authority and value. The commander of the captured frigate would lose everything. His previous successes, his whole career would be sacrificed to wipe the slate clean.

But Bolitho knew how easily it could happen. Back and forth, up and down, in every sort of sea and wind, the weather-beaten ships of the blockading squadrons often became over-confident, too certain that the French would be sensible enough to stay in port rather than risk a fight.

Ropars must have timed it well. With the patrol captured, his own heavier ships were out and away before dawn.

The courier brig's information was scanty but for one thing. Ropars had sailed north. Not west to the Caribbean or south to the Mediterranean, but north.

Herrick said despairingly, 'With Admiral Damerum relieved by our smaller squadron, sir, and you away, as I thought, in Copenhagen, I was split in halves. The Admiralty thinks Ropars has sailed to assist an invasion and uprising in Ireland. Our fleet is so thinly spread, it might be a good moment to try.'

Bolitho nodded, his mind busy. 'Five years ago, when I was Sir Charles Thelwall's flag captain in *Euryalus*, I saw enough misery on that station. The French tried it then. They just might make another attempt, Thomas.'

Herrick shaded his eyes to squint up at the topgallant yards where some seamen were clinging on with hands and feet as the sails ballooned violently to the wind.

He said, 'But I decided I could do no useful thing by running for Ireland, sir. We have too few ships.' He looked Bolitho straight in the eyes. 'In any case, sir, *you* are my flag officer.'

Bolitho smiled. With him in Copenhagen it must have been

a hard decision for Herrick. If he had decided wrongly his head
would be on the block with his admiral's, loyalty or not.

But he said warmly, 'That was well said, Thomas. I'll see you
with your own broad pendant before long, mark my words.'

Herrick grimaced. 'I'd not thank you for it, sir!'

He shifted his feet and said, 'The French admiral's strength
is a squadron, no more. That we do know. And I'll wager every
ship from the Channel Fleet is prowling the enemy's ports in
case they try to reinforce this Ropars.'

Bolitho released his grip from the nettings. It did not take
long to get used to the change of motion. From the wild plunges
of a frigate to the slow, ponderous tilt of a ship of the line.

'Well, Thomas? I'm waiting.'

Herrick bit his lip, as if wishing he had remained silent.

'I heard what you did in the Baltic. I questioned the master
of one of the merchantmen you set free. It was a fine piece of
work, sir, with just the *Styx* to carry it out.'

Bolitho looked at the grey sea alongside, willing Herrick to
get on with it, but equally afraid to break the thread of his ideas.

'I think it unlike the Frogs to send one frigate for that task,
sir. They would know your squadron would prevent any attempt
to escort the merchantmen to France.' He spread his hands. 'And
for the life of me I can see no other reason for their actions!'

Bolitho stared at him. 'Time and distance, Thomas, is that
it?'

Herrick nodded. 'Aye, sir. I believe that the Frogs intended
to draw our squadron to the west to assist the Channel Fleet
and to cut Ropars retreat if his attack on Ireland failed.'

Bolitho gripped his arm. 'And all the while Ropars is really
sailing further north, around Scotland maybe, and then down
the coast of Norway, is *that* what you believe?'

Herrick licked his lips. 'Well, er, yes, sir. They'll come south.'
He looked at the hazy outline of the Danish coast. 'To here.'

'Where they hope to find the back door open for them, eh?'
It was so simple it had to be wrong.

Bolitho said, 'Signal the squadron to steer west, Thomas, with
Relentless and *Lookout* as far in the lead as possible without
losing visual contact. When you are satisfied with them, come
aft and bring the master with you. We'll study the charts and
share our ideas.'

Herrick looked at him, less certain now.

'I may be quite wrong, sir. Is it worth the risk?'

'If we fight here, we will be on the lee shore. No, we shall meet them in open water, if at all. Cripple some and send the rest running. I have heard of Admiral Ropars, Thomas. This is just the sort of thing he would attempt.'

Herrick said ruefully, 'A bit like you then, sir?'

'Not too much, I hope. Otherwise he may be outguessing us already!'

Bolitho made his way aft to his quarters, past the rigid marine sentry, and then ducked automatically as if he was still aboard the frigate.

For a while he moved restlessly about the cabin, thinking of all that had happened in so short a time. The fragment of chance when *Lookout* had taken the French brig *Echo*. Their arrival in Copenhagen, the attack through the snowstorm, men dying, others cheering.

He heard cheering now, as if his thoughts had come to life, but when he peered through the stern windows he saw the frigate *Styx* close-hauled under a full pyramid of canvas and steering past the slower moving two-deckers. The squadron was cheering one of its own. A scarred victor, going home for repairs and perhaps a hero's welcome.

Allday entered the cabin and replaced the presentation sword on its rack below the other one.

He said, 'I was a mite worried back there, sir. Just for a while.'

Bolitho shrugged. 'Fate is a strange thing.'

Allday grinned, obviously relieved. 'The folk in Falmouth would have been caught aback if you'd broken it, and that's no error, sir!'

Bolitho sat down, suddenly tired. 'Fetch me something to drink, if you please.' Then he smiled gravely. 'And let us both stop pretending, shall we?'

7

Prepare for Battle

It was a very cold morning, and when Bolitho went on deck
for his customary walk he felt the chill in the air as he had off
Gotland.

He looked at the sky, almost devoid of cloud but, like the
sea, leaden grey, without welcome.

With the aid of a telescope he sought out the other ships,
studying the early morning activity, sails being set or retrimmed
to bring each vessel into a slow-moving line. Of the *Lookout*
there was no sign as yet, although the masthead might already
be able to see her.

The first lieutenant was pacing along the lee side, his ginger
hair flapping beneath his hat to make the only bright colour on
deck.

His was not to reason or criticize. Wolfe was the first
lieutenant, with a command of his own before too long if he
was fortunate. To run the *Benbow* like a perfectly tuned instru-
ment and hand her to his captain in first degree readiness was
his sole purpose for being here.

Bolitho dragged his thoughts from the daily routine and considered his own position. Two days they had been heading
slowly west and then north. Two days with their Baltic patrol
left unattended. Suppose he was wrong? Suppose he had been
so eager to exploit the success of the squadron, even in the face
of Inskip's doubts and warnings, that he had missed the obvious?

The excitement at seeing *Styx* and her battle scars could not
last forever. Soon now and he would have to decide. To continue, or to return to the inshore station. Failing to take his
ships, or some of them, to Irish waters, and then missing any
sort of contact with the French squadron because of an hap-

hazard idea would not go down at all well with Damerum or the Admiralty.

He paused as he heard Wolfe say in his harsh tones, 'Now then, Mr Pascoe, what is all this I hear about you requesting a transfer for the landman Babbage? To the afterguard, y'say?' He leaned forward, towering above the young lieutenant like an ungainly giant.

Pascoe replied, 'Well, sir, he was pressed at Plymouth. He comes from Bodmin, and . . .'

Wolfe growled impatiently, 'And *I* come from bloody Bristol, so where does that get us, eh?'

Pascoe tried again. 'Mr Midshipman Penels asked for the transfer, sir. They grew up together. Babbage worked for Penels' mother when his father died.'

'Is that all?' Wolfe nodded, satisfied. 'Well, I already knew that. Which is why I kept 'em separate, when I got to hear of their connection, so to speak.'

'I see, sir.'

'Oh no you don't, Mr Pascoe, but never mind. You asked, I said no. Now take some men to the foretop and attend the barricade. Mr Swale assures me that it is already cracked with strain. The devils probably used condemned timber when they built it, damn them!'

Pascoe touched his hat and strode to the gangway.

When he was out of earshot Bolitho called, 'Mr Wolfe. A moment please.'

Bolitho was quite tall, but Wolfe made him feel like a dwarf.

'Sir?'

'I could not help but overhear that. Perhaps you could share your information with *me*?'

Wolfe grinned, unabashed. 'Most certainly, sir. I met the officer in charge of the press at Plymouth when he brought some hands aboard for us. He told me about Babbage. How he had been sent to Plymouth with a message for a storekeeper there.'

'A long way from Bodmin, Mr Wolfe.'

'Aye, sir. It is that. Someone wanted him out of the way. Sent him where his capture would not be discussed or gossiped about, if you get my meaning, sir?'

Bolitho frowned. 'Penels' mother?'

'I expect so, sir. With her son at sea, and her man dead, she'd be seeking a new er, husband. Babbage could be a nuisance. Living at the house. Seeing and hearing everything. She couldn't have known Babbage would end up crossing his hawse with our young Mr Penels.'

'Thank you for telling me.'

Bolitho thought of the luckless Babbage. It was not unknown for employers and landowners to get rid of an unwanted servant in this fashion. Send him on a mission and then inform a crimp or the press-gang. The rest was easy.

Wolfe added, 'Mr Pascoe will be a good officer, sir. An' I'm not saying that to win your favours. He will learn about the wiles of women all in good time. Time enough then to bother him with such things.' He touched his hat and strode away humming to himself.

Bolitho continued his pacing. There were other sides to the ungainly first lieutenant, he thought. *Not saying that to win your favours.* You only had to look at him to know that!

'Deck there! *Lookout* in sight on the weather bow!'

Bolitho saw the officer of the watch make a note in the log about the first sighting of the day. Far beyond the sloop, Captain Rowley Peel in his *Relentless* would be eagerly scanning a brightening horizon. Thinking of *Styx*'s hard-won fight, hoping for a chance for himself and his ship. He was twenty-six, and that was about all Bolitho knew of him. Yet.

There was a clatter of feet on the lee gangway and a tough-looking boatswain's mate trudged aft and knuckled his forehead to the same lieutenant who was about to cover the log with its canvas hood.

'Beg pardon, Mr Speke, sir, there's bin a fight on the lower gundeck. Man struck a petty officer with a stool, sir.'

Speke was the second lieutenant, a competent officer, according to Herrick, but inclined to lose his temper too easily.

He said sharply, 'Very well, Jones. Tell the master-at-arms, and I will note it in the log for the first lieutenant's attention. Who is it, by the way?'

Somehow, and yet for no sane reason, Bolitho had known who it would be.

'Babbage, sir. Mr Pascoe's division.' As an afterthought he

added bluntly, 'He's put the petty officer in the sick-bay, sir. Split his skull, he did.'

Speke nodded severely. 'That's it then. My compliments to Mr Swale. Tell him a grating will have to be rigged sometime today.'

Bolitho walked to the companionway, his appetite for break-fast gone.

Sailing to seek out an enemy, to die if need be, was hard enough. To have a flogging as well would not help at all.

'Have you any new orders for me, sir?' Herrick stood just inside the screen door, his hat beneath his arm, his faded sea-going coat at odds with the newly furnished cabin.

Bolitho listened to the silence, the ship holding her breath around her company of six hundred and twenty men and boys. It was almost noon. The sky was still free of cloud and rain, and yet between-decks the air was damp and musty, with a touch of the wintry weather to come. Nothing had been reported by the frigate or the sloop, except for a fast-moving schooner which had headed away immediately. Privateer, smuggler or just some hardworking trader trying to stay clear of trouble?

Bolitho looked at his friend, knowing what was bothering him. It was unfair on Herrick, he thought. It had been his idea to disregard the advice brought by the courier brig. His plan to quit their proper station to meet the enemy in open water. It was wrong that he had this new worry on his mind as well.

Gently he asked, 'Can I help, Thomas? It is this matter of punishment, am I right?'

Herrick stared at him. 'Aye, sir. I am fair turned-about by it. Young Adam came to me about Babbage. Takes the blame on himself. He'll think me a bloody tyrant if I don't interfere.'

'You know about Babbage?'

Herrick nodded. 'I do now. Mr Wolfe told me.' He looked up at the deckhead and added, 'I'm not blaming him, of course. He sees it as plain duty to keep such matters away from his captain.' He tried to smile. 'As I used to from you.'

'I was thinking that.'

Herrick said, 'I've looked into the matter fully. The petty

T.I.S.—D

officer provoked Babbage, probably without knowing it. Babbage is an orphan, which only makes it worse.'

Bolitho nodded. No wonder his nephew was upset. He was an orphan also.

'We are involved, Thomas.'

'Aye, sir. That's the curse of it. If it was any other man I'd have no hesitation. Right or wrong, I'll not have my petty officers laid low and damn near killed. I hate flogging, as you well know, sir, but this sort of thing cannot be tolerated.'

Bolitho stood up. 'Would you like me to come on deck? My presence might show that is not merely a whim but a requirement of duty.'

Herrick's blue eyes were unwavering. 'No, sir, this is my ship. If there was a fault, I should have seen it for myself.'

'Whatever you say.' Bolitho smiled gravely. 'It does you credit, Thomas, to worry about one man at a time like this.'

Herrick moved to the door. 'Will you speak with Adam, sir?'

'He is my nephew, Thomas, and very close to me. But as you said when I hoisted my broad pendant aboard your old *Lysander*, he is one of *your* officers.'

Herrick sighed. 'I shall think twice in future before I venture such remarks.'

The door closed and another opened as Yovell, the clerk, entered with one of his files.

As the calls shrilled along the gundecks and the boatswain's mates yelled, 'All hands! All hands lay aft to witness punishment!' Yovell looked up at the skylight and murmured, 'Will Oi close the lower shutter, zur?'

'No.'

They were all doing it. Shielding him from a world he had known since he had been twelve years old.

'Prepare to write some new orders for the squadron. We will alter course this afternoon and return to our station.'

He heard Herrick's voice, as if through a padded wall. Slow and clear, like the man.

He found he was tensing his stomach muscles, and knew Yovell was watching him.

The drum rolled, and he heard the lash cut across the man's naked back like a pistol shot. Bolitho could see it exactly as if

he were there on deck. Grim faces, the ship carrying them along
while the punishment continued.

At the third stroke of the lash he heard Babbage scream,
wildly, in terror, like a woman in agony.

Crack.

Yovell muttered, 'Lord love us, zur, 'e's taking it badly.'

Two dozen lashes were the absolute minimum for Babbage's
assault. Many captains would have awarded a hundred or worse.
Herrick would make it as little as possible. To spare the victim
without destroying the petty officer's authority when he eventually returned to duty.

Crack.

Bolitho stood up violently, the awful screams probing his
ears like knives.

The drum faltered and someone shouted to restore order.

Then Bolitho heard another cry, far away, from the dizzy
masthead.

'*Lookout*'s signalling, sir!'

Bolitho sat down again, his heart drumming against his ribs,
his fingers gripping the arms of the chair. The screaming was
still going on but the flogging had stopped.

It took physical effort to remain seated.

He said, 'Now, tell me about the despatches you wish me to
sign.'

Yovell swallowed hard. ' 'Ere, zur.' He laid the canvas file
in which he carried his carefully penned letters on the table.

Bolitho ran his eyes over the round handwriting but saw
nothing but the little sloop-of-war showing her hoist of signal
flags which she was no doubt repeating from the *Relentless*.

There was a tap at the door and Browne entered carefully.

'Signal from *Relentless*, sir. *Five sail to the north-west*.'

Bolitho stood up. 'Thank you. Keep me informed.' As the
flag lieutenant made to withdraw he asked, 'What happened on
deck?'

Browne looked at him blankly. 'The man under punishment
could not stand the pain, sir. Five blows and the surgeon asked
for the boatswain's mate to desist while he examined him.' He
smiled briefly. 'He should thank the masthead lookout for keeping his eyes open. He's a lucky fellow.'

'That's one way of looking at it, I suppose.'

Bolitho made up his mind. 'I shall come on deck with you directly.' He looked round for his hat and Ozzard appeared with it like a small magician.

Together they walked beneath the poop and out into the cold, clinging wind.

The grating was still rigged on the gangway, and a few droplets of dark blood were already being swabbed away by some of the duty watch.

Herrick strode to meet him, his round face questioning.

Bolitho smiled. 'I came to hear more about the five sail.' He saw the strain being eased from Herrick's eyes. 'Was it bad?'

'Bad enough. I'd have stopped it anyway. At least, I *hope* I would.'

Herrick turned to watch the repeated signal breaking from the *Benbow*'s yards for the benefit of the other ships, the way the flags were streaming towards the starboard bow.

He said, 'The newcomers, whoever they are, will have the wind-gage, sir.'

Bolitho nodded, satisfied. Herrick's mind, his professional attention to detail, had taken over again. Almost.

He said, 'It will be close on two hours before we sight anything. Have the people fed before we clear for action.'

Herrick regarded him grimly. 'You really believe it is Ropars and his squadron, sir?'

Loveys, the white-faced surgeon, was making his way aft to report on Babbage's condition. He looked like the walking-dead himself.

Bolitho asked, 'Don't *you*, Thomas?'

Herrick grimaced. 'I never thought I should welcome the sight of an enemy. But after this last spectacle I'm making an exception!'

Bolitho listened to the clatter of hurrying feet and guessed that Herrick's lookouts had at last sighted the other vessels. He gulped down another cup of strong coffee and glared at Allday as he tasted brandy in it.

'You know I never drink at times like these!'

Allday was unmoved. 'We're usually in warmer climes, sir. This will give you strength.'

The marine sentry called through the door, 'Midshipman of the watch, sir!'

It was Aggett, *Benbow*'s senior 'young gentleman'.

Bolitho looked at him as calmly as he could.

'Mr Browne's respects, sir, and we have just received another signal from *Relentless*.'

Bolitho said patiently, 'Well, Mr Aggett, I am afraid I am no mind-reader!'

The youth flushed. '*Eight strange sail to the nor'-west, sir.*'

Bolitho digested this new information. So it was eight now. The odds were getting worse.

He said, 'My compliments to the flag lieutenant. Tell him to make to *Lookout*, repeated to *Relentless*, *reconnoitre the ships in view and report to the admiral.*'

Captain Peel would need no urging, but it might give him comfort to know he had the support of his flagship. With *Styx* gone from the squadron his role was doubly important, even vital.

Allday took down the old sword and waited for Bolitho to lift his arm so that he could clip it to his belt.

'That's more like it, sir.'

Bolitho handed the empty cup to Ozzard. 'You're too sentimental, Allday.'

Then, with a quick glance through the stern windows to ensure that neither wind nor light had altered, he went on deck.

The signalling parties were working like demons, flags dashing up and down the yards, repeating, acknowledging, questioning. He noticed once again that these specialists seemed to like and respect the outwardly casual Browne.

Browne did not miss a thing. Perhaps Inskip had been right, and he should find a place in Whitehall or Parliament.

Herrick and Wolfe were training their glasses above the tightly packed hammock nettings, as were several unemployed officers.

A master's mate coughed a polite warning, and Herrick turned to greet his superior.

'You heard, sir? Well, I've got the sixth lieutenant in the mainmast cross-trees with his glass, and the other ships are in sight. Eight, we know of, though of what strength I cannot tell as yet.'

Browne called, 'From *Lookout*, sir. *Enemy in sight*.'

Bolitho looked at him impassively. 'Acknowledge, then make a general signal. *Prepare for battle*.'

He ignored the sudden excitement, the busy squeal of halliards, and said to Herrick, 'You were *right*, Thomas.'

Herrick grinned. 'Now I'm not so sure if I'm glad about it.'

Wolfe touched his hat and said fiercely, 'Permission to clear for action, sir?'

'Aye. Let's be about it.'

As the drums beat out their staccato call to quarters, seamen and marines poured up through hatches and companionways in a living tide. They had all been expecting it, and for the most part had been totally unaware of their captain's misgivings, their admiral's doubts.

Bolitho heard the screens being ripped down throughout the hull, every obstruction, chest or piece of furniture being carried below the water-line to leave the ship free to act to full advantage. The lower gundeck would be one long double battery from bow to stern, the thirty-two-pounders already manned, their breechings cast off even as the ship's boys ladled sand around the feet of their crews. On the upper gundeck the twenty-eight eighteen-pounders, each partly covered by gangways which ran along either side joining forecastle to quarter-deck, were equally busy.

Bolitho watched the quarterdeck gun crews, moving as if to an unspoken drill as they checked the tackles of their nine-pounders, examined their equipment like surgeons, while the scarlet caterpillars of marines passed through them to poop or forecastle, to the fighting tops, or to the less popular tasks of guarding the hatchways to prevent any terrified man from running below.

It was a fact that such things were necessary. Men, driven out of their sanity by the thundering roar of artillery, the awful sights of close combat around them, would often try to seek refuge in the depths of the hull.

He heard Wolfe exclaim angrily, 'Dammee, Mr Speke, sir! The *Indomitable* has cut her time again! Beaten us to it!'

Browne said, 'From *Relentless*, sir.' He was squinting down at the midshipman's slate. '*Five sail of the line, two frigates and one transport*.'

Bolitho took a telescope from a master's mate and climbed into the shrouds, aware that the nearest gun crews were staring up at him as if expecting something more than a mere man inside the fine coat with its bright epaulettes.

He waited, steadying the glass against the vibrating ratlines, until *Benbow* lifted lazily on a long roller which passed diagonally beneath her keel before allowing her to slide into the next trough.

In those seconds Bolitho saw the enemy for the first time. Not just blotches of tanned sails against a dull sky, but as ships. He had no doubt that the French commander was watching him, too.

Six large vessels in two columns. The second one in the weather column wore the flag of a vice-admiral. If there had been any remaining doubt in Bolitho's mind it was gone now.

Beyond the two columns were the frigates, probably waiting well clear of their squadron until they knew Bolitho's strength, especially in fifth-rates like themselves.

He called, 'I estimate their course to be sou'-east, Captain Herrick.'

Herrick, equally formal with half the quarterdeck straining to hear him, replied, 'My view, too, sir.'

Bolitho waited for the next slow lift beneath *Benbow*'s massive bilges and then searched for the transport. She was probably the rearmost ship in the lee column, he decided. In the best place to tack clear or seek protection from the frigates if so ordered. What would she be carrying? Surely not stores. More likely some of Napoleon's crack soldiers, men who barely knew the meaning of defeat. The Tsar of Russia would certainly need some of their professional instruction before he ventured into the spreading arena of war. Or maybe they were troops being sent to guard the captured British merchantmen. Well, Bolitho thought grimly, whatever is decided today, those ships will be safe from Ropars, and *Styx*'s action might make the Swedes or the Prussians less eager to support the Tsar's ambitions.

He climbed down to the deck and saw Midshipman Penels looking across at him like someone under sentence of death.

'Mr Penels, come here.'

The boy hurried to obey, bringing a few grins from the seamen as he caught his foot on a ring-bolt.

'It has been a bad day for you, it seems.' He watched the boy flinch under his gaze. Twelve years old, no father, sent off to sea to find his way as a King's officer. He would take it badly over his friend Babbage.

Penels sniffed. 'He was a good friend to me, sir. Now I don't know what I'll say when next we meet.'

Bolitho thought of Wolfe's casual acceptance of it. Penels' mother turning to another man. God knows, it happened enough to the wives of sailors. But Penels was only dressed as an officer. He was still a boy. A child.

Bolitho said quietly, 'Mr Pascoe did what he could. Perhaps after this Babbage will need your help more rather than less. I suspect it has always been the other way round in the past?'

Penels stared at him, speechless. That his admiral should care must seem incredible. That he was also right in his assumption about Babbage even more astounding.

He stammered, 'I – I shall try, sir.'

Wolfe tapped one great foot impatiently, and as Penels hurried back to his station on the starboard side he barked, 'Assist the flag lieutenant, Mr Penels. Though, God damn me, I'd feel safer with a Frenchie than with you, sir!' He glanced at Lieutenant Speke and winked.

Old Ben Grubb blew his nose noisily and remarked, 'Wind's steady, sir. Westerly with barely a shift either way.' He peered at the half-hour-glass by the binnacle and added, 'Not long now, I'd say.'

Bolitho looked at Herrick and shrugged. Not long for what? he wondered. Early darkness, victory or death? The sailing master seemed to enjoy tossing in these strange observations. He had one massive fist in the pocket of his shabby watch-coat, and Bolitho guessed he was holding his tin whistle, ready to play them into hell itself if need be.

Herrick was less charitable. 'Grubb's getting old, sir. Should be ashore somewhere with a good woman to take care of him.'

Bolitho smiled. 'Heavens, Thomas! Since you took to marriage you cannot help replanning others' lives!'

Allday, lounging by the mainmast trunk, relaxed slightly. He always gauged his own chances by watching Bolitho at such moments. He looked over the weather gangway and studied the other ships. The enemy. Both squadrons were moving towards each other like a great arrowhead, the steady wind parting their courses like a shaft. But the French had the wind's advantage, and there were more of them. He turned to watch the men near him. The old hands checking their gear. Flintlocks and powder-horns, sponges and rammers, screws and prickers, even though they had already done it several times. And when they had finished they would begin again. They had seen it all before. The slow, deadly approach, the huddle of sails and masts changing to individual vessels and formations. It took nerve to stand and wait for the final, inevitable embrace.

The youngsters saw it through different eyes. Excitement touched with the ice of fear. The need to be doing something at last instead of the endless backbreaking work and drills.

Slightly separated from the individual gun crews and the men who would work the ship throughout a battle, the petty officers went through their lists and examined their own parts of the whole. Here and there along the divisions of guns were small patches of blue and white, the lieutenants, warrant officers and midshipmen, and below on the other gundeck the pattern was repeated in the eerie darkness behind sealed gunports.

Lieutenant Marston of the marines was up forward talking with the crews of the two big carronades, and Allday recalled the *Styx*'s marine officer sitting with his head in his hands, struck blind by flying splinters.

Major Clinton was right aft with Sergeant Rombilow, pointing up at the swivel gun in the mizzen top with his black stick. Allday considered that all marines were probably a little mad. Clinton was no exception, and always carried his walking-stick when the ship went to quarters, while his orderly nursed his sword like a bearer.

Allday saw Pascoe walking slowly behind each of his forward guns. If the ships continued on their same tack, his guns would engage the enemy first. How like Bolitho he looked. He thought suddenly of Babbage, of the sickening spectacle of him writhing and screaming under the lash. Even the boatswain's mate who had been using the cat-o'-nine-tails had looked shocked by the outburst.

Next to Bolitho, Allday would do anything for Pascoe. They had lived, fought and suffered together, and if Babbage was to be the cause of Pascoe's worried expression, then Allday found good reason for hating him.

The ship was about to sail into battle. Allday cared very little for the rights and wrongs of it, the 'cause' which was drawing the whole world into a war. You fought for those you cared about, for the ship around you, and for little else.

The rich and powerful could drink their port and gamble away their fortunes, Allday thought, but this was his world while it lasted. And if Pascoe had his mind even partly occupied by some fool's problems he would be in more danger than the rest of them.

Bolitho watched his coxswain and said quietly to Herrick, 'See him, Thomas? I can almost read his mind from here.'

Herrick followed Allday's glance and answered, 'Aye, sir. He's a good hand, though he'd blast your eyes rather than agree with you!'

The air reverberated to the sudden boom of gunfire, and Wolfe said, 'The Frenchies are putting a few shots at the *Relentless*, I shouldn't wonder, sir.'

Herrick looked at Bolitho. 'I'll withdraw her and *Lookout* to our lee, sir. They've taken enough risks for the moment.'

Bolitho watched him speaking with the flag lieutenant as the signal was bent on to the halliards. Herrick had come a long, long way since he had been appointed as flag captain in the *Lysander*. The hesitations were few, and when he decided on something it was with the authority of confidence.

Browne called, 'They have acknowledged, sir.'

Herrick asked, 'What d'you think the French will do, sir?'

'Leaving the frigates out of it for the present, I would say that Ropars will put his full weight against us. If I were Ropars I would form a single line, otherwise the first engagement will be our four to his three. In line of battle the odds will be five to four against us.'

Herrick faced him, his eyes hopeful. 'But you don't intend that, do you, sir?'

'No.' He clapped him on the shoulder. 'We will break the enemy's line in two places.'

Wolfe said, 'The Frenchies *are* forming into line, sir.' He grinned with admiration. 'And the transport seems to be standing well astern of the main column.'

Bolitho barely heard him. 'We will attack in two subdivisions. *Benbow* and *Indomitable*, while the second one, *Nicator* and *Odin*, will tack in succession. Tell Browne's men to have the signal ready.'

He moved away and trained a telescope on the French line. It was still in disarray, but he noticed immediately that the flagship was remaining in second place in the line. To watch Bolitho's tactics before he himself acted. Or perhaps to allow one of his captains to take the first brunt of battle.

He walked aft again past the helmsmen and looked at Grubb's chart which was fixed on a little table below the poop. To save Grubb the extra effort of carrying his great bulk to the chart room, Bolitho thought.

To all appearances the two squadrons were in a landless ocean, and yet some fifty miles to the north-east was Norway, and further away to the south-east the coast of Denmark, with the Skagerrak cradled between them.

Bolitho wondered briefly what Inskip was doing, and if it had really been the Crown Prince he had met.

He shut them all from his mind.

'We will alter course, Captain Herrick. The squadron will steer nor'-east by east.'

He walked past the bustling afterguard and watched the *Relentless* shortening sail to steer a parallel course with the squadron, *Lookout* following astern like her cub.

The French ships did not alter course or change a single sail.

Herrick studied his own canvas as the yards steadied again, and remarked, 'That'll get him guessing, sir.'

Bolitho watched the leading French ship. About the same size as *Benbow*, she was already running out her guns. It must seem worse to some of the French sailors, he thought. They had been too long in harbour to withstand the strain of this slow approach. Their officers were keeping them busy, they would be firing a few sighting-shots soon to give them heart for a fight.

Grubb said dourly, 'Two miles, sir. We'll be up to them in 'alf an hour.' He tapped the sand-glass with a thick finger.

There was a dull bang, and seconds later a thin waterspout shot skywards well clear of the larboard bow. A few of the seamen jeered, and some of the older hands looked aft, impatient now that the game had begun.

'Load and run out, if you please. Tell your gun crews we will be engaging on both sides today, but the starboard ports will remain closed until we are amongst the enemy.'

Bolitho moved to the opposite side of the quarterdeck, hemmed in by gun crews and marines, officers and messengers, and yet completely alone.

The French squadron was more powerful, but he had seen worse odds. What his own ships lacked in men and guns they made up in experience. The two lines were drawing toward some point on this grey water, as if being warped by invisible hawsers.

Bolitho dropped his hand and rested it on the well-worn sword at his hip.

Almost to himself he said, 'We will put ourselves against the French flagship. They are all far from home. If Ropars' flag falls, the rest will soon scatter.'

The leading French ship, a seventy-four, vanished momentarily behind a billowing barrier of smoke.

Grubb said to his master's mate, 'Note it in the log, Mr Daws. The enemy 'as opened fire.'

8

Outwitted

Bolitho watched the fall of the French broadside from the leading ship. She had fired at extreme range, and he guessed her captain was using the broadside as an exercise. It was more than likely that his gun crews had had little opportunity of aiming at a real enemy before.

British sailors could curse and swear all they wished, but when it came to a fight it was sea-time which counted as much as the weight of armament.

He could not recall seeing the complete contents of a broadside fall before in open water. It was like a violent upsurge from something beneath the surface, hurling spray and smoke in a long, jagged barrier. Even when the last ball had fallen the sea still writhed, the surface painted with great daubs of hissing salt.

Herrick remarked, 'Waste of good powder and shot.'

Several others nodded, and Wolfe said, 'They're shortening sail, sir.'

Herrick nodded. 'Do likewise, Mr Wolfe.'

Bolitho walked away. It was the usual practice, once enemies had been committed to a course of action. Enough canvas to give steerage-way and to manoeuvre, but not enough to encourage an outburst of fire. A flaming wad from a gun, a lantern knocked over by a stray ball, anything could change these fine pyramids of sail into a roaring inferno.

Bolitho watched the maincourse being gathered up to its yard, the sudden activity along the deck as the order was obeyed. Along the slow-moving British line the others followed suit, stripping for combat.

And still the two columns continued remorselessly towards one another. The second French ship, with Ropars' flag at the

fore, fired some ranging shots from each deck. Much nearer
than the first impressive broadside. Bolitho followed a ball's
progress as it tore low across the wavecrests, cutting a path of
spurting spray, until it struck hard into the sea and vanished.
It fell less than a cable from *Benbow's* larboard bow.

Bolitho said, 'When we engage, Mr Browne, make to *Relentless, attack and harass enemy's rear*. I will keep *Lookout* with us
to give the French something to ponder on.'

Somebody laughed. A short, nervous sound. One of the new
hands probably. The sudden burst of cannon fire, the over-
whelming weight of iron as it had scythed into the sea had been
less dangerous than the carefully pointed shots from Ropars'
flagship. But to an inexperienced eye it would seem awe-
some.

Lieutenant Speke had left the quarterdeck and was walking
between the lines of eighteen-pounders, hands behind his back
until he joined Pascoe by the foremast bitts.

Gun captains watched them apprehensively, while here and
there a handspike moved to point a cannon more accurately,
while another seaman made a small adjustment with a quoin.
It was as if the whole ship was on the edge of tension, and even
the braced fore-topsail gave two sharp, impatient flaps, making
one of the ship's boys peer round in alarm.

Bolitho turned as the leading Frenchman fired again. Much
closer, some of the spray falling so near they could hear it, like
tropical rain.

Bolitho trained a glass on the French line. Along the five
vessels, all seventy-fours, he could see the sails changing, being
reefed or filling again to the wind as their captains did everything to hold the distances and yet be ready to react to their
enemy.

He said, 'Alter course two points starboard, Captain Herrick.
The squadron will follow.'

Men hurried to the braces, and he heard the wheel being
hauled over rapidly as if the quartermaster and helmsmen had
been expecting the order.

Grubb said, 'Steady as she goes, sir. East by north.'

The British line had edged slightly away from the other
squadron, so that for a moment it appeared as if the French
were falling astern. The yards squeaked to the pull of blocks

and braces, and at the masthead Bolitho saw the pendant flapping almost directly forward.

He could feel the ship responding, as with the wind under her coat-tails she forged eagerly ahead.

'French have made more sail, sir.' Herrick looked at him. 'Do I set the courses on her again?'

'No.' Bolitho walked three paces to the nearest gun and back again. 'I want them to believe we're more interested in delaying their progress than closing to point-blank range.'

He watched the French topgallant yards changing shape and direction as the ships spread more sail and increased speed accordingly. Less than a mile separated them now.

'Be ready, Mr Browne.'

He pictured the captains following in *Benbow*'s wake. He had explained this very tactic to them when he had first met them as a squadron. The minimum of signals. The maximum of initiative. He could see them now. Keverne, Keen and good old Inch. Waiting for the solitary flag which was already bent on and ready. As he had said at the time, 'The French can read our signals, too, so why share our knowledge with them?'

'I think we may open fire, Captain Herrick.'

Bolitho saw his words being passed forward along the gun-deck by whisper and gesture with the speed of light.

'No broadside. Tell your gun captains to shoot on the uproll and to fire at will.'

Herrick nodded. 'Aye, sir. That will get the Frogs moving. They'll not want to be dismasted or crippled by a random shot at this stage of the game. They've a fair way to go in either direction!'

A midshipman ran down the main hatch with the message, and seconds later a whistle shrilled out from the forecastle.

It was hard to see who fired first, and to what effect. Down the engaged side the guns came crashing inboard on their tackles, the crews jumping instantly to sponge out the steaming muzzles and reload. Gun captains, stooped like old men, peered through their ports, watching the sails of the leading French ship jerk wildly as if in a whirlwind.

From the lower gundeck the recoiling thirty-two-pounders made the timbers quiver, while streaming past her beakhead the drifting smoke fanned out on either bow like a fog.

'We've hit her, by God!'

Another voice yelled, 'That was our gun, lads! Run out now an' we'll make 'em dance another jig!'

The rest of Bolitho's line were firing now, the shots cutting through the waves, some falling short and others hitting sails and hulls in a confusion of bursting spray and smoke.

'The French have altered course again, sir.' Herrick could barely control his excitement. 'Here they come.'

He winced as the second ship vanished in a wall of smoke and the long orange tongues flashed through it with the sound of thunder.

Water deluged across the forecastle, and beneath his feet Bolitho felt the massive hull stagger to the enemy's iron. Five, maybe six hits, but not a stay or shroud had been parted.

'Sponge out, that man!' A gun captain had to punch one of his men in the shoulder to bring him back to his senses. 'Now load, you bugger!'

Crash . . . crash . . . crash. All along *Benbow*'s painted tumblehome the guns came roaring inboard on their tackles. Alone, in pairs or whole sections their captains aimed and pulled their trigger lines, unhampered by the restricting demands of a fixed broadside.

Men were cheering from up forward as the leading Frenchman's main-topgallant mast vanished into the smoke. There were black dots drifting past the ships; wreckage, burned hammocks from the nettings or perhaps corpses thrown overboard to keep the guns firing.

'Again, lads! *Hit them!*' Herrick was yelling through his cupped hands, a far cry from the quiet-faced man who had stood at the altar in Kent.

The French line were all firing now, and each British ship was being damaged, or so deluged in falling spray she appeared to be.

A ball punched through the main-topsail and other holes appeared in the fore.

A few severed lines swung lazily above the guns, like dead weed, while Swale, the boatswain, Big Tom, matched his voice to the din as he urged his men aloft to splice and effect repairs before something vital carried away.

Bolitho flinched as metal clanged against a gun on the starboard side and the broken splinters cracked around him like musket fire. A seaman fell headlong to the deck, and Bolitho saw that beneath his pigtail his vertebrae had been laid bare. Nearby a petty officer had dropped to his knees and was trying to hold his entrails in his hands, his mouth wide in a soundless scream.

'Steady, lads! Point! Ready! *Fire!*'

The quarterdeck nine-pounders fired together, their sharper note making some of the men gasp with pain.

'And *again!*'

Bolitho swallowed hard as more enemy shots beat into the hull. He heard one smash through an open port on the lower gundeck, pictured the horror as it ploughed through men already blinded by smoke and half-mad from the deafening explosions.

'*Fire!*'

The leading French ship was overreaching *Benbow*, in spite of her missing topgallant mast. She was firing wildly, but some of the shots were hitting the hull. Bolitho looked along the upper gundeck at the men moving back and forth, jumping clear as each gun came squealing and crashing inboard.

Some lay where they had been dragged to await treatment. Others would not move again. Pascoe was walking behind his men, shouting something, then waving his hat. One of his gun captains turned to grin at him and fell dead as a ball whipped past his stomach without even touching him. On the opposite side it thundered into the bulwark and killed another seaman even as he ducked away.

'*Fire!*'

Bolitho cleared his throat. 'We are rightly placed, I think.' He peered up at the flapping pendant, his eyes smarting with smoke. 'Be ready, Mr Browne!'

He heard Herrick yelling, 'Stand by to come about, Mr Grubb! Mr Speke!' He had to borrow Wolfe's trumpet to make the lieutenant hear through the noise. 'We will engage with both batteries! Prepare to raise the starboard port lids!' He watched to ensure that his message had been carried to the lower gundeck and then turned to add, 'By God, our people are doing well today, sir!'

Bolitho took him by the arm. 'Walk about, Thomas. When

we break the enemy's line they will try to mark us down from the tops!'

Somewhere in the smoke a man gave a shrill scream, and blood ran along the larboard scuppers in an unbroken thread.

He measured the distance. It was time. Later and the French might cripple them, or might try to separate them from each other.

'Make your signal, Mr Browne!'

The solitary flag broke from the yard, to be acknowledged all along the line.

Browne wiped his mouth with his hand. His hat was awry and there was blood on his white breeches.

'Close up, sir!'

Bolitho looked at the men ready at the braces, the ones at the big double-wheel taking the strain on the spokes while they tried to concentrate on Grubb, on everything but the crash and roar of cannon fire.

A marine fell from the maintop, hit a net and rolled over the side into the sea.

A powder-monkey, running towards the larboard guns, turned on his toes like a dancer then fell kicking to the deck. Before he looked away Bolitho saw that his eyes had been blasted from his head.

'*Now!*'

The yards came round like great, straining bows, and as the helm went over Bolitho saw the French ships suddenly loom above the larboard bow. Then they stood before the bowsprit as *Benbow* continued to turn until her yards were all but braced fore and aft.

With canvas thundering and flapping in protest, *Benbow* held on her new tack, her tapering jib-boom pointing directly at the gilded gallery of the French flagship. He could see the sudden consternation on her poop and quarterdeck, the flags appearing frantically above the drifting smoke as she endeavoured to rally support.

'Make your other signal to *Relentless*.'

Bolitho watched narrowly as the deck heeled to starboard under the tightly braced sails. Would they manage it? Break astern of the flagship and smash her poop to fragments, or would *Benbow* ram her instead and impale her on the bowsprit like a lance?

He heard more cheering, rising from the fog of battle to drown the cries and groans of the wounded. *Indomitable* was following close astern and, seeming much further away now, *Nicator*, with Inch's smaller sixty-four, *Odin*, in her wake, was heading to break the enemy's line. With luck, Captain Keen would pass between the fourth and the rearmost ship in the French squadron. If he could cut out the last ship and cripple her, the big transport would be at his mercy.

'Open your ports! Run out the starboard battery!'

The guns squealed to the ports as one, as if eager to discard their previous roles of spectators.

Herrick said between his teeth, 'Easy, Mr Grubb. You can let her fall off a point now.' He slammed one hand into the other. '*Got him!*'

They were so close to the other flagship that *Benbow*'s jib-boom and tattered staysails threw faint shadows across her counter and stern windows.

Bolitho heard Speke yell, 'As you bear! *Ready!*'

Right up forward Bolitho saw the two carronades poking their ugly snouts outboard. The starboard one at least could hardly miss.

Muskets cracked through the din, and Bolitho saw the hammocks jump in the nettings as the French marksmen tested their aim. In *Benbow*'s tops the marines were also firing, pointing out their opposite numbers to each other as they tried to mark down anyone in authority.

The blast and thunder of gunfire from the scattered ships was mounting to a terrible crescendo. Bolitho saw the starboard carronade fire, but the effect of its devastating charge of tightly packed grape was lost in smoke and thrown spray. Through it all *Benbow*'s men were yelling and cheering like demented beings. Their figures were blurred in smoke, their eyes staring and white as they threw themselves to their guns or ran to trim the yards in response to Wolfe's trumpeting voice from the quarterdeck.

Bolitho wiped his stinging eyes and peered at the Frenchman's stern as it loomed over the starboard bow. He could vaguely see her name, *La Loire*, the fine gilt lettering splintered by grape-shot and canister, while above it the stern windows were smashed to a shambles.

He heard Browne yelling at him and saw him pointing wildly to the opposite beam.

The third ship in the French line, the one which Bolitho had intended to isolate from *La Loire*, had suddenly hoisted an admiral's command flag to the fore, and even as the signal broke from her yards she began to tack round, following *Benbow*'s slow turn as if they were linked together.

Browne shouted incredulously, '*La Loire* has hauled down her flag, sir!'

Bolitho pushed past him, feeling the sudden despair drop across the wildness of battle like a blanket. The French admiral had planned it perfectly, the lure of his false flag breaking the British and not his own squadron into pieces.

Herrick was waving his sword. 'At 'em, lads! Engage to larboard again, Mr Speke!'

Thwarted by the enemy's unexpected change of direction, the *Nicator* and *Odin* were almost in irons, their reduced sails flapping in wild confusion as they tried to re-form into line.

Ropars' ship was surging level with *Benbow*'s quarter, her forward guns firing rapidly across a narrowing strip of water. To the dazed seamen around Bolitho it must seem as if each ball was finding a target.

There was not even a cheer as the foremast of the false French flagship staggered overboard in one great mass of canvas, broken spars and rigging. *La Loire* had been badly mauled, but her sacrifice looked like changing a battle into a total defeat for Bolitho's squadron.

In poor light, made worse by the billowing smoke, the ships lurched drunkenly against one another, guns pounding mercilessly at point-blank range. It was like being surrounded by a forest of masts and whipping flags, like being in hell itself.

Herrick seemed to be everywhere. Directing and rallying, shouting encouragement here, demanding greater effort there.

The young sixth lieutenant, Courtenay, the one Allday had ousted from his barge, was sprawled on his face, his shoes drumming on the deck as some of the marines dragged him towards the quarterdeck ladder. He had been hit by a French sharpshooter and his lower jaw had been completely shot away.

Browne shouted, '*Relentless* is attacking the transport, sir!'
He lowered his glass. 'The two French frigates are after him,
and *Lookout* requests permission to engage!'

'Denied.' Bolitho wiped his face. 'We may need her yet.'

For what purpose? To pick up survivors or to carry news of
a crushing defeat to England?

He said, 'General signal. *Take suitable stations for mutual
support. Engage the enemy in succession.*'

Some of the flags spilled over the deck as a ball ploughed
through the hurrying seamen, but despite the horror and the
screams the signal broke to the yards with barely a delay. Bolitho
doubted if it would make much difference. His captains knew
what to do, and were doing their best. But as the flags broke
above the rolling smoke it might show that their force was still
one, with a head and mind to control it.

Bolitho stared bitterly at a limping, sobbing seaman. *What
have I brought you to?*

Herrick said, '*Indomitable*'s in trouble, sir. Her mizzen just
went down.'

Grubb said, 'Aye, but old *Nicator*'s spread more sail to cover
'er flank!'

'All have acknowledged, sir.' Browne looked at the spattered
blood on his breeches, seeing it for the first time. 'Hell's teeth!'

Bolitho stared fixedly at Ropars' flagship. Less than half a
cable away. She was shortening sail, her gangways alive with
armed men, while her starboard batteries continued to fire as
rapidly as ever.

Herrick yelled, 'She'll be down on us soon, sir!'

Bolitho looked up at the *Benbow*'s pitted sails. Ropars' captain was acting like a true professional. Taking the wind out of
Benbow's sails, cutting away her power to manoeuvre even as
he poised for the final embrace.

Wolfe bellowed, 'Prepare to repel boarders!'

Overhead, a swivel crashed sharply and the hail of canister
raked a bloody path through some of the massed French seamen
and marines.

The taut faces of the crouching gun crews glowed in a vivid
red light, and seconds later an explosion rocked the embattled
ships like toy boats in a storm.

Smoking fragments fell hissing all around them, and Bolitho

knew that *La Loire* had caught fire unnoticed in the fight, and now her magazine had exploded.

Men dashed past to obey the boatswain's lisping bellow, buckets of water poised to douse any piece of burning wood or fabric as it fell on their own ship.

'From *Indomitable*, sir. *Request assistance!*'

Bolitho looked at his flag lieutenant but saw only Keverne. He shook his head.

'We can't. We must hold together.'

Browne watched him curiously and then nodded to his assistants.

'Acknowledge.'

Indomitable was being attacked by the two ships which had been at the rear of the enemy squadron. Hampered by a broken mast and trailing rigging, she was falling slowly astern, while *Nicator* and *Odin* forged past in pursuit of their own flagship, spreading more canvas and firing as fast as they could reload.

Ropars' flagship was making a lot of signals, too, and Bolitho thought that most of them were being directed to his frigates and heavy transport. The last thing he would wish was for the transport to be so damaged that she and her cargo, troops or otherwise, would fall in to enemy hands.

Bolitho shouted hoarsely, 'Stand fast, lads! It's going to be now or never!' He gripped Herrick's arm. 'Make our people cheer, Thomas! Get them on the gangway as if they want to board the enemy!'

Herrick stared at him. 'I will *try*, sir!'

Bolitho tore off his brightly laced hat and waved it above his head. 'A *cheer!*' He strode along the larboard gangway above the overheated guns and past ripped and punctured hammocks. 'Huzza, lads! Show them what we can do!'

The most ignorant man aboard knew that *Benbow* had been outmanoeuvred and outwitted by the French admiral. If they faltered now they were finished, with every likelihood of *Benbow* being taken intact to sail in a French line of battle.

It was too terrible to contemplate, and Bolitho did not even see Herrick's alarm or the concern on Allday's face as he ran to follow him along the exposed gangway.

But they were responding. As more shots hammered into the hull or clipped away rigging like some invisible scythe, the

Benbow's people stood back from the guns to cheer, to arm themselves, and climb to join Bolitho at the boarding nets.

The depleted gun crews were busily reloading, held under control by threat and physical strength, as Speke yelled, '*Full broadside! Ready!*'

Bolitho gripped the nettings and stared at the sea splashing alongside. It must soon end.

He could feel the grin fixed to his lips like a painful bit, hear the voices of the seamen blurred and distorted around him as they shouted towards the enemy. Like baying hounds, eager to kill even at the expense of death.

'Broadside! *Fire!*'

The shock almost hurled Bolitho headlong, and when he looked behind him he thought it was like standing on an abandoned footbridge, for the smoke, as it billowed inboard through every port, hid the entire gundeck from view.

Somewhere a trumpet blared with sudden urgency, and in disbelief Bolitho saw Ropars' ship standing away, her mizzen-topmast gone completely, her side and gunports streaming smoke. There were sparks, too, with running figures throwing water to fight the sailor's greatest fear of all.

Allday shouted wildly, 'The Frogs are hauling off, sir! You did for 'em!'

Men were cheering in spite of the shots which still hissed and whimpered overhead.

Bolitho's mind cringed to the noise, but the realization was stronger. It would soon be too dark to chase the enemy, even if his battered ships were able. Ropars, too, would be unable to regroup in time to give battle, and a complete escape was no doubt uppermost on his mind.

He saw Pascoe hurrying along the gangway, his face strained and somehow defenceless.

He turned and then winced with pain as something struck him hard in the left thigh. For a brief instant he imagined someone had kicked him or had struck him with a musket or pike in the excitement of the moment. Then as he stared at the great pattern of blood pumping across his leg the agony slammed into him like a white-hot iron.

Bolitho could not think clearly, and heard himself cry out as his cheek scraped on the deck planking. He felt himself falling

and falling, even though his body was motionless on the gangway.

He thought he heard Herrick shouting from a long way off,
and Allday calling his name. Then Pascoe was above him, looking down at his face, his fingers pushing the hair from his eyes
as the final darkness closed in and offered him oblivion.

Bolitho moved his head from side to side, conscious of little else
but a terrible screaming, which for a few moments he imagined
was coming from his own throat. Everything was dark, yet held
patches of swaying light and blurred colours.

A voice said urgently, 'He is conscious. Get ready to move
him!'

A red haze faded above him, and he realized it was Major
Clinton's coat. He and some of his men must have carried him
below. Sweat broke like ice water across his chest. *Carried below.*
He was on the orlop deck, and the scream was someone already
under the surgeon's knife.

He heard Allday, his voice almost unrecognizable as he said,
'We must take him aft, Major.'

Another voice, demented in terror, said, 'Oh no, *oh no*!
Please!'

Bolitho felt his head being raised slightly and realized a hand
was supporting it. Water trickled through his lips while his
eyes probed the semi-darkness of the orlop as he tried to swal-
low. Another scene from Hades. Men propped against the
Benbow's massive timbers. Inert shapes, and others which
rocked about in their separate agonies.

Beneath a cluster of lanterns Loveys, the surgeon, stooped
over his makeshift table, his apron spattered with blood like a
butcher's.

The man who had been screaming was lying spreadeagled on
the table, his cries stopped by a leather strap between his
clenched teeth. He was naked, and held rigid by Loveys' mates.
Only his eyes moved, like marbles as he stared at the surgeon,
pleaded with him.

Bolitho saw that the man's arm had been split open, smashed
by an enemy ball or a large fragment of iron.

The knife glittered in Loveys' hand, and for what seemed

like an eternity he held the edge of the blade on the soft flesh above the wound, barely inches from the point of the shoulder. With a quick nod to his mates he cut down and round, his face like stone. Another assistant handed him his saw, and in minutes it was done, the severed limb thrown into a bucket below the gyrating lanterns.

Someone whispered, 'Thank the Lord, he's fainted, poor bugger!'

Allday was behind Bolitho's head. 'Let us carry you aft, sir. Please, this is no place for you!'

Bolitho strained his head round to look at him. He wanted to console him, to explain that he had to remain here, if only to share the pain he had brought to the men around him. But no words came, and he was shocked to see the tears running down Allday's face.

Bolitho gritted his teeth. 'Where is Captain Herrick?'

Browne was on his knees beside him. 'He is attending to the squadron, sir. He will be down again soon.'

Again? So much to do; the dead to be buried, the repairs to be carried out before a storm found them, yet Herrick had already been here to see him.

Loveys was looking down at him, his wispy hair shining in the lamplight.

'Now, sir, let me see.'

Loveys knelt down, his skull-like features showing no sign of fatigue or dismay. He had just flensed a man's arm and amputated it, and God knew how many before that. For so frail a man he seemed to have more strength than any of them.

Bolitho closed his eyes. The pain was already so bad he barely felt the probing fingers, the slicing movement of a knife through his breeches.

Loveys said, 'Musket ball, but it is somehow deflected.' He stood up slowly. 'I will do what I can, sir.'

Browne whispered, 'Your nephew is coming, sir. Shall I send him away?'

'No.'

Even one word was agony. The thing he had always dreaded. This was no scar, no spent ball in the shoulder. This was deep in his thigh. His leg and foot were on fire, and he tried not to think of the man he had just seen on the table.

'Let him come to me.'

Pascoe knelt beside him, his face very still, like one of the old portraits at Falmouth.

'I'm here, Uncle.' He took Bolitho's hand in his. 'How are you?'

Bolitho looked at the deckhead. Above it, and the next above that, the guns were still.

He said thickly, 'I have been better, Adam.' He felt the grip tighten. 'Is everything all right with the squadron?'

He saw Pascoe trying to shield him from a man who was carrying the bloodied bucket to the companion ladder.

Pascoe nodded. 'You beat them, Uncle. You *showed* them!'

Bolitho tried to hold the pain at bay, to estimate the damage to his body his wild gesture had cost him.

Loveys was back again.

'I will have to remove your clothes, sir.'

Allday said, 'I'll do it!' He could barely look at Bolitho as he fumbled with his shirt and slashed breeches.

Loveys watched patiently. 'Better leave the rest to my loblolly boys.' He gestured to his assistants. 'Lively there!'

It was then that Bolitho wanted to say so much. To tell Adam about his father and what had really happened to him. But hands were already lifting him up and over some motionless figures. Drugged with rum, bandaged against infection, they might yet live. He felt something like terror, claws of fear exploring his insides.

He exclaimed, 'I want you to take the house in Falmouth. Everything. There is a letter . . .'

Pascoe looked desperately at Allday. 'Oh God, I cannot bear it.'

Allday said brokenly, 'He'll be all right, won't he?'

His words shocked Pascoe into reality. He had never known Allday show doubt, in fact he had always looked to the burly coxswain for assurance in the past.

He gripped Allday's sleeve. 'Be certain of it.'

Bolitho lay on the table, seeing little beyond the circle of swaying lanterns.

He had always expected it to be swift when it found him. One instant in battle, the next in death. But not like this, a useless cripple to be pitied or ridiculed.

Loveys said calmly, 'I will not deceive you, sir. You are in mortal peril of losing your leg. I will do my best.'

A hand came round Bolitho's head and the man placed a pad between his teeth. It was sodden with brandy.

Loveys said, 'Bite well, sir.'

Bolitho felt the terror rising like a phantom. Fear that the moment was here and now, and that he would show it in front of all the unseen watchers.

Fingers gripped his arms and legs like manacles, and he saw Loveys' right shoulder draw back and then come down suddenly, the pain exploding in his thigh like molten lead.

He tried to move his head from side to side, but Loveys' men knew their trade well. On and on, the agony spreading and probing, cutting, and hesitating whenever the ship gave an unexpected roll.

Through the haze of agony and fear he heard a voice call, ' 'Old on, Dick! Not long now!'

The interruption by the unknown sailor or marine gave Loveys the seconds he needed.

With a final twist of his thin wrist he gouged the flattened musket ball from the blackened flesh and dropped it in a tray.

His senior assistant murmured, ' 'E's fainted away, sir.'

'Good.' Loveys made another, deeper probe. 'One more piece.' He watched the man swab away the blood. 'Hold him fast now.'

Herrick approached the table slowly, his men parting to let him through. It was wrong to see Bolitho like this, naked and helpless. But in his heart he knew Bolitho would have it no other way. He had to clear his throat before he could speak.

'Is it done?'

Loveys snapped his fingers for another dressing. 'Aye, sir, for the present.' He gestured to the tray. 'The ball split one of his buttons and drove it and some fabric deep into the wound.' He met Herrick's anxious gaze. 'You and I have been in the King's service for a long time, sir. You know what can happen. Later I may regret that I did not remove the leg here and now.'

Herrick saw Bolitho stir, heard him moan quietly as a man removed the pad from his mouth.

He asked, 'Can we move him?'

Loveys signalled to his men. 'To my sick-bay. I dare not risk a longer journey.'

As they carried him into the shadows of the orlop Loveys seemed to thrust him momentarily from his mind. He pointed to a man whose head was swathed in bandages. 'Get him!' Then to Herrick he added simply, 'This place, these conditions, are all I have, sir. What do the Admiralty expect of me?'

Herrick walked past the man who was next on the table. To Pascoe he said, 'I'd take it as a favour if you'd stay with him.' He selected his words carefully, sensing Pascoe's sudden anxiety as he added, 'If things go badly, I need to know at once.' He looked at the young lieutenant gravely. 'And *he* will want to know you are close by.'

He turned on his heel and beckoned to Browne. 'Come. We'll walk through the gundecks and speak with our people. They did well today, bless 'em.'

Browne followed him towards the companion ladder, to the cleansing air of the upper deck.

Under his breath he said, 'And so did you, Captain Herrick, and I know what it is costing you at this very moment.'

When Herrick eventually returned to the quarterdeck the work was still under way. Aloft and below men were splicing and cutting wood for repairs under Wolfe's watchful eye.

Speke, who had taken over the watch, touched his hat and said, '*Indomitable* has rigged a jury-mast for her mizzen, sir, and the squadron is under command.'

It was strange, Herrick thought, he had not even considered his sudden authority of overall responsibility. Nor did it seem to matter now. He clenched his jaw as a man cried out pitifully from the lower gundeck. Then he took a telescope and levelled it on the other ships. The line was uneven, and the sails were more holes than canvas. But Herrick knew that given time ships could be put to rights, their hurts repaired. He thought of the terrible scene on the orlop. With people it was not so simple.

Herrick turned towards Browne. It would soon be too dark to pass or exchange signals. He had already ordered that the squadron should steer south-east in the best formation they could manage.

'I will require a list of all casualties and damage, Mr Browne. Mr Speke will assist you. At daylight you will signal the squadron and request the same from each ship in turn.' He swallowed hard and turned his face away. 'Our admiral is bound to ask me that first when he is up and about again.'

Speke was an unimaginative man. 'Will he recover, sir?'

Herrick swung on him, his eyes blazing. 'What are you saying, man! Just you attend your damn duties!'

As the two lieutenants hurried away, Major Clinton came out of the gloom and said, 'Be easy, sir. I'm sure he meant no harm.'

Herrick nodded. 'I expect you're right.' Then he moved to the weather side and began to pace up and down.'

Old Grubb blew his nose noisily and plodded over to the marine. 'Leave 'im, Major. With all respect, *leave 'im be*. This'll be a black day for the cap'n, be certain of that, an' for many more beside.'

Clinton smiled sadly and then climbed up to the poop deck where some of his men had fallen that afternoon.

He had heard many stories about Bolitho and Herrick, that they had obviously been true was even more surprising, he thought.

9

Waiting

Captain Thomas Herrick leaned moodily on his elbow and leafed through the purser's daily report. His mind and body ached from worry and work, and neither was helped by the *Benbow*'s uncomfortable motion. She would roll steeply into a trough, the movement ending each time with a long-drawn-out shudder which ran through every deck and timber.

She was, like the other ships of the line, anchored under the protection of Skaw Point. After the slow crawl from the position on the chart where they had fought Ropars' squadron, and another day at anchor, they were still working. Mending or replacing sails, paying seams, hammering and sawing, splicing and blacking-down rigging. It was just as if they were in the security of a dockyard instead of being out here in the bleak North Sea.

There was a tap at the door, and Herrick steeled himself for the moment he had been dreading.

'Enter!'

Loveys, the surgeon, closed the door behind him and took a proffered chair. He appeared exactly as before, deathly white, and yet tireless.

Loveys said, 'You look worn out, Captain.'

Herrick thrust all the affairs of the squadron and his ship aside like dead leaves. Even though he had been forced to attend to his daily work without respite, he had not once forgotten his friend in the stern cabin.

Men to be promoted to fill the gaps of dead or crippled comrades. Midshipman Aggett appointed as acting lieutenant in place of young Courtenay. With his lower jaw shot away and his mind completely unhinged, it was a miracle Courtenay had survived this long. The watch and quarter bills had had to be rearranged to share out the experienced hands. The purser had been complaining about rations, about the total loss of some salt beef casks which had been shattered by a stray cannon-ball. The grim business of sea burials, of answering questions and maintaining contact with the other captains, all had taken a brutal toll of his resources.

'Never mind that.' He calmed his tone with an effort. 'How is he today?'

Loveys looked at his strong fingers. 'The wound is very inflamed, sir. I have repeatedly changed the dressings, and am now using a dry stupe on it.' He shook his head. 'I'm not certain, sir. I cannot smell gangrene as yet, but the wound is a bad one.' Loveys made a gesture like scissors with his fingers. 'The enemy ball was flattened on impact with flesh and bone, but that is normal enough. The button was split like a claw and I fear there may be fragments left in the wound, even pieces of cloth which could encourage rotting.'

'Is he bearing up well?'

Loveys gave a rare smile. 'You will know that better than I, sir.' The smile vanished. 'He needs proper care ashore. Each jerk of his cot is agony, each movement could be the one to start gangrene. I give him an opiate at night but I cannot weaken him further.' He looked Herrick in the eyes. 'I may have to probe again, or worse, take off the leg. That can kill even the strongest, or a man given power by the lust for battle.'

Herrick nodded. 'Thank you.' It was as he had expected, although he had searched for hope, for his 'Lady Luck'.

Loveys made to leave. 'I suggest you send Mr Pascoe to his normal duties, sir.' He silenced Herrick's unspoken protest by adding, 'Our admiral might die, but young Mr Pascoe will have to fight again. He is wearing down his very soul by staying aft with him.'

'Very well. Ask Mr Wolfe to attend to it for me.'

Alone once more, Herrick tried to decide what he should do. With *Styx* away from the squadron he could not spare *Relentless* to carry Bolitho to England. *Relentless* had amazed everyone. By harrying the heavy transport, which Captain Peel had confirmed to be packed with French soldiers, she had drawn off Ropars' frigates from the real fight. That, plus *Benbow*'s unexpected challenge, had turned the tables. In spite of all that, *Relentless* had been barely marked.

Herrick had thought of detaching *Lookout* from the squadron. After Loveys' discouraging report there seemed no alternative.

He would get no thanks from Bolitho. He had always put duty before personal involvement, no matter what hurt it had caused him. But in this case . . .

Herrick started as someone tapped at the door and Lyb, who had taken over from Aggett as senior midshipman, peered in at him.

'Mr Byrd's respects, sir, and *Lookout* has just reported a sail to the west'rd.'

Herrick stood up, uncertain and reluctant. 'Tell the fourth lieutenant I will be on deck shortly, and inform the squadron. Is *Relentless* in sight?'

Lyb frowned at the unexpected question. He was a pleasant-looking youth of sixteen with hair the same colour as Wolfe's. He must have had to take some cruel comments on that, Herrick thought.

'Aye, sir. She is still to the nor'-west of us.'

'My compliments to Mr Byrd. Tell him to repeat the signal to *Relentless*. Just in case.'

Lyb stared. 'In case, sir?'

'Dammit, Mr Lyb, do I have to repeat every word?'

He gripped the chairback and steadied himself. *Just in case.* It had been unthinkable to voice his caution aloud. It gave some hint of the strain which held him like a vice.

He called, 'Mr Lyb!'

The youth came back, trying not to look frightened.

'Sir?'

'I had no cause to abuse you just then. Now please carry my message to the fourth lieutenant.'

Lyb backed away, mystified. At the sudden outburst, which was quite unlike the captain, but more so at the apology, which was unlike *any* captain.

Herrick picked up his hat and made his way aft. Every day he had tried to act out his part, to pretend for Bolitho's sake that all was as before. Even when he had found Bolitho drowsing, or barely aware of what was happening, he had made his

report, his comments about the ship and the weather. It was his
own way of offering something which might break through the
barrier of anguish, might also help to remind Bolitho of the
world they shared.

He found Allday sitting in a chair and Ozzard collecting
some soiled dressings from the sleeping cabin.

He waved Allday down as he made to rise. 'Easy, man. These
are bad times for us all. How does he seem?'

Allday saw nothing unusual in being asked the question by a
captain. Herrick was different. A true friend.

Allday spread his big hands. 'He's so weak, sir. I gave him
some soup but he couldn't keep it down. I've tried brandy, an'
I asked Ozzard to read to him, him being an educated man, so
to speak.'

Herrick nodded, touched by Allday's simplicity.

'I'll make my report.'

He entered the small sleeping compartment and walked hesitantly to the swinging cot. It was always the same. The horri-
fying dread of gangrene, of what it could do to a man.

He said, 'Good morning, sir. *Lookout* has just sighted a sail
to the west'rd. Likely a Dane, or some other lucky neutral. I
have ordered *Relentless* to be ready to run down and intercept.'

Herrick watched Bolitho's strained face. He was sweating
badly and the lock of black hair which usually hid the terrible
scar on his temple was plastered aside. Herrick looked at the
scar. That must also have been a close thing. But Bolitho had
been a youthful lieutenant when it had happened, younger than
Pascoe or even the wretched Lieutenant Courtenay.

With a start he realized that Bolitho had opened his eyes.
They were like the only things alive in the man.

'A sail, you say?'

Very carefully Herrick answered, 'Aye. Probably nothing
important.'

'Must get word to the admiral, Thomas.' The words were
hurting him to utter. 'Tell him about Ropars and the big transport. As soon as we sight a scouting frigate from the fleet you
must . . .'

Herrick bent over the cot, feeling his friend's despair, his
suffering.

T.I.S.—E

'I will attend to all that. Have no fear.'

Bolitho tried to smile at him. 'I am in hell, Thomas. At times I am afire. Sometimes I can feel nothing at all.'

Herrick wiped Bolitho's face and neck with a flannel. 'Rest now.'

Bolitho gripped his wrist. 'Rest? D'you see yourself? You look worse than I do!' He coughed, and then groaned as the movement awakened the pain.

Then he asked, 'How is the ship? How many did we lose?'

Herrick said, 'Thirty killed, sir, and about four to follow them, I fear. Throughout the squadron we have lost a hundred dead and seriously wounded.'

'Too many, Thomas.' He was speaking very quietly. 'Where is Adam?'

'I put him to work, sir. He has a lot on his mind.'

Herrick was amazed that Bolitho could manage a smile.

'Trust you to think of that.'

'Actually, it was the surgeon.'

'That man.' Bolitho tried to move his arm. 'He is like the Reaper. Waiting.'

'A better surgeon than some, sir.' Herrick stood up. 'I must go and attend to this newcomer. I shall return soon.'

Impetuously he reached down and touched Bolitho's shoulder. But he had drowsed off into semi-consciousness again. Very gently Herrick pulled down the blanket and after some hesitation laid his hand on Loveys' carefully prepared stupe. He withdrew it swiftly and left the cabin. Even through the dressing Bolitho's thigh had felt like fire. As if his body was being consumed from within.

Allday saw his face. 'Shall I go to him, sir?'

'Let him sleep.' Herrick studied him sadly. 'He spoke to me quite well, but . . .' He did not finish and went straight out to the quarterdeck.

In the dull light of the forenoon he saw that most of the lieutenants who were discussing the strange sail were careful to avoid his eye as he appeared.

He heard Wolfe saying, 'I understand how you must feel, Mr Pascoe. But duty is duty, an' I'm short-handed enough without you staying away from your division.'

Wolfe touched his hat to Herrick and said, 'All done, sir. It's better from me. He can loathe my guts as much as he wants, provided he does his work.'

Midshipman Lyb called, '*Lookout*'s signalling, sir. The other vessel is . . .' He craned over a fellow midshipman's arm to study the list of numbers. 'She's *Marguerite*, brig, sir.'

Wolfe released a great sigh. 'News, mebbee?'

Then he glared at Lyb and roared, 'Pork and molasses, sir! Acknowledge *Lookout*'s signal, *if you please*!'

Herrick turned away. It was better to be like Wolfe. Uninvolved, and therefore unreachable. Even as he thought it he knew it was a lie.

The ship's company went to their midday meal, and by the time they had turned to for work again the lively little brig *Marguerite* was already standing into the wind while she lowered a boat alongside.

Herrick said heavily, 'Man the side, Mr Wolfe. The brig's commanding officer is coming across, it seems.'

Further aft in his cot, Bolitho strained his body on to one side as he listened to the familiar sounds from the quarterdeck. Preparing to receive the other vessel's captain. Allday had told him the brig's name, and Bolitho had sent him on deck to discover what was happening.

The pain seemed to pounce on his thigh like a savage beast. Sweating and sobbing, Bolitho pulled himself further and further up the side of the cot. In his reeling mind it was suddenly vital that he should see the water again, the other ships, and cling on to what he saw like a life-line.

It was like that day on the gangway. One second standing there, the next feeling his face grinding against the planking, with no memory in-between.

Outside the screen door the startled marine sentry yelled, 'Sir! Sir!'

Allday came running, thrusting the sentry aside as he rushed into the cabin and then stared aghast at Bolitho's sprawled figure on the deck.

The black and white chequered canvas beneath him was stained with discoloured blood, and it was spreading even as Allday shouted, 'Fetch the surgeon!'

He gathered Bolitho in his arms and held him firmly.

When Herrick and Loveys entered, followed by the brig's

astonished commander, neither Allday nor Bolitho had moved.

Loveys knelt on the deck and said tersely, 'It's broken the wound.' He looked at Herrick. 'Please send someone for my instruments.' He was thinking aloud.

Herrick stared at him as Ozzard ran to fetch Loveys' assistants. 'Not his leg?'

When the surgeon remained silent he said, 'You'll not take off his leg?'

Allday exclaimed brokenly. ' 'Twas my fault. He sent me away. I should have *known*!'

Loveys eyed him sharply. 'Known what?'

Allday jerked his head towards the stern windows. 'He wanted to get to the sea. It's his life, don't you understand?'

Men were crowding into the cabin, with orders being passed as rapidly as any musketry drill.

Loveys cut away the dressing, and the lieutenant who commanded the brig recoiled saying, 'My God, he must have been in agony!'

Loveys shot him a chilling glance. 'Be off with you, sir, if you've nothing but slops to offer!'

In a gentler tone Loveys said to Allday, 'Go, too. Trust me.'

Allday reluctantly released hold of Bolitho's limp body as the surgeon's men grouped around him like ghouls.

In the adjoining cabin Herrick said quietly, 'Now, what do you have to tell me, Lieutenant?'

Still wilting from the surgeon's anger, the lieutenant answered, 'I brought a despatch for your flag officer, sir. The French squadron did not go to Ireland. It is almost certain it may try to enter the Baltic. Commodore Rice of the Downs Squadron is coming to give you support.'

Herrick tried not to listen to the movements beyond the closed door.

Then he answered simply, 'We met with Vice-Admiral Ropars three days ago. That man you just saw, who may well die before another hour is out, dispersed the enemy and destroyed one of his seventy-fours.' In the silent cabin his words were like pistol shots.

The lieutenant said shakily, 'That was bravely done, sir. Do you have orders for me?'

Herrick looked at the door. 'Presently.'

Lieutenant the Honourable Oliver Browne watched Herrick's stocky shadow sweeping back and forth beyond the cabin lanterns.

The ship's motion had got a good deal worse during the day, and Browne could not even imagine the surgeon's difficulties in such conditions. Now, it was early dark, and it was obvious that Herrick was driving himself to a complete collapse unless he rested from his work. Browne knew why Herrick was keeping himself busy when others could have done some of the tasks needing attention, but he did not know *how*.

The masthead lookouts had reported a signal from *Relentless* as she prowled along her patrol line to the north-west of the anchored ships. Commodore Rice's Downs Squadron had been sighted, but even as the signal had been read and repeated to the other captains, dusk, aided by a fast-moving rain-squall, had blotted out everything from view.

Herrick said, 'I shall inform Commodore Rice of our situation. We can fight, but some hull damage needs more careful attention. I will ask permission to leave the area and return to port.'

Browne nodded. The *Benbow* had certainly taken the worst of the battering, with more than a third of the squadron's total casualties. Two more men had been buried that day, surprisingly, neither had been expected to die at all.

Herrick threw his papers on the table and said desperately, 'What is that damned butcher *doing*?'

'His best, sir.' It sounded so trite, so far short of what he had meant that Browne expected Herrick to fly at him.

Instead Herrick said, 'I have never cared more for any man, d'you know that? We have seen action together from here to the Great South Sea. I could tell you things which would make you shake with fear and with pride.'

Herrick was looking at Browne as he spoke but his blue eyes were far-away, reliving moments which Browne knew full well he could never share.

Herrick said, 'Storms, raging gales which threatened to tear the sticks out of the ship, but we saw them through, we *managed*, d'you understand me?'

'I – I think so, sir.'

'I was the one who had to take him the message about his young wife. They said it came better from me, but how can terrible news like that ever be *better*?'

Herrick sat on the edge of the cabin table and leaned towards the lieutenant as if to emphasize his words.

'Down on the orlop, one of our people shouted out to him and called him Dick.' He gave a sad smile. 'In his frigate *Phalarope* they used to call him that. *Equality Dick*. He cares, you see.'

Herrick stared past Browne's head as the cabin door swung open, the other shipboard noises intruding like strangers.

Allday stood there, filling the entrance, his face like stone.

Herrick leapt to his feet. 'What is it, man?'

Browne strode across the cabin and gripped Allday's arm. 'For God's sake!'

Allday said in a small voice, 'I would relish a glass of something strong, sir.' He made a great effort. 'The surgeon says he'll live, sir.'

He sounded stunned, as if he was only half aware of what was happening to him. The three of them stood together, swaying in time with *Benbow*'s deep roll, each wanting to speak but only Allday with the words.

Then Herrick said, 'Go on.'

He backed across the cabin as if by taking his eyes off Allday he would destroy everything. He groped for a bottle and some glasses.

Allday took the brandy and swallowed it without apparently noticing.

Herrick said gently, 'I thought the surgeon told you to leave?'

'You know better than that, sir.' Allday held out the glass to be refilled. 'Hours they were. All that blood. Even old Loveys . . .' He shook himself. 'Meaning no disrespect, sir, but he was taken aback by it.'

Herrick listened, fascinated, reliving it through Allday's hesitant words.

Allday continued, 'The surgeon said that if he hadn't fallen from the cot he would have lost the leg. The wound burst, and Mr Loveys found another splinter of metal and some more cloth with his forceps.'

Herrick sat down heavily. 'Thank God.' He had thought until now that Bolitho had lived but had lost his leg.

Allday looked round the cabin, his face still stricken. 'I – I'm sorry, sir, I shouldn't have burst in here without so much as a by-your-leave.'

Herrick handed him the bottle. 'Go to your quarters and drink what is left. I think you've done enough.'

Allday nodded slowly and walked towards the door. Then he turned and murmured, 'He opened his eyes, sir.' Allday rubbed his chin to confirm it. 'And d'you know the first thing he said to me?'

Herrick did not speak, unable to watch the tears on Allday's stubbled cheeks.

' "You've not shaved, you ruffian!" *That's* what he said, sir!'

Browne closed the door quietly. Allday had left it swinging to the ship's motion. He was in a world all of his own.

Browne sat down and looked at the deck. '*Now* I understand, sir.'

When Herrick said nothing he realized the captain had fallen asleep in his chair.

Very carefully Browne left the cabin and made his way to the companion ladder. He almost collided with the surgeon who was holding to the ladder while he waited for the ship to sway upright again. Browne noticed that Loveys' hands were like red gloves.

He said, 'Come to the wardroom and I will open a bottle, you more than deserve it.'

Loveys regarded him suspiciously. 'I'm not a wizard, you know. Rear-Admiral Bolitho may have a relapse, and at best he will probably endure pain and a limp for the rest of his life.' He smiled unexpectedly, and for once the strain showed itself to its full extent. 'Mind you, Mr Browne, I'm *quite* pleased myself.'

Herrick left his chair and groped his way from the cabin. His exhaustion had been a useful excuse. Had he continued to speak with Browne he knew that he, like Allday, would have been unable to hide his emotion.

He stepped on to the quarterdeck, his eyes distinguishing the darker shapes in the gloom, the guns, the nettings finely etched against the evening sky.

The master's mate of the watch was by the poop ladder, while one of the midshipmen was writing something on his slate as he held it against the compass light.

All around the ship groaned and clattered as she swung heavily to her cable, her decks shining with rain, the sea air like ice.

Herrick saw the officer of the watch on the far side of the deck and called, 'Mr Pascoe!'

Pascoe hurried towards him, his shoes making little sound on the wet planking.

He hesitated, his eyes trying to pierce the darkness as he said, 'You want me, sir?'

'It's over, Adam. He's going to live, and with two legs.' He turned away, adding, 'I shall be in my cabin if needed.'

'Aye, aye, sir!'

Pascoe waited until he had disappeared and then clapped his hands together.

The midshipman gasped, 'Sir? Is something wrong?'

Pascoe had to share it, to tell somebody. 'Not any more! I've never felt better!'

He strode away, leaving the midshipman as mystified as before. He cared about the admiral, of course, but in a midshipman's life there were so many things to worry about. These calculations, for instance. Old Grubb, the master, wanted them before morning. He would take no excuses from anyone.

The slate shook as the youth relived that terrible and splendid moment. The rear-admiral waving his hat and defying the enemy's blazing guns. Men cheering and dying.

And he, Mr Midshipman Edward Graham of the County of Hampshire, had survived.

Unknown to the thirteen-year-old midshipman, Richard Bolitho was thinking very much the same.

10

The Fantasy

After one of the stormiest passages Bolitho could recall, *Benbow* had at last dropped anchor at Spithead. They had been away for nearly three months, a short time to any experienced sea officer, but Bolitho had not expected to see Spithead again, or anywhere else for that matter.

The tossing waves with curling crests of dirty yellow were almost beautiful, and the clinging damp air of the cabin no longer seemed irksome.

Bolitho stood back carefully from the stern windows, taking the strain on his wounded leg, trying not to cry aloud as the pain lanced upwards. Each day, supported by Allday or Ozzard, and on the stormiest days by both, he had forced himself to take a few steps.

Pride, anger – he was still not certain which – had made him start on the road to recovery. He suspected that Commodore Rice of the Downs Squadron had quite unsuspectingly had a lot to do with it.

Herrick had requested that Rice should take over the charge of the combined squadrons while he sailed *Benbow* to a dockyard for proper inspection and repair.

Rice had almost snubbed Herrick, probably eager to get back to his own, less arduous station, and he likely imagined Bolitho already dying and Herrick too junior for his consideration. Whatever it had been, Bolitho had called for Yovell and had dictated a curt despatch for the commodore. Rice would remain in temporary command of the combined squadron until otherwise instructed. If Ropars or other enemy ships attempted to enter the Baltic they would have to face a much larger force and at far greater risk.

Herrick tapped on the door and entered. 'We are anchored,

sir.' He watched Bolitho doubtfully and added, 'You should rest.'

'Would you have me dropped in the boat by bosun's chair, Thomas? Like that surgeon we once had, or some piece of unwanted cargo?' He winced as the deck tilted steeply. 'But I *will* take care.'

Herrick smiled. 'Aye, sir. As soon as the tide turns I intend to enter Portsmouth Dockyard. I have sent word to the port admiral to that effect.' He added gravely, 'The sixth lieutenant has just died. So near to home.'

Bolitho nodded. It was kinder this way. A young officer with half of his face blown away and his mind equally crippled would be an embarrassment ashore. Now, his memory would be cherished by his family.

He said, 'A lot of good men, Thomas. I hope they did not die in vain.'

Herrick smiled. 'Put it behind you, sir. We've had to do that often enough.'

'And what will you do?'

'Once docked, I will send the midshipmen and some of the married men to their homes.'

Bolitho understood. By married men Herrick meant lieutenants and warrant officers. Seamen, no matter how loyal, might soon desert when they found the comfort of their homes again.

Herrick was saying, 'I will remain with the ship, of course. Please God, my wife will join me here.'

Bolitho sat down with great care. 'The best of both worlds, Thomas, and rightly so.'

'That is true. I am lucky.' He sounded almost unhappy at the thought. 'Will you be going to the Admiralty, sir?'

Bolitho grimaced. 'Yes. I would rather do ten crossings in this ship than aboard the London coach!'

Allday looked through the door. He was smartly dressed in his gilt-buttoned coat and buckled shoes.

'I have ordered the barge crew to muster, sir.'

Herrick stared at him, appalled. 'You don't intend to be pulled ashore, sir! We will be in the yard by tonight. You can catch the coach from the George tomorrow forenoon.'

Bolitho smiled at his concern. 'I must learn to walk again, Thomas. And something tells me not to drag my feet here.'

Herrick sighed. 'If you have made up your mind. . . .'

Allday grinned. 'We both know about that, eh, sir?'

Beyond the cabin Bolitho heard the stamp of feet and the squeal of tackles. *Benbow* was home again, but to watchers on the foreshore she would be just another ship. Safer at a distance, better to read about in the *Gazette* than to examine at close quarters. To those uninvolved a ship was a ship. Not muscle and bone, blood and fear.

Bolitho allowed Ozzard to help him into his coat. He kept his face impassive but guessed that neither Herrick nor Allday was fooled. He was sweating with pain, and every effort was like a separate challenge to his resources. Sword and belt, then his hat, while Ozzard rearranged his queue over the gold-laced collar.

Allday adjusted the sword-belt and muttered, 'If you get a mite thinner, sir, this will be no bigger than a hound's collar!'

Browne appeared in the doorway, already wearing his boat-cloak.

'Barge alongside, sir.'

He ran his eyes over Bolitho's appearance and nodded with approval.

With Herrick in the lead they walked out beneath the poop and on to the wet quarterdeck.

Bolitho stared at the great crowd of seamen in the shrouds and massed along the gangways.

Herrick said quickly, 'I gave no order, sir.'

Bolitho removed his hat and walked slowly towards the side. The entry port seemed a mile away, and each slow tilt of the deck threatened to hurl him down. He felt light-headed, dazed by the experience of living. It was his first time on deck since the musket ball had smashed him down. Pain, loss of blood, he needed no reminding at this moment.

Browne hissed, 'Lean on me, sir.' Even he had lost his usual calm. 'I beg of you.'

Quite suddenly a man gave a cheer, to be backed up instantly by a great roar of voices which ran through the ship like a tide-race.

Pascoe was waving his hat with the rest, his smile telling everything.

Grubb in his shabby coat, the towering shape of Lieutenant Wolfe, all the faces which had become names. *People.*

'Carry on, Mr Browne.' Bolitho held out his hand to Herrick. 'I'll keep you informed, Thomas. My regards to your lady.' He was speaking between his teeth to contain the pain.

He looked down at the swaying boat below, the bargemen in their neat checkered shirts and tarred hats, the oars very white against the dull sea.

Now or never. Bolitho stepped outboard and concentrated his full attention on the boat, on Allday, stiff-backed, with his hat in one hand while he watched, ready to aid his descent.

The squeal of calls, the cheers of the seamen, helped to cover his discomfort, each gasping step, until with a final effort he reached the barge.

As the boat pulled away Bolitho looked up at the *Benbow*'s tumblehome, at the makeshift repairs to the shot holes, to the clawing scars of grape and canister along the gangway.

As the oarsmen found their stroke, Bolitho looked astern towards the pointing figurehead. Vice-Admiral Benbow had lost his leg. Bolitho had almost joined him.

It was a long hard pull, and yet in some ways it helped to restore Bolitho's strength. The boat's liveliness, the darting fingers of spray across his face made a change from the third-rate's damp confines.

Some marine pickets forced a way for Bolitho and his companions through a cluster of onlookers who had come to watch his arrival.

In Falmouth, even Plymouth, he would have been recognized on sight. Here, they saw far more senior admirals than Bolitho coming and going with the tides.

A woman held up her small child and shouted, 'Is it Nelson?'

Another said, 'He's been in a battle, whoever he is.'

Bolitho stared at an elegant carriage which was waiting in the shelter of the wall.

Browne explained almost apologetically, 'I sent word as soon as we anchored, sir. It belongs to a friend of the family, and I am thankful he was able to get it here in time.'

Bolitho smiled. The carriage was beautifully sprung and would be vastly different from the London coach.

'You never cease to surprise me.'

A young lieutenant stepped forward and removed his hat. 'I am to give you these despatches, sir.' He was watching Bolitho with an unwinking stare as if to memorize every detail. 'From the port admiral, and from Whitehall, sir.'

Browne took them and handed them to Allday. 'Put them in the carriage, then tell your second coxswain to return with the barge to *Benbow*.' He added dryly, 'I *assume* you are intending to come with us?'

Allday grinned. 'I have packed a small bag, sir.'

Browne sighed. Allday had expanded like the tropical sun since Bolitho's recovery.

'My respects to the port admiral.' Bolitho pictured Herrick dictating his own lengthy reports for the dockyard, a task he hated, as did most captains. 'Please give him my greetings.'

Browne gave the lieutenant, the admiral's messenger boy, a withering stare as he melted into the crowd.

Allday returned and climbed up beside the heavily muffled coachman.

But Bolitho hesitated, and turned to glance through the sally-port gate towards the anchorage. There were many vessels at anchor, but he was looking at the *Benbow*. In two weeks it would be another year. Eighteen hundred and one. What might it bring for the *Benbow* and all she carried within her fat hull?

He climbed up and into the carriage, sinking into the soft cushions with relief.

'Does it give much pain, sir? We can stay here awhile if you wish. The carriage and horses are yours for as long as you need them.'

Bolitho eased his legs gingerly back and forth. 'He must be a good friend.'

'He owns half the county, sir.'

Bolitho forced his limbs to relax a fibre at a time 'Drive on The surgeon's work appears to be holding together.'

He lay back and closed his eyes, remembering those first fleeting moments.

Allday's face, the surgeon's assistants all around him, the pain, his own voice groaning and pleading like a stranger's.

And this morning. The sailors cheering him. He had taken them to the verge of death and they could still wish him well.

The carriage's motion was like a hull in choppy water, and

as the clatter of hoofs and wheels across the cobbled street changed to the duller sound of a muddy road, Bolitho fell asleep.

'*Whoa*, Ned! *Whoa there*, Blazer!'

Bolitho came out of his sleep with a start, aware of several things all at once. That it was much colder, and there was sleet gathering at the corners of the carriage windows. Also that his seat was rocking violently. More to the point, Browne was trying to lower a window, a cocked pistol in his hand.

Browne muttered, 'Goddammit, it's jammed!' He realized Bolitho was awake and added unnecessarily, 'Trouble, by the sound of it, sir. Footpads, or gentlemen of the road maybe.'

The window dropped like a guillotine and the freezing air filled the carriage in seconds.

Bolitho heard the horses coming under control, the slither and stamp of hoofs in mud. It was a fine place for a robbery. It looked like the end of nowhere.

The carriage stopped, and a man with a set of white eyebrows peered up at them.

Bolitho pushed Browne's pistol aside. It was Allday, his face and chest glistening in sleet and snow.

Allday said, 'Carriage, sir! Off the road! Someone's hurt!'

Browne climbed down and turned to protest as Bolitho clambered after him.

There was quite a strong wind, and as the two officers struggled after Allday their boat-cloaks streamed behind them like banners. The coachman stayed where he was, soothing his horses which were stamping nervously, their bodies steaming with heat.

The other carriage was a small one, and was lying on its side in a ditch beside the road. A horse was standing nearby, seemingly indifferent to what had happened, and there was a patch of blood near the rear wheel, vivid against the sleety mud.

Allday said, 'Down here, sir!' He staggered up the slope, a man in his arms. One of the man's legs jerked at an unnatural angle, obviously broken.

'Easy, man!' Browne knelt beside him. 'Stunned, poor devil.'

Allday said, 'Looks like he was trying to crawl away. To get help, most probably.'

They all stared at each other, and Bolitho snapped, 'Look in the coach. Here, pull me up!'

With some difficulty they dragged the door open and upwards like a gunport, the other being buried in the mud.

Bolitho said, 'It's a woman. On her own.' He gripped the side of the door until the splintered wood pierced his skin.

It had not happened. He was still asleep and this was one more cruel twist to torture him.

He felt Allday beside him. 'You all right, sir?'

'Look inside.' He could barely control his voice.

Allday thrust his leg through the door and gingerly eased himself inside. Out of the bitter wind and wet the interior seemed almost warm.

He reached out and touched the body, then started with alarm as her head lolled slowly towards him.

'Oh, my God!'

Bolitho said, 'Help me inside.'

He did not even feel his bandaged thigh jar against the door. All he could see and feel was the woman's body, her velvet cloak flung to her feet by the impact. The same long chestnut hair, almost the same face, feature by feature. She would even be about Cheney's age, he thought despairingly.

Hardly daring to breathe, he cradled her shoulders in his arm, and after another hesitation he thrust his hand under her breast. Nothing. He licked his lips, sensing Allday's strength, willing her to live.

There it was, a slight beat under his fingers.

Allday said hoarsely, 'Nothing broken, I'd say, sir. Nasty bruise on her temple.' With surprising gentleness he brushed some hair from her face. 'I'd not believe it if you'd not been here, an' that's no lie.'

Bolitho held her carefully, feeling her low breathing, the warmth of her body growing against his own.

He heard Browne calling from the road. 'What is happening, sir?'

Poor Browne, he could probably see nothing from his place beside the injured coachman.

And what *was* happening? Bolitho wondered helplessly. A

girl who looked so like Cheney, but was not. A twist of fate
which had brought them together on the empty road, but not for
long.

Allday said, 'We'd best get her to our carriage, sir.' He was
watching Bolitho worriedly. 'Reckon she'd have died in this
cold, but for us.'

Bolitho climbed out of the coach, his mind confused. Even
the setting was as he had always imagined it. The coach smashed
and overturned. Cheney carrying their unborn child, trapped
inside. The coachman had been killed, but Ferguson, Bolitho's
one-armed steward, had been with her. Ferguson had somehow
carried her two miles to find help, but to no avail. Bolitho had
gone over it so often. If these strangers had been actors they
could not have recreated it more truly, more savagely.

Browne said, 'I've fashioned a splint for his leg. He's a bit
stunned.' He looked vaguely through the sleet, his cocked hat
shining like glass. 'Lord Swinburne has an estate near here.' He
shouted at the coachman, 'Do you know it?'

The coachman nodded, probably unwilling to become further
involved. 'Yes, sir.'

It was then Browne sensed that something else was happening. He watched Allday carry the limp body to the carriage and
turned to ask Bolitho about her. But he was already climbing
into the carriage, his face a mask of concentration.

Allday came back again and looked at the injured coachman.
Browne whispered fiercely, 'What is it, man?'

Allday regarded him more calmly than he felt. 'Mr Browne,
sir, if you want to assist, I suggest you help search the other
coach for baggage. There'll be thieves aplenty here soon. Like
crows round a gibbet. Then, if you would, you can tie that stray
horse on behind us. I'm not much of a hand with horses.'

As Browne obediently started for the coach Allday added,
'He will tell you if he wants to, sir. No disrespect to you, an'
none taken, I hope.'

He said it so bluntly that Browne knew he meant that he
could go to hell if he chose to.

Then something he had heard seemed to rouse his mind like
a voice.

'She's like his dead wife, is that it?'

Allday sighed. 'That's the strength of it, sir. I knew her well.

I couldn't believe my eyes just now.' He stared at the other carriage, its outline blurred in the steady sleet. 'As if he doesn't have enough on his mind.'

He said it with such bitterness that Browne decided to leave it there.

Later, as the carriage turned warily on to another road, the freed horse trotting obediently behind, Browne watched Bolitho as he and Allday protected the woman against any sudden lurch.

Pale from shock, and yet her skin held more than a hint of sunlight. She had obviously been abroad, and quite recently, he thought. Browne put her age at about thirty. She was lovely, there was no other description. A gentle mouth, which even the pain and shock could not spoil.

And her hair, he had never known such a fine rich colour.

One of her hands fell from beneath her cloak, and Browne saw Bolitho reach out to lift it back again. Watched him falter in a manner he had not seen before. Perhaps it was the ring on her finger. Someone else's, which was only to be expected, he thought. He saw the sadness in Bolitho's eyes and felt strangely moved. In fantasy such things should never happen. Browne often had dreams of his own. Of the perfect girl riding towards him. Taking so long that the pain was only endurable because of the perfect ending which would some day be his.

The ring had prevented even a dream for Bolitho.

Allday said, 'We're passing a lodge, sir.' He cocked his head to listen as the coachman shouted something to the gatekeeper.

To himself he added bitterly, 'I wish to God we'd done what Captain Herrick asked and stayed aboard for another night. Then he'd never have known about her.'

The coach came to a halt and female voices seemed to flood into it.

'Lawd bless us, sea officers, no less! Lend a hand there! You, tell Andy to saddle up and ride for the doctor!'

Browne said, 'Lucky I remembered this place, sir.'

But Bolitho did not hear him, he was already following the others towards the entrance of the big house.

Lord Swinburne seemed far too small a man to command so much authority and in such a magnificent house.

He stood with his buttocks dangerously close to a roaring fire and looked from Bolitho to Browne with the searching intelligence of a winter robin.

'Damn me, what a story, sir. And it's good to have you with us, er, Bolitho. King's officers are rare out here. The army and the fleet have taken all the young men away. How my steward manages to run things I dare not ask!'

A servant girl entered the tall double doors and curtsied.

'Beg pardon, m'lord, but the doctor has arrived.'

'Damn yer eyes, girl, show him to the room! Tell him I've something to warm his tripes when he's done!'

The girl curtsied again, giggled and fled.

Swinburne chuckled. 'You're off to London y'say, sir? Well, why not stay with us tonight? My head groom says this will blow over soon. You'll be a damn sight more comfortable here than in some flea-infested inn, I daresay!' He was enjoying his unexpected visitors.

Bolitho stretched his leg and felt the heat from the fire easing away the throbbing pain.

Swinburne said with sudden gravity, 'Good to know we have some young men to command our fleets. God knows, we're going to need 'em. I hear that Nelson is back from the Mediterranean and already with the Channel Fleet. There are big events in the making, I'd say.'

Bolitho took a glass from another servant. The wine was clear and cool. Made on the estate from some ancient receipt, most likely. The way they did it in Cornwall, and all such counties which had to live off their own resources.

Lord Swinburne knew more than he did. But he could drum up no excitement or interest. All he could think of was the girl upstairs. The touch of her. The scent of her hair as he had held her in the carriage. He was a fool, mad even, to compare her with Cheney. It was over. Sooner or later, by some method or other, he would have to find a release.

Browne said, 'I should like to stay here, m'lord. My father often speaks of you.' He looked at Bolitho. 'Will it suit, sir?'

Bolitho was about to refuse, to show rudeness if necessary, if only to escape and hide with his despair. But he saw a round little man with glasses coming through the room and knew he was the doctor.

'Well, how is she?'

The doctor took a goblet of brandy and held it admiringly against the fire.

'Nothing broken, but she needs to rest. It was a bad shock, and she has bruises on her body like a prize-fighter.'

Browne tried to appear unconcerned, but he was thinking of that lovely girl naked and helpless under the doctor's eyes.

The doctor added, 'She's conscious now, thank God. Her ladyship is looking after her, so she's in good hands.' He held out the goblet to be refilled. 'By God, m'lord, I'd no idea the smugglers ran their cargoes as far as this!'

Lord Swinburne grinned fiercely. 'You impertinent devil! If there was another doctor in five miles you'd not set foot in here again!'

They were obviously very good friends.

The doctor placed his goblet down carefully and crossed to Bolitho.

'Please be still, sir.'

Bolitho made to protest and then saw the blood glinting in the firelight like a cruel eye. The doctor was already unbuttoning his coat.

'Will you allow me to take you to another room?'

Browne watched fascinated, Bolitho's resentment changing to embarrassment as the doctor added gently, 'I have seen enough brave men to know a wound, sir.'

As they left the room, the tall officer leaning against the rotund doctor, Swinburne said, 'You serve a remarkable man, Oliver. It might be the making of you yet.'

'If Rear-Admiral Bolitho is unfit to continue tomorrow I shall leave without him, m'lord.' Browne considered his decision. It would almost be worth it just to see Sir George Beauchamp's face when he marched into the Admiralty on his own with Bolitho's despatches. 'I think he would only fret and worry otherwise.'

'Good thinking, Oliver, m'boy. The roads are not what they should be.'

The doctor returned, buttoning his coat, as if that was his way of showing he was no longer working.

He dropped his voice. 'This is a terrible wound, Lieutenant. A good man did the work, but it needs far more patience than your superior is prepared to give.' He held his hands to the fire. 'He was lucky to have such a good surgeon from what I have heard and read.'

Swinburne said, '*Well?* What are you doing about it?'

'I'll keep him here, if I may. I believe he is a lonely man. The sudden change from swift action to life ashore might do him more harm than good.' He gestured around the great pillared room. 'But in this *humble* abode, and with Christmas almost on us once more, I think he might fare better!'

Swinburne winked at Browne. 'Done! You go to those blockheads of Admiralty if you must. But be back here in time for our celebrations.' He rubbed his hands. 'It will be just like the old days!'

When Bolitho returned he knew it was pointless to protest or argue. Sometimes it was better to give in. Fate, Herrick's Lady Luck, or whatever you chose to call it. Something had decided he should leave *Benbow* at the first possibility. Something had prompted Browne to borrow the comfortable coach instead of catching the London Mail. If he had insisted on the latter it would have taken another, busier road.

He tried to smother the ridiculous hope, to destroy it before it destroyed him.

Swinburne said loudly, 'Of course, dammit! *Bolitho*! I did not realize it was you. I've been reading about you in the *Gazette* and *The Times*.' He shook his fist at Browne. 'You're a bigger fool than your father, Oliver! You didn't tell me! God damn your eyes, man!' He was beside himself with pleasure.

Browne said smoothly, 'You did not give me much of an opportunity, m'lord.'

A servant threw open the doors, and Lady Swinburne, moving with the stately confidence of a ship of the line, swept in to greet her guests.

She nodded to Browne. 'Ah, Oliver.'

That was all she said, but Bolitho guessed that it meant far more.

She took Bolitho's hand and studied him curiously. She was a very large lady, a head and shoulders taller than her husband.

'Rear-Admiral Bolitho, you are very welcome. You are like I would have wished our oldest son to be. He fell in battle at the Chesapeake.'

Swinburne said, 'Don't distress yourself, Mildred. It's a long time ago.'

Bolitho squeezed her hand. 'Not to me, my lady. I was there also.'

She nodded. 'I thought you were of an age.' A smile swept her sudden sadness aside.

She said, 'There is a young lady upstairs who wishes to see you. To thank you for what you did.' She saw the doctor give a quick shake of the head and then realized there was a bloodstain on Bolitho's breeches which even some of the doctor's spirit had failed to remove. 'Well, later then.' She beamed at the others. 'A wounded hero and a lady in distress, what better ingredients for Christmas, eh?'

II

An Old Score

Bolitho stood uncertainly by a newly laid fire and listened to the sleet lashing the windows. It was evening, and for all he knew he could have been quite alone in the great house. They had not even roused him for a midday meal, but had allowed him to sleep in a small room on the ground floor.

When he had at last awakened he had discovered his clothes neatly laid out, his breeches as white as new with no trace of the bloodstain.

The house was very old, he decided, and had probably been added to through the various generations of the Swinburne family. This room was lined with well-used books which reminded him of the one in Copenhagen where he had supposedly met the Crown Prince. That, too, seemed like part of a dream. Only the painful reminder of his wound kept the rest alive in his mind.

He tried to think of the girl from the wrecked carriage as a total stranger, as he would have done had she been different. It was like standing well back to examine a portrait, to fit the pieces together which were blurred by being too close.

The door opened quietly and he turned, expecting it to be Browne or one of Swinburne's attentive servants.

She stood framed against the lights in the other room, her face and arms shining in the fire's glow.

Bolitho was about to cross the room when she said, 'No, please. Remain where you are. I have heard about your injury. By helping to save my life on the road you could have risked your own.'

She moved into the reflected firelight, her gown swishing across the floor. It was white with a yellow flowered pattern.

Her long chestnut hair was tied back in a ribbon of the same yellow.

She saw him staring and explained, 'It is not mine. Lady Swinburne's daughter loaned it to me. My luggage has already gone ahead to London.' She hesitated and held out her hand. 'I am indebted to you and your friends.'

Bolitho took her hand and sought helplessly for the right words.

'I am thankful we were in time.'

She released her hand gently and sat down in one of the chairs.

'You are Rear-Admiral Bolitho.' She smiled gravely. 'I am Mrs Belinda Laidlaw.'

Bolitho sat opposite her. Her eyes were not like Cheney's at all. They were dark brown.

He said, 'We were also going to London. To the Admiralty. We have just returned from duty.' He tried not to look at his leg. 'I had the misfortune to stand up when I should have been lying down!'

She did not respond to his feeble joke.

'I, too, have just returned to England from India. It all seems changed here.' She gave a shiver. 'Not just the climate, everything. The war seems so near I can almost picture the enemy across the Channel waiting to invade us.'

'I can think of several good reasons why the French will never come.' He smiled awkwardly. 'Though they may try.'

'I suppose so.' She looked lost, wistful.

Bolitho thought that the bruises and concussion might have been worse than the doctor had realized.

He asked gently, 'Is your husband with you?'

Her eyes darkened in shadow as she looked towards the closed door.

'He is dead.'

Bolitho stared at her. 'I am so sorry. It was wrong of me to pry. Please forgive me.'

She faced him again, her expression one of curiosity.

'You really mean that. But I am through the worst of it, I think. He was with the East India Company. At Bombay he was happy, dealing with the company's mercantile affairs, trade, all the expanding business he was helping to build. He had been a soldier, but was a gentle man and glad to be rid of his commission.'

She gave a brief shrug, the movement stabbing at Bolitho's concern like a knife.

'Then he became ill. Some fever he caught when he was away on a mission inland.' Her eyes, like her tone, were dreamy, as if she was remembering each moment. 'It got worse and worse, until he could not even move from his bed. I nursed him for three years. It became part of life, something to accept without pity or hope. Then one morning he died. What I did not know was that he had been doing some private business of his own. He'd hinted at it sometimes, of how he was going to break away from the company and not just be a link in their chain. But he left me no details of whatever he was doing and, needless to say, none of his "friends" came forward to explain. In just a few hours of his death I discovered that I was penniless and completely alone.'

Bolitho tried to imagine what it must have been like for her. And yet she spoke without bitterness or rancour. Perhaps, like her husband's long-drawn-out suffering, she had been forced to accept it.

He said, 'I should like to make it plain that if there is anything I can do . . .'

She raised her hand and smiled at his concern. 'You have done enough. I will go on to London as soon as the road is clear and begin my new life.'

'May I ask what that may be?'

'When I was in Bombay I encountered the only piece of good fortune I can recall. Quite by chance I met with one of the company's officials, and to our astonishment we discovered that we were related.' She smiled at the recollection. 'Very distantly, and very remotely, but it was like finding a willing hand when you are about to drown.'

Bolitho looked at the carpet, his mind reeling.

'Rupert Seton.'

'How on earth could you know that?'

He replied, 'I was in Copenhagen recently. I heard that he had passed through there on his way to England.'

She watched his expression anxiously. 'What is wrong?'

'I was married to his sister.' His words were dull and without hope. 'She was killed in a coaching accident while I was at sea. When I saw you in the coach this morning, your hair, I thought, I imagined . . .' He took several seconds to complete it. 'You are so like her.'

In the long silence he heard a clock ticking, the beat of his own heart, and somewhere far away a dog barking with sudden excitement.

She said softly, 'So I did not imagine all of it. Nor was I delirious. The way you were holding me. I knew somehow that I was going to be all right.'

The door opened and Browne said, 'I beg your pardon, sir. I thought you were alone.'

The girl said, 'Please come in, Lieutenant. This house makes you feel like a fugitive!'

Browne rubbed his hands in front of the fire. 'You look much better after that rest, sir. I have been speaking with Lord Swinburne's steward. He says that the road will be clear soon after first light. The snow is changing to rain again.'

When Bolitho said nothing he hurried on, 'So with your permission I will take the carriage to London with your despatches.'

'Very well.' Bolitho looked at the fold in his breeches, hating the wound. 'I will wait here for your return.'

Her gown swished across the floor and she said, 'May I share your carriage, Lieutenant? I think they will be alarmed if I am any later in arriving.'

Browne looked from one to the other, unusually confused. 'Well, ma'am, that is to say, well, I will be delighted to be of assistance.'

She turned and waited as Bolitho got to his feet. 'I would have liked to have continued our talk.' She laid one hand on his arm. 'But I fear it might have done both of us harm. So I will thank you again for all your kindness, and now I will go to bed in readiness for an early start. It has been a very demanding day, one way and the other.'

Bolitho stared at her hand as she removed it from his arm. The brief contact was broken. It had never begun.

Browne stared helplessly as the door closed behind her.

'I am really sorry, sir!'

'Sorry? *For what?*' Bolitho turned towards the fire and said in a calmer tone, 'There, you made me break an old rule. I had no cause to use my hurt on you.' He knew Browne was going to speak and added, 'You are a good fellow, Browne. At first I hated the idea of having a flag lieutenant, someone to share my confidences. But I have come to know you well, and have grown fond of you.'

'Thank you for that, sir.' Browne sounded astonished.

'Say no more of this. I was a fool to myself and an embarass-ment to the lady. I have been a sailor too long to change now. My place is on the sea, Browne, and when I am no further use then I were better under it!'

Browne moved silently from the room and shut the door. If only Pascoe or Herrick were here, he thought. Even Allday was powerless to break past the chain of command of Swinburne's household. And Bolitho needed somebody.

Browne thought of the despatches, of the other nagging doubts he had nursed since Bolitho's appointment to the Inshore Squadron. He would be as fast as he could. He glanced back at the closed door, recalling Bolitho's words. *Grown fond of you.* In Browne's world nobody ever said things like that and it had deeply affected him.

He saw a footman gliding towards a stairway, a silver tray beneath one arm. He beckoned him over and said, 'Would you take a drink to my admiral?'

The footman regarded him bleakly. Like a frog. *'French* brandy, sir?'

'No, not that. My admiral has been at war with the French for seven years and before that also.' He saw that his words were finding no response in the froglike face and added, 'Some cool wine from the countryside. He seems to like it.'

As the footman moved away Browne saw Lord Swinburne coming down the great stairway.

Swinburne asked, 'All well, Oliver?'

'I have a favour to ask, m'lord.'

'Huh. That doesn't surprise me. Just like yer father.' He chuckled. 'Well?'

'Would it be possible for my admiral to have his coxswain with him?'

'His coxswain? *Here?*' His robin's eyes sparkled. 'Of course, he has not brought a man with him. I will speak with my steward. Has he *asked* for his coxswain?'

Browne shook his head. 'No, m'lord. It is just a feeling I have.'

His lordship shuffled away, shaking his head. 'Quite mad, just like yer father!'

Later, as the same footman was about to enter the room with his tray, Allday touched his arm and said abruptly, 'Here, matey, I'll take it.'

The footman glared at Allday, and then saw his expression and the size of his fists.

Allday balanced the tray in one hand and opened the door. There may be a squall and a few damn and blasts, he thought. After that . . . we shall see.

Bolitho fidgeted impatiently while Allday painstakingly adjusted his neckcloth and collar and wondered how he was going to get through the evening. It was Christmas Day, a day of many comings and goings at the big house. Farmers and neighbours, tradesmen with last-minute additions for the dinner which Swinburne's kitchen must have been preparing for weeks.

He could hear the lively music of violins from below and toyed with the idea of saying he was too tired to join Swinburne and his guests. But the lie would be churlish and unforgivable after the way he had been cared for and treated.

It was snowing outside, but without much substance, so that the carriageway and the roofs of the outbuildings glistened in a dozen colours from the lanterns which had been hung to guide the new arrivals to the entrance.

Bolitho had moved to the room from the floor below, but even the change of view did little to settle his thoughts. He wished now he had gone to London in the carriage and damn the consequences for his wound.

Allday stood back and said, 'Good, sir. You look your old self again.'

Bolitho noticed how Allday kept his voice level, his gaze shuttered off in case he did or said something to provoke him.

Bolitho felt ashamed. He must have given Allday a difficult time.

He said, 'I wish you could take my place at table.' He glanced at Allday's reflection in the mirror. 'You deserve it, and far more.'

Allday met his gaze in the mirror and grinned, the strain slipping from his face as he replied, 'With all those fine ladies, sir? God bless you, I'd be in *real* trouble, an' that's no error!'

Somewhere a gong boomed importantly. Allday took Bolitho's best coat and held it out for him. 'I've got a pretty little wench to press it for you, sir.'

Bolitho slipped his arms into the sleeves. 'No doubt you will *repay* her for the kindness?'

Allday followed him to the door and stood aside for him. 'No doubt, sir.'

Bolitho paused. 'I owe you an apology, Allday. I seem to be trampling on everyone who is trying to help me these days.' He turned, listening to the voices and music surging up the great stairway like an invisible throng.

Allday said quietly, 'Best be about it, sir. You'll not escape by backing your tops'ls!'

Bolitho nodded and made his way slowly down the stairs, feeling vaguely unsure of himself without hat or sword.

He barely recognized the hall as the same place. It was packed with brightly coloured gowns, half-bared bosoms, the red coats of the military, and such a mixed array of people he wondered where they all came from.

A footman saw him coming and called, 'Rear-Admiral Richard Bolitho.'

A few heads turned towards him, but most of the guests had not even heard the announcement above the din.

Swinburne bounced from the crowd. 'Ah, Bolitho, good fellow!' He steered him through the less important fringe of the gathering and muttered, 'Want you to meet me friends. Most of 'em have never set eyes on a fightin' man before.' He lowered his voice as they passed a scarlet-faced major who looked old enough to have been in two previous wars and added, 'Him, for instance. Supposed to be recruitin' for the Colours. God, the country lads take one look at him and run off to join the French, I shouldn't wonder!'

A glass appeared in his hand, while a footman hovered nearby with a tray of replenishments, and within seconds Bolitho found himself hemmed in a corner by smiling, curious faces.

Questions came from every angle, and perhaps for the first time Bolitho sensed the unease and anxiety which even the Christmas cheer could not disperse.

Sometimes during his service Bolitho had felt irritation, even contempt for such outwardly privileged people. At sea, men died every day from one cause or another, while on land the military fared little better. In spite of her enemies and difficulties, Britain's trade and influence abroad was growing, but it took the whole navy and endless outposts and garrisons of redcoats to maintain it.

Hearing their questions, feeling their uncertainty as they tried to form a picture of the country's defences or the weaknesses which might allow a French invasion, Bolitho was closer to understanding the war's other face than he could recall.

Lady Swinburne swept through the crowd and said, 'Time to dine.' She offered her arm to Bolitho. 'We will lead.'

As they passed through the beaming faces and curtseying ladies she remarked, 'An ordeal for you, I expect. But you are among friends. They want to understand, to know their fate by looking at you. This may be a temporary refuge for you, but it is escape for them.'

They reached the long, glittering table when there was a small disturbance in the outer hall.

Bolitho heard Swinburne barking at one of his footmen. 'Arthur! Lay another place for the lieutenant!' Browne had returned.

While the guests moved slowly to their allotted places at the heavily laden table, Browne managed to cross the room and say, 'The despatches are delivered, sir. Sir George Beauchamp is most eager to see you when you are able to travel.' He lowered his voice, aware that several people were craning their necks to listen, still surprised at his unexpected entrance. Like a scene from a play. The dishevelled young officer riding from the lines to report to his general. *The French are out. The cavalry are coming.* 'Things are warming up in the Baltic as you feared, sir.'

There was a great rustle of gowns and scraping of chairs as the guests sank down to admire the mountains of food which all but hid one line of heads from those opposite them.

Bolitho turned to find himself looking directly into the eyes of a young, attractive woman. Her gown was cut so low that

he wondered how it was staying in position, and even so it left
little to the imagination.

She met his eyes boldly. 'You are staring, sir!' She smiled,
her tongue running along her lower lip as she asked, 'Do you
like what you see?'

A heavy-jowled face thrust round her bare shoulder and said
thickly, 'Watch this one, m'dear fellow. A wildcat, an' worse!'

She did not even flinch but kept her gaze on Bolitho. 'My
husband. A lout.'

Bolitho was almost grateful when the meal eventually began.
And what a feast it was. It would have fed every midshipman
in the squadron for a week and still left enough to pass around.

The courses were presented by a well-trained line of footmen,
and the plates and bowls removed with equal precision. Bolitho
was amazed to see that most were wiped clean, whereas he was
already feeling uncomfortably full.

There were various kinds of fish. One Bolitho recognized as
turbot, and another, although almost swamped in a rich sauce,
he thought was baked whiting.

On and on, each course larger and more lavishly decorated
than the one before.

A massive baron of beef, roasted on a slow fire, baked ham
and boiled turkey, all washed down by Lord Swinburne's rich
selection of wines.

Bolitho felt the girl's knee against his, and when he moved
slightly she pressed harder, the sensation insistent and sensuous.
But when he looked at her she was eating busily, her hands
reaching out for various portions with the trained performance
of a musician.

He saw Browne watching him from the other end of the
table. He appeared to be clearing his dishes with the best of
them. His life in London had been an obvious advantage.

The girl beside him said, 'Are you on a secret mission?'

Her eyes looked less steady now and had the far-away stare
of someone who had gone beyond caution.

He smiled. 'No. I have been resting for a few days.'

'Ah yes.'

One hand disappeared beneath the table and he felt her
fingers moving caressingly up his thigh.

'You were wounded. I heard it somewhere.'

Bolitho saw the footman on the opposite side of the table. His face was expressionless but his eyes spoke volumes.

'Easy, ma'am, d'you wish your husband to call me out?'

She threw back her head and laughed. 'Him? He will be dead drunk before the ladies retire, unconscious soon afterwards!' Her tone changed, pleading but direct. 'That is why I am seated here beside you. Our host thinks me to be a bitch. To him I am just a necessary animal, to be used, or mated.'

'And now . . .' Swinburne was on his feet, a full goblet in his hand. 'Before the ladies retire I will give you the loyal toast!'

Chairs scraped back again and footmen darted in to shield silk gowns from fallen scraps of food and upturned glasses.

Bolitho was caught off guard, being used to remaining seated as was the naval custom.

'To His Britannic Majesty, King George!'

How solemn they all suddenly appeared, Bolitho thought. Then the mood passed again and the ladies made their departure. Bolitho's companion paused and patted his arm with her fan.

'Later.'

She had been right about one thing, Bolitho thought. Her husband was lying with his head on his arms, his hair daubed with a mixture of trifle and Dutch flummery.

Long pipes were brought and the port was passed slowly around the table. The air was soon heavy with tobacco smoke which mingled with that from the log fire made the eyes smart and sting.

Bolitho pretended to drowse like the others, to let the conversation wash around him. It was mostly talk of farming and shortage, of prices and poor labour. It was their war, the one which was alien to Bolitho as a gundeck would be to them.

He tried to think of his coming visit to the Admiralty. How long would Herrick take to complete repairs? What were the French doing? The Danes, the Russians?

But he kept seeing her face between him and his conclusions. The way she had looked at him before she had gone to her bed. Had gone to escape from his ridiculous fantasies.

She was probably already settled in some fine London house,

her mind too full with beginning her new life to remember him for long.

Browne dropped into the empty chair beside him.

'That was a fine dinner, sir.'

'Tell me about London. How did the journey go?'

'Quite well, sir. The nearer we got to London the better the road became. We stopped several times, of course, and we were fortunate with our choice of inns.'

The 'we' and the 'our' made Bolitho helplessly jealous.

Browne was saying, 'Sir George was his usual crusty self, sir. I think Admiral Damerum had been with him. Something Sir George said made me wonder.'

'What did he *say*?'

'Nothing much.' Browne fidgeted under his stare. 'But the talk in the Admiralty is that the Tsar of Russia has continued to harass our merchantmen in the Baltic. I believe those which you cut out from the French frigate will be the last until this affair is settled.'

Bolitho nodded. 'I hoped for the best, but in my heart I suspected it would end like this. Denmark will have no choice. Neither shall we.'

Browne reached out and grasped an abandoned goblet of brandy. He hesitated and then downed it with a fierce gulp, his eyes misting over as the fire surged through him.

Then he said stiffly, 'May I speak out, sir?'

'I have always told you . . .' He stopped, seeing the lieutenant's uncertainty. 'Whatever it is. Tell me.'

'I have never had much to do with sea-going officers, sir. My father insisted I should don the King's coat and used his influence to arrange the appointment.' Browne smiled sadly. 'I have always *carried* the uniform but have never earned it. My life became that of a courier, a messenger-boy, a privileged onlooker, or whatever my admiral demanded of me. Only since I have been serving you, and I mean this, sir, have I found any real pride in myself.' He gave a wry grin. 'But for the matter of a certain lady, I doubt if I would ever have left Sir George's service!'

He had been using his words and the brandy as a barricade. When he spoke again it was like someone entirely different.

'I was troubled about your appointment, sir, and more so at

the way Admiral Damerum quit the inshore station without giving you all the intelligence he must have gathered from his patrols.' He stared at Bolitho as if expecting to be silenced for abusing their new friendship. 'Your late brother, sir.' He licked his lips. 'I – I am not sure I can continue.'

Bolitho looked at the floor. So it was back again, not buried after all. Nor would it be.

He said quietly, 'My brother was a renegade, a traitor if you like.' He saw his words hit home. 'He was a terrible gambler, and always had a nasty temper, even as a boy. He fought a duel with a brother officer aboard his ship and the man died. My brother fled to America and eventually rose to command a privateer during the Revolution. He was killed after the war by a runaway horse in Boston.' That final part was a lie, but he had become so used to it, it no longer mattered. He looked at Browne calmly. 'Is that what you were going to say?'

Browne stared at his goblet but it was empty.

'Thank you for sharing it with me, sir.' He fixed his eyes on a point above Bolitho's shoulder. 'Did you know the other officer, the one who was killed?'

'No. I was in the Caribbean. When I got home my father told me. The shock nearly killed him.' Something in Browne's tone made him ask sharply, 'Why?'

'His name was Damerum, sir. Sir Samuel's brother.'

Bolitho recalled the first meeting with the admiral aboard his flagship *Tantalus*. No hint. Not a single sign of memory or connexion with the past.

In just a few minutes Browne seemed to have become very drunk.

In a slurred, confidential tone he murmured, 'An' if you think he wouldn't let his personal feelings come before duty, then, shir, you are mishtaken!'

Bolitho stood up. 'I think it might be wise to retire.' He nodded to Swinburne, but he, too, seemed barely aware what was happening.

Up the stairway once more, Browne becoming looser and more unsteady with each step.

By the door of his room Bolitho saw Allday sitting on a dainty gilt stool which looked as if it might collapse under him at any moment.

T.I.S.—F

He saw Browne and grinned. 'Bit too much for a poor luff, eh, sir?'

'Put him on my bed, Allday.' He straightened his coat as Allday thrust one arm round the lieutenant's waist. Another moment and Browne would have fallen on his face. 'I will return to the hall.' He forced a smile for Allday's benefit. 'As the only representative of the King's Navy in attendance, I must not let us down.'

Allday pushed open the door and dragged the limp figure towards the bed.

'Is he to sleep here, sir?'

Bolitho glanced at the clock. 'Yes. But I suspect he will not be alone for long. There may be a young lady arriving directly, so do not stand in her way.'

Allday stared at him. 'An' she'll be thinking it's *your* room?'

Bolitho turned towards the stairs. 'I suspect that neither of them will care, nor will they remember a thing about it to-morrow, I'm sure of that also!'

Allday watched him until he had vanished down the stairs and then sighed with envy. He toyed with the idea of carrying the lieutenant to another room and taking his place in the bed.

Then he thought of the servant girl who was waiting for him at the other end of the house.

He touched his forehead to the door and said, 'Sleep well, Mr Browne with an "e". You are a very lucky man even though you may never know it!'

12

Love and Hate

Admiral Sir George Beauchamp remained with his back to the high-ceilinged room and stared distastefully at the breadth of Whitehall beyond the window.

It was a cold, wet day, but there were plenty of carriages and traders' carts on the move. Bustling, muffled figures, steaming horses. To Beauchamp with his clear, ordered mind it looked a shambles.

Bolitho sat in a straight-backed chair and tried not to reach down to his thigh.

It had been a long drive from Swinburne's fine house on the Hampshire/Surrey border. Browne had, for once, been poor company, and had been unable to prevent himself from groaning or retching each time one of the wheels had lurched into a deep rut.

When they had paused at an inn in Guildford, Allday had whispered cheerfully, 'Your plan must have been a great success, sir. He looks like death!'

Bolitho had been ushered into this room with some haste, and he had seen an unfortunate officer turned away from an appointment even as he had topped the stairs.

Beauchamp had shaken his hand stiffly, his eyes examining Bolitho's face and general condition, much as a good horseman will study a badly used mount.

Then, with his wizened fingers pressed together, he had sat dwarfed in his big chair while Bolitho had explained his actions, the attack on the French frigate, and the following encounter with Ropars' squadron.

Occasionally, Beauchamp would lean forward to check something or relate it to a note or part of Bolitho's despatches, but he made no interruption.

Bolitho had finished his report by saying, 'I would like to

emphasize that every incident which led to any success was due to the initiative and skill of my captains.'

Beauchamp turned from his place at the window. He had gone there as Bolitho completed his summing up, as if it were a signal or to give him time to form an opinion.

He said suddenly, 'I have heard from your friend Inskip. Your action seems to have been somewhat at odds with his ideas of diplomacy.' He gave a wry smile. 'There are more rumours going through the corridors of St James's and the Admiralty than when the French beheaded their king!' He pursed his lips. 'Some are saying that your attack on the *Ajax* was an act of aggression in neutral waters. Tsar Paul of Russia has certainly used it to gather more strength for his plan to become Bonaparte's ally. Had the Danish batteries fired on *Styx* when you sailed into Copenhagen, it would have been war in an instant, and one which we would have had little hope of containing, let alone winning, with all our other commitments. No, Bolitho, there are some who are hinting my choice for command of the Inshore Squadron was hasty, even foolish.'

Bolitho stared at the window above the admiral's chair, the long rivulets of rain running down each pane.

He recalled starkly the marine officer with his bloodied hands to his face. *Benbow*'s junior lieutenant with his jaw shot away. Other faces, inflamed with the hate and terror of battle, swept through his mind like souls in torment. It had all been for nothing. Tsar Paul had lost six prize-ships which he had unlawfully seized, but *Styx*'s swift vengeance had given him the lever he required just the same.

'Turning for a moment to your encounter with Ropars' squadron.'

Beauchamp's precise tones brought Bolitho back to the room again.

'Our intelligence sources tell me that the French transport was indeed carrying soldiers to aid and train the Tsar's army. Your action, particularly the destruction of the enemy seventy-four, scattered Ropars' ships, and he also lost a frigate to the blockading squadron in the Channel.'

'So that *was* approved, sir?' Bolitho could not hide the bitterness he felt.

Beauchamp snapped, 'Do not act like a junior lieutenant,

Bolitho! I am dealing with hearsay as well as the facts. As a flag officer you would do well to follow my example!' He was calm again. 'Of course it was approved, dammit! The story, largely exaggerated and distorted by the people who write such things, went through London like a lion. If Ropars had got into the Baltic it would have taken an act of God to force him out again. With French soldiers, no matter how few, and all those ships, Tsar Paul's unholy alliance would have been at our throats. I am told with equal authority that plans were in readiness to launch an invasion from the Channel ports to coincide with the big thrust from the Baltic. Now, whatever the outcome later on, your victory has given us time. Before the ice melts around Paul's ports and bases, *we must be ready*!'

Bolitho wondered what would have happened if another admiral had been facing him across this desk. Beauchamp was ruthless when he needed to be, but he was known for his fairness, too.

The little admiral continued, 'Even so, there are the critics who ask why your flag captain failed to act on the courier brig's report that Ropars was making for Ireland. It would make good sense to many. The King has only recently approved the alteration of the Union Flag to conform with our union with Ireland. From January the first, that is next week, it would outwardly appear less simple to rouse a rebellion there.'

'Captain Herrick acted wisely as it turned out, sir. Had he done as you suggest, there would have been nothing to stop Ropars.'

'Possibly. But I did warn you when you accepted the appointment. Envy is never far away.'

Beyond the tall doors someone coughed discreetly, and Beauchamp peered at the clock.

'You will be tired after your journey.'

The interview was over.

Bolitho stood up and tested his weight on his leg. His thigh felt as if it was asleep, lifeless. He waited for the first tingling stab to move through it and asked, 'Will you be requiring my presence again, sir?'

'It is possible. I took the liberty of arranging some comfortable quarters for you. My secretary will give the address to your flag lieutenant. How is he, by the way?'

Bolitho walked with him to the door. He still could not determine whether the admiral was supporting his actions or merely preparing judgement on them.

'I can't imagine how I managed without him, sir.' He looked him in the eyes. 'He is extremely competent.'

Beauchamp grimaced. 'Impertinent, too, when the mood takes him.'

With one hand resting on the door Beauchamp said quietly, 'The next months are going to be demanding, even critical. We shall need every good officer, every loyal hand if we are to survive, let alone win through.' He studied Bolitho's impassive features and added, 'You know about Sir Samuel Damerum, of course. I can see it on your face as plain as a pikestaff. My spies told me that Browne had been ferreting around for information, and the rest was simple reasoning.'

'I have no intention of involving you or my appointment, sir.' He got no further.

Beauchamp said, 'I like you, Bolitho, and I admire your courage as well as your humanity. But you involve *anyone* and *there will be no appointment*, do I make myself clear? You are above it now. Remain so.'

He opened the door and about six officers who had been waiting moved hopefully towards it.

Browne got to his feet from a bench seat and groaned. His face was ashen.

'I have the address, sir.' He quickened his pace to keep up with Bolitho. 'Was everything satisfactory, sir?'

'If you call being made to feel like a grubby schoolboy satisfactory, then yes, it was. If you imagine that obeying every order, even if written by a blindfolded donkey, and no matter what you know to be the truth, then again I must say yes!'

Browne said shakily. 'It was not a success then, sir.'

'No.' Bolitho turned at the foot of the stairs. 'Do you still wish to serve with the squadron?'

He could not help smiling at Browne's crest-fallen expression, his appearance of complete exhaustion. His companion at dinner must have roused herself enough to torment Browne to the point of collapse.

Browne straightened up. 'I do, sir.' He squinted at a piece of paper. 'The residence is not too far away. I know Cavendish

Square quite well, sir.' He added in a pained voice, 'We shall
not be on the fashionable side of it, I'm afraid.'

Allday was waiting outside by the carriage, patting the horses
and chatting with the coachman.

Bolitho climbed into the carriage and drew his cloak around
him, remembering the girl lolling against his body as they had
headed off the road to Lord Swinburne's estate.

The carriage rocked on its fine springs as Browne clambered
up beside him.

'You remember the young lady, Browne?'

Browne stared at him blankly. 'Mrs Laidlaw, sir?'

'Yes.' He almost said, *of course.* 'Did you discover where she
is staying?'

'The house belongs to an elderly judge, sir. He has, I understand, an equally old wife, who is also disagreeable to boot.'

'*Well?*'

Browne was obviously getting his own back.

Browne spread his hands. 'That is all, sir. The judge is often
on the Assize circuit and away from home a great deal.' He
swallowed hard under Bolitho's eyes. 'The young lady will be a
companion to the judge's wife, sir.'

'*Good God!*'

Browne recoiled. 'I – I am sorry, sir. Did I do or say something wrong?'

Bolitho did not hear him. *A companion.* It was common
enough for widows these days to be forced into such positions.
But surely not her? Young, vital, desirable. His mind reeled to
his anger and concern. Rupert Seton had offered to help her,
and had in fact arranged passage home for her from India.
Seton was a rich man and could easily have made some allow-
ance for her care and protection. It was so unlike the Seton he
had known, whose sister he had loved, he could scarcely believe
it.

But what could he do about it? One thing was certain, he
would not leave things as they were, even at the expense of
making himself look a fool again.

The carriage came to a halt outside an elegant building with
a broad pillared entrance. Another temporary headquarters, and
even if, according to Browne, it was not the fashionable side of
the square, it was impressive in its own right.

Browne nodded weakly to two servants who were hurrying down the steps to greet them.

To Bolitho he said, 'Will you be needing me, sir?'

'Go and rest your head. When you are refreshed and restored from your orgy, I would ask you to take a letter for me.'

'A letter.' Browne nodded again, his eyes vacant.

'Yes. To that judge's house you mentioned.'

Browne grappled with it and asked, 'Is it wise, sir?'

'Probably not. But at the moment it seems I am not much in demand for my wisdom.'

Allday watched him from the door as the servants hauled their chests into the warm hallway.

That's more like it, my captain. They want fire, you give it them, damn their eyes.

He turned as a woman's voice asked, 'Are you ready for some food, sir?'

Allday ran his eye over her approvingly. Must be the cook. She had a very full figure, and her round, plump arms were half-whitened with flour. But her face was gentle and friendly.

He replied lazily, 'Just you call me John, my dear.' He touched her bare arm and added, 'Here, I'll give you a hand if you like. You know what they say about sailors.'

The kitchen door swung shut behind them.

Captain Thomas Herrick sipped slowly at a tankard of strong ale and ran his eyes over the remaining pile of books and papers which awaited his attention.

It was strange to feel the *Benbow* so still, which, plus hard work and the excellent ale, was making him drowsy.

Anchored within the sheltered stretch of Portsmouth Harbour was far different from the lively Solent, or that bleak rendez-vous he had shared with the squadron at Skaw Point.

He went over the repairs and the replenishments for the hundredth time, looking for a flaw, expecting to discover a forgotten item.

Herrick felt justifiably proud of what he and his company had achieved. It could not have been easy for most of them, working without let-up, knowing all the while that over in the town, and throughout the country, others were celebrating

Christmas to the full extent of their means.

From his own pocket Herrick had provided something of a feast for his sailors and marines. Some of them had got so drunk that they had to be forcibly restrained. But it had been worth it, he decided, and when they had turned to for work again he had felt the change run through the ship like a lively shanty.

He thought of his wife, waiting for him to come ashore when he had finished his duties for the day. It was all so new and wonderful to Herrick. A nice, snug little inn run by a friendly landlord and his wife. A parlour of their own when Herrick went to share his dreams and hopes with his Dulcie.

With a deep sigh he turned his attention to the lists and ledgers. Progress of work book, muster book, details of stores, gunnery equipment, canvas, every fibre and nerve of a full-rigged fighting ship of the line.

Herrick had thought a great deal about Bolitho, had wondered how he was getting on in London. He knew Bolitho had never been at ease in the capital. Streets piled with horse dung, a place being poisoned by its own stench, he had once said. The streets had become so overcrowded with vehicles of every sort that the richer houses had to spread straw on the cobbles to muffle the din of iron-shod wheels.

He often examined his own feelings about the battle with the French admiral, Ropars. Herrick had faced death alongside Bolitho many times, and each threat seemed to get worse than the one before. Without effort he could see Bolitho on *Benbow*'s gangway, waving his hat to torment the French marksmen and give his own sailors heart to continue their fight against odds.

A lot of men had died or been wounded that day. Herrick's lieutenants had roamed the backstreets of Portsmouth and further out to the Hampshire villages and farms in search of men. Herrick had even had some handbills printed and distributed to inns and village halls where they could be read aloud by someone with education to inspire or coax a man to join the Colours.

Relentless had dropped anchor that forenoon, having been relieved on station by the hastily repaired *Styx*. Despatches had been exchanged, new hands signed on. The Navy allowed little time for rest or complacency. He glanced at the big Union Flag which the boatswain had brought aft to show him. The new

flag, with the additional Cross of St Patrick sewn on it. A lot
of those had gone out to the squadron, too. To Herrick's prac-
tical mind it seemed a waste of effort to change a flag when the
world was intent on destroying itself.

Yovell, Bolitho's clerk, padded into the cabin, a fresh bunch
of papers in his hands for signature. With Herrick's own clerk,
Yovell had been a tower of strength. Herrick hated paper, the
need to form sentences so that no victualling yard or chandler
could misinterpret them.

'More?'

Yovell smiled. 'A few, zur. There is one to sign for the
London courier.'

Herrick glanced at it uneasily. That was another thing he
found hard to get used to. Running his own ship was quite
enough. But as flag captain he had to put his thoughts to the
affairs of the whole squadron, which included *Relentless*.

Captain Peel had reported that his third lieutenant, wounded
in the leg during the fight with the enemy squadron, had had
his leg amputated and was now ashore in the naval hospital at
Haslar.

He required a replacement immediately, as none of his midshipmen had the age or seniority for the appointment. *Relentless*
hoped to weigh and rejoin the squadron without additional
delay. Herrick thought immediately of Pascoe and dismissed the
idea. It might be days, weeks before Bolitho was back. It would
be unfair to send the boy away in this fashion.

Yovell watched him impassively. 'Shall I prepare a letter for
the port admiral, zur?'

Herrick rubbed his chin. There were several men-of-war in
harbour completing repairs of storm or battle. One of them
would have a replacement, a young officer who would give his
soul for a place with Captain Peel.

'I shall think about it.'

He knew Yovell was shaking his head sadly. He might have a
word with Peel. Invite him to dine with Dulcie. Herrick bright-
ened immediately. She would know what to do. She had given
him such confidence he could scarcely believe it.

Herrick stood up and crossed to the side of his cabin. He
wiped the damp haze off the glass and peered across the harbour. It was afternoon, but it was almost dark. He could barely

see the two great three-deckers which were anchored abeam, and there were already some small lights bobbing on the water as boats plied back and forth like beetles.

One more day and he would be writing those all important words in his despatch.

Being in all respects ready for sea . . .

After this stay in harbour it would be hard to stomach.

There was a tap at the door and Speke, the second lieutenant, stepped over the coaming, his eyes glinting in the lamplight.

'What is it?'

Speke shot a quick glance at the clerk and Herrick said, 'Later, Yovell. Leave us just now.' Speke's cold expression had swept away his feeling of satisfaction and comfort like a breaking wave.

'I believe Mr Pascoe may be in trouble, sir.'

'You *what*?' Herrick stared at him. 'Spit it out, man!'

'He was officer of the watch, sir. I relieved him when he asked permission to go ashore. He said it was urgent.' Speke gave a brief shrug. 'Young he may be, but he is more experienced than many of our people. I did not question his reasons.'

'Go on.'

Herrick forced himself to sit down, to display calm as he had seen Bolitho do so many times.

'There was a freshwater lighter alongside for most of the day, sir. When it cast off it appears that one of the working party went with it. Deserted. Mr Midshipman Penels was in charge of the party. Just a handful of landmen. And after a quick muster I discovered the missing one is Babbage, whose punishment was stood over by you, sir.'

Herrick studied him grimly. 'You are suggesting that the midshipman helped Babbage to run?'

Speke met his gaze complacently. 'Yes, sir. He admitted it. But only after Mr Pascoe had gone ashore. He was so ashamed at what he had done, he thought he should own up to Mr Pascoe. The young fool. Babbage will be caught and run up to the mainyard anyway. As it is . . .'

'As it is, Mr Speke, the third lieutenant has gone ashore to recover the deserter, to bring him back before anyone discovers he is missing?'

'Correct, sir. But for Penels . . .'

'Fetch him here.'

Herrick shifted in his chair, his mind thrashing about like a snared fish. It would be just like Pascoe, he thought. What Bolitho would have done. *What I would have done. Once.*

Speke thrust the terrified boy through the door and closed it behind him, saying angrily, 'You can thank your miserable stars it was I and not the senior who found out. Mr Wolfe would have torn you in halves!'

'*Easy!*' Herrick's tone silenced him. 'What did you arrange with the man Babbage?'

'I – I just thought I could help him, sir. After all he did for me at home.' Penels was sniffing and close to tears. 'He was so afraid of being hurt again. I *had* to help him, sir.'

'Where was he going, did he tell you?' Herrick felt his patience draining away. 'Come on, boy, Mr Pascoe may be in danger. And he tried to help *you*, remember?'

Herrick hated the shame and despair he was causing but knew there was worse to come.

In a small voice Penels whispered, 'He said he would find a place called The Grapes. One of the old hands had spoken of it.'

Speke groaned. 'A truly foul place, sir. Even the press would not go there without a full squad.'

Penels, lost in his misery, continued, 'He was going to wait until I could get some money. Then he was hoping to return to Cornwall.'

Herrick looked at the tankard. It was empty and his throat felt like dust.

'My compliments to Major Clinton. Ask him to see me.'

Speke hurried away and Herrick said, 'Well, Penels, at least you had the wit to tell Mr Speke what you had done. It is not much but it may help.'

The marine entered and said, 'Can I assist, sir?'

Clinton did not even glance at the wretched midshipman, and Herrick guessed Speke had told him what had happened. It was probably over the whole ship by now.

'Mr Pascoe is at The Grapes, Major. Does that mean anything?'

Clinton nodded. 'A lot, sir.' He added, 'With your permission I'd like to go ashore without delay. I'll take Mr Marston and some of my lads.'

'Thank you, Major Clinton. I'm obliged.'

Moments later he heard the twitter of calls and the grating clatter of tackles as a boat was swayed up and over the gangway. Then boots, as some hand-picked marines hurried to obey Clinton's unexpected summons.

Herrick regarded the sniffing midshipman for several seconds.

Then he said, 'I agreed to take you aboard as a favour to an old friend. What this will do to him, let alone your mother, I cannot imagine. Now take yourself below and report to the senior master's mate.'

As Penels groped blindly for the door Herrick said quietly, 'While you are in your berth, think on this. One day you would have had men depending on your judgement. Ask yourself if you think that is right.'

Yovell entered as the midshipman departed.

'Bad, zur.'

Herrick glanced at the round handwriting, the place below for his signature.

'I shall want to send a message to my wife. I'll not be ashore tonight, I'm thinking.'

He listened for the sound of the boat but it had already left the *Benbow*'s side.

Pascoe strode along yet another narrow street, his boat-cloak billowing around him in the stiff wind. He did not know Portsmouth very well, but the officer of the guard had explained where The Grapes was situated. The officer had suggested that Pascoe should stay away from such a hell-hole, as he had described it. Pascoe had told him he was to meet a party of armed seamen nearby in the hope of seizing some likely recruits. It had been surprising how easily the lie had come. The officer of the guard had not even been interested. Anyone foolish enough to hope for pressed men in Portsmouth would have to have more than luck.

One street seemed very like the next. Narrow, squalid, but never empty of movement. In doorways and beneath arches, at windows, or merely in the form of sounds. Drunken laughter,

shrieks and terrible oaths. As if the miserable dwellings and not
their occupants were giving voice.

Once a girl reached out to touch his shoulder as he passed.
Even in the gloom he could tell she was no more than fourteen
or fifteen.

Pascoe thrust her away and heard her shrill voice pursuing
him around the next corner.

'You bloody bastard! I 'ope the Frogs spill yer guts from
you!'

Quite suddenly it was there. A square, sombre building,
protected on either side by smaller houses, and the street was
littered with filth which stank like a sewer.

Pascoe had once been used to poverty, and as a midshipman
had seen and suffered hardship in plenty. But all this unnecessary filth seemed needless, disgusting.

He stared up at a flaking board above the main entrance,
feeling the rain bouncing on his hat and face. The Grapes.

Beneath his cloak he loosened his hanger and then banged
on the door with his fist.

A panel flew inwards, as if the man had been poised there,
waiting.

'Yes? Who is it?' Two white eyes swivelled back and forth
across Pascoe's shoulders, but seeing no armed seamen or
marines, seemed satisfied. 'A young gentleman, is it?'

Even the man's crooning voice made Pascoe feel sick.

'Cat got your tongue, has it? Ah well, we'll soon sort that
out for you!'

The panel snapped shut, and seconds later the great door
swung inwards and Pascoe stepped inside. It was like being
swallowed up. Suffocated.

It must have been a fine house once, he thought. Big stair-
case, now damaged and covered in dust. Carpets, too, once rich
and thick, were full of holes and covered in stains. A merchant's
house perhaps, when Portsmouth had been busier for commerce
and not plagued by the French and the privateers which were
too close for comfort.

An immense woman stepped from a room. She was tall,
muscular and without any femininity. Even her piled hair and
the great red slash of a mouth made her look like a ploughman
dressed for a village play.

The doorkeeper said in a wheedling voice, 'He's an officer, ma'am!'

She moved towards Pascoe, her deepset eyes fixed on his face. Like the house, she seemed to engulf him. He could see the skin of her partly bared bosom, feel her power. He could even smell her. Gin and sweat.

'Are you with the press, young fellow?' She put her hand under his chin and looked at him searchingly. 'Pretty boy. No, you're here for some fun, eh?'

Pascoe said carefully, 'I believe a man is hiding here.' He saw her eyes flash dangerously and added, 'I want no trouble. If I can get him back to the ship he will have nothing to fear.'

She chuckled, the sound rising through her great body until it broke into the hall like a guffaw.

'Nothing to fear? That's a bloody good one that is, eh, Charlie?'

The doorkeeper tittered uncertainly. 'Yes, ma'am.'

Pascoe stood very still as the woman unclipped his boat-cloak and lifted it from his shoulders.

'I've two good girls for you, Lieutenant.' But she sounded defensive, as if even she was impressed.

Pascoe put his left hand on his hanger and very slowly drew it upwards and then fully out of its scabbard. Her eyes never wavered from his, and he knew there were other hidden watchers nearby, ready to cut him down if he attempted to use his hanger.

He turned it in his hand and turned the hilt towards her.

'See? Now I am unarmed.'

She tossed the blade carelessly to the pop-eyed doorkeeper and said, 'Come with me, dearie. A glass of Geneva while I think a bit. This man you are trying to help.' She could not repress a grin. 'His name?'

'Babbage.'

'And you'll be Mr . . .?'

A girl's grubby hand came out of the shadows and gave Pascoe a glass of gin.

He said, 'Pascoe, ma'am.'

'Damn me, I *believe* you!'

She walked from the room. 'Stay here, dearie. I'm not saying I *know* the man. But if he is here, without me knowing, of course, I will put your case to him.' She turned and stared at him boldly. 'Don't fret, pretty boy. He'll not run if I say different.'

It was warm in the musty-smelling room and yet Pascoe felt the sweat on his spine like ice. A stupid, crazy gesture. And for what? To help Penels, or to prove to himself that he could do it? His hanger was gone, and at any moment he might be rushed, his throat cut merely for the price of his clothes.

While he waited he became aware of the rest of the house. It was alive with furtive sounds and muffled voices. Every room must be occupied, he thought.

He looked at the girl who was holding the stone gin bottle to her breast. Thin, sunken-eyed, worn out and probably diseased to add to her misery.

She looked back at him and smiled, letting her shabby dress fall from one shoulder as she did so.

It made her look pitiful instead of provocative.

A door banged open and men's voices boomed down the stairs urgent and angry.

Pascoe walked from the room and looked up the stairway. There were three men at the top landing, and cowering against the wall was a fourth, Babbage.

The biggest of the men pointed at Pascoe and barked, 'That him?'

Pascoe noticed that he was wearing the white breeches and shirt of a sea officer and had probably been disturbed at his pleasure. Whatever the reason, it was a relief to know he was not entirely alone.

Babbage said huskily, 'Yes, sir. That's Mr Pascoe.'

The man came down the stairs slowly. He was heavily built and in his middle twenties, with thick, curly hair and a hard, aggressive face.

'Well, well, well.' He paused on the bottom stair and rocked back on his heels. 'I was going to meet you, Mr Pascoe, but I never thought you'd fall from the sky like this.'

'I don't understand?'

The big man turned and waved his arm to his companions. 'Though I suppose Mr Pascoe would be well at home here, eh, lads?'

They laughed, and one stooped to seize Babbage as he tried

to crawl away. There was blood on his mouth and he had obviously been beaten.

'I order you to hand over that man to me, whoever you are!'

'He *orders*! This youth, masquerading as a King's officer, orders me!'

The woman of the house pushed past the others and placed herself between them and Pascoe.

She said angrily, 'Leave him be, damn you! He means no harm.'

'Oh, I'm certain of that, Ruby! Mr Pascoe's own mother was a whore, and his bloody father a traitor to his country, so what harm could *he* do?'

Pascoe swayed on his feet, stunned by the man's grating voice. He could feel himself shivering, the anger and hate tearing at his insides like claws.

It could not be possible, was not happening. Not now, after all this time, the dreams, the pretence.

The woman was looking at him anxiously. 'You'd better be off. Lively now. I want no trouble here. I've that enough as it is.'

Pascoe brushed past her, seeing nothing but the towering, grinning face on the stairway.

'Well, Mr Pascoe?' He was enjoying it. 'Is your uncle still protecting his brother's bastard?'

Pascoe sprang forward and drove his fist into the man's face. He saw the shock and surprise, felt the pain lance up his arm from the force of the blow. But the face was still there, the unexpected strength of Pascoe's punch already bringing blood to his lip.

'Well now, you've struck me!' He dabbed his mouth, his eyes hidden in shadow. 'To be touched by the likes of you is like getting the plague! I think this can be settled, that is, if you have learned how to ape the gentleman?'

Pascoe met his challenge with sudden calmness, or was it resignation?

He heard himself say, 'Swords?'

'I think not.' The other man was still dabbing his lip, watching Pascoe, measuring his resistance, his hurt. 'Pistols I believe would be better. But before we part . . .'

He snapped his fingers and Pascoe found his arms being pinioned to his sides.

'. . . I will give you a lesson in manners.'

He swung round, caught off guard, as Babbage darted past them, his head covered by his hands as he ran for the door. With a frantic gasp he dragged it open and was gone.

The big man drew back his fist. 'That's the last we'll see of him!'

Pascoe tensed for the blow which was aimed at his stomach.

He was dimly aware of running feet, a sharp challenge and the sudden bang of a musket.

Major Clinton entered the doorway, swinging his black stick carelessly as he said, 'That was Babbage. My men challenged him but he ran.' He waited until the others had released Pascoe's arms and said, 'You were too late for him, Mr Pascoe.' He nodded to the man with the cut lip. 'But you were in time, I take it, Mr Roche?'

The man he had named as Roche shrugged. 'Just high spirits, Major. It is not forbidden for us to come here.'

Clinton snapped, 'You are leaving now! And I do not care if you do serve on the admiral's staff. Your courage would not last for long in battle, I suspect!'

The three men retrieved their coats and left, but not before Pascoe had seen that Roche was a naval lieutenant, as were his companions.

'I am sorry to involve you, sir.'

Pascoe followed the marine into the wet street. Clinton's lieutenant, Marston, and a file of marines were standing by a sprawled corpse. For Babbage at least it was over.

'I cannot discuss it further.' Clinton looked at his men. 'Get rid of this body.' Then he fell in step beside Pascoe and added wearily, 'Roche is on the staff of the port admiral. He will never be promoted for he now has means of his own. He is a dangerous man. Did he provoke you into a challenge?'

'That is something which *I* cannot discuss, sir.'

Clinton remembered Herrick's face and thought otherwise.

13

Three Minutes to Live

Bolitho waited hesitantly in the neat London square and looked at the house. He had made himself walk from his temporary residence for several reasons. To exercise his leg and to give himself time to prepare what he was going to say.

He had asked Browne if he had seen Belinda Laidlaw when he had called to deliver the letter, but Browne had shaken his head.

'Just a servant, sir. It was so glum there, it was like a tomb.'

Bolitho could now understand Browne's brief description. The house was a twin of the one alongside it. Tall, elegant and of fine proportions. There was no other similarity. It looked cold and unwelcoming, and yet he had the distinct impression it was watching him, as if the whole square was holding its breath to see what a visitor was doing here.

After his walk, the bustle and noise around the many shops and wine merchants, he felt less sure of himself.

It was ridiculous. He strode up the steps and reached for the bell-pull, but the door opened before him as if by magic.

A miserable-looking footman regarded him curiously.

'Sir?'

Bolitho was in no mood for argument. He released his cloak from his throat and handed it to the footman, then his hat.

'My name is Richard Bolitho. Mrs Laidlaw is expecting me.'

As he examined his appearance in a tall, heavily framed mirror, Bolitho saw the man backing up the hallway, staring from the hat and cloak to the visitor with something like awe. Bolitho guessed that they had few guests here, and certainly not any uncouth junior flag officer.

He straightened his coat and turned to face the interior.

Everything looked old and heavy. Owned once by people now long dead, he thought.

The footman returned empty-handed. Bolitho tried to remain impassive, to hide his relief. He had expected she might refuse to see him, if only to avoid embarrassment.

The man said in a doleful tone, 'This way, sir.'

They reached a pair of fine inlaid doors on the opposite side of the house, and with great care the footman opened them together and closed them soundlessly as Bolitho stepped into the room.

It was vast, and again filled with grand furniture and imposing portraits, mostly, it appeared, of senior judges.

In a gilded chair to one side of the fire was the judge's wife. She had to be, Bolitho thought grimly. She was massive and well upholstered, like one of her chairs, and her pale features were deeply lined with disapproval.

Nearby, an open book on her lap, was Mrs Belinda Laidlaw. She wore a plain, dove-blue gown which was more like some kind of uniform than Bolitho would have expected. She was watching him steadily, as if by showing some sign of pleasure or sudden animation she would shatter the peace of the room.

Bolitho said, 'I am temporarily in London, ma'am.' He looked at the judge's wife but meant his words for the girl. 'I asked to call, for in my profession we never know when we may touch land again.'

It sounded heavy and pompous, like the room. Perhaps it had that effect on visitors, Bolitho decided.

The old lady's arm came out from her skirt and directed Bolitho to an uncomfortable-looking chair opposite her. She pointed with a thin black stick, very like the one carried by Major Clinton.

There were some windows facing Bolitho, empty of houses or trees, so that the hard light changed the girl into a silhouette without face or expression.

The judge's wife said, 'We shall have tea presently, er . . .' She peered at Bolitho's epaulettes. 'Captain, is it?'

The girl said quickly, 'Rear-admiral, ma'am.'

Bolitho caught the tension in her tone and knew that the judge's wife had been told all about him and probably a lot more beside.

'I am afraid such things are beyond our calling.' She nodded slowly. 'I gather you stayed at Lord Swinburne's Hampshire estate?' It sounded like an accusation.

Bolitho said, 'He was very helpful.' He tried again. 'It seems likely I shall be rejoining the squadron directly.' He turned towards her silhouette. 'I trust you are settled in, as we sailors say?'

'I am comfortable, thank you.'

And that was how it continued. A question from Bolitho which was immediately parried. A mention of some place he had been or the animals, ships or natives he had seen in far-off countries which was politely ended with a nod or a patient smile.

'The judge is so often called away to administer the law that we rarely find the time to travel.'

Bolitho shifted his leg carefully. She always spoke of the judge. Never by name or as a husband. Her remark about travel made Bolitho's descriptions of life at sea seem like idle enjoyment.

She was saying in the same dry voice, 'The war brings so much lawlessness. The judge is hard put to complete his work. But he is dedicated, and duty should be reward enough.'

Bolitho could pity any man appearing before this particular judge for sentence. If he was anything like his wife there would be neither mercy nor compassion.

A bell chimed, the sound echoing down the passageways like a funeral lament.

The old lady poked a log on the fire with her stick and said coldly, '*More* visitors, Mrs Laidlaw? We are becoming popular.'

The footman crept soundlessly through the door and said, 'I crave pardon for disturbing you, ma'am.' He sounded as if he was used to being cowed. 'There is another naval gentleman here.' He shifted his gaze to Bolitho. 'He is asking to see you, sir.'

Bolitho got up from the chair. He could almost feel the girl watching his efforts to appear relaxed and free of pain.

'I am sorry. It must be urgent.'

As he left the room he heard the old lady say, 'I do not think we will need tea, Simkins.'

Browne was standing in the lower hall, his cloak spotted with droplets of rain.

Bolitho asked, 'What is it? The French, are they at sea?'

Browne glanced quickly around him. 'It concerns your nephew, sir.' He reached out as if to reassure him. 'He is safe, but it was a close-run thing. Captain Herrick sent a fast rider to let you know at once.'

In short, disjointed sentences Browne explained about Pascoe and his meeting with Lieutenant Roche.

Browne said, 'When I read Captain Herrick's message I was appalled, sir. Roche is a bully and a professional duellist. Pascoe met him while he was on some personal mission ashore. Roche made a remark to him and Pascoe struck him.' He shrugged wearily. 'Captain Herrick did not elaborate but bade me tell you that he has dealt with the matter.' He forced a smile. '*Relentless* had a vacancy for third lieutenant. It has now been filled.'

Bolitho was looking round for the footman.

'You do not understand. It is not finished, nor will it be until . . .' He stopped as he saw the girl moving from the shadows towards him. 'I am sorry. But I must leave.'

Browne insisted, 'But he will be safe now, sir.'

'Safe? Have you already forgotten what you discovered about my family? It will never be settled until the truth is out.'

He said in a calmer tone, 'I apologize for all this bother, ma'am. I expected we might talk. I had even hoped . . .'

He watched her face as if to fix it in his mind. The brown eyes, the perfectly shaped mouth, her lips slightly parted with concern at his anxiety.

She said, 'I am sorry, too. After all you did for me, and you were made to sit there like a tradesman. I felt ashamed.'

Impetuously Bolitho reached out and took her hands in his. 'There is never any time!'

She did not remove her hands but said in the same low voice, 'For what? What is it you wish to tell me? That I am so like your dead wife that you wish me to replace her?' She shook her head slowly. 'You know that would be wrong. I would have to be wanted as me, not as a memory of someone else.'

Browne said awkwardly, 'I'll wait outside, sir.'

Bolitho faced him. 'I shall want a fast horse and a list of

post-houses along the Portsmouth Road. Tell Allday to follow
with the carriage and our chests.'

Browne stared at him with disbelief. 'Horses, sir?'

'I *can* ride, Browne!'

Browne stood his ground his face determined. 'With all
respect, sir, your wound is barely healed, and then there may
be a conference at the Admiralty which would require your
presence.'

'Blast the Admiralty, Browne, and damn their politics!' He
gave a brief smile which failed to reach his eyes. 'And should
you care to arrange for *two* horses, I'll show you whether or not
my injury will prevent my beating you to Portsdown Hill!'

Browne hurried away, leaving the front door open in his confusion.

Bolitho said, 'Excuse the language. I forgot myself.' He
regarded her searchingly. 'I'll not lie to you, I was overcome by
the likeness. I have been too long with hope, or perhaps too
long with none at all. But I needed the time for you to like me.
I could not bear the thought of your being here. Now I have
seen the place I am even more convinced it is not for you, even
as a temporary remedy.'

'I have to stand on my own feet.' She brushed some hair from
her face. 'Rupert Seton wished me to take money from him.
Other men made varying offers. As my circumstances worsened
so their offers became less delicately put.'

He took her hand and raised it to his lips. 'Please remember
me. I will never forget you.'

She stood back as the footman appeared with Bolitho's hat
and cloak.

'Your aide was anxious about you riding to Portsmouth. Must
you go?'

'It is something which has been haunting me for years. And
time is running out.'

He looked at her gravely. 'I wish you all the luck in the
world. Happiness, too.'

He did not remember leaving the house, but when he looked
back the front door was shut. It was just as if he had imagined
all of it. That he was still preparing what he would say when
he met her.

When Bolitho reached the house in Cavendish Square he saw

two powerful looking horses waiting outside. Browne had a lot of friends and no little influence, he thought.

Inside the hallway there was complete confusion. Browne trying to pacify Allday, the cook weeping in the background although she could barely know what it was all about.

Allday turned towards Bolitho, his voice pleading. 'You can't go without me! It's not fair. You know I can't ride, sir.' He looked brokenly at the floor. 'It's not *right*, Mr Browne here is a good man, sir, but he don't know *you*!'

Bolitho was deeply moved by Allday's despair.

'I have to ride. It will be much faster. You follow in the carriage.'

Allday had not heard. To Browne he said imploringly, 'You stop him, sir! I know him of old. He's going to fight that bugger.' He looked desperately at Bolitho again. 'With pistols!'

Bolitho said, 'You should not have told him!'

Browne replied quietly, 'It seemed only right, sir.'

Allday stepped between them. 'You're a fine swordsman. One of the best I've ever seen, an' that's no error.' He gripped Bolitho's sleeve. 'But you're no hand with a pistol, sir. You couldn't hit a man at thirty paces, an' you know it!'

'If we're to change horses at Guildford, sir.' Browne looked meaningly at his watch. 'We should leave now.'

Bolitho nodded. 'Wait for me.'

He could not walk away from Allday and leave him like this. They had been together so long, perhaps too long. Like the man and his loyal dog, each worrying for the other, and the one who would eventually be left behind.

He said, 'Listen to me, my friend. If there was another way I'd take it. But Adam is being used to destroy me. If not now in England then elsewhere at some other time. We can't have that, can we?'

'It's not fair, sir. I should be with you.'

Bolitho touched his arm. 'You are. And you will be.'

He walked out into the growing drizzle and climbed up into the saddle.

Browne glanced at him questioningly. 'All done, sir?'

'Aye. How far is it?'

Browne tried not to show his concern. 'Sixty miles and a bit, sir.'

'Let's be about it then.'

Bolitho nodded to the groom who released his grip on the bridle. He thought of Allday's words. *No hand with a pistol.* So what chance would Adam have stood against a professional killer?

The thought seemed to give him added strength and he snapped, 'At least when you are fighting another ship you know where the shots will come from. It seems it is not so easy when you are among civilized people!'

As the guard-boat pulled lustily across the swirling currents of Portsmouth harbour Bolitho had to grit his teeth to prevent them from chattering with cold. The ride from London had been like part of a nightmare, confused and seemingly unending. Small inns, a few moments to gulp down a hot drink while weary-eyed ostlers led the horses away and saddled fresh mounts for the next stretch of the journey.

Winding coach roads, bushes standing darkly by the side like hunched groups of footpads, cold wind and the stinging cut of rain to keep his mind awake.

Now it was almost dawn, and in the dull grey light even Portsmouth looked like a dream's interpretation, without reality.

The boat's coxswain swung the tiller and headed towards a solitary top-light which Bolitho knew to be his flagship.

Browne had said very little during the hard ride, and was slumped beside him, either too tired to speak or immersed in some plan of his own.

The officer of the guard snapped, 'Show the lantern!'

He was a lieutenant with a terrible facial disfigurement from some sea-fight in the past.

The bowman slid the shutter of his lantern and held it above his head.

Bolitho could imagine *Benbow*'s drowsy watchkeepers, the marine sentries on the forecastle and poop, the pandemonium which would begin as soon as they realized he was returning.

Across the dark water came the age-old challenge. '*Boat ahoy?*'

The coxswain cupped his hands, probably enjoying the chaos he was about to cause.

'Flag! Benbow!'

Bolitho said, 'I hope to God Captain Herrick is aboard.'

He despised himself immediately for thinking otherwise. Of course he would be here.

Like a rounded cliff *Benbow*'s side loomed over the boat, and high above, more starkly etched against the dull sky, her masts and yards made a black pattern all of their own.

'Toss your oars!'

The boat glided the last few yards to the main chains, but when Bolitho made to rise from his seat he almost cried out with pain as his leg buckled beneath him.

Browne whispered urgently, 'Here, sir, let me help!'

Bolitho stared up at the entry port, his vision misting with pain. What had he expected? A ride like that was enough to break any wound. His sense of urgency, his need to get here had made him lie to Browne. He had barely ridden a horse, and certainly not so hard, for several years.

He said, 'No. I must manage. *Must.*'

The lieutenant raised his hat, and the oarsmen sat in their boat, panting with exertion, as they watched Bolitho climb slowly up the *Benbow*'s side.

Herrick was there, dishevelled and anxious as he hurried forward to meet him.

Bolitho said huskily, 'Later, Thomas. Come aft with me now.'

Startled figures moved from and then retreated to the shadows. Acting Lieutenant Aggett, in charge of the hated morning watch. Perhaps he was already regretting his unexpected promotion after the death of the sixth lieutenant.

Others, too, but Bolitho had thoughts only for his cabin. To reach it and find the peace to think.

The marine sentry outside his cabin stamped to attention, his uniform very bright beneath the solitary lantern.

Bolitho limped past him. 'Good morning, Williams.' He did not see the pleasure on the man's face that he had found time to remember his name.

Ozzard was in the stern cabin, bustling and muttering as he lit the lanterns and brought life to the green leather and the heavy-beamed deckhead.

Herrick stared at Bolitho as he sank into a chair and gasped, 'Get my boots off, Ozzard.'

Browne warned, 'Easy, man.'

Herrick saw the broad patch of blood on Bolitho's thigh.

'God Almighty!'

Bolitho tensed against the pain. 'Tell me, Thomas. About this damned duel.'

Herrick said, 'I passed all I knew to Browne, sir. I was not sure where you might be at that time. But *Relentless* sails on the morning tide. Pascoe will be out of harm's way.'

He winced as Bolitho gave a sharp cry.

'I'll pass the word for the surgeon.'

'*Later.*' Bolitho turned to Ozzard. 'A drink, please. Anything. As fast as you like.' To Herrick he said, 'How did Adam take it?'

'Badly, sir. He spoke of honour, of your trust in him, and of causing you trouble because of his dead father.' Herrick frowned, reliving and hating it. 'I had to use my authority in the end. That was almost the worst part.'

Bolitho nodded. 'To think Adam has always dreamed of joining a frigate. To have it spoiled in this way is bad, but you acted well, Thomas. Captain Rowley Peel is young and ambitious, and has proved his skill at arms. More than that, he is a stranger to me, so he has no axe to grind. Dear Inch would say black was white if he thought it would please me. Like you in that respect.'

He took a goblet from Ozzard and drank deeply. It was ice-cold hock which Ozzard had been keeping in his secret store in the bilges.

Bolitho sank back and said, 'Another. And fetch some for Captain Herrick and my flag lieutenant.' He looked at each of them in turn. 'I am indebted to you both for more reasons than I can name.'

Browne blurted out, 'Do you intend to face Roche, sir?'

Herrick almost choked on his wine. '*What?*'

Bolitho asked, 'When is the meet?'

'This morning at eight, sir. On the Gosport side. But it is not necessary now. I can inform the port admiral and have Roche charged.'

'Do you think that anyone who would use Adam to get at me would not try again? It is no coincidence.' He saw Herrick's expression. 'You've remembered something?'

Herrick licked his lips. 'Your nephew made a strange remark, sir. This Lieutenant Roche remarked that he had been looking for him. *I was going to meet you* or something of that sort.'

'That settles it.'

He thought suddenly of her face. But whose, Cheney's, or the girl he had left in London at that sombre house?

Browne said, 'He means it.'

Bolitho smiled. 'Now you may fetch the surgeon. I'll need a new dressing, and some fresh breeches and shoes.'

Browne replied, 'And shirt.' He hesitated. 'In case of the worst, sir.'

As he left the cabin Herrick said, 'I'll come with you.'

'Major Clinton is probably better used to such matters. You are too close, Thomas.' He thought of Allday. 'It is better this way.'

Browne returned, out of breath. 'Surgeon's coming aft, sir.'

'Good. Arrange for a boat, and a carriage of some kind if it's any distance.'

He closed his eyes as the pain returned. But for Herrick's message he would still be in London. Any delay and the time for the duel would have been past.

If Damerum was behind it, he would be waiting to gloat over Roche's victory.

He said quietly, 'There is a letter in my strongbox, Thomas.' He saw Herrick's eyes widen with alarm. 'I am a coward. I should have told Adam about his father's death. It is all written in the letter. Give it to him if I fall today.'

Herrick exclaimed, 'You could not tell him, sir. By so doing you would have revealed yourself for harbouring a traitor. And then your brother would have been taken and Pascoe would have seen him hang.'

'That is what I told myself, Thomas. Maybe that, too, was a lie. Perhaps I was frightened Adam would hate me for the deceit. I think that is what it was.'

The surgeon entered the cabin and glared at Bolitho like an enraged skull.

'With all respect, sir, do you *want* to die?'

Herrick said heavily, 'Hold your tongue and do what is required.' As he made for the screen door he added, 'You might as well try to stop a charging bull.'

But there was no humour in his voice, and long after he had gone his words seemed to hang in the air.

Major Clinton said, 'I think it best that we should stop now, sir.' He peered through the small window. 'It is reckless to advertise such matters.'

Bolitho climbed down from the small carriage and looked at the sky. It was almost eight o'clock but the light was still poor.

Clinton tucked his case of pistols under his cloak and added, 'I shall see the fellow's second, sir. I'll not be long.' But still he hesitated. 'If you are really intent on this?'

'I am. Remember, confine your remarks to Roche's second to the minimum.'

Clinton nodded. 'I'll not forget, sir. Just as you told me. Although . . .' He did not finish it.

Bolitho placed his hat on the carriage seat and tugged his cloak more tightly around him. Small things stood out. Some early sparrows searching for food. The fact that the muffled coachman had got down from his seat to stand by his horses' heads. To pacify them at the first pistol shots. That his hands were damp with sweat.

What it must be like for a condemned man, he thought vaguely. Trying to hold on to small, ordinary things, as if by so doing he could stop time itself.

Clinton came back, his face grim. 'They're waiting, sir.'

Bolitho walked beside him through the wet grass to a small clearing, beyond which Clinton had said there was a bog.

Clinton said, 'The pistols are examined and accepted, sir.'

'What did he say to annoy you so much, Major?'

'Damned impudence! When I told him Mr Pascoe had been ordered to sea and that another sea officer of the Bolitho family was to take his place, he just laughed! *It won't save his honour or his life*, he said!'

Bolitho saw two carriages standing discreetly beneath some trees. One for his opponent, the other for some trustworthy doctor, no doubt.

He watched Roche and his second striding purposefully to meet them. Roche was a powerful-looking man, and he was almost swaggering with conceit and confidence.

They faced each other, and Roche's second said crisply, 'You will each take fifteen paces, turn and fire. If neither falls, each of you will advance five paces and fire again.'

Roche bared his teeth in a grin. 'Let's begin. I need a drink.'

Bolitho looked at the two open cases, his mind empty of everything but that by using two pistols it would have been even easier for a trained marksman to kill his opponent.

He said, 'Take my cloak, Major.'

He tried not to look at Roche's face as he threw the cloak from his shoulders. In the grey light, and set against the bare, dripping trees, his uniform stood out like a painting. The bright epaulettes, the single gold stripe on his sleeve, the buttons, one of which on another coat had almost cost him his leg.

Eventually he did turn to face Roche. The transformation was complete. Instead of his sneering amusement at the thought of another kill he was staring at Bolitho as if he was having a seizure or that his neckcloth was choking him.

'Well, Mr Roche?'

'But – but I cannot fight with . . .'

'With a rear-admiral? Does rank decide who will live or die, Mr Roche?'

He nodded to Clinton, thankful that he at least was outwardly in control of his feelings.

'Let us get on with it.'

He heard Roche mutter, 'Tell him, John. I'll stand down.'

Bolitho lifted the two long-barrelled pistols from their case and cocked them. His heart was pounding so hard that he thought Roche and the others must hear it.

Bolitho said, 'But I will not.'

He turned his back and waited, the pistols pointing at the clouds.

If Roche decided to go through with it he would be dead in about three minutes.

The second cleared his throat. There was no other sound now, even the sparrows were silent.

'Fifteen paces. *Begin!*'

Bolitho fixed his eyes on a straight elm tree and walked carefully towards it, counting each step like the beat of his heart.

Adam would have been doing it at this very moment. If by

any chance Roche had failed to kill him with the first ball the second would have finished him. Those extra paces, after being narrowly missed by a professional duellist, or maybe wounded, would have destroyed any remaining confidence.

'Thirteen . . . fourteen . . . *fifteen*!'

Bolitho's shoes squeaked on the grass as he turned and dropped his right arm. He saw Roche's shirt outlined above the smooth barrel and then realized that his arms were at his sides, his pistols pointing to the ground.

Roche called hoarsely, 'I cannot shoot you, sir! *Please!*'

His second turned to stare at him, more used to hearing a victim pleading before Roche had cut him down.

Bolitho kept his aim steady although the pistol felt like a cannon ball.

He said, 'If you finish me, Mr Roche, do you imagine that whoever paid you to kill my nephew will stand by you? At best you will be transported for life. But my guess is that there are many who would use their influence to see you dance on a gibbet like the common felon you are!'

The pistol was getting so heavy Bolitho wondered how he was keeping it so steady.

He called, 'On the other hand, *when* I kill you, there will be an end to it, for your patron will hardly be likely to admit that he was party to this!'

The second called shakily, 'I must insist, gentlemen!' A handkerchief appeared above his head. 'When I drop this, you will fire!'

Bolitho nodded. 'I am ready!'

Roche's shape narrowed as he turned his right side towards Bolitho, the pistol coming up firmly to point directly at him.

It had not worked. How long now? he wondered. Three seconds?

The handkerchief moved, and then Roche threw himself on his knees, his pistols hurled away into the grass.

'Please! *Please have mercy!*'

Bolitho walked slowly towards him, each step agonizing as his wound tore at the thick dressing. But the pain was more like a spur than a handicap. He did not take his eyes from the kneeling, whimpering lieutenant until he was standing less than a yard away.

Roche stopped pleading and babbling and stared at the black muzzle, afraid even to blink.

Bolitho said coldly, 'I have seen better men than you'll ever be die for less reason than you. My nephew, whom you chose to mock, to humiliate without cause, has done things which your sort do not even bother to read about. You sicken me, and I can think of no valid reason to let you live a moment longer!'

His finger tightened on the trigger and then he heard Clinton say gently, 'If you like, sir, I'll put the pieces in their case.' He took the pistol from Bolitho's hand and added, 'Mr Roche's courage today will be all over Portsmouth by noon. By tomorrow, who can say where the tale will be told and heard,' he swung on the terrified Roche, '*with relish*, damn your bloody eyes!'

Bolitho nodded to the second and then turned towards the waiting carriage.

Clinton strode beside him, his breath like steam in the cold air.

'Scum, sir! I had my heart in my teeth, all the same.'

Bolitho looked down at the blood on his breeches. It was like wet paint in the dull light.

'Yes, Major. Scum. But the really terrible thing was, I *wanted* to kill him. But for you?' He shook his head. 'Now I'll never know.'

Clinton grinned with relief. 'Neither will he, sir!'

14

Belinda

Edmund Loveys, *Benbow*'s surgeon, straightened his narrow shoulders and regarded Bolitho with as much defiance as his profession allowed.

'You have all but ruined my work, sir.' He reached down and dabbed a swab against the raw wound, barely able to conceal his malice. 'It's a wonder to me you didn't get gangrene started on the ride south from London, and never mind the duel.'

Bolitho lay back on the bench seat beneath the stern windows and stared up at the salt-stained glass.

As his mind regained some of its control he began to see the madness of his actions. He had ridden from London without a word to the Admiralty, where even now they might be convening a meeting to discuss strategy. By challenging Roche to open combat he had gone against his word to Beauchamp, but even that seemed unimportant.

He said, 'I apologize. It was necessary.'

Loveys pouted. 'I have heard little else, sir. It is all over the port about your meet with Lieutenant Roche.'

Bolitho sat up slowly. *It would be.* There were no secrets for long in the fleet.

He looked at his thigh, the livid scars which showed around the thick dressing which Loveys was about to secure once more. It was strange, he thought vaguely, but as a young lieutenant he had never thought of a captain, let alone a flag officer, as a mere mortal. Now, here he sat, as naked as the day he was born, with just a blanket across his shoulders, and that was because of the cold and not modesty.

Herrick had been to see him more often than necessary, and he guessed that he was trying to keep up his spirits. With *Benbow* almost ready for sea again, her holds, magazines and water casks filled to full capacity, Herrick had a lot to do. New men were still being gathered and sworn in, a lieutenant named Oughton had arrived to replace Pascoe, all these details which were mainly Herrick's concern were part of his plan to keep Bolitho from brooding.

He wondered how Pascoe was settling in aboard the *Relentless*. The frigate would be standing out into the North Sea by now, another separate world into which Pascoe would soon be as one. It was a pity he had not been able to see him before he had sailed. He had even missed the frigate when she had weighed and spread her canvas in the dawn air. While he had been making plans to bluff Roche or die because of a gesture.

Loveys said, 'Try to rest it, sir. You'll have a limp otherwise. If nothing worse.'

'I see. Thank you.'

Bolitho groaned as he lurched to his feet. Ozzard was ready with some steaming coffee, but had learned not to show any concern as Bolitho took his first steps towards his table. His wound felt like fire, as if he had indeed been shot during a duel.

He wondered what Allday was doing. He should have arrived in Portsmouth with the borrowed carriage by now. He recalled his stricken, pleading face and knew he needed him here, if only to reassure him, to prove he was still alive.

Herrick entered the cabin and regarded Bolitho's nakedness without expression.

'I'd like to move out to Spithead tomorrow, sir, as soon as we've completed provisioning. The wind's fair, and I'd not wish to wait in harbour.'

'Inform the port admiral, Thomas. I'll not be sorry to return to the squadron. There's nothing for me here.' He relented instantly and said, 'Forgive me, I was thinking only of myself.' He shrugged. 'Again.'

Herrick smiled. 'I understand. I have never known such happiness as that shared with Dulcie. But I'll not save it by staying here. This is a new year, perhaps with peace as part of its promise. To all accounts, the enemy is massing along the Channel ports again, but at least your action against Ropars and the *Ajax* delayed, if not prevented, a full scale attack from the

Baltic. Even those ungrateful dolts at the Admiralty must see that.'

Bolitho sipped his coffee and marvelled how their friendship had endured everything.

'It will be blockade and patrol for us, Thomas. At least until the ice melts in the Baltic and Tsar Paul decides which way he will jump.'

Bolitho crossed to the quarter gallery, his clothes forgotten as he heard someone hailing a boat from the poop.

It was one of *Benbow*'s cutters. It contained a few anonymous sacks, same small casks, two frightened looking men who had probably been handed over by the local magistrate rather than deport or hang them, and in the sternsheets, Allday.

Bolitho sighed. With the memory of the overturned coach still fixed in his thoughts he had been worried about Allday's safety.

There was no sign of Browne in the boat, however. He had been in the dockyard all morning to pester the admiral's staff about possible orders from London.

Herrick joined him by the windows and said, 'Allday knows already. He's grinning all over his face.' He added more seriously, 'I hope there are no more threats against you, sir.'

'There will be, Thomas. But against *me*, not Adam.' His hand shook. 'When I think what would have happened but for your prompt actions, Thomas, I feel mad with anger. Never mind that killer, Roche, I'd have called out Damerum himself, God help me!'

Feet pounded along the passageway, and after a hasty knock Allday strode into the cabin, his face reddened by wind and spray.

'You are safe, sir! I knew you had a trick to play!'

'You are a liar, Allday, but thank you.' Impetuously he thrust out his hand. 'Very much.'

Herrick smiled, the anxiety slipping from his face. 'Did you hand over the carriage in one piece? Mr Browne's friend will have words to utter if you've wrecked it.'

There was a shout from the marine sentry. 'Midshipman of the watch, sir!'

Midshipman Lyb entered the cabin and said, 'First lieutenant's respects, sir, and may he hoist all but the duty boats inboard?' He was careful to keep his eyes averted from Bolitho's nakedness.

Bolitho recalled his own time as captain. Two years ago, and yet he could remember well the internal dramas of his various ships. Like poor Lyb, for instance. Equal in seniority and just slightly older than Midshipman Aggett, but the latter had been promoted to replace the dead Lieutenant Courtenay. It was just a fragment, a mere speck when set against the great strategy of a fleet at war. And yet Lyb's downcast expression revealed so much.

Herrick said doubtfully, 'It's a mite early, Mr Lyb. I'd better come up and see what Mr Wolfe intends.' He picked up his hat and said, 'I'll leave you in this ruffian's hands, sir.'

The door closed and Allday said, 'I'm afraid Mr Lyb may have got that message wrong.'

Bolitho took a clean shirt from Ozzard and slipped it over his head.

'Why is that?'

'I, that is,' Allday looked momentarily off balance, 'I wanted to speak with you alone.' He glared at Ozzard, who seemed to shrink in size before he left the cabin.

Bolitho exclaimed, 'You *did* wreck the carriage?'

'No, sir.' Allday fiddled with his gilt buttons. 'Fact is, after you'd ridden from the house with Mr Browne the lady came.' He nodded to Bolitho's disbelief. 'Aye, sir, *the* lady.'

Bolitho looked away. 'Tell me. What did she say?'

Allday replied, 'I was so bothered by you riding off without me I can't remember exactly, sir. She was most upset. About you, that you'd think her heartless when you had so much on your mind about your nephew. She fired so many questions at me when she found I'd been with you for so long I could barely get the chests packed.'

'When she found out? You mean, you told her everything?'

'I expect so.' Allday looked at him with sudden determination. 'I'd better tell you without further delay, sir. I brought her with me. We met Mr Browne by accident an' he put her in The George.' He took a deep breath. 'She's waiting there. Now.'

Bolitho sat down in a chair and looked at his hands. 'Does she know about the duel?'

Allday beamed. 'Oh yes, sir. We heard about that before we came through Wymer Parish. I think Mr Roche must have had a lot of enemies!'

Bolitho did not know what to say. She was waiting to see him, here in Portsmouth. When she had heard he was safe she could have gone about and returned to London without seeing him. If it had been only pity, or common courtesy, she would have sent a brief message perhaps, nothing more.

He said, 'I will go ashore.'

'Bless you, sir, not like that!' Allday was grinning hugely. 'Better put some breeches on!'

Ozzard answered Bolitho's call a bit too quickly for one who had been out of earshot. But Bolitho was too confused, too aware of possible disappointment, and barely noticed.

Allday marched round the cabin issuing instructions. 'Best coat, now. Fetch the hat with the black binding, not the gold-laced one.'

Bolitho paused in his efforts to finish dressing. 'Why is that?'

Allday regarded him calmly. 'Ladies need to see the man, sir, not just the uniform.'

Bolitho shook his head. 'You never fail to amaze me, Allday.'

Allday examined him carefully. 'About right, sir. Now, if you will excuse me, I'll muster my bargemen.' He stepped aside as Herrick returned.

Herrick said, 'Lyb got it all wrong, as usual.' He stiffened as he saw Bolitho's changed appearance. 'Hell, sir, you look just fine. If only . . .' He broke off, his blue eyes clearing with understanding. 'Allday! He got me away from here! And I think I know why!'

Bolitho took the hat from Ozzard. As ordered by Allday, it was the plain one with black cockade and simple lace edging.

'I am to meet her now, Thomas.' He looked up, his eyes searching. 'I will probably make a fool of myself.'

Herrick said, 'I think not.' He followed him through the screen door. 'I had a feeling about this. And bear in mind I've not yet laid eyes on the lady. But I know you, and I almost understand Allday by now, so the rest was easy.' He gripped his hand firmly. 'Good luck, sir.'

They strode out on to the damp deck, Bolitho treading very carefully to avoid disturbing the dressing on his wound. He

thought he saw Loveys watching him from a companion, probably cursing him for not heeding his warning.

At the entry port, where the side party was lined up to honour
his departure, and below which the *Benbow*'s barge rolled impatiently on an incoming tide, Herrick said quietly, 'I'm not
much of a hand at praying. But I'll be doing the next best
thing.'

They stood apart and Bolitho raised his hat formally to the
quarterdeck. It was only when he reached down to ensure that
his scabbard would not tangle in his legs that he realized Allday
had clipped the old sword to his belt.

Where luck was concerned, nobody was taking any chances.

The room was very small and situated right at the top of the
old George Inn. As Bolitho paused outside the door to regain
his breath after a hasty climb up three flights of stairs he guessed
that Browne had had to use bribes as well as influence to obtain
it with Portsmouth so crowded with sea officers and the military.

He tapped on the door, his mind suddenly empty of words
or conversation.

It opened and he saw her standing very still, one hand
around the edge of the door, as if unsure whether to welcome
him or shut it in his face.

'Come in.' She watched him pass, her gaze dropping to his
leg as he limped towards a small window and looked across the
neighbouring roof-tops. 'I have sent for some tea. You were
very quick. In fact, I was not sure you'd come at all. That you'd
wish to come.'

Bolitho studied her as she took his hat and cloak. 'It's so
good to see you. I've thought a lot about you. I am sorry about
my visit to your house. I wanted you to like me so much.' He
tried to smile. 'Like using too much canvas in a gale, you can lose
everything.'

She ushered him to a chair near a fire. 'Your Mr Allday told
me a great deal. If one man can love another, then he must be
such a person. All the way on that journey he kept talking. I
suspect it was as much to calm his own fears as to help with
mine.'

'Why did you come?' Bolitho reached out as if to touch her.

'I am sorry. That was badly put. Forgive my crudeness. I'd give so much to please you, even in a small way.'

She watched him gravely. 'You must not apologize. You have done nothing. I did not really understand. Perhaps I was too proud, too sure I could make my way without favours from others. Every smile, each hint I received was like a smirk, a bargain. And I was alone.' She tossed the hair from her face. The brief gesture was both defiant and helpless.

She said, 'Your nephew. Tell me about him.'

Bolitho looked at the flickering flames. 'His father was named a traitor when he ran from the Navy to America. There, he joined up with the privateers, and by some cruel fate I was captured by his ship during the campaign. His desertion, his acts against his own country, destroyed my father. When I heard that my brother Hugh had died in an accident in Boston I could feel no pity, no sense of loss. Then one day, Adam, my nephew, walked out of nowhere with nothing but a letter from his dead mother. He wanted to be part of his real family. *Mine.* He had never met his father, nor had Hugh known about his existence.'

Without realizing he had moved, Bolitho was at the small window again, staring at the windswept waterfront, the anchored ships beyond.

'But my brother had not died. He had been hiding and running for too long when quite by chance he was rescued from the sea and brought to me, of all people. He was hiding in a dead man's uniform and using his name. Where better to find refuge than in the one life he really knew?'

He felt her staring at him, her fingers clenched in her lap, as if she was afraid to speak and break the spell.

'But it was my ship he found. And his son was serving in her as a midshipman.'

'And your nephew knows nothing of this?'

'Nothing. His father died during a battle. Killed by throwing himself between Adam and a French pistol. I'll never forget it. Never.'

'I guessed part of it.' She stood up lightly and took his arm with her hand. 'Please sit down. You must be tired, worn out.'

Bolitho felt her nearness, her warmth against him.

He said, 'If I had not come to Portsmouth Adam would be dead. It is all part of one hate. My brother killed a man for cheating at cards. Now that man's brother wishes to harm me, to destroy me by reviving the old memories and, as in this case, by hurting those I hold very dear.'

'Thank you for telling me. It could not have been easy.'

Bolitho smiled. 'Surprisingly, it was easier than I would have imagined. Maybe I needed to speak out, to share it.'

She looked at her hands, once more resting in her lap. As she did so, her long hair fell about her shoulders very slowly, as in a dream.

She said quietly, 'Will you tell him now?'

'Yes. It is his right. Although . . .'

'You think you will lose his affection? Is that it?'

'It makes me seem selfish. But at the time it was dangerous. If Hugh had been taken he would have hanged. But only when I tell Adam will I know why I really contained the secret.'

There was a quiet tap at the door and a homely looking inn servant entered with a tray.

'Your tea, ma'am.' She shot Bolitho a quick glance and curtsied. 'Bless me, sir!' She peered at him closely. 'Captain Bolitho, isn't it?'

Bolitho stood up. 'Well, yes. What can I do for you?'

'You'll not remember, of course, sir.' But her eyes were pleading. 'My name is Mrs Huxley.'

Bolitho knew it was terribly important but could not think why. Then, like the drawing of a curtain, he saw a man's face. Not moving, but like one in a portrait.

Quietly he said, 'Of course, I remember. Your husband was a quartermaster in my ship, the old *Hyperion*.'

She clasped her work-reddened hands together and stared at him for several seconds.

'Aye, sir. Tom often spoke of you. You sent me money afterwards. That was so good of you, sir. Not being able to write, I didn't know how to thank you. Then I saw you just now. Just like that day when you brought the *Hyperion* back to Plymouth.'

Bolitho gripped her hands. 'He was a brave man. We lost a lot of fine sailors that day. Your husband is in good company.'

It was incredible. Just a word, a name, and there he was, plucked from memory to join them in this room.

'Are you all right here in Portsmouth?'

'Aye, sir.' She looked at the fire, her eyes misty. 'I couldn't face Plymouth no more. Watching the sea, waiting for Tom, an' all the while knowing he was dead.'

She made a sudden effort and added, 'I just wanted to speak, sir. I've never forgotten what Tom said of you. It makes him seem nearer somehow.'

Bolitho stared at the door as it shut behind her.

'Poor woman.' He turned bitterly towards the fire. 'Like all those others. Watching the horizon for the ship which never comes. *Will* never come.'

He broke off as he saw her face in the firelight, the tears running down her cheeks.

But she smiled at him and said softly, 'As I sat here waiting for you I wondered what you were like, *really* like. Allday told me a lot, but I think that sailor's widow said far more.'

Bolitho crossed to the chair and looked down at her.

'I want you so much. If I speak my inner thoughts I could drive you away. If I remain silent you may leave without a glance.' He took her hands in his, expecting her to draw away, tensing his body as if to control his words. 'I am not speaking like this because you are in need, but because *I need you*, Belinda. If you cannot love me, I will find enough love for us both.' He dropped on one knee. 'Please . . .'

But she looked at him with alarm. 'Your wound! What are you doing?'

He released one hand and touched her face, feeling the tears on his fingers.

'My injury must wait. Right now I feel more vulnerable and defenceless than on any gundeck.'

He watched her eyes lift and settle on his. Saw the guard dropping away, as if she were stripping herself before him.

She said in a low voice, 'I can love you.' She rested her head on his shoulder, hiding her face. 'There will be no rivals, no cruel memories.'

She took his hand and opened it in hers. 'I am no wanton, and I am disturbed by the way I feel.' Then she pressed his hand around her breast, holding it there while she slowly raised her eyes to his.

'Can you feel it? *There* is my answer.'

Down in one of the coffee rooms Browne sat with a glass of port by his elbow, a pack of despatches on the bench beside him.

It was growing dark, and some of the servants were moving about, lighting candles and preparing for the inn's visitors from the London coach or the usual throng of officers from the dock-yard.

Browne glanced at the tall, dignified clock and smiled to himself.

He had been here for hours. But as far as he was concerned, the despatches, the *Benbow*, even the war could wait a while longer before he disturbed the couple in the little room at the top of the inn.

15

Lay the Ghost

His Britannic Majesty's ship *Benbow* tilted steeply on the swell, her hull and gangways soaked with spray. The Solent was covered with cruising white horses as the wind hissed through the rigging and furled sails.

Bolitho signed one more letter and waited for his clerk to put it with all the others. The ship was groaning and muttering all around him, as if she could sense the meaning of her change of anchorage. From harbour to Spithead.

Yovell said, 'I'll have this lot sent across in the duty boat, zur.' He watched Bolitho's profile curiously, as if startled by his change of demeanour.

Yovell was not so simple that he did not understand some of it. At first he had imagined Bolitho had been unable to conceal his relief over the duel's outcome. But for Roche's cowardice he might well be dead and the repercussions from the Admiralty would have affected everyone, even a lowly clerk.

Bolitho said, 'Good. If being at sea is a hardship, it also favours those who hate wording despatches, especially as they may never be read.'

There was a tap at the door and Herrick entered, his uniform glittering with spray.

'I am ready to up-anchor, sir. Just as soon as you are ready.'

Bolitho nodded to Yovell who swept the despatches into a canvas bag and hurried from the cabin.

'Very well, Thomas. We shall rejoin the squadron and resume our original duties.' He tapped the drawer of his table. 'I received a full set of instructions from Admiral Beauchamp. I think he is so eager to get me to sea he will not spare the time to see me.' He smiled wryly. 'But I cannot complain. He has been more than patient.'

Herrick exclaimed, '*Patient*, sir? After all you did? Bless *me*, I should damn well think so!'

Bolitho called for Ozzard and said, 'I am glad of your loyalty, Thomas. However, but for our successes and the information I put in my report about the Danish galleys, I fear even Beauchamp's importance would not have protected me.'

'Back to the squadron, eh?' Herrick watched as Ozzard poured two glasses of madeira. 'It will be different for you this time, sir.'

Bolitho nodded. 'It was good of your wife to assist in this matter.'

'Good?' Herrick grinned. 'She loves organizing poor sailor-men! She is even bent on arranging my sister's wedding.' He became serious. 'God, your lady is a beautiful one, sir. You will be so right for each other.'

Bolitho let his mind drift away. In just a few days his whole life had changed. Belinda Laidlaw had left her employment as the judge's wife's companion and had accepted Mrs Herrick's offer of accommodation with only the briefest hesitation.

She had said, 'Only if I am allowed to help you in return.'

Dulcie Herrick had laughed. 'Bless you, my dear, you'll be worn out with my whims and fancies.'

But they had both been pleased at the arrangement.

Bolitho had managed to hold his one real fear at bay. That after he had been at sea for weeks, even months, she might regret her decision and go elsewhere. As Herrick had said, she was beautiful, and desirable.

As the fear re-entered his thoughts he said, 'I am grateful as well as proud, Thomas. I tried to write to her, but it took two attempts before I could find the words. Even so, they are empty against what I feel.' He looked at his friend. 'I talk like a lovesick midshipman. I cannot help it.'

Herrick downed his drink and said, 'It shows, sir. In your manner, on your face. It suits well.' He stood up. 'I will be ready to weigh as soon as the boat returns.'

He hesitated by the door. 'It will seem better somehow. Knowing they're both keeping company with each other while we're on that damned blockade.'

Bolitho sat for a long time sifting through his thoughts. There was a lot which Herrick did not know. For instance, that

Damerum was back in overall command of the station, that he would decide where the Inshore Squadron might best be placed. No, better for Herrick to be left in peace for as long as possible. To have to look over his shoulder at a hostile authority when he should be watching the enemy was asking for an early grave.

Two hours later, as her great anchor broke from the ground, the *Benbow* staggered heavily downwind, her canvas thrashing in apparent confusion until under full rudder and close-reefed topsails she ploughed contemptuously through the first deep trough.

Bolitho stood at the side of the quarterdeck, oblivious to the wet wind and the bustling seamen at halliards and braces.

He took a telescope from the midshipman of the watch and moved it slowly across the walls of the Portsmouth forts and batteries. They looked like gleaming metal instead of stone, he thought, and already so far away. Beyond reach.

Something moved in the corner of the lens and he trained the glass carefully towards it.

It was too far to see her face, but she was wearing the same blue cloak as she had worn in the overturned coach. Her hair was free and streaming in the wind as she waved a kerchief high above her head.

Bolitho took a few paces further aft as part of a flanking battery wall moved inexorably across the side of his lens, attempting to shut her off like a door.

He hurried up the larboard poop ladder, and with the glass to his eye removed his hat to wave it slowly back and forth, even though it was unlikely she would see him.

Bolitho returned to the quarterdeck and handed the telescope to the midshipman.

When he moved to the nettings the angle from the shore had increased even more, and the small patch of blue with the streaming chestnut hair above was hidden from view.

He remembered her as he had last seen her, the feel of her supple body in his arms.

'*Belinda.*'

Lieutenant Speke turned towards him anxiously.

'Beg pardon, sir?'

Bolitho had not realized he had spoken her name aloud.

'Er, nothing, Mr Speke.'

Herrick had heard him, too, and turned away to hide a smile and to thank the good fortune which had given Bolitho such unexpected happiness.

Old Ben Grubb did not miss much either. He blew his nose noisily and remarked, 'Fair wind, all bein' well. An' 'tis only right an' proper in my book.'

Back on the spray-soaked ramparts Dulcie Herrick called, 'Better come down now, my dear. You'll catch your death of cold otherwise.'

She had desperately wanted to share *Benbow*'s departure, to wave at the ship as she spread more canvas and heeled ponderously to the wind. But she knew from her own short experience how important this moment was. Too important to share with anyone.

The girl turned and looked down at her, her brown eyes misty as she said, 'Did you hear the sailors singing?'

'A shanty, yes. It always moves me. Especially now.'

The girl climbed down the stone steps and slipped her hand through her arm.

'There is so much I want to know about him. About his world.' She squeezed her companion's arm and added huskily, 'I was nearly such a fool, Dulcie. I could have lost him.'

The days which followed *Benbow*'s return to the squadron were marked only by their emptiness, their dreary similarity. As they dragged into weeks, and Bolitho's weatherbeaten ships beat back and forth on their endless patrol, it seemed to many that they were the only living beings, that the rest of the world had forgotten them.

Even the sloop and lively frigates found little to report. Nothing moved in or from the Baltic, and only by keeping their people busy or otherwise engaged in contests amongst themselves could the captains cling to a disciplined routine.

Bolitho released one ship at a time for a brief call to a home port. As each vessel left the little squadron the remaining ones began to count the days for her return and their own chance of parole.

Relentless, being the larger of the two frigates, was employed around the Skaw and down into the Kattegat. Whenever she made contact with the flagship, which was rare, it was through the *Styx* or the sloop *Lookout*, and Bolitho often wondered how his nephew was getting on, and if he was still brooding over the duel and the cause of it.

The last ship to return from her short reprieve in an English harbour was Captain Inch's sixty-four, *Odin*. As Bolitho stood on the quarterdeck and watched the two-decker running down towards the squadron he felt in his bones that she was to be the last, and it was with no surprise that he heard Oughton, the new lieutenant, call, 'Signal from *Odin*, sir! Captain requests to come aboard!'

Herrick moved to Bolitho's side. 'I wonder what news he has for us, sir?'

Bolitho saw some of the off duty hands on the weather gangway, so hardened now to the bitter weather that most were bare-armed, some even without shoes. They would also be wondering. The blockade was to be withdrawn. The war was over. The French had invaded.

He said, 'Whatever the news, Thomas, Inch is eager to tell it. Much more canvas and he'll dismast his ship!'

They both smiled. Inch had never been renowned for his ship-handling. But his courage and his dogged loyalty made up for that and much more.

Odin was already standing into the wind, her sails banging and puffing in torment as Inch took the way off his ship.

Wolfe said, 'Boat's in the water, sir.' He glared at a boatswain's mate. 'Man the side!'

Herrick muttered, 'It had better be something useful. Here we are, in March now, and no nearer a solution than when we left Spithead last September.' He ran his gaze over his command and added, 'But we've made our mark, none the less.'

Inch clambered through the entry port, his hat awry, his long horse-face bobbing to the side party and saluting marines.

He saw Bolitho and Herrick and almost ran towards them.

Bolitho smiled. 'Easy, you'll have the people thinking we are on the retreat!'

Inch allowed himself to be led aft to the cabin before he

burst out with, 'We are mustering a great fleet, sir. Admiral Sir Hyde Parker is to command. He will break through the Sound and attack Copenhagen!'

Bolitho nodded slowly. It was much as Beauchamp had hinted. With the respite given to the Navy's scattered resources by the Baltic ice, it would soon be time to act. Before Tsar Paul could combine the strength of Sweden, Prussia and his own forces for an all-out attack, it would be necessary to intimidate the most vulnerable power, and Denmark was the obvious choice.

Bolitho felt no satisfaction in his heart. He remembered the green spires, the pleasant people, the elegant buildings of the city.

Herrick asked, 'Who is Hyde Parker's second-in-command?'

Inch looked perplexed. 'That is something I did not understand. It is Vice-Admiral Nelson.'

Herrick banged his palms together. 'Typical! Nelson, the man who beat the Frenchies at the Nile, somebody who Jack would follow into the teeth of hell itself if need be, is expected to serve under Hyde Parker!'

Bolitho said nothing, but he knew what Herrick meant. It was like condemning Nelson for being a victor, a hero in his country's eyes. Hyde Parker was twenty years older than Nelson and very rich, and that was about all Bolitho knew of him. Except that he had a wife young enough to be his daughter, who was known throughout the fleet somewhat irreverently as Batter-Pudding.

Inch dragged a long envelope from inside his coat and handed it to Bolitho.

'Orders, sir.' He swallowed hard, his eyes trying to pierce the sealed cover. '*Our* part.'

Herrick took the cue. 'Come to my cabin, Francis. We will drink a glass and you can tell me the latest scandal.'

Bolitho sat down slowly and slit open the envelope.

It was neatly and precisely laid down, and he could almost hear Beauchamp's dry tones as he read through the list of ships, some famous, many of which he had seen several times throughout his service. Their captains, too. As boys, as lieutenants, then as experienced commanders. It was a formidable fleet, but if the enemy was allowed to combine its forces, Hyde Parker's ships of the line, including Bolitho's, would be outnumbered by more than three to one.

He recalled what he had seen and learned in Copenhagen, the talk of block-ships and moored batteries, of the galleys and gun-brigs, bomb vessels, and knew this was to be no skirmish, no show of force to deter a would-be attacker. This was in deadly earnest, and the Danes would react with equal determination.

He called for Ozzard but Allday entered the cabin instead.

'We are to attack, Allday.' It was strange how simple it was to speak with him. 'Would you ask Captain Herrick to come aft again, please?'

Allday nodded grimly. 'Aye, sir.' He glanced at the two swords on their rack. 'And I thought we might get away with it this time, sir. I reckon we've done our share.'

Bolitho smiled. 'There are no shares.'

He loosely outlined the content of the despatch to Herrick and Inch without emotion. Their part in the attack was not yet clear. Admiral Damerum was to command the supporting squadron to protect supply vessels, prevent interference from any French ships which might try and slip through the blockade to join with the battle. It did not seem that his role was to be of much importance.

Herrick said at length, 'We'll just have to make the best of it.'

Inch was more definite. 'Pity our Nel is not in the van, with our own rear-admiral in support!'

Herrick nodded glumly. 'I'll drink to that sentiment, Francis!'

Bolitho lowered his face to hide a smile. Inch's supreme confidence in what he could do was unnerving.

He said, 'The fleet will rendezvous outside the Sound towards the end of the month.'

He tried not to think of her face, what she would have to endure when the news broke in England. The end of the month, he had said. It was barely two weeks away.

'After that, it will be up to Sir Hyde Parker.'

He pictured the narrow Sound Channel with the great battery of Elsinore beyond. If the Swedish guns opened fire, too, the squadrons would be cut to pieces from both directions at once.

Inch said, 'I should like to return to my ship, sir.' He looked suddenly troubled. 'I have some letters for the squadron.'

As the two captains left the cabin Bolitho heard Herrick ask, 'How is your wife?'

'Hannah is well, thank you. We are expecting our first child.' The rest was cut off by the closing door.

Bolitho stood up and paced restlessly about the cabin. Once, none of them had cared very much beyond the day, or the one to follow. Now, Herrick and Inch had wives. He stopped by the stern windows, feeling the shudder of the tiller-head beneath his cabin as Herrick brought the ship around to make a lee for *Odin*'s gig.

This was what the flag, *his* flag at the mizzen truck really meant. Not just another fight, a bewildering duty which required only obedience and courage, it was people. Men like Herrick and Inch with wives who had their own sort of battle to fight each time a man-of-war weighed anchor. Ordinary men with hopes and problems who had no choice but to trust their commander.

He remembered with sudden clarity her words as they had held each other in that last embrace.

'Come back safely to me, Richard. I ask for nothing more.'

Now, he had that kind of responsibility, too.

He watched *Odin*'s misty shape lengthening as she changed tack, shivering through the thick glass panes, her sails like wings against the dull clouds.

An hour later, with the squadron once more sailing in a tight line, Herrick came to him again. Bolitho was still at the window, his hands on the sill as he took the weight off his aching leg.

Bolitho saw Herrick's reflection in the salt-spattered glass and said, 'We will call all the captains aboard when we know what is expected of us. I should like to see them before we give battle.' He thought of Browne. *We happy few*. 'Make a signal to *Lookout* to recall *Relentless* from her patrol.'

Herrick nodded. 'I'll do it now. The light is getting poor.' He watched Bolitho's uncertainty. 'Will you tell him, sir?'

Bolitho did not have to ask whom he meant. 'It is his right, Thomas. None of it was Adam's doing.'

Herrick eyed him sadly. 'Or yours, sir.'

'Perhaps.' He turned and faced him. 'Now be off and make that signal. Then we will have supper together, eh?'

Alone again, Bolitho sat at his table and listened to the ship's voices. Rigging and spars, timbers and tackle, all murmuring their own private conspiracy.

Then he dragged some paper from a drawer and lifted a pen from its stand which had been made by Tregoye, the carpenter. A fellow Cornishman, he said little, but had left the stand as a present, knowing Bolitho would understand in some way.

He thought for a few moments, remembering how she had held him, and also the moments of peace, her hands folded in her lap like a child.

Then, without hesitation, he began to write.

My dearest Belinda . . .

If the courier brig found them in time before the battle she would eventually read it. By then it would all be over, but at least she would know what he was thinking at this moment, as with *Benbow* in the lead the little squadron sailed towards the shadows of evening.

Bolitho listened to the muffled squeal of calls and knew it marked the arrival of another of his captains for the brief conference. And it *had* to be short, for with so many ships in the vicinity, backed up by patrolling frigates and brigs, supply vessels and the rest, they were not free to anchor.

The last week had been busy but less tense. Once committed to a plan of battle, no matter how hazy it must appear to an ordinary seaman or marine, the people went to work with a will. Shifting stores, powder and shot to retrim the hulls which had for the most part been living too long off their own fat.

During daylight hours the masthead lookouts reported sighting more ships of Hyde Parker's fleet as it gathered together for the first perilous thrust through the Sound Channel.

There was a tap at the door and Bolitho heard feet moving beyond it, like players waiting to emerge on stage.

Browne peered in and said, 'All present, sir.' As an afterthought he added, 'Wind's as before, sir, and Mr Grubb says there's little chance of a change.'

'Let them enter.' Bolitho walked to the door to greet and shake hands with each of his young captains.

Veitch of the *Lookout* and Keverne of the *Indomitable*. The latter had changed not at all in spite of his authority. He still had the gipsy good looks which Bolitho remembered when he had been first lieutenant in his own *Euryalus*. Inch and, of course, Neale of the *Styx*, followed closely by Captain Peel of the *Relentless*.

The last one to enter with Herrick was Captain Valentine Keen of the *Nicator*. They had shared so much together before the war, in the East Indies and later in the Great South Sea where Bolitho had all but died of fever.

Bolitho shook his hand warmly. 'How is everything with you?'

Keen knew that Bolitho's question had a double edge. *Nicator*'s previous captain had been a coward and a liar, and it was said he had died from a ball fired by one of his own company. *Nicator* had been an unhappy ship then, but under Keen's command had prospered with surprising swiftness.

'Aye, sir. I am ready.' He gave a smile. 'You can depend on it.'

Herrick clapped him on the shoulder. 'Enough said, young Val! Let's get this meeting completed in time for a glass, eh?'

Bolitho stood behind his table, his feet taking the gentle roll and plunge of the deck.

'I have received the final instructions, gentlemen.' He saw them watching him, eager, anxious, some trying to hide their feelings completely.

'More intelligence has been received about the armed galleys which Captain Neale and I observed when we made our little venture into the Baltic.' He saw a few smiles. 'The Danes have many more than first believed, and have been keeping them to the south of Copenhagen. They present an obvious threat to any slower vessels sailing in single-line. It has been agreed that Vice-Admiral Nelson will lead the main assault on the defences and moored men-of-war, and all else which the Danes have prepared for us.'

Even Hyde Parker must have been embarrassed by agreeing to his junior accepting the hardest part of the battle. Bolitho saw Neale nudge Inch with his elbow and guessed they were thinking along the same tack.

'It is now definite that the Danish batteries will open fire as soon as we attempt to enter the Baltic. The Swedish commander has made no comment, but we must assume they may follow that example. When I was in Copenhagen I heard talk of the Danes removing buoys and steering-marks from the channel.'

They were no longer smiling. Without definite knowledge of the channel it would mean a more cautious approach. Just two ships running aground could turn an orderly advance into a shambles long before they reached their objectives.

'So,' Bolitho paused and glanced down at the neatly written instructions, 'this squadron will enter the channel under cover of darkness to bypass the harbour defences and attack the galleys before they can get amongst our main fleet.'

He had to speak carefully to conceal his dismay.

'Soundings will be taken by the boats of the squadron, each to be under the charge of an experienced lieutenant or warrant officer. Close contact will be maintained at all times, but with a minimum of signals. It seems certain that we will not complete the passage without detection, and some casualties and damage must be expected. For this and other reasons we will keep to the Swedish side of the channel and make it as hard as possible for the Danish gunners, understood?'

Most of them nodded, but Peel stood up abruptly to ask, 'If the main fleet is held by the Danish defences, sir, what will become of us?'

Bolitho said, 'Ask me when it happens.'

He liked the appearance of Captain Rowley Peel. At twenty-six he had earned a fine reputation as a frigate captain, although he looked more like a young farmer than a sea officer. It was hardly surprising, Bolitho thought, as Peel came from a long line of landowners and would be as much at home with his beasts and crops as on a quarterdeck.

Peel grinned. 'Aye, sir. With Nelson at one end and you at t'other, I think we shall live!'

Bolitho leaned on his hands and looked at each face in turn.

'Now to the order of battle. *Relentless*, being the larger of the frigates, will lead, with *Lookout* in close support.'

He turned to Neale, seeing his crestfallen expression as he added, 'You will follow astern of the squadron to repeat signals from the fleet or pass information to it.'

You would think he had just ordered Neale's court martial rather than saving him from the first crushing broadsides.

For a moment all their faces seemed to fade and he felt alone in the cabin.

Relentless's part was vital and the choice left no alternative.

When Damerum had put his suggestions to Hyde Parker he must have found it hard to conceal his elation. He would have discovered about Pascoe's appointment to the frigate and would have known how precarious that position would soon become.

A few questions came and went, answered by either Herrick or Browne.

Ozzard appeared with a tray of goblets and each man was soon drinking the loyal toast.

Then Bolitho said quietly, 'Most of us have known each other for a long time. In war that is a fortunate thing. During the fight ahead, our knowledge of each other will be as important as gunnery and seamanship, and to me, most of all, it will be a great encouragement to know I am among friends.'

Herrick raised his goblet. *'To us!'*

Then they began to take their leave, each probably devising the best way to explain what was expected to his own ship's company.

Herrick and Browne left the cabin to see the captains into their waiting boats, but Peel hung back, his face embarrassed.

'What is it, Captain Peel?'

'Well, sir, it's not for me to say, of course. But it's fairly common knowledge through the squadron about your clash with Admiral Damerum. I can understand why this dangerous course must be followed, and for my part I am proud to be in the van when we attack. If Sir Hyde Parker needs all his gun-brigs and bomb vessels for the assault on Copenhagen harbour, then it is obvious that we must play our part and scatter the galleys.'

Bolitho nodded. 'That is a fair summing up, Captain Peel.'

Peel said stubbornly, 'But there is nothing to state that your nephew must be in my ship when it happens, sir! After all that's gone before, it would be the least I could do to replace him.'

Bolitho faced him gravely. 'Thank you. That could not have been easy for you.'

Peel swallowed hard. 'He came aboard with me anyway, sir, to speak with the flag captain. I should like to consult your sailing master on some recent charts.' He raised an eyebrow. 'Shall I send Mr Pascoe aft, sir?'

'Yes. And I am grateful for your concern.'

It seemed an age before Pascoe came to the cabin. He looked very pale, as if he was in fever.

Bolitho said, 'Sit down, Adam.'

Pascoe asked quietly, 'You are surely not removing me from *Relentless*, sir?'

'No. I understand you better than you realize. My one regret is that I have left it so late to say so much. That scum Roche cleared my head if nothing else.'

Pascoe said, 'I heard all about it. The risk you took. He might have killed you.'

'Or you, Adam, have you thought of that?'

Bolitho walked to the stern windows and stared out at the shifting grey line of the sea, rocking back and forth as if to tip the ships over the edge into oblivion.

'I will not hide my feelings from you, Adam. You mean a great deal to me, more than I can say. I had hoped you might one day take on my family name, as you so rightly deserve.'

He saw Pascoe's reflection in the glass as he moved to protest.

'No, hear me. You have had to bear the shame of your father's actions for too long.' He could feel his heart pounding in time with the ache in his wound. 'I'll prolong it no more, even at the risk of losing your friendship. Your father, *my brother*, killed a man in a senseless duel. That man was Admiral Damerum's brother, so you see the hate has never washed away.'

'I understand, sir.'

'You don't. You think of your father as a traitor who died in ignominy.' He swung round, ignoring the sudden pain as he added sharply, 'The master's mate, Mr Selby, who lost his life to save yours aboard the *Hyperion*. He was Hugh, your father!'

If he had struck Pascoe he could not have made him recoil more.

Before he could speak Bolitho continued remorselessly, 'I thought it could be buried, forgotten. Hugh did not even know of your existence, but when he did, I can assure you he was a proud man. I made him promise to keep the secret from you. To do otherwise would have cost him his life, and you something even more dear. As it happened, he died bravely, and for no better cause.'

He realized Pascoe was on his feet, his body swaying against the roll of the hull as if he had lost his self-control.

Pascoe said quietly, 'I must think about this.' He stared round the cabin desperately like a trapped animal. 'I – I don't know what to say! Mr Selby? I grew to like him very much. If I'd only known . . .'

'Yes.'

Bolitho watched his confusion and despair and felt his hope draining away like sand from a glass.

He looked up at the skylight as feet pounded overhead. The squadron was preparing to move towards the final rendezvous before the Sound Channel.

Pascoe said suddenly, 'I had better return to my ship, sir. I came to see Captain Herrick about the man Babbage and Midshipman Penels.' He looked at the deck. 'And, of course, to visit you.'

'Thank you for that, Adam.'

Pascoe still hesitated, his fingers resting on the door.

'Will you tell me more of my father one day? Now that I know the truth?'

Bolitho strode across the cabin and gripped his shoulders tightly.

'Of course I will, did you doubt it?'

Pascoe stood very still now, his eyes fixed on Bolitho's as he replied, 'And you, Uncle did you doubt my feelings? After all you have done for me, the happiness and pride we have shared, do you imagine I could feel anything but love for you?'

They stood back from each other, neither able to speak further.

Then Bolitho said, 'Take care, Adam. I'll be thinking of you.'

Pascoe tossed some hair back from his forehead and jammed his hat on his head.

'And I'll be looking for your flag, Uncle.'

Then he turned blindly and almost blundered into Allday who was waiting outside the door.

Allday said bluntly, 'He knows then, sir?'

'Aye, he does.'

Allday padded past him to look for a clean goblet.

Then he said, 'Bursting with it, he was, fair bursting!' He nodded with grim approval. 'Just as well, seeing it was you what looked after him. Otherwise, luff or not, I'd have put the young devil across my knee!'

Bolitho sipped the drink without even noticing what it was. In two days or so they would be fighting for their lives.

But the ghost was driven out, once and for all.

16

'*All Gone!*'

Lieutenant the Honourable Oliver Browne lowered his telescope and said, 'Signal repeated from *Elephant*, sir. *The Inshore Squadron will anchor when ready.*'

Bolitho, too, had a glass to his eye, but he was studying the long, overlapping folds of the land. It never seemed to get any nearer, but held a strange menace, as if the whole shore-line was waiting for their first move into the channel.

The burden on individual captains was severe in these enclosed waters, but with a commander like Nelson some of the strain was removed. There would be no unnecessary signals, no wasted time, and Bolitho guessed that the Hero of the Nile must have worked on Hyde Parker to get him to a point of attack so quickly.

All day, as the squadrons and distant patrols had headed south through the Kattegat, Bolitho had felt the finality of it. With the coasts of Sweden and Denmark on either beam, even when invisible, it was like leading his ships into a poacher's bag.

Even now, with brigs and ships' boats under sail darting through the ponderous lines of two-deckers, there would be unseen eyes watching their movements. Nelson had signalled the whole fleet to anchor, even though he knew Bolitho's squadron would get under way again as soon as it was dark. He rarely forgot anything. He had even shifted his flag from the big ninety-eight-gun *St George* to the *Elephant* because the latter was smaller and had a shallower draught so that she could get closer to the shore without grounding.

Bolitho lowered the glass and glanced around at the familiar faces of the watch on deck.

Old Grubb, squinting at his traverse-board with his master's mates. Wolfe, staring up at the maintop where some marines were exercising with a swivel-gun on the barricade. Browne, standing almost knee-deep in bright flags as his midshipman and assistants brought down another hoist of signals from the yards.

And Herrick, he seemed to be everywhere, as usual.

Bolitho said, 'Anchor when it suits you.' He glanced at the masthead pendant. 'Wind's dropped a bit. It has to be perfect for our work.'

Herrick nodded and crossed to join the sailing master by the wheel.

'Be ready to box the ship off, Mr Grubb.' To Wolfe he called, 'Shorten sail. Take in the t'gan's'ls and maincourse, if you please.'

Calls shrilled again and men dashed to their stations for reducing *Benbow*'s display of canvas.

Bolitho watched them, the patterns they made as they scurried up the ratlines to the topgallant yards, or loosened belaying pins while they awaited the next order from aft. Hardly any hesitation now, even amongst the latest recruits or pressed hands. *Men not ships.* Herrick's comment of six months back seemed to be fixed in his mind.

He saw Midshipman Penels by the mizzen shrouds, dwarfed by a boatswain's mate and a handful of seamen. He moved like a puppet and rarely showed interest in anything around him. Herrick had told Bolitho about Pascoe's visit, how he had tried to defend what Penels had done. The rights and wrongs seemed small in comparison with the next few days, and only Babbage's unfortunate death was indisputable fact.

Herrick had been unusually uncharitable about Penels. 'Not fit to receive a commission, sir. A mother's boy. I should never have accepted him.'

Bolitho thought he could understand Herrick's attitude, just as he could sympathize with Pascoe's rash attempt to recover the deserter.

Herrick had never had an easy time. From a poor family, he had been made to win each single advance without favour in high places. But he loved the Navy all the more because he had earned it, and seemed unshakable when it came to others less determined.

When Bolitho had tried to find some excuse for Penels' behaviour, Herrick had said scathingly, 'See the *Styx* over yonder, sir? Her captain was Penels' age when we put down that bloody mutiny together! I didn't hear him moaning for his mother!'

But whatever the outcome, Penels would have to stand the hardship and horror of battle with everyone else in the fleet.

Bolitho made up his mind and beckoned to his flag lieutenant.

'Yes, sir?'

Browne more than anyone seemed to have thrived on the austere life at sea and monotonous food. The change from Admiralty to wardroom had been remarkable.

'Young Penels. Could you use him in your party?'

'Well, sir.' His face cleared of protest as quickly as it had appeared. 'If so ordered, I could.' He gave a gentle smile. 'Of course, sir, I could make the point that but for him Babbage would be alive, or at best still running for his life. Your nephew would not have been called out, and *you*, sir?'

'What about *me*?'

'I'll take him, sir. I have just remembered something. But for your nephew's challenge you would not have ridden me raw to Portsmouth. In which case your lady might not have come after you.'

Bolitho swung away. 'Damn you to hell for your impertinence! You are as bad as my coxswain. No wonder Sir George Beauchamp was glad to be rid of you!'

Browne smiled at his back. 'Sir George has an eye for the ladies, sir. Quite unfairly, of course, he may have seen me as a rival.'

'Of *course*.' Bolitho smiled. 'I did wonder.'

In plodding procession the four ships of the line headed into the wind to drop anchor while their smaller consorts stood further to windward before following suit. Even here, with so many ships in company, you could never drop the guard against attack, either singly or in strength.

Eventually, Herrick lowered his telescope, apparently satisfied.

'All anchored, sir.'

'Very well, Thomas.' They walked away from the nearest seamen and Bolitho added, 'At dusk you can put the people to work. Rig top-chains to the yards and have nets spread in good time. There will be little moving in the channel after dark, but there may be just one vessel to raise an alarm. We must be ready. If the worst happens and we touch ground, we must be lively and warp her off without delay.'

Herrick nodded, glad to share his own views and anxieties. '*Benbow* is sheathed with the best Anglesey copper, but I'd not risk it on the bottom hereabouts!'

He paused to watch some men hurrying past with buckets of grease and fat. Every loose bit of tackle, from driver-boom to capstan, had to be well covered with it.

From a deck of a ship at night the sounds of wind and sails seemed terrifyingly loud, but, in fact, it was the isolated metallic noise which carried best across the water.

Herrick said, 'The selected boats from the squadron will begin sounding as soon as we are under way. It will give them confidence and practice. When we are through, or if we are attacked, I have ordered the boats to return to their ships only if they do not impede progress. *Styx* can collect them later if need be.'

Bolitho looked at him searchingly. Even in the dying light Herrick's eyes were clear and blue.

'I think we have thought of everything, Thomas. Beyond that, your Lady Luck will have to give us some assistance.'

Herrick grinned. 'I've already put in my bid.'

A figure flitted past like a shadow. It was Loveys, the surgeon. Bolitho felt a chill dart up his spine as he remembered the pain, the intent stare in Loveys' deepset eyes as he had probed into the torn flesh.

The squadron surgeons would be in demand in hours rather than days, he thought grimly.

He said, 'I am going to my cabin. Perhaps you can join me presently.'

Herrick nodded. 'I'd like to clear for action when the people have been fed, sir.'

Bolitho agreed. He had left it to each individual captain to prepare for battle when he thought fit. Herrick would take it badly, none the less, if one of them beat the flagship to it.

The cabin looked larger than usual, and Bolitho realized that Ozzard had had most of the furniture carried below the water-line. It always made him feel uneasy. A sense of committal and finality.

Allday had taken down the bright presentation sword and was cleaning the other one with a soft cloth.

'I've arranged supper for you, sir. Nothing heavy.'

Bolitho sat down and stretched out his legs.

'Doesn't the prospect of another battle worry you?'

'It does, sir.' He peered along the blade and nodded with satisfaction. 'But where your flag goes the others will follow and the enemy will be the thickest. That's far more to worry about than a few bloody noses!'

Bolitho allowed Allday to continue with his own private routine. The courier brig would be in England now with any luck. A day or so on the roads and his letter would eventually reach Herrick's home in Kent where Belinda was staying.

Ozzard entered with his tray covered by a cloth.

He said, 'They are about to clear for action, sir.' He sounded outraged by the disturbance it would cause. 'But Mr Wolfe has assured me that this cabin will remain as it is until you have finished.' He placed the tray on the table.

'Salt beef again, I'm afraid, sir.'

Bolitho smiled, recalling Damerum's mention of his London grocer. Mr Fortnum? Perhaps he would go there with Belinda one day.

Far away, as if aboard another ship, he heard the cry, growing louder as deck above deck the boatswain's mates and petty officers dashed through the hull.

'All hands! All hands! *Clear for action!*'

Benbow seemed to shiver as hundreds of feet pounded along her decks, as if she herself was stirring to give battle.

Bolitho looked at the tough meat and Ozzard's attempt to make it appear palatable.

He heard himself say, 'Looks well, Ozzard. I'll take a glass of madeira with it.'

Allday walked from the cabin, his huge, outdated cutlass beneath his arm. He would take it to the gunner's grindstone himself. Trust it to a seaman or ship's boy and it would come back looking like a woodsman's saw.

He had heard Bolitho's comment. So like the man, he

thought. At a time like this he would eat that rock-hard meat rather than hurt Ozzard's feelings.

He strolled between the lines of guns, through the hurrying figures and bawling warrant officers.

Allday had seen it all before, and had often been one of these bustling shapes.

But as Bolitho's personal coxswain he was above it, unreachable afloat or ashore until fate decided otherwise.

Tom Swale, the boatswain, gave Allday a great gap-toothed grin as he passed.

'Busy, John?'

Allday nodded companionably. 'Aye, Swain, busy.'

It was a game and they both knew it. Without it they would be useless when the guns began to speak.

One by one Bolitho's ships up-anchored as soon as it was completely dark, and like ghostly shadows moved slowly away from the rest of the fleet.

Bolitho rested both hands on the quarterdeck rail and strained his eyes directly ahead. He could see the pale uprights of the masts, the bulky webs of rigging stretching up into the night, but little else. *Relentless* and *Lookout* were invisible, as were most of the pulling boats as they moved ahead and abeam of their great charges like wary hounds.

A chain of men lined each of *Benbow*'s gangways ready to pass back soundings from the leadsmen in the bows to Grubb and his assistants by the helm.

The wind hissed and slapped playfully at the reefed topsails, and against the ship's hull Bolitho heard the gentle sluice of water, almost the only sign that *Benbow* was under way.

There was a harder shadow to larboard, the Swedish coast creeping out towards them as if it and not the ships were moving.

'By th' mark ten, sir!'

Bolitho heard Herrick whispering with Grubb, someone's pencil squeaking on a slate as the depth was recorded.

Bolitho knew that the *Indomitable*, next astern, was very close, but was afraid to climb to the poop and seek her out. It was as if he would miss something, or by turning away he might leave a gap in his own defences.

Surely the Danish batteries would be expecting something like this? He knew it was unlikely but, nevertheless, found it hard to accept. No admiral in his right mind would attempt to lead a fleet through the narrows under those powerful guns, so what would be the point of sending a mere handful like Bolitho's?

It had sounded all right in the cabin, but as the brooding shoreline hardened still further towards the larboard bow it was less easy to digest.

He thought of the leading boat pulling well ahead of the men-of-war. Busy with lead and line, watching for a prowling guard-boat, listening for an unusual sound. It must be like a black desert. He wondered which lieutenant was in charge. He had not asked. If he needed their trust, he must trust them also.

The boats had been cast off an hour before they had reached the start of the narrows. The oarsmen would be getting tired now, more conscious of their fatigue than the need for absolute vigilance.

He stepped back from the rail, cursing himself for his anxieties. It was done.

Herrick stepped out of the gloom. 'Seems fairly quiet, sir.'

'Yes. My guess is that the Danes have made such massive preparations for a frontal attack on the port that they are as reluctant as we are to move in the darkness.'

A few more hours and Nelson's ships would be roused and under way, ready to follow the same route through the Sound Channel and then head for an anchorage at Hven Island where they could lick their wounds before the final assault on the Danish forts and blockships.

The heads along the larboard gangway bobbed together with sudden urgency until the last man in the chain called, 'Shoal on the larboard bow, sir!'

Herrick snapped, 'Bring her up a point, Mr Grubb.'

Bolitho resisted the temptation to join some of the nine-pounder crews at the nettings as they peered down into the darkness. It must have been *Benbow*'s second cutter which had seen and signalled the danger.

Sails rustled together as the yards were trimmed, and Bolitho looked across to the opposite beam, wondering if any sleepy sentry had noticed the cutter's shaded lantern as the warning was flashed to the flagship.

But he doubted if the Danes were very different from Englishmen. It took a lot to get a sentry to rouse his officer and possibly the whole garrison merely because he *thought* he had seen something. Whole campaigns, let alone one fight, had been lost and won because of military protocol.

He pictured Wolfe somewhere up there in the bows. The first lieutenant had no particular duty for the moment. His experience, his hoard of skills gained in every sea in the world, was enough. He might see or feel something. Sense some dangerous shallows perhaps which even the leadsmen had missed.

Herrick murmured, 'How many of these miniature gunboats d'you reckon we'll find, sir?'

'The exact number is not known, Thomas. But more than twenty, and that is too many. Vice-Admiral Nelson intends to anchor eventually at the Middle Ground Shoal before he closes with the Danish ships. He will do it, no matter what we discover. But if those galleys can work through his line of battle, it could be disastrous.'

'Deep twelve!'

Grubb sighed. 'That's more like it.' He even managed a chuckle.

As one hour dragged into the next, it felt to Bolitho as if he had been carrying some great weight. Each one of his muscles ached with strain, and he knew it was affecting everyone from captain to ship's boy.

There were several startled cries as a boat moved sluggishly down the starboard side. But it was one of the squadron's, the oarsmen bent double across their looms, barely able to breathe from exhaustion. A lieutenant, his white lapels very clear in the darkness, waved up at the flagship, and a marine said huskily, 'We're through, sir! That's what he said!'

Herrick said quietly, 'Pass the word! Not a sound, d'you hear? They'll begin to cheer otherwise, it'd be just like them!' He looked at Bolitho, his teeth bared in a grin. 'I feel a bit that way myself, sir!'

Bolitho gripped his hands together to steady his nerves. Not a shot fired nor a man lost. It would be different in daylight when the main fleet started its advance.

'Give it another turn of the glass, Thomas. Then we can recall the boats.'

Grubb said, 'Dawn'll be up in two hours, sir.' He rubbed his red hands together. 'I'm fair parched after that little lot!'

Herrick laughed. 'I understand, Mr Grubb. Pass the word to the purser. Break out a double tot of rum for each man, and no arguments from that miser or I'll skin him alive!'

Bolitho felt the tension draining away around him, even though the fight was still to come. *Benbow* was through, and that was something each man could understand. As Allday had remarked, they fought for each other, not some plan from high authority.

The half-hour glass squeaked round beside the compass and Grubb said, 'Time, sir.'

Herrick called, 'Tell the cutter to inform *Indomitable* that we are recalling the boats.'

Bolitho could imagine the relief in the various boats as the message was passed down the line. There would be a few blisters and aching backs when daylight found them.

Bolitho felt a tankard being put into his hands and heard Browne say, 'Don't fret, sir. 'Tis brandy, not rum. I know you do not take kindly to *that*!'

Bolitho was about to reply when he felt some of the spirit splash across his fingers and realized Browne was shaking.

'What is wrong?'

Browne looked towards the hidden land. 'What is wrong? You can ask that, sir?' He tried to laugh it off. 'I am a fair hand at matters of ceremonial and Admiralty duty. I can use a sword or pistol better than most, and can hold my own at the tables.' He shuddered. 'But this sort of thing, this dreadful, long-drawn-out crawl towards hell, I have no stomach for it, sir!'

'It will pass.' Bolitho was shocked to see Browne in such distress.

Browne said quietly, 'I was just thinking. It will be the first of April tomorrow. By the end of the second day I might be *nothing*!'

'You are not alone. Everyone in this ship, except the mindless fool, will be thinking like that.'

'You, too, sir?'

'Aye. I feel it now, just as I fear it.' He tried to shrug. 'But I have taught myself to accept it.'

He watched Browne move away into the shadows and reflected on his words.

The first day of April. In Cornwall it would be green again, the snow and mist gone for another year. He could almost smell the hedgerows, the richer aromas of the farms.

And the house would be waiting, as it had done so often for a hundred and fifty years, for a Bolitho to return home.

Stop it now! It was useless to wallow in false hope and self-pity.

He stared up at the mizzen truck but his flag was still lost against the dull clouds.

It was chilling to accept that this small group of ships contained the last two sailors of the Bolitho family.

Lieutenant Wolfe strode to the nettings, his head cocked, as the first rumble of gunfire rolled over the ships like thunder.

'By God, listen to that!'

On the gundeck many of the seamen were standing back from the long eighteen-pounders to stare aft at the officers, as if to determine what was happening.

Bolitho shaded his eyes and glanced up at the masthead lookouts. At first light he had managed to overcome his hatred of heights to climb as high as the maintop and watch the Danish shoreline, the towers and steeples misty and unreal. With the aid of a telescope, and watched curiously by the marine marksmen there, he had studied the span of Copenhagen's defences.

His own small squadron had no intention of drawing within range of the many batteries arranged along the coast. His duty was to find the galleys and destroy as many of them as possible before they could join in the fight.

From his many written instructions he knew much of what Nelson would have to face. At least eighteen moored ships, presenting an impregnable line of fixed broadsides, and the massive Three Crowns battery on Amager Island which mounted sixty-six heavy guns. To say nothing of other men-of-war, bomb vessels and military artillery ranged along the shore.

Against such a force Nelson would be leading just twelve seventy-fours, provided they could get through the last part of the channel without being crippled.

Now, as he listened to the continuous rumble of cannon fire he marvelled at the audacity or perhaps the recklessness of the plan. More so at the cool nerve of the man who was back there in command with his flag in the *Elephant*.

Herrick moved up beside him, his face worried.

'I wish we were with the fleet instead of here, sir. It seems wrong to leave them like this. Every extra gun will be needed just now.'

Bolitho did not answer immediately. He was watching the *Relentless*, a distant pyramid of gently flapping canvas as she changed tack slightly to larboard. Well astern of her the sloop-of-war *Lookout* was end on, one eye no doubt on the flagship.

Bolitho said, 'The Danes will not act until Nelson has committed himself. When the fleet weighs again tomorrow, and stands around the Middle Ground, *that* is the moment *I* would choose. Our ships would be caught in cross-fire from three directions at least.'

He watched the smoke spreading up and across the sky, blotting out the distant ships and also the city. Men were fighting and dying, and yet from *Benbow*'s quarterdeck it held no threat, no sense of danger.

Browne lowered his glass and said, 'Signal from *Relentless*, sir, repeated by *Lookout*. *Strange sail bearing south-east.*' He added, '*Relentless* is already making more sail, sir.'

Bolitho nodded, concealing his sudden doubt from the others. Captain Peel was acting as instructed, not wasting time passing vague sighting reports back and forth.

But surely the whole Danish fleet would be under orders for the attack. And no lone merchantman would be foolhardy enough to sail between two powerful fleets.

Relentless was drawing rapidly away from her smaller consort, and Bolitho knew Peel must have picked his masthead lookouts with care to make such a quick sighting.

'Gunfire's slackening, sir.' Wolfe crossed to the deck-log to make a brief scribble to that effect. 'Our Nel must be through.'

As if to confirm this, Browne called, 'From *Indomitable*, sir. *Styx* has reported that our fleet is in sight and already changing tack.'

Herrick wiped his brow with his handkerchief. 'That's a relief. At least we'll know we're not alone for the return passage!'

'Deck there!' The forgotten masthead lookout made every head lift towards him. 'Gunfire to the south'rd!'

Herrick swore. 'What the *hell*! Peel must be engaging!'

'Signal from *Lookout*, sir. She's requesting permission to give assistance.'

Herrick shook his head and then glanced questioningly at Bolitho.

Bolitho said quietly, 'Denied. It would take *Lookout* two hours to catch up with the frigate. And if we sight the galleys she will be needed to head them off.'

Browne watched the flag dashing up the yard and breaking to the wind. To see the quick exchange of glances between Bolitho and Herrick had pushed his own troubles into the background. He knew what they were thinking. What it must always cost a senior officer to place a friend or relative at risk.

The gunfire was reaching the quarterdeck now, savage, intermittent and very distinct, which suggested that the two or more vessels were firing at close range.

Herrick said, 'Mr Speke! Aloft with you and tell me what you think.'

The lieutenant scrambled up the shrouds, his coat tails flying in the wind.

Wolfe touched his hat. 'Shall I pass the order to load and run out, sir?'

Bolitho said, 'No. There's no point.'

It was strange. In a matter of seconds the battle, Copenhagen, even their reason for being here at all, had been sponged away.

Somewhere on the horizon's misty edge one of their own was fighting. It sounded like two ships. Russian, Swedish or Danish made no difference now.

He recalled Peel's quiet competence and knew he would not be one to act foolishly. He thought, too, of Pascoe's expression as he had turned away from the cabin after he had heard about his father.

'Smoke, sir!' Speke's voice sounded shrill. 'Ship afire!'

Bolitho bit his lip. 'Signal to the squadron, Mr Browne. *Make more sail.*'

Herrick caught his mood and shouted, 'Mr Wolfe! Hands aloft and set t'gan's'ls! Then break out the driver!'

Wolfe strode about the deck, ginger hair flapping, his speaking trumpet swinging as he bellowed for the afterguard to be piped to the braces even as the topmen swarmed to the uppermost yards.

Benbow responded instantly, as under more canvas she heeled heavily to the thrust. Astern, down the line, the other ships were following her example, and to a landsman's inexperienced eye they would seem to be flying like frigates. In fact, Bolitho knew that in these moderate winds they were barely making five knots through the water.

The horizon seemed to shiver and then erupt to a single, violent explosion. Nobody on the quarterdeck said anything. Only a ship's magazine could sound like that.

Browne cleared his throat. 'From *Lookout*, sir. *Sail in sight.*'

Herrick stared at *Benbow*'s flapping topsails with fixed attention. 'But *which one*, for God's sake?'

Speke called, 'One ship has gone down, sir. The other seems to be crippled!'

The masthead pendant whipped out, and Bolitho felt the deck give a sudden tremble as the strengthening gust pushed over the quarter to fill the sails.

He trained a telescope through the rigging, saw a man's face leap into focus as it passed over the carronades on the forecastle to reach far ahead of the ship.

He saw the pall of smoke, two masts with yards and sails in holed fragments standing above it like mute witnesses of the fight.

Then he heard the lookout cry, 'She's a Frenchie, sir!'

Bolitho looked at Browne. 'The *Ajax*.'

Allday came from the poop and watched with the others. 'She'd done her repairs an' was trying to get back to France, I reckon.'

'Probably.'

Bolitho gripped his sword hilt until the pain made him think

more clearly. Allday was right, had to be. After such a mauling
from *Styx* the French captain would have needed at least five
months to effect repairs. He had probably chosen a port which
had become hemmed in by the ice, and now here he was, bringing with him a terrible revenge.

He said harshly, 'Tell *Lookout* to investigate but not to engage.' He turned and glanced at the sailing master's ruined
features and added, 'Lay a course to take the wind-gage off that
one, Mr Grubb.'

Herrick lowered his telescope. '*Ajax* is not moving. She's lost
her mizzen, and I think her steering may have gone.'

The torment of waiting, watching the battered frigate growing larger and larger while *Lookout* moved warily nearby like
a hunter who has discovered a wounded lion, was made more
terrible by the silence.

Then Wolfe said, '*Lookout*'s dropped her boats, sir. Looking
for survivors, though after that explosion . . .' He fell silent as
Herrick shot him an angry glance.

Major Clinton had left his marines to join Herrick by the
quarterdeck rail. Suddenly he pointed with his stick and said, 'I
think the Frenchman's getting under way!'

Wolfe nodded. 'He's cut the wreckage free. Now he's set
another topsail.'

They faced Bolitho as he said, 'Run out the lower battery,
Mr Wolfe.'

Even the repeated order was hushed. Then the deck gave a
long quiver as the great thirty-two-pounders trundled noisily up
to their open ports.

'Run out, sir!'

Blackened woodwork and a length of trailing rigging clattered along the *Benbow*'s side. There were corpses, too, or what
was left of them.

'Fire a warning shot, Mr Wolfe.'

The gun nearest the bows erupted with a violent bang, and as
the smoke fanned out over the water Bolitho saw the great ball
slam down almost in line with *Ajax*'s figurehead.

But the tricolour which had replaced the one lost overboard
on the mizzen showed no sign of dipping, and even as he
watched Bolitho saw the frigate's shape shortening as she began
to turn away.

Wolfe asked, 'Broadside, sir?'

Bolitho stared past him, the French ship blurred in his vision
as if through thick glass.

At a range of just over a mile, a full broadside from those
great guns would smash the damaged frigate to fragments. The
leaks caused by her fight with *Relentless* and the weight of her
own artillery would finish it.

He heard Clinton exclaim, 'That captain is a fool!'

Bolitho shook his head. 'Tell the gun captains to fire in succession.'

The second ball smashed through the *Ajax*'s quarter, hurling
wreckage and shattered spars high into the air like straw in a
wind.

Bolitho watched the tricolour as it was hauled down and
added quietly, 'He is also a brave man, Major.'

A master's mate said, '*Lookout*'s boats have picked up some
people, sir!'

Bolitho barely recognized his own voice. 'Alter course to
intercept *Lookout*. Make a signal to *Indomitable* to board the
Ajax and take off her company.' He hardened his voice. 'Then
sink her.'

Speke, still on his lofty perch in the cross-trees, yelled, 'Six
hands, sir! Five seamen and a marine!'

Bolitho ducked beneath the furled boarding nets and stood
on the starboard gangway as he watched the slow-moving boats,
the drifting remains of Peel's command. Flotsam, burned timber, fire-blackened canvas. And men. Men so torn and disfigured
that they would have known very little about it.

He gripped the shrouds and almost cried out as his wounded
thigh grated against the iron-hard cordage.

A hand reached up and he saw Midshipman Penels staring at
him. 'Let me, sir!'

'Thank you.' Bolitho rested his elbow on the boy's shoulder
as he waited for the pain to ebb away.

Damerum, however unwittingly, had found an assassin after
all.

He made himself look at the procession of bobbing remnants
as they parted beneath *Benbow*'s staring figurehead.

Behind him he could hear some of the seamen yelling, con-
gratulating each other on preventing *Ajax*'s escape.

Penels said in a small voice, 'Sir, I think I saw something move out there.'

Bolitho raised his glass and followed the direction of his arm. Half of an upturned boat and a long spar with one end blasted off like chalk.

There were several corpses floating nearby, and for a moment he thought Penels had imagined it, or had wanted to say something to please him.

He said, 'I see it!' It was just an arm, sticking up over the spar. But it was moving. Alive. Someone who had survived. Who might know . . .

He was gripped by something like panic. Even in these few moments the ship had moved some fifty yards.

'Captain Herrick! Man in the water, starboard side! Quarter boat, *quick*!'

He almost fell as Penels darted from beneath his elbow. He had a vague impression of the boy's terrified face, matched only by some last spark of determination, before he was up and diving straight for the water. He broke to the surface and was swimming strongly before Herrick understood what had happened.

Bolitho saw the quarter boat appear around the stern, the coxswain staring blankly at his officers.

Herrick cupped his hands. 'Follow that boy, Winslade! Fast as you can!'

Bolitho climbed back to the quarterdeck as Browne said apologetically, 'I am sorry, sir, but *Indomitable* has signalled to say that the *Ajax* will be destroyed once we are standing clear of the danger.'

Loveys, the surgeon, hurried across the quarterdeck, his white face alien amongst the guns and the seamen.

He said calmly, 'The boat is returning, sir. I took the liberty of borrowing a telescope. There are two survivors.' He relented slightly. 'One is Mr Pascoe.'

Bolitho clasped his arm then hurried past him to the rail as the boat nudged carefully alongside.

Winslade, the boat's coxswain, waited for more seamen to climb down the tumblehome to assist and then called, 'Just the two, sir!' He swallowed hard before adding, 'I'm afraid we lost young Mr Penels, sir! He just seemed to give up as he reached the boat!'

Bolitho reached the entry port as the two limp figures were handed through. The first he did not recognize, a pigtailed seaman with one arm so badly burned it looked inhuman.

Loveys was on his knees running his hands over Pascoe's body while his aproned assistants hovered behind him like butchers.

Bolitho watched the painful rise and fall of his nephew's chest, the sea water running from beneath his closed lashes like tears. His clothes had been all but blasted from his body and he gave a quiet groan as the surgeon's boney fingers felt for internal damage.

Loveys said at length, 'He's young and fit, of course. Nothing broken. He's lucky.'

He turned to the seaman and said, 'Now, let me have a look at you.'

The seaman muttered vaguely, 'I didn't hear nothin'. One minute the cap'n was yellin' and cussin' about fire.' He shook his head and winced as Loveys touched his burned arm. 'Next thing I was deep underwater. Goin' down. I can't swim, y'see?' He realized that Bolitho and Herrick were there and stammered, 'Beggin' yer pardon, sir!'

Bolitho smiled. 'Easy now. What happened next?'

'Our new third lieutenant, sir. Mr Pascoe 'ere, 'e pulls me to some floatin' wreckage, then goes back for my mate, Arthur. But he died afore the boat come for us. It was just me an' Mr Pascoe, sir. The rest is all gone.' He had to repeat it as if he still could not accept the enormity of it. '*All gone!*'

As the seaman was carried away to the sick-bay, Pascoe opened his eyes. Surprisingly, he smiled and said weakly, 'I've come back after all, Uncle!' Then he fainted.

17

The Prime Target

Bolitho sat at a small table in the stern cabin, a pen poised above his report. Someone would read it, he thought grimly, log books and written reports always seemed to survive no matter what.

It was a strange feeling, like sitting in an abandoned house. The furniture had all been taken below, and without looking up from the table he knew that the gun crews of the nearest nine-pounders were sharing the space with him. Screens had been taken down, and the ship, as she moved very slowly towards the Danish coastline once again, was cleared for battle from bow to stern.

Unlike Nelson's fleet, Bolitho's squadron had been under way throughout the night, his four ships of the line divided into two short columns so that they could watch as much of the area as possible.

The seamen and marines had worked watch and watch, snatching a few hours rest beside their guns and nourished by neat rum and stale food. The galley fire had long since been doused for safety's sake, for each ship in the squadron had to be prepared to fight at minutes' notice.

Bolitho looked at the lines he had written about Mr Midshipman George Penels, aged twelve years and nine months, who had died the previous day in one desperate act of courage.

What had the boy been thinking of? Of Pascoe, whom he had got involved in Babbage's desertion, of his admiral, who had cared enough to put him in Browne's charge when everyone else had shunned him?

This carefully worded report might help the boy's mother when the news eventually reached her in Cornwall. Bolitho had no doubt that Herrick would make certain no mention of Babbage would mar his memory for her.

Allday walked to an open port and leaned down to watch the sea, cold and grey in the morning light. Two cables abeam, *Nicator*, followed by Inch's *Odin*, brought life to the dreary scene.

He said, 'Not long now, sir.'

Bolitho waited for Yovell to seal the envelope and replied, 'The attack will begin in two hours, if everything is timed correctly.'

He glanced along the deck, past where the screen door would normally be, to the gloom beneath the poop and beyond to the crowded activity of the quarterdeck.

'Our part will happen at any moment.' He stood up and tested his leg warily. 'Get my sword, will you?'

How quiet the ship was, he thought. The excitement of the *Ajax*'s capture and her terrible end when the fuses had been fired in her magazine had been dulled by the loss of Peel's ship. Altogether, *Lookout* had found ten survivivors. With Pascoe and the burned seaman also rescued, that meant a total bill of some two hundred sailors and marines killed. It was too much of a price to pay.

Bolitho had visited his nephew several times during the night. Each occasion had found Pascoe wide awake, defying Loveys' efforts to make him rest and save his strength.

Perhaps those last moments in the water were too stark in his mind, as if by going to sleep he would never reawake and find his survival only part of a nightmare.

But Pascoe's descriptions, brief though they were, completed a full and horrific picture.

The cruellest part of it had been that Peel had been winning. But some last fury had brought the *Ajax* too close, so that both frigates had collided bowsprit to bowsprit, bringing down the Frenchman's mizzen and hurling many of the men from their feet.

Pascoe vaguely remembered Peel shouting about smoke even as *Relentless*'s cheering boarders had rushed to grapple the enemy hand to hand.

He had been on the quarterdeck, the second lieutenant having been killed in the opening broadsides. The next minute he had felt himself flying through the air and then being smashed, choking, into the sea.

Pascoe had started to swim for a drifting boat when one of the *Relentless*'s topmasts had dropped from the sky like a giant's lance and had cut the boat in half and some struggling men with it.

The thing which Pascoe had not been able to accept was the actual explosion. It had blasted the thirty-six-gun frigate to pieces, yet he had heard nothing.

The collision between the two ships had probably caught a man off balance below decks. A lantern overturned, some powder spilled as a boy ran to serve his gun, or even a flaming wad from the enemy's broadside, it could have been caused by any one of many things.

Bolitho walked slowly beneath the poop, his head ducking automatically between the deckhead beams.

Faces turned to watch him pass, faces which after nearly seven months were no longer strangers.

The figures on the quarterdeck came alive as he stepped out into the morning light, and he saw Herrick with a telescope trained across the nettings towards the *Lookout* which stood well away on the larboard bow.

The sea was rising and falling in a slow swell, with no crests to break the surface or the motion. There was quite a lot of haze about, and far ahead of the two columns of ships it looked pale green. A trick of the eye and distance. The haze was real enough but the green layer was land. Denmark.

Herrick saw him and touched his hat.

'Wind's backed two more points, sir. More than I hoped. I shall continue on this tack, nor'-nor'-east, until I can make a proper landfall.' Some of the old, uncertain Herrick stepped out of memory as he added, 'With your permission, that is.'

'Aye, Thomas. That should suit us well.'

He strode to the nettings and peered across the opposite quarter. There was *Styx*, alone and watchful, ready to dash downwind and assist when required.

Ajax's captain had probably imagined the *Relentless* to be her, Bolitho thought. It would be just enough to drive him to the last edge of anger and hatred.

Midshipman Keys, who was assisting Browne, called excitedly, 'Signal from *Lookout*, sir. *Two strange sail to the north-west!*'

Men bustled around in a flurry of lively flags as the signal was repeated down the line and to the distant *Styx*.

'Two sail, eh?' Herrick rubbed his chin.

Bolitho said, 'General signal, please. *Prepare for battle.*'

Wolfe chuckled and gestured abeam to the *Nicator*. 'Listen, sir! They're cheering already!'

Browne reported, 'All acknowledged, sir.'

Bolitho met his eyes. 'All right now?'

The flag lieutenant smiled stiffly. 'Better, sir. A bit better.'

'Deck there! Enemy in sight! Two sail of the line!'

Wolfe strode back and forth, his ungainly feet miraculously missing ring-bolts and the crouching gun crews with their rammers and handspikes.

'No frigates then? That's something!'

Herrick stiffened and held his glass in direct line with the larboard cathead.

'*Got 'em!*'

Bolitho raised his own glass and saw the two towering spans of canvas emerging from the mist as the other ships continued towards him on a converging tack.

Two-deckers, each with a great curling flag at her gaff, red with a white cross, the Danish colours.

Benbow's forecourse lifted and puffed itself out like a huge chest as a strengthening breeze pushed across the dull water.

Bolitho said, 'They're holding their course, Thomas. Strange. They're heavily outnumbered.'

Herrick grinned. 'Makes a change, sir.'

Bolitho thought of the man in the book-lined room at the Danish Palace. What was he doing at this moment? Did he still remember their brief meeting, with Inskip hovering around like a nursemaid?

Somebody chuckled, the sound unnatural in the tension of the quarterdeck.

Bolitho turned and saw Pascoe coming from the poop, very pale but trying not to show his uncertainty. He was wearing a borrowed uniform which was far too large for him.

He touched his hat and said lamely, 'Reporting for duty, sir.'

Herrick stared at him. 'My God, Mr Pascoe, what are you thinking of?'

But Bolitho said, 'Welcome back.'

Pascoe smiled at the grinning seamen nearby. 'The coat belongs to Mr Oughton, sir. He is a bit, well, larger.'

Bolitho nodded. 'If you feel weak, say so.'

He could understand Pascoe's need to get on deck. After his experience in *Relentless*, he would be unwilling to stay on the orlop with its grim reminders.

Pascoe said simply, 'I heard about Penels, sir. I feel to blame. When he first came to see me . . .'

Herrick interrupted, 'There was nothing you could have prevented. If wrong was done, then I must bear it, too. He needed advice, and I damned him for his one foolish act.'

'Deck there!' The lookout hesitated, as if unable to describe what he saw. 'Galleys! Between the two ships!' His voice cracked in disbelief. 'So many I can't count 'em!'

Bolitho levelled his glass just in time to see another hoist of signals appear on *Lookout*'s yards. He did not need to read it. Between the two oncoming ships was a veritable flotilla of galleys, sweeps rising and falling like crimson wings, flags streaming above the hidden oarsmen and each massive bow-gun.

'Load and run out, Captain Herrick.' His sharp formality swept away the momentary easing of tension. 'Upper gundeck with grape and bar-shot.'

He turned towards the marine officers. 'Major Clinton, there'll be work for your best shots today.'

The two marines touched their hats and hurried away to their men.

Speaking his thought aloud, Bolitho said, 'They will try to separate us. Signal *Styx* and *Lookout* to harry the enemy's rear as soon as we are engaged.'

The young midshipman who had taken the place of the dead Penels wrote scratchily on his slate and then waited, his mouth half open, as if he could not get his breath.

Bolitho looked at him impassively, seeing in those few seconds his youth, his hopes and his trust.

'Now, Mr Keys, you may hoist number sixteen, and make sure it stays flying.'

The youth nodded jerkily and then ran back to his seamen.
He yelled, 'Jump to it, Stewart! Hoist the signal for *Close
Action*!'

At a guess, Keys was about fourteen. If he lived after today
he would remember this moment forever, Bolitho thought.

Slowly and inexorably the two formations continued to close
one another. It was as if they were being drawn by some irre-
sistible force, or that their captains were blind and unaware of
the approaching danger.

Herrick asked, 'Line of battle, sir?'

Bolitho did not reply immediately. He moved his glass carefully from ship to ship, each with her broadsides run out like
dull teeth, her yards and taut canvas unchanged.

During the night Bolitho's squadron had kept to the carefully
rehearsed plan. After standing well clear of Copenhagen the
squadron had slowly changed tack, taking advantage of the
wind's backing to move closer again to the land, like drawing
the noose of a halter. At first glance the plan had worked perfectly. Here were the galleys, heading north towards Copenhagen to offer their massive support just as soon as the British
admiral made his move to attack. Bolitho could either continue
to close with them or could harry them all the way to their
objective.

The presence of the two third-rates puzzled him. Big men-of-
war rarely worked with fast-moving vessels under oars. The
varying scales of mobility and fire-power would hinder rather
than help.

Perhaps the Danes were merely sending the ships to add to
their fleet in Copenhagen, using the cluster of galleys as a useful
escort for the passage there.

He said, 'No. We will remain in two columns. I am not happy
about the enemy's intentions. In a fixed line of battle we would
be more vulnerable.'

Herrick sounded surprised. 'They will not dare to attack us,
sir! I'd stake *Benbow*'s chances alone against the pair of 'em!'

Bolitho lowered the telescope and wiped his eye. 'Have you
ever seen galleys at work?'

'Well, I've no personal experience, sir, but . . .'

Bolitho nodded. 'Aye, Thomas, *but.*'

He thought of the picture he had just seen compressed in the lens. Two, maybe three lines of galleys gliding abreast between the two big men-of-war. There was something unnerving about their unwavering approach, how it must have been in ancient days at Actium and Salamis.

He said, 'We will test their range. The first four guns of the lower battery. Maximum elevation, Thomas. See if that deters them.'

Herrick beckoned to a midshipman. 'My compliments to Mr Byrd. Tell him to open fire with four ranging shots. Gun by gun, so that I can watch it.'

The midshipman vanished below, and Bolitho could picture the men turning from their ports and loaded thirty-two-pounders to watch him scamper to the lieutenant in charge. The lower gundeck was always an eerie place. With the lanterns extinguished, the only light filtered around the guns in their ports. Sounds and events were shut off from the many men who waited there. The sides were painted in red, a grim reminder that in battle it would hide some of the horror even if it could not lessen the pain.

Bang. Some of the men on the upper deck stood to cheer as the gun spouted smoke and fire from below the forecastle.

Herrick commented, 'Very close.'

Bolitho watched the second ball ricochet and then splash down in direct line with the right-hand ship.

Grubb rumbled uneasily, 'Still comin', the buggers!'

'Continue firing, sir?' Herrick watched the widening array of craft, still expecting a change of direction.

'No.'

Bolitho moved the glass towards the galleys. Still too far away to pick out details properly. Except for the precision of the stroke, tireless and easy, as if no human hand was needed. And the gun above each prow, the only ugly thing there was, like a tusk.

He flinched, even though he was expecting it, as the leading galleys faded momentarily in a swirling curtain of smoke.

Then came the sound, a jarring roar, intermingled and threatening, as the great guns lurched back on their slides.

In the few remaining seconds Bolitho heard the angry shriek

of gulls which had only just returned to the water after *Ben-bow*'s opening shots.

'Pork and molasses!' Wolfe fell back with astonishment as the sea erupted in a leaping torment of spray and smoke. 'Did you see *that*, for God's sake?'

Herrick exclaimed, 'That was too near for comfort, sir. They must be thirty-two-pounders, bigger maybe!'

Browne said, 'The Danish ships are changing tack, sir.'

Bolitho watched. It was like a cumbersome ballet, he thought. The two Danish ships were turning slowly to larboard, presenting themselves broadside on and heading roughly north-east. Passing ahead, through and astern of them the crimson galleys were splitting into smaller subdivisions, three or four to a section.

'Close the range, Thomas. Bring her up two points if you can.'

He fell silent and waited, counting seconds as the Danish guns fired again. He felt the hull shudder as some of the iron fell close alongside and flung cascades of spray high above the gangway to reach even the hard-braced foresail.

Bolitho recalled Allday's words to him. The enemy were certainly concentrating their opening fire on the flagship.

He said, 'Mr Browne, make to *Nicator*, *Lee column will not engage.*'

He glanced up at the sails as they banged and protested to the change of course. *Benbow* was standing as close to the wind as Grubb could manage, but the Danes still held the advantage, their canvas full-bellied and perfectly set.

Herrick was watching an arrowhead of galleys forging past the leading two-decker.

He said, 'Those devils are going to attack us from ahead, if we let 'em!'

Bolitho nodded. 'There is nothing we can do at present. If we alter course to lee'rd to gain agility the Danish ships will rake our sterns. Even at this range it could do untold harm before we are to grips with them.'

As he spoke he saw the cool reasoning of the Danish commander. Like sharks around a helpless whale, the galleys could cut *Benbow* down to the bones without risking a single man.

He said harshly, 'Signal *Lookout* to engage.'

Herrick turned away to watch Wolfe directing more men to the weather braces.

He knows, Bolitho thought bitterly. *Lookout* was fast and lively, but her slender hull was no match for heavy cannon.

Browne called, 'She's acknowledged, sir.'

Bolitho saw the sloop spreading her topgallants and sweeping round with her lee gunports almost awash. Like his own first command, he thought, so full of promise and high hopes. In his mind's eye he pictured Veitch, her commander, and prayed that he was using all his experience and shutting *Relentless*'s fate from his thoughts.

The gunfire was growing and spreading as *Indomitable* loosed her first timed and aimed broadside at the enemy. Another crimson formation of galleys was pulling around the rear of the squadron, but with less confidence than the others as *Styx* altered course to meet them.

The sea's face was covered in a drifting mist of powder smoke, and the air shook to the screech and plunge of shot with barely a break.

In one brief lull Bolitho heard a deeper, heavier sound which seemed to drive through the water and lift the keel higher in his imagination.

Grubb ambled towards the deck-log. 'Reckon the fleet is attackin' now, sir!'

Wolfe turned and gave a fierce grin. ' 'Bout bloody time, Mr Grubb! I'm fair sick of being the prime target!'

The hull gave a violent lurch as a ball smashed deep into the bilges, and Bolitho heard the boatswain urging some of his spare hands below to assist.

'*Lookout*'s in trouble, sir!'

Bolitho looked at the sloop, his mind like ice as he saw her foremast topple into the smoke, wreckage tearing adrift from her engaged side. The galleys were closing in on her, their guns hammering as fast as they could reload. One had been too daring and was lifting slowly like a pointer, spilling sweeps and bodies from the shattered hull before diving to the bottom.

Someone yelled, '*Styx* has done for two of them!'

More cries and shouts came from below as another great ball punched into the side like a battering-ram.

Bolitho heard Wolfe yell through his speaking trumpet, 'On the uproll, gun captains!'

The men at the upper battery waited like crouching statues, their eyes blind as they tensed for the broadside.

Wolfe yelled, *'Fire!'*

Bolitho watched the leading Danish two-decker, felt his mouth go dry as the packed mass of grape and whirling bar-shot swept through the enemy's rigging. Sails and cordage, then the main-topmast itself fell together in a devastating avalanche of destruction. The bar-shot, masses of spade-shaped metal linked together by rings, was hard to aim, but when it found a target it could reduce a vessel's canvas and rigging to shreds in seconds.

Inflamed by the Danes' superior tactics and manoeuvrability, the effect of the broadside brought new heart to the gun crews. Sponging out and shouting meaningless words into the drifting smoke they worked like demons, their arms and backs streaming sweat despite the chill air.

'Fire!'

Bolitho moved further aft, his eyes fixed on the leading ship as she began to fall downwind towards the *Benbow's* murderous broadsides.

All the months and weeks of drills born from dreary monotony were paying off now. Only a few distant waterspouts told of misses, and the majority of the shots, both ball and bar, were hitting their target. The Danes' fore-topgallant mast was falling, slewing round drunkenly as it fought against the pull of shrouds and stays before thundering over the side in a tremendous splash.

Benbow received another massive ball from somewhere ahead, and Bolitho saw two galleys moving towards the ship, firing as they approached. His heart sank as he saw *Lookout* beyond the billowing smoke. All but her mizzen had gone and she was drifting helplessly to the mercy of the galleys' bombardment with only a few of her guns still able to reply.

'Try and mark down those galleys with the bow-chasers!'

Bolitho could feel the rage rising within him. Not one of despair or frustration, but something more terrible. It was cold, gripping his insides like a vice as he stared at the embattled vessels around him.

It was all suddenly stark and clear. Like Damerum's efforts to place him and his squadron here. Like his attempt to get Pascoe killed by a hired duellist. Now this. The sudden reality of defeat had acted as a spur rather than the opposite.

'Signal *Nicator* to engage the other ship *now*!' He felt metal hiss overhead and crash hard into the poop. '*Styx* will support *Nicator* and *Odin*.'

He swung round, seeking the nearest galleys, as the Danish two-decker staggered heavily downwind to be hammered again by *Indomitable* as she kept station on her flagship.

'Full broadside, Thomas! We will alter course to starboard and engage with both sides.' He watched *Nicator* and then *Odin* as they acknowledged his signal and then snapped, 'Steer east-nor'-east!'

Men ran from side to side as both batteries of guns prepared to fire.

Bolitho shouted, 'It will have to be quick or the galleys will outpace us before we can rake them!'

By turning downwind and away from the remaining enemy two-decker it might seem that *Benbow* was withdrawing from the fight. And by ordering Keen and Inch to attack the rest of the enemy formation he knew he might be sacrificing them and every man under their command.

But he had to hit the galleys and destroy their confidence. Otherwise his whole squadron would be overwhelmed. No blame would lie with Damerum, for the Inshore Squadron would have served its purpose even in the blood of its own destruction. Nelson was at the gates of Copenhagen, and nothing which the galleys or anyone else could do would change that now.

Bolitho saw Pascoe walking between the guns, his borrowed hat gone, his black hair blowing across his face as he spoke to some of the seamen. He must be feeling the shock more deeply now, Bolitho thought, and even along the length of the deck he could see his unnatural stiffness.

He heard Herrick explaining to Wolfe and Grubb exactly what he wanted, saw the seamen manning the braces and staring aloft at the sails, most of which were patterned with shot holes.

'Stand by on the quarterdeck!'

More shots hit the hull, but in the tension nobody cried out.

Gun crews stood by their tackles, the captains testing the trigger lines and picturing their targets.

'*Now!* Put up your helm! Lee braces there! *Roundly*, lads!'

Bolitho felt the deck begin to tilt, saw an upended fire-bucket spill water across the pale planking as once again *Benbow* responded to her masters.

'The galleys are re-forming, sir!' Browne broke off choking in gunsmoke as the upper batteries crashed inboard once more from their ports.

Bolitho strode to the nettings, seeing *Nicator* and *Odin*, their hulls overlapping as they closed the range with the Danish ships. Galleys milled around them, sweeps pulling and then backing with equal precision as their commanders handled them as if they and the guns were one weapon.

Odin was pouring smoke from her side and poop, but Keen's *Nicator* was firing at point-blank range at her adversary, so that as a full broadside smashed into the Danish ship she appeared to rock over as if struck by a mountainous sea.

Benbow's alteration of course had not only taken her away from the squadron, but had also isolated her amongst the galleys. Her first massive broadsides as she had swung down-wind had taken the galleys completely by surprise, and seven of them had been sunk or smashed beyond recognition. Figures floundered amongst floating timbers and broken spars, and Bolitho guessed that some were survivors from the *Lookout* which had foundered without anyone seeing her final moments.

Bolitho stared along the upper deck at the seamen and marines who had been working and firing, pulling wreckage and wounded men aside without a break since the opening shots. The hull was being hit again and again, and despite the din he could hear the occasional clank of pumps.

'*Odin*'s signalling, sir! *Require assistance!*'

Bolitho glanced across at Herrick and said, 'Inch will have to hold on, Thomas.'

He turned as a man fell kicking and choking on his own blood, cut down by a fragment of iron.

Someone found the breath for a cheer as another galley rolled over, gutted by a packed charge of round-shot and grape.

Falling further and further astern of her flagship, the *Indomitable* was fighting off attacks from both bow and quarter, the great balls slamming through the stern and forecastle, up-ending guns and forcing their crews to cower down for protection.

Herrick, his hat gone, a pistol gripped in his hand, peered through the smoke and shouted, 'Two more of 'em are closing astern!'

There was a great crash, and Grubb yelled hoarsely, 'Steerin' carried away, sir!'

A wildly flapping shadow swept overhead, and Bolitho felt himself being dragged roughly aside as the mizzen-topmast, spars and trailing creepers of cut rigging clattered and thundered over the larboard side.

It was like being left naked. Guns crashed and recoiled as before, but as *Benbow* swung helplessly out of control the aim was lost. Men lay buried beneath great coils of fallen rope and blocks, others crept about on hands and knees like terrified dogs. There were many dead, too, including the marine lieutenant, Marston, an overturned cannon had crushed his chest and stomach to bloody pulp.

Swale, the boatswain, was already there with his men, axes flashing, more concerned with freeing their ship from the trailing anchor of wreckage than with their fallen comrades.

Herrick assisted Bolitho to his feet, his eyes wild as he shouted at his first lieutenant.

'Send a master's mate below, Mr Wolfe! Rig emergency steering tackle!'

Bolitho nodded to Allday who had pulled him away from the splintered topmast as it fell.

Major Clinton at the head of some marines charged aft and up to the poop to reinforce his men there as four and then five galleys closed around the *Benbow*'s unprotected stern. Again and again the deck jumped and quivered as ball after ball slammed through the counter and quarter gallery, against which the crack of Clinton's muskets sounded puny and useless.

A swivel blasted canister from the maintop, and Bolitho realized that the first Danish ship, which had been totally disabled by *Benbow*'s broadsides, had drifted down towards them and was barely fifty yards away. Shots banged back and forth across the narrowing arrowhead of water, and marksmen joined in to try and seek their enemy's officers and add further to the confusion and death.

The midshipman named Keys staggered and toppled sideways, but Allday caught him before he hit the deck.

He stared past Allday at Bolitho, his eyes glazing rapidly as he managed to whisper, 'Number . . . sixteen . . . still . . . flies . . . sir!' Then he died.

Bolitho looked up blindly, seeing another midshipman swarming up the main-topgallant mast with his rear-admiral's flag trailing behind him like a banner.

Wolfe jumped back as the last of the mizzen's severed rigging slithered across the deck and vanished over the side.

But he pivoted round again as Major Clinton shouted, 'They're boarding us, sir!'

Herrick waved his pistol, but Bolitho shouted, 'Save your ship, Thomas!' Then he beckoned to the gun crews at the disengaged side and added, 'With me, Benbows!'

Whooping and yelling like demented beings they charged through the poop and down the companion, half of which had been reduced to splinters. Steel clashed on steel, and in the semi-darkness men staggered and reeled through the smoke, cutlasses and boarding axes painting the deckhead and timbers in shining patterns of blood.

A pistol banged out, and through the wardroom's shattered stern windows Bolitho saw men leaping up from the galleys which were hooking on to the counter and fighting their way inboard. Many fell to Clinton's muskets, but still more appeared, yelling and cursing as they grappled with *Benbow*'s seamen. Even in the cruel madness of battle they would be well aware that the only way to stay alive now was to win.

Lieutenant Oughton aimed his pistol at a Danish officer, pulled the trigger and gaped at the weapon in horror as it misfired.

The Danish officer parried a sailor's cutlass aside and drove his blade through Oughton's stomach once, and then again, before he had time to cry out.

As Oughton fell the Danish officer saw Bolitho, his eyes widening as in those brief seconds he took in his rank and authority.

Bolitho felt the man's blade slide across his own, saw the Dane's first determination give way to desperation as the hilts locked and Bolitho twisted his wrist as he had done so often in the past.

But as he took the weight on his wounded leg it seemed to weaken under him, the pain making him gasp as he lost the advantage and fell back against the press of men behind him.

Allday's great cutlass flashed across his vision and sank into the officer's forehead like an axe into a log. Allday wrenched it free and swung again at a man who was trying to duck past him. The man screamed and fell, trodden instantly underfoot as the hacking, gasping men fought savagely to hold their ground.

Then it was done, the surviving boarders running to the broken stern to climb back to their galleys or to drop into the sea to escape the reddened cutlasses and pikes.

Wolfe appeared, his face like stone as he stared at the corpses and the glittering runnels of blood.

'We are almost alongside the enemy, sir!'

He saw a man's hand creeping from the shadows to retrieve a fallen pistol. One great foot pinioned the man's wrist to the deck, and with almost contemptuous ease Wolfe struck down with his hanger, cutting off the scream almost before it had begun.

Bolitho gasped, 'Leave some spare hands here!'

He heard Allday hurrying after him to the companion, saw the most forward gun crews fading into deeper shadow as the drifting enemy floated slowly alongside. But they continued to fire, cheering and swearing, aware of nothing but the pock-marked hull opposite their muzzles. Men lay dead and dying around the guns but only the other ship seemed to mean anything. Deafened, half-blinded, sickened by the stench of killing, it was likely that some of them had not even noticed the attempt to board their ship from astern.

Bolitho walked across the shot-pitted quarterdeck, his eyes fixed on the enemy. Men fired muskets, swivels and pistols, while others, driven almost mad, stood and shook their cutlasses and pikes at the Danes.

Herrick had one hand inside his coat and there was blood on his wrist.

Browne was on his knees bandaging Acting Lieutenant Aggett's leg which had been laid open by a wood splinter.

'*Repel boarders!*'

With a grinding shudder the two hulls came together in a powerful embrace, yards and rigging snared, gun muzzles overlapping and grating as they continued to drift helplessly downwind.

Clinton waved his stick. 'At 'em, marines!'

The red-coated marines ran to the attack, bayonets probing and stabbing through the nets as the first Danish seamen attempted to cut their way through.

Men fell screaming between the hulls, human fenders as the ships rocked and ground together on the swell. Others tried to get away, to be trodden down by their companions or shot in the back in sight of safety.

A pike jabbed through the nets and narrowly missed Allday's chest. Browne parried it away and slashed the attacker across the face before despatching him with a full thrust.

Like survivors on a rock, Grubb and his helmsmen stood clustered around the useless wheel, firing pistols at the figures on the enemy's poop and gangway while their wounded companions reloaded for them as best they could.

Pascoe came running aft with the carronade crews, his hanger flashing dully through the smoke.

Then he skidded to a halt, his feet and legs splattered with blood, as he shouted, 'Sir! *Indomitable*'s signalling!'

Herrick swore savagely and fired his remaining pistol at a man's head below the nettings.

'Signals? God dammit, we've no time for *them*!'

Browne wiped his mouth and lowered his sword. Then he said hoarsely, '*Indomitable*'s repeating a signal from the fleet. *Discontinue the engagement!* Number thirty-nine, sir!'

Bolitho stared past the *Indomitable*'s battered hull and trailing shrouds. A frigate, one of Nelson's, was standing far beyond the smoke like an intruder, the signal still flapping to the wind.

'*Cease firing!*'

Wolfe pointed his hanger at the ship alongside as one by one the Danish seamen dropped their weapons and stood like stricken creatures, knowing that for them it was all over.

Herrick said, 'Take charge of our prize, Mr Wolfe!' He

urned to look at the ships and at the galleys which even now were fading away into the smoke to seek refuge in their harbour.

The sea was littered with flotsam and broken timber of every ort. Men, friend and enemy alike, clung together for mutual support and awaited rescue, too beaten and shocked to care much who had won. There were many corpses, too, and Inch's *Odin* was so deep by the bows that she looked as if she might capsize at any moment.

Only the *Styx* seemed unmarked, distance hiding her hurt and scars as she shortened sail to search amongst the debris of battle.

Bolitho put his arm round his nephew's shoulder and asked, 'D'you still want a frigate, Adam?'

But the reply was lost in a growing wave of cheering, wilder and louder as it spread from ship to ship, with even the wounded croaking at the sky, grateful to be alive, to have come through it once more, or for the first dreadful time.

Herrick picked up his hat and banged it against his knee. Then he put it on his head and said quietly, '*Benbow*'s a good ship. I'm *proud* of her!'

Bolitho smiled at his friend, feeling the tiredness and the pain as he glanced at the grinning, smoke-blackened faces around him.

'*Men*, not ships, you once said, Thomas. Remember?'

Grubb blew his nose and then said, 'Rudder's answerin', sir!'

Bolitho looked at Browne. It had been a near thing. Even now he was not certain how it might have ended had the frigate not appeared. Perhaps the English and the Danes were too much alike to fight. If so, there would have been no man alive by nightfall.

Browne asked huskily, 'Signal, sir?'

'Aye. General signal. *Squadron to form line ahead and astern of flagship as convenient.*'

The flag for close action rippled down from the yard, and as it was removed from the halliards Allday took it and laid it across the face of the dead midshipman.

Bolitho watched and then said quietly, 'We will rejoin the fleet, Captain Herrick.'

They looked at each other. Bolitho, Herrick, Pascoe and Allday. Each had had something to sustain him throughout the battle. And this time there was something to hope for in the future.

Even if the weather remained kind to the mauled and bloodied squadron there was much to be done. Friends to be contacted, the dead to be buried, the ships to be made safe for the passage home.

But for this one precious moment, this escape from hell, a new hope would suffice.

Epilogue

The open carriage paused at the top of a rise while the horses regained their breath and the dust settled around them.

Bolitho removed his cocked hat and allowed the June sunlight to play across his face, his ear picking up the many sounds of insects in the hedgerows, the distant lowing of cattle, the voices of the countryside.

By his side Adam Pascoe stared ahead towards the rooftops of Falmouth, the glassy reflection of Carrick Roads beyond. On the opposite seat, his feet planted firmly on several sea-chests, Allday glanced contentedly around him, lost in his own thoughts and the moment of peace after the jolting ride from Plymouth.

The journey over moorland and past isolated farmsteads and small hamlets had been like a cleansing, Bolitho thought. After all the weeks and months, and those final devasting broadsides before Nelson had ordered a ceasefire and had declared a truce, the Cornish landscape had affected Bolitho and his companions deeply.

Now, *Benbow* was anchored at Plymouth with the other scarred survivors of the Inshore Squadron. With the exception of Inch's *Odin*, which because of her severe underwater damage had only just managed to reach the safety of the Nore.

Two months since they had watched the crimson galleys returning to harbour like guilty assassins, and now it was difficult to believe any of it had happened.

The green hills, the sheep dotting their slopes, the slow comings and goings of farm waggons and carriers' carts were far removed from the discipline and suffering of a man-of-war.

Only the marked absence of young men in the villages and

fields gave a hint of war, otherwise it was as Bolitho had alway remembered, had clung to when he had been in far-off place and on other seas.

The Battle of Copenhagen, as it was now being called, wa: hailed as a great victory. By their determined action the British squadrons had immobilized Denmark completely, and Tsa: Paul's hopes of a powerful alliance had been smashed.

Against that, the price had been equally impressive, althougl far less remarked upon in press and Parliament. The British had lost more men dead and wounded than at the Nile. The Danes' total casualties in killed, wounded and taken prisoner, quite apart from the destruction or capture of their ships, were three times as great.

Bolitho thought of the faces he would not see again. Veitch, who had gone down in his sloop-of-war *Lookout*. Keverne, killed in the last stages of the fight aboard his *Indomitable*. Peel of the *Relentless*, and so many more beside.

And now, while Herrick, soon to be joined at Plymouth by his wife, dealt with the damage to his own command, Bolitho and his nephew had come home.

The carriage started to move once more, downhill this time, the horses nodding their heads together as if aware that food and rest were drawing closer with each turn of the wheels.

Bolitho thought of Lieutenant Browne. After obtaining this carriage for the journey to Falmouth he had made his own way to London. Bolitho had made it perfectly clear to him. If he wished to return to his service when the *Benbow* was put back in commission he would be more than welcome. But if he chose another life in London, using his talents to better effect, that, too, Bolitho would understand. After such a baptism of fire and death, he doubted if Browne's view of daily life would ever be the same again.

Two farm workers, spades over their shoulders, doffed their hats as the carriage rolled past.

Bolitho smiled gravely. The word would soon be round, the grey house on the headland would have lights in the windows tonight. A Bolitho was back again.

Pascoe said suddenly, 'I never thought to see this place again, Uncle.'

He said it so forcefully that Bolitho was moved.

He answered, 'I know that feeling, Adam.' He touched his arm. 'We shall make the most of this stay.'

They spoke little for the last part of the journey. Bolitho felt unsettled, vaguely apprehensive as the wheels clattered on to the hard cobbles of the town.

He looked for familiar faces as they turned to watch the two sea officers being carried through the square. One so young, the other with the bright epaulettes on his shoulders.

A girl, shaking a tablecloth from an inn door, saw Allday and waved to him. Bolitho smiled. Allday at least was recognized, and welcome.

The road narrowed into a lane, lined on either side by mossy flint walls. Flowers barely moved in the warm air, and the grey house appeared to rise from the ground itself as the horses pounded up the last stretch towards the open gates.

Bolitho licked his lips as he saw Ferguson, his one-armed steward, running to meet the carriage, his wife close behind him, already crying with pleasure.

He steeled himself. The first moments were always the hardest, in spite of the warm welcome and good intentions.

'Home, Adam. Yours and mine.'

The youth looked at him searchingly, his eyes bright. 'I want to talk about it, Uncle. All of it. After losing *Relentless* I don't think I shall ever be so afraid again.'

Allday waved to some people by the gates, his face split into a grin. But he sounded serious as he said, 'I still think it's wrong and damn unfair, sir, an' nothing will make me change my mind!'

Bolitho watched him wearily. 'Why so?' He already knew, but it was better to let Allday get it out of his system so that he could enjoy their homecoming in his own way.

Allday gripped the door as the carriage swung round towards the stone steps.

'All them others, sir, getting the glory and the praise. But for you they'd have been wallowing in their own guts long since! You should have got a *knighthood*, an' that's no error!' He looked at Pascoe for support. 'Ain't that right?'

Then he saw Pascoe's expression and turned his head towards the doorway at the top of the steps.

Bolitho held his breath, barely able to trust his own senses.

She stood motionless, her slim figure and long chestnut hair framed against the house's inner darkness, one hand held out towards him as if to consume the last few yards.

Bolitho said quietly, 'Thank you, Allday, old friend, but now I know I have won a far greater reward.'

He climbed from the carriage and took her in his arms. Then, watched in silence by Pascoe and Allday, they walked into the house. Together.

Hutchinson & Co. (Publishers) Ltd
3 Fitzroy Square, London WIP 6JD

London Melbourne Sydney Auckland
Wellington Johannesburg and agencies
throughout the world

First published 1978
© Bolitho Maritime Productions Ltd 1978

Set in Intertype Garamond

Printed in Great Britain by
The Anchor Press Ltd and bound by
Wm Brendon & Son Ltd
both of Tiptree, Essex

ISBN 0 09 134580 4

ALEXANDER KENT

The Inshore Squadron

HUTCHINSON OF LONDON